BUG-EYED MONSTERS & BIMBOS

THE CHRONICLES OF LUCIFER JONES

by Mike Resnick

Volume I—1922-1926: Adventures

Volume II—1926-1931: Exploits

Volume III—1931-1934: Encounters

Lucifer Jones, the most irrepressible, unabashed rogue to emerge from the pen of Mike Resnick, takes us on one hilarious journey after another.

BUG-EYED MONSTERS & BIMBOS

EDITED BY
MIKE RESNICK

PHOENIX PICK

an imprint of

ARC
MANOR
Rockville, Maryland

ISBN: 978-1-61242-032-5

www.PhoenixPick.com

**Great Science Fiction & Fantasy
Free Ebook Every Month**

Published by Phoenix Pick
an imprint of Arc Manor
P. O. Box 10339
Rockville, MD 20849-0339
www.ArcManor.com

COPYRIGHT ACKNOWLEDGMENTS

For Carol, as always,

And for the Four Horsemen of New Orleans:
George Alec Effinger
John Guidry
Guy Lillian III
Justin Winston

♈

CONTENTS

INTRODUCTION

to the 2012 edition of
Bug-Eyed Monsters and Bimbos

THIS IS THE FIRST anthology I ever edited. I was the Toastmaster at Nolacon II, the 1988 Worldcon, and the committee asked me if I'd be willing to edit an anthology on any topic that appealed to me. I've always loved humor, so I agreed if I could put together a book of science fiction parodies.

I titled it Shaggy B.E.M. Stories (in science fiction parlance, a B.E.M. is a Bug-Eyed Monster). I scoured the professional magazines, but also the fanzines, and finally came up with some 30 stories, some by superstars like Asimov and Clarke, some by relatively unknown fans.

I turned in the manuscript, and they went to press...but none of them had ever been involved in publishing, and they didn't know that they were supposed to return the galleys to the editor and the authors for proof-reading, so the final version had about 200 typos in it. (And even so, it was still a damned funny book.)

Shaggy B.E.M. Stories was a limited edition, and about 75% of the print run sold out the weekend of the convention. Finally, after a dozen years or so, I decided it was time to bring it out again, and I sold it to Byron Preiss, who promptly re-titled it Dirty Rotten Aliens. Money changed hands, I paid all the writers a second time—and then Byron was killed in a tragic accident, and the book never came out.

Move the clock ahead another decade, and I thought I'd try again. And now you hold in your hands the second edition, proudly wearing yet its third title, this time Bug-Eyed Monsters and Bimbos.

And you know what?

Whatever they call it, it's still a totally delightful collection of some of the best parodies of science fiction ever written.

Enjoy,

Mike Resnick

Michael F. Flynn

Writing as Rowland Shew

(Author's Note) This came to me on the west-bound rail platform of the LIRR when I was leaving I-Con a number of years ago. Writers had been bemoaning, as is their wont, the cover art with which their progeny had been afflicted. I noted that my book In the Country of the Blind *featured a white man on the cover even though the main character was a black woman. Okay, it was "high concept," but a one-eyed man never appears in the novel. Roger MacBride Allen showed me his own book,* The Ring of Charon, *crying, "There's a bimbo on the cover of my book!" And such a character never appeared in the book. I thought, on the railroad platform: That scans, and began subvocalizing it to the tune of "She'll be Coming 'Round the Mountain." The mean and hairy monster graced the cover of my collection,* The Nanotech Chronicles. *The space ships and ray guns covered books by Harry Turtledove and Nancy Kress, although I no longer recall the titles. (All subsequent notes are by the editor.)*

THERE'S A BIMBO ON THE COVER

Or

The Art Director's Fight Song
(Sung to the Tune of "She'll be Coming 'Round the Mountain.")

There's a bimbo on the cover of the book.
There's a bimbo on the cover of the book.
She is dumb and she is sexy.

She is nowhere in the text. She
Is a bimbo on the cover of the book.

There's a monster on the cover of the book.
There's a monster on the cover of the book.
He is mean and he is hairy,
Though the story's not that scary.
There's a monster on the cover of the book.

There's a white male on the cover of the book.
There's a white male on the cover of the book.
Though the heroine is black,
With Art that cuts no slack.
So, there's a white male on the cover of the book.

There are death rays on the cover of the book.
There are death rays on the cover of the book.
It's a philosophical story,
But the cover must be gory.
So, there are death rays on the cover of the book.

There's a space ship on the cover of the book.
There's a space ship on the cover of the book.
The connection's very iffy,
But if the story's sci-fi[1]
There'll be space ships on the cover of the book.

---

1   Pronounced "skiffy" by the cognoscenti.

Clive Jackson

The only thing I know about Clive Jackson is that he originally wrote this piece for a fanzine in 1950. I first read it in Fred Brown's and Mack Reynolds' SCIENCE FICTION CARNIVAL—and if there is a better parody of the entire space opera genre, I've yet to come across it.

THE SWORDSMEN OF VARNIS

THE TWIN MOONS BROODED over the red deserts of Mars and the ruined city of Khua-Loanis. The night wind sighed around the fragile spires and whispered at the fretted lattice windows of the empty temples, and the red dust made it like a city of copper.

It was close to midnight when the distant rumble of racing hooves reached the city, and soon the riders thundered in under the ancient gateway. Tharn, Warrior Lord of Loanis, leading his pursuers by a scant twenty yards, realized wearily that his lead was shortening, and raked the scaly flanks of his six-legged vorkl with cruel spurs. The faithful beast gave a low cry of despair and it tried to obey and failed.

In front of Tharn in the big double saddle sat Lehni-tal-Loanis, Royal Lady of Mars, riding the ungainly animal with easy grace, leaning forward along its arching neck to murmur swift words of encouragement into its flattened ears. Then she lay back against Tharn's mailed chest and turned her lovely face up to his, flushed and vivid with the excitement of the chase, amber eyes aflame with love for her strange hero from beyond time and space.

"We shall win this race, my Tharn!" she cried. "Yonder through that archway lies the Temple of the Living Vapor, and once there we can defy all the Hordes of Varnis!" Looking down at the unearthly beauty of her, at the subtle curve of throat and breast and thigh, revealed as the wind tore at her scanty garments, Tharn knew that even if the Swordsmen of Varnis struck him down his strange odyssey would not have been in vain.

But the girl had judged the distance correctly and Tharn brought their snorting vorkl to a sliding, rearing halt at the great doors of the Temple, just as the Swordsmen reached the outer archway and jammed there in a struggling, cursing mass. In seconds they had sorted themselves out and came streaming across the courtyard, but the delay had given Tharn time to dismount and make his stand in one of the great doorways. He knew that if he could hold it for a few moments while Lehni-tal-Loanis got the door open, then the secret of the Living Vapor would be theirs, and with it mastery of all the lands of Loanis.

The Swordsmen tried first to ride him down, but the doorway was so narrow and deep that Tharn had only to drive his sword-point upward into the first vorkl's throat and leap backward as the dying beast fell. Its rider was stunned by the fall, and Tharn bounded up onto the dead animal and beheaded the unfortunate Swordsman without compunction. There were ten of his enemies left and they came at him now on foot, but the confining doorway prevented them from attacking more than four abreast, and Tharn's elevated position upon the huge carcass gave him the advantage he needed. The fire of battle was in his veins now, and he bared his teeth and laughed in their faces, and his reddened sword wove a pattern of cold death which none could pass.

Lehni-tal-Loanis, running quick cool fingers over the pitted bronze of the door, found the radiation lock and pressed her glowing opalescent thumb-ring into the socket, then gave a little sob of relief as she heard hidden tumblers falling. With agonized slowness the ancient mechanism began to open the door; soon Tharn heard the girl's clear voice call above the clashing steel: "Inside, my Tharn, the secret of the Living Vapor is ours!"

But Tharn, with four of his foes dead now, and seven to go, could not retreat from his position on top of the dead vorkl without grave risk of being cut down, and Lehni-tal-Loanis, quickly realizing this, sprang up beside him, drawing her own slim blade and crying "Aie, my love! I will be your left arm!"

Now the cold hand of defeat gripped the hearts of the Swordsmen of Varnis: two, three, four more of them mingled their blood with the red dust of the courtyard as Tharn and his fighting princess swung their merciless blades in perfect unison. It seemed that nothing could prevent them now from winning the mysterious secret of the Living Vapor, but they reckoned without the treachery of one of the remaining Swordsmen.

Leaping backward out of the conflict he flung his sword on the ground in disgust. "Aw, the hell with it!" he grunted, and unclipping his proton gun from his belt, he blasted Lehni-tal-Loanis and her Warrior Lord out of existence with a searing energy beam.

Randall Garrett

This is perhaps the most famous of the late Randall Garrett's many science fiction parodies, and was approved by E.E. "Doc" Smith himself (who even suggested that the Dauntless become the Dentless). Like the best of its type, it not only makes you laugh—but it also makes you want to go back and re-read the original.

BACKSTAGE LENSMAN

ON A PLANET DISTANT indeed from Tellus, on a frigid, lightless globe situated within an almost completely enclosing hollow sphere of black interstellar dust, in a cavern far beneath the surface of that abysmally cold planet, a group of entities indescribable by, or to, man stood, sat, or slumped around a circular conference table.

Though they had no spines, they were something like porcupines; though they had no tentacles, they reminded one of octopuses; though they had no wings or beaks, they seemed similar to vultures; and though they had neither scales nor fins, there was definitely something fishy about them.

These, then, composed the Council of the Meich, frigid-blooded poison-breathers whose existence at temperatures only a few degrees above zero absolute required them to have extensions into the fourth and fifth dimensions, rendering them horribly indescribable and indescribably horrible to human sight.

Their leader, Meichfrite, or, more formally, Frite of the Meich, radiated harshly to others of the Council: "The time has now come to consider the problem of our current losses in the other galaxy. Meichrobe, as Second of the Meich, you will report first."

That worthy pondered judiciously for long moments, then: "I presume you wish to hear nothing about the missing strawberries?"

"Nothing," agreed the other.

"Then," came Meichrobe's rasping thought, "we must consider the pernicious activities of the Tellurian Lensman whose workings are not, and have not been, ascribed to Star A Star.

"The activities and behavior of all members of the never-to-be-sufficiently-damned Galactic Patrol have, as you know, been subjected to rigid statistical analysis. Our computers have come to the conclusion that, with a probability of point oh oh one, the Lensman known as Gimble Ginnison either is or is not the agent whom we seek."

"A cogent report indeed," Meichfrite complimented. "Next, the report of Meichron, Third of this Council."

"As a psychologist," Meichron replied, "I feel that there is an equal probability that the agent whom we seek is one of the fire-blooded, oxygen-breathing Tellurians. Perhaps one of the immoral Palanians, who emmfoze in public."

"That, too, must be considered," Meichfrite noted. "Now to Meichrotch, Fourth of the Meich…"

And so it went, through member after member of that dark Council. How they arrived at any decision whatever is starkly unknowable to the human mind.

On green, warm Tellus, many megaparsecs from the black cloud which enveloped the eternally and infernally frigid planet of the Meich, Lensman Gimble Ginnison, having been released from the hospital at Prime Base, was talking to Surgeon-Major Macy, who had just given him his final check-up.

"How am I, Doc?" he asked respectfully. "QX for duty?"

"Well, you were in pretty bad shape when you came in," the Lensman surgeon said thoughtfully. "We almost had to clone you to keep you around, son. Those Axlemen really shot you up."

"Check. But how am I now?"

The older Lensman looked at the sheaf of charts, films, tapes, and reports on his desk. "Mmm. Your skeleton seems in good shape, but I wonder about the rest of you. The most beautiful nurses in the Service attended you during your convalescence, and you never made a pass—never even patted a fanny."

"Gosh," Ginnison flushed hotly, "was I expected to?"

"Not by me," the older man said cryptically.

"Well, am I QX for duty? I have to do a flit."

Surgeon-Major Macy handed Ginnison an envelope. "Take this to the Starboard Admiral's office. He'll let you know. Where are you flitting for?"

"I'm not sure yet," Ginnison said evasively, taking the envelope.

"Right. Clear ether, Gimble."

"Clear ether, Macy."

True to an old tradition, these two friends never told each other anything.

The Starboard Admiral slit open the envelope and took in its contents at a glance. "According to Macy, you're fit for duty, son. Congratulations. And, in spite of everything, that was a right smart piece of work you did on Mulligans II."

Ginnison looked at the tips of his polished boots. "Gee whiz!" he said, blushing. Then, looking up: "If I'm fit for duty, sir, I'd like to make a request. That mess on Cadilax needs to be cleaned up. I'm ready to try it, sir, and I await your orders."

The Starboard Admiral looked up into the gray eyes of the young, handsome, broad-shouldered, lean, lithe, tough, hard, finely-trained, well-muscled, stubborn, powerful man who stood before him.

"Gim," he said firmly, "you have disobeyed every order I have ever given you. It always comes out all right, so I can't gripe, but, as of now, I'm getting out from under. I've talked to the Galactic Council, and they agree. We are giving you your release."

The release! The goal toward which every Lensman worked and so few attained! He was now an Unattached Lensman, responsible to no one and nothing save his own conscience. He was no longer merely a small cog in the mighty machine of the Galactic Patrol—

He was a Big Wheel!

"Jeepers!" he said feelingly. "Goshamighty!"

"It's all of that," the Starboard Admiral agreed. "Now go put on your Grays, take the *Dentless*, and get the hell out of here!"

"Yes, sir!" And Ginnison was gone.

He went back to his quarters and took off the black-and-silver uniform. Then he proudly donned the starkly utilitarian gray leather uniform which was the garb of the Unattached Lensman. And as he did so, he made that curious gesture known as Gray Seal. No entity has ever donned or ever will don that Gray uniform without making that gesture. It is the only way you can get the zipper closed.

In his office, solidly sealed against both thought and spy-ray beams, the Starboard Admiral sat and stared at the glowing Lens on his wrist, the Lens which was, and is, the symbol of rank and power of every Lensman of the Galactic Patrol.

But it is far more than merely a symbol.

It is a lenticular structure of hundreds and thousands of tiny crystalloids, and each is built and tuned to match the ego of one individual entity. It is not, strictly speaking, alive, but its pseudo-life is such that when it is in circuit with the living entity to whom it is synchronized, it gives off a strong, changing, characteristically polychromatic light. It is a telepathic communicator of astounding power and range, and kills any being besides its owner who attempts to wear it.

Thus, it is both pretty and useful.

Manufactured and issued by the mysterious beings of dread and dreaded Arisia, it cannot be counterfeited, and is given only to those entities of the highest honor, integrity, honesty, and intelligence. That knowledge made the Starboard Admiral, as, indeed, it did all Lensmen, feel smug.

The mighty *Dentless*, from needle prow to flaring jets, was armed and armored, screened and shielded as was no other ship of her class and rating. Under the almost inconceivable thrust of her mighty driving jets, she drilled a hole through the void at her cruising velocity of a hundred parsecs per hour.

Not in the inert state could she so have done, for no body with *inertial* mass can travel faster than the velocity of light, which, in the vast reaches of the galaxy, is the veriest crawl.

But her Bergenholm, that intricate machine which renders a spaceship inertialess, or "free," permitted her to move at whatever velocity her ravening jets could achieve against the meager resistance of the almost perfect vacuum of interstellar space. Unfortunately, the Bergenholm, while it could completely neutralize inertial mass, never quite knew what to do with *gravitational* mass, which seems to come and go as circumstances require.

As the *Dentless* bored on through the awesome void toward her goal, Ginnison and Chief Firing Officer Flatworthy checked and rechecked her mighty armament. Hot and tight were her ravening primary beams, against which no material object, inert or free, can offer any resistance whatever. When struck by the irresistible torrents of energy from a primary, any form of matter, however hard, however resistant, however refractory, becomes, in a minute fraction of a second, an unimaginably hot cloud of totally ionized gases.

Equally tight, but not so hot, were the ultrapowerful secondaries, whose beams could liquefy or gasify tungsten or even the ultra-resistant neocarballoy in the blink of an eye.

The inspection over, Ginnison lit a cigarette with a tertiary and Lensed a thought to an entity in another part of the ship. "Woozle, old snake. I hate to disturb your contemplations, but could you come down to my cabin? We have things to discuss."

"Immediately, Ginnison," that worthy replied, and shortly thereafter Ginnison's door opened and there entered a leather-winged, crocodile-headed, thirty-foot-long, crooked-arm, pythonish, reptilian nightmare. He draped himself across a couple of parallel bars, tied himself into a tasteful bow-knot, and extended a few weirdly-stalked eyes. "Well?"

Ginnison looked affectionately at the horribly monstrous Lensman. "Concerning *l'affaire Cadilax*," he began.

"I know nothing about it, fortunately," Woozle interrupted. "That gives you a chance to explain everything."

"Very well, then. As you well know, I have spent a long time searching for clues that will lead me to the top echelon of Boskonia—Boskonia, that frightful, inimical, soul-destroying, inter-galactic organization which is so ineradicably opposed to all the moral values which we of Civilization hold so dear."

Woozle closed a few eyes. "Yes. Continue."

"On Leanonabar," Ginnison continued, "I got a line through Banjo Freeko, the planetary dictator, but only after I blew up the mining industry on his planet and killed a few thousand innocent people—regretfully, of course. But I do that all the time. It revolts me, but I do it."

"What boots it?" Woozle asked. "You got your line, didn't you? You humans are so squeamish."

"To continue," said Ginnison. "This is the line I traced."

And in Woozle's mind there appeared a three-dimensional representation of intergalactic space. Two galaxies floated there in the awesome awfulness of the unimaginable vastness of the intergalactic void.

From Leanonabar, in the First, or Tellurian, Galaxy, a thin, hard red line ran straight through and past the Second Galaxy, out into the vast reaches of the intergalactic space beyond.

"Isn't that rather overdoing it?" came Woozle's thought. "You think this line may extend *beyond*—?"

Ginnison shook his head. "Not really. There's nothing along that line for half a billion parsecs, and that's a Seyfert Galaxy."

"Tough about them," Woozle opinioned. "Let's get back to Cadilax."

"Oh, yes. Well, Cadilax is clear across the Galaxy from Leanonabar, so that would give us a good baseline for our second triangulation."

"I trust," Woozle thought, "that you have a better reason than that for picking Cadilax."

"Certainly." Rising from his seat, Ginnison paced across the deck of his cabin, turned, and paced back. "In the past several months, all hell has broken loose on Cadilax. The drug trade has gone up three hundred percent. Thionite, heroin, hashish, nitrolabe, cocaine, bentlam, and caffeine—all of them have increased tremendously, and Narcotics can't find the source. The adolescents have gone wild; the boys are wearing their hair long, and the girls have given up perms. Illicit sex is rampant. They live in unstructured social groups." He took a deep breath, and said, in a hushed voice: "There have even been demonstrations against the way the Patrol is running the Boskonian War!"

"Madness, indeed," Woozle agreed, "but are you certain that your information is up-to-date?"

"Reasonably certain," Ginnison pondered. "The latest information we have—"

At that point, a sharp, cold, Lensed thought intruded.

"Lensman Ginnison, greetings. I humbly request communication with you."

Ginnison recognized that thought. It was that of Shadrack, a poison-blooded, frigid-breathing Lensman he had known of yore.

"Sure, little chum: what is it?"

"I do not interrupt?" Shadrack quavered.

"Not at all. Go ahead."

"I trust I do not intrude upon matters of far greater importance than that of my own meager and faulty information?"

"Certainly not," Ginnison reassured.

"As is well known," continued the soft thought, "I am a yellow-bellied, chicken-livered, jelly-gutted coward—a racial characteristic which

I cannot and do not deny. Therefore, I most humbly apologize for this unwarranted intrusion upon your thoughts."

"No need to overdo it, little chum," said Ginnison. "A simple grovel will be enough."

"Thank you, Ginnison," Shadrack snivelled gravely. "Then may I inquire, in my own small way, if you are aware of the existence of an entity known as Banlon of Downlo? He is, like myself, a creature accustomed to temperatures scarcely above zero absolute, but of far greater courage and bravery than any of my own race possesses."

"BANLON!" Ginnison's Lensed thought fairly shrieked. "Klono, yes, I know of him!" Then, more calmly: "He's been out after my hide since we destroyed Downlo."

"That, I fear, is true," Shadrack commented. "Even now, he has, according to the information which my poor powers have allowed me to glean, englobed the *Dentless* with a fleet of twelve ships which are prepared to blast you out of the ether."

"Klono's curving carballoy claws and gilded gadolinium gizzard!" Ginnison roared mentally. "Why didn't you say so in the first place?"

"I am devastated," Shadrack replied. "It is, again, a racial characteristic which I cannot avoid. It took me too long to apologize." A pause, then: "I fear, even now, that I may have been too late," Shadrack apologized.

"Clear ether, little chum."

The Lensed connection cut off, and Ginnison flashed a thought to the control room, only to discover that, indeed, the *Dentless* was surrounded.

In a black, undetectable, refrigerated speedster, many parsecs from the soon-to-be scene of battle, that entity known as Banlon of Downlo gloated over his instruments as he watched the englobement of the *Dentless* take form.

Like the Meich, and like Shadrack, he was of a race whose normal temperature was near that of boiling helium, and thus required extra-dimensional extensions in order to gather enough energy to survive. Superficially, that sounds glib enough, but, unfortunately, your historian knows less about dimensional analysis than you do, so let's drop it right here.

To return to our narrative, Banlon, a safe distance away from the impending conflict, observed minutely the behavior of the Boskonian squadron which had englobed the *Dentless*. Each captain of the twelve Boskonian warships had done his job to perfection.

"Very well," Banlon radiated harshly to his minions, "englobement is now complete. Tractors and pressors out! Cut your Bergenholms and go inert! Blast that ship out of the ether!"

Inertialess as she was, the mighty *Dentless*, caught in a web of tractor and pressor beams, could not continue at speed against resistance of an inert combined mass twelve times that of her own. Relative to the Boskonian squadron, she came to a dead halt in space, easy prey for the Boskonians.

At Banlon's order, all twelve Boskonian ships fired at once toward the center of their englobement, where the apparently helpless Patrol ship floated.

Beams, rods, cones, stilettoes, ice picks, corkscrews, knives, forks, and spoons of energy raved against the screens of the *Dentless*. Quasi-solid bolts of horrendous power chewed, gnawed, flared, snarled, and growled against the energy screens of the Patrol ship, seeking eagerly to blast through them to the hull metal. All of circumambient space was filled with the frightful discharge of those tremendous bolts of power.

The screens of the *Dentless* flared red, orange, yellow, green, blue, and into the violet. From there, they went into the ultraviolet and x-ray spectrum. But still they held.

Gimble Ginnison, teeth clenched and jaw muscles knotted, stared with unblinking gaze of gray eyes at the plate before him, listening to the reports from the officers commanding the various functions of the ship. But only one of those reports was really important.

"Screens holding, Lensman!"

"Fire secondaries," the Lensman ordered crisply.

The prodigious might of the Patrol ship's secondaries flared out toward the twelve Boskonian ships. Those screens, too, blazed up the spectrum toward the ultraviolet, then toward blackness.

"Primaries one through twelve! Ready?"

"Ready, sir!"

"At my order, then." Ginnison watched his plate closely.

"Five seconds! Four...Three...Two...One...FIRE!"

Twelve primary batteries flamed forth as one, each ravening beam smashing into, through, and past the already weakened shields of the Boskonian battleships. Like tissue paper in the flame of an oxyhydrogen torch, the dozen ships dissolved into white-hot gas.

As far as his detectors could scan, Ginnison could see that there was not a single threat in the ether about the *Dentless*.

"Navigator," he ordered crisply, "continue toward Cadilax."

From his coign of vantage, so many parsecs away, Banlon stared in disbelief at his instruments, knowing to the full what they had reported. But after that first momentary shock, the ultrahard logic of his ultracold brain reasserted itself.

"Shit!" he thought. And, flipping his speedster end-for-end, he turned around and ran.

Came, betimes, to Cadilax, a bum.

He showed up, unobtrusively, in the streets of Ardis, the capital of that disturbed planet. He was, apparently, a man approaching sixty—graying, flabby, rheumy-eyed, alcoholic, and not too bright. He was so typical of his kind that no one noticed him: he was merely one of ten thousand such who wandered about the streets of the various cities of Cadilax. He hung around the bars and bistros of the spaceport, cadging drinks, begging for small change, leering innocuously at the hookers, and telling stories of the days of his youth, when he was a "somebody." He claimed to have been a doctor, a lawyer, a pimp, a confidence man, a bartender, a judge, a police officer, a religious minister, and other such members of highly respected occupations, but he could never produce any proof that he had ever been any one of them.

And no one expected him to, for that was the *sine qua non* of the spaceport bum. He was what he was, and no one expected more of him. He called himself Goniff, and, because of his vaguely erudite manner of speech, soon became known as "Professor" Goniff.

He was never completely sober, and never completely drunk.

The student of history has, of course, already surmised that beneath this guise lay the keen mind and brain of Gimble Ginnison, Gray Lensman, and he is right.

Throughout this time, Ginnison was searching out and finding a wight bedight Gauntluth.

It had taken time. The Gray Lensman's mind had probed into the depths of degradation, the valleys of vileness, the caverns of corruption, in the dregs of the noxious minds of the foulest folk of a planet before finding that name and individual. He might have found him earlier, had he not been enjoying himself so much.

At first, only vaguely had he been able to construct from the clues available a picture of the all-powerful drug baron and pirate who ruthlessly ruled the underworld of Cadilax. Then, as time went on and more and more data came in, his visualization of Gauntluth became complete.

Gauntluth was tall, lean, and tough, with the all-pervading cadaverous blue of a Kalonian. His headquarters were in the Queen Ardis Hotel, the biggest luxury hotel on the planet, which catered only to the top fringe of the upper crust of the ultra-ultra.

There, in his superbly screened and shielded suite of offices, Gauntluth controlled, through an intricate webwork of communications, and by a highly efficiently organized army of minions, the drug traffic on half a dozen different solar systems.

For long Ginnison pondered, and came to the obvious conclusion that "Professor" Goniff could in no wise gain admission to the elite society of the Queen Ardis Hotel. Therefore Goniff the bum vanished.

Instead, it was Lester Q. Twodyce, cosmopolitan, and wealthy playboy, who checked into the Queen Ardis with an entourage of flunkies and yes-men, not one of whom could easily be detected as an officer of the Galactic Patrol. As was de rigeur on Cadilax, every one of Twodyce's men wore a thought-screen.

Carefully, step by step, Ginnison laid his trap. Throughout the highest ranks of Gauntluth's organization, it became known that Lester Q. Twodyce had something valuable that he was eager to sell. It became clear, even to Gauntluth, that whatever it was Twodyce had, it was certainly worth investigating.

Thus it came about that one evening, when the impeccably dressed Mr. Twodyce was seated at a table in the grand dining room of the hotel with two of his hard-faced gunmen, he was approached by two equally well-dressed men who bowed politely and smiled pleasantly.

One of them said: "Good evening, Mr. Twodyce. I trust we do not interrupt your repast?"

Twodyce looked up. "Not at all," he said. "Will you be seated?"

Then, almost as an afterthought: "May I order you drinks? Such distinguished gentlemen as yourselves deserve only the best, of course."

"You know, then, who we are?" asked the spokesman.

"Certainly, Mr. Thord," replied the Lensman suavely, "you and Mr. Thield are hardly anonymous." Drinks were brought.

"These—" he gestured toward the men on either side of him, "—are my associates, Mr. Kokomo and Mr. De Katur."

After several minutes of preliminary conversation, the ape-faced Thord finally broached the subject which they had all been anticipating.

"I hear, Mr. Twodyce," he said, "you are here to do business."

"Not primarily," said the Lensman nonchalantly. "I am here to enjoy myself. Business is not a primary concern of mine."

"I understand," said Thord, "for such a man as yourself..."

"Nevertheless," continued Ginnison, "I do have a small trifle which I am willing to dispose of for a proper price."

The lizard-like Mr. Thield spoke. "And that is?"

Twodyce said off-handedly, "Fifty grams of clear-quill thionite."

There was stunned silence from Thord and Thield.

Thionite! Thionite, that dreadful and dreadfully expensive drug which, in microgram doses, induces in the user clear, three-dimensional, stereo-sonic visions in which he indulges his every desire to the point of ecstasy. Every desire, base or noble, mental or physical, conscious or subconscious. Whatever pleasurable experience he wishes for himself, he experiences. It is addictive to the nth degree. It is the ultimate high, but the slightest overdose is deadly.

It is also purple.

One milligram of that dire drug was enough for two thousand doses, and the insouciant Mr. Twodyce was offering fifty thousand times that amount!

"Gad!" murmured Mr. Thield.

"Indeed?" said Thord. "If that is true, we are prepared to offer..."

"You will offer nothing," Ginnison said calmly. "I do not deal with underlings."

Thord's face darkened. "Underling? *Underlings?* To whom do you think you are speaking, *Mister* Twodyce?"

"To underlings," said the unruffled Twodyce. "And you may tell Gaunt-luth I said so."

There was a momentary silence from Thord and Thield as their eyes darted from Ginnison's face to those of the bodyguards. Each body-guard was fingering his necktie, his right hand only inches away from the DeLameter that was undoubtedly in a shoulder holster concealed by the loose-fitting dress jacket that each man wore.

Thord and Thield rose, superficially regaining their composure. "We will speak to you later, Mr. Twodyce," said Thord.

"You will not," said Ginnison in a low, deadly voice. "I have no desire to see either of you again. Gauntluth may contact me if he so wishes. Tell Gauntluth that I caution him to think of a hamburger."

"A...a hamburger?" gasped Thord.

"Precisely. A hamburger."

"—But—"

"You may not be able to figure it out," Ginnison said coldly, "but your boss will. Now go."

Without another word, the two underlings turned out and went.

That night, in his own suite, Lester Q. Twodyce was Lensing a thought to Lieutenant-Admiral Partisipple, the Lensman in charge of the Patrol Base on Cadilax.

"Partisipple?"

"Yes, Ginnison, what is it?" came the Lensman-Admiral's thought.

"This thing's about to bust wide open," Ginnison declared, "and I'll need some help."

"Anything you want, Gray Lensman."

"Good. Can you get me about fifty logons?"

"Logons?" Lensed the base commander in astonishment. "LOGONS?"

There was a reason for his astonishment, for the logon, or Cadiligian rateagle, is one of the nastiest, most vicious, and intractable beasts in the galaxy. Its warped mind is capable of containing but one emotion: HA-TRED! The Cadiligian rateagle hates anything and everything living, the only desire in the small compass of its mind being to reduce that life to something edible. The logon resembles the Tellurian rat at its worst, but is the size of a Tellurian terrier and has the wings and claws of an eagle. Logons do not make nice pets.

"Yes, logons," Ginnison replied. "I can control them."

"With your superior mental equipment," the base commander thought humbly, "I am sure you can. How do you want them packaged?"

"Put them in a 'copter. Have the pilot ready to release them on my order, within one kilometer of the roof of the Queen Ardis Hotel."

"Certainly. Clear ether, Gray Lensman."

"Clear ether, Partisipple."

Then, another Lensed thought to Woozle, in the *Dentless*, hovering invisibly in orbit high above the surface of Cadilax. "Woozle, old serpent, here's the story so far." And in flashing thoughts he told the reptilian Lensman his plans. "So have Lieutenant Hess von Baschenvolks and his company of Dutch Valerians down here and ready to go."

"Will do, Ginnison. Clear ether."

"Clear ether."

In the office on the top floor of the Queen Ardis Hotel, the inscrutable face of Gauntluth stared thoughtfully at the banks of screens, meters, switches, dials, indicators, knobs, buttons, and flickering lights on the panels and control boards which surrounded him.

Finally, after long pondering, he touched a button on one of his control panels. "Give me suite 3305," he said.

Ginnison was waiting for the call when it came. The cadaverous blue face of the gaunt Gauntluth appeared on his visiscreen. "Yes?" he said calmly.

"I am told," came Gauntluth's rasping voice, "that you are in a position to deal with me concerning a certain—ah—article."

"As long as the deal is on the up-and-up, I am," replied Ginnison. "Of course, the usual precautions must be taken on both sides."

"Of course, my dear fellow," Gauntluth said agreeably. "Shall we, then, make arrangements that are agreeable to both sides?"

"Let us do so," said Ginnison.

On cold and distant Jugavine, the planet of the Meich, the First of the frightful Council, Meichfrite, radiated harshly to the others: "You have all scanned the tapes containing the report of our agent, Banlon of Downlo. Somehow, by what means we know not, the Lensman, Ginnison, escaped the trap Banlon set for him. Twelve of our ships have vanished utterly, and Banlon's report is neither complete nor conclusive. I would now like to hear your comments, Meichrobe."

"It seems to me," that worthy radiated, "that the strawberries are—"

"Forget the goddamn strawberries!" Meichfrite riposted. *"What about Ginnison?"*

"Well, then," Meichrobe thought raspingly, "our computers have calculated that with a probability of point oh oh four, Gimble Ginnison has either gone to Cadilax or somewhere else."

"Indeed," Meichfrite thought thoughtfully. "Meichrodot, Fifth of the Meich, give us your thoughts on this subject."

"Our reports from Cadilax," informed Meichrodot, "indicate that all is going smoothly. There is no trace of the Lensman on or near the planet. However, Banlon's agent Gauntluth has reported through Banlon that he is running short of thionite. He wants to make a buy."

Meichfrite turned his attention to the Sixth of the Meich. "Meichroft, this is your department."

"Banlon," Meichroft emitted, "must go to Trenco."

Trenco! That planet was, and is, unique. Its atmosphere and its liquid are its two outstanding peculiarities. Half of the atmosphere and almost all of the liquid of the planet is a compound with an extremely low heat of vaporization. It has a boiling point such that during the day it is a vapor and it condenses to a liquid at night. The days are intensely hot, the nights intensely cold.

The planet rotates on its axis in a little less than twenty-six hours: during the night it rains exactly forty-seven feet, five inches—no more and no less—every night of every year.

The winds are of more than hurricane velocity, rising to some eight hundred miles per hour, accompanied by blinding, almost continuous lightning discharges.

What makes the planet unique, however, is that, with compounds of such low latent heat, the energy transfer is almost nil. Theoretically, the hot days should evaporate that liquid as quietly and gently as a ghost evaporates in a spotlight, and during the night it should condense as softly as dew from heaven falling on the place beneath. Thermodynamically speaking, the planet Trenco should be about as turbulent as a goldfish bowl. Nobody can figure out where those winds or the lightning come from.

Be that as it may, Trenco was, and is, the only planet where the plant known as Trenconian broadleaf grows, and that plant is the only source of thionite in any of several galaxies.

In addition, Trenco has a strong Galactic Patrol base, manned by Rigellian Patrolmen whose sole job it is to kill anyone who comes to Trenco. One can well understand why thionite was, and is, so expensive.

"Ah, a cogent thought indeed!" radiated Meichfrite. "Very well, then, relay to Banlon that he is to proceed at speed to Trenco and pick up a cargo of broadleaf, to bring here for processing. Meantime, he is to order his underling Gauntluth to report directly to us."

In his office atop the Queen Ardis, Gauntluth the Kalonian watched with hard, steel-blue eyes as a figure on his spy-ray plate moved toward his suite of offices.

Twodyce, with the exception of the DeLameter in his shoulder holster, was unarmed; he was carrying nothing else but the hermetically sealed container which bore within itself fifty grams of almost impalpable purple powder.

A smile twisted Gauntluth's face. "Fool!" he gritted harshly under his breath.

He continued to watch as Twodyce came to the outer door and activated the announcer. He activated the door-opener. "Come in, Mr. Twodyce," he spoke into a microphone. "Down the hall and first door to your left."

Gimble Ginnison, fully alert, strode down the corridor and opened the door. Alone behind his desk sat the unsuspecting Kalonian.

"I perceive," said the zwilnik[1], "that you have brought the thionite with you."

"I have," said the Lensman. "Have you the payment ready?"

"Certainly. Half in bar platinum, half in Patrol credits, as specified. But first, of course, I must test the Thionite."

"First I test the platinum," said Twodyce impassively.

Gauntluth blinked. "We seem to be at an impasse," he murmured. "However, I think I see a way around it. Know, Twodyce, that you stand now in the focus of a complex of robotic devices which, with rays and beams of tremendous power, will reduce you to a crisp unless you hand over that thionite container instantly."

"Since it is inevitable," Ginnison said calmly, "I might as well enjoy it." He carefully put the container on Gauntluth's desk.

Gauntluth needed no further check. Directing his thought toward a lump of force in a nearby corner of the room, he sent a message to Jugavine.

This was the moment for which Ginnison had been waiting. In an instant, he effortlessly took over the zwilnik's[2] mind. He allowed Gauntluth to send the message, since it would only further confuse all those concerned. Gauntluth reported in full to Meichfrite that he had, indeed, obtained a goodly supply of thionite.

"Excellent," the cold thought returned. "There will be more coming. End communication."

By main force and awkwardness, Ginnison held Gauntluth's mind in thrall. He now had his second line to the Boskonian base, but Gauntluth, although taken by surprise at first, was now fighting Ginnison's mental control with every mega-erg of his hard Kalonian mind.

"Think you can succeed, even now?" sneered the still-rigid Kalonian mentally. And, with a tremendous effort of will, he moved a pinkie a fraction of a millimeter to cover a photocell. Every alarm in the building went off.

Ginnison's mind clamped down instantly to paralyze the hapless zwilnik.[3] With a mirthless smile on his face, Ginnison said: "I permitted

---

1   A zwilnik is anyone connected with the drug trade.
2   A zwilnik is still a zwilnik.
3   See above.

that as a gesture of futility. You did not, as I suggested, contemplate a hamburger."

"Bah!" came Gauntluth's thought. "That childishness?"

"Not childishness," said the Lensman coldly. "A hamburger is so constructed that most of the meat is hidden by the bun. My resources are far greater than those which appear around the edge."

Then Ginnison invaded Gauntluth's mind and took every iota of relevant information therein, following which, he hurled a bolt of mental energy calculated to slay any living thing. Perforce, Gauntluth ceased to be a living thing.

Meanwhile, from a hidden and shielded barracks in a sub-basement of the Queen Ardis came a full squadron of armed and armored space-thugs, swarming up stairways and elevators to reach the late Gauntluth's suite. Closer, and, at this point in space and time, far more dangerous, were the DeLameter-armed, thought-screened executives and plug-uglies who were even now battering down the doors of the suite.

Calmly and with deliberation, Ginnison flashed a thought to Woozle: "HE-E-E-ELP!"

"At speed, Ginnison," came the reply.

Ginnison went into action. Snatching the hermetically sealed thionite container from the desk at which lay the cooling corpse of Gauntluth, he broke the seal and emptied the contents into the intake vent of the air conditioner. He had, of course, taken the precaution of putting anti-thionite plugs in his nostrils; all he had to do was to keep his mouth shut and he would be perfectly safe.

The impalpable purple powder permeated the atmosphere of the hotel. There was enough of the active principle of that deadly drug to turn on fifty million people; since the slightest overdose could kill, every person in the hotel not wearing anti-thionite plugs or space armor died in blissful ecstasy. Most of Gauntluth's thugs were wearing one or the other, but at least the Galactic Patrol need no longer worry about interference from innocent bystanders.

With lightning speed, Ginnison grabbed a heavy-caliber, water-cooled machine rifle that just happened to be standing near Gauntluth's desk, swiveled it to face the doors of the office, and waited.

At the same moment, a borazon-hard, bronze-beryllium-steel-prowed landing craft smashed into the side of the Hotel Queen Ardis at the fifteenth floor. Steel girders, ferroconcrete walls, and brick facing alike splattered aside as that hard-driven, specially-designed space boat, hitting its reverse jets at the last second to bring it to a dead halt, crashed into and through the bridal suite. The port slammed open and from it leaped, strode, jumped and strutted a company of Dutch Valerians in full space armor, swinging their mighty thirty-pound space axes.

No bifurcate race, wherever situate, will voluntarily face a Valerian in battle. Those mighty warriors, bred in a gravitational field three times that of Tellus, have no ruth for any of Civilization's foes. The smallest Valerian can, in full armor, do a standing high jump of nearly fifteen feet in a field of one Tellurian gravity; he can feint, parry, lunge, swing, and duck with a speed utterly impossible for any of the lesser breeds of man. Like all jocks, they are not too bright.

Led by Lieutenant Hess von Baschenvolks, they charged in to block off the armed and armored space-thugs who were heading toward the top floor. As they charged in, the Lieutenant shouted their battle-cry.

"Kill! Bash! Smash! Cut! Hack! Destroy! Bleed, you bastards! Bleed and die!" And, of course, they did.

A thirty-pound space axe driven by the muscles of a Valerian can cut its way through any armor. Heads fell; arms lopped off; gallons of gore flowed over the expensive carpetry. Leaving behind them dozens of corpses, the Valerians charged upward, toward the suite of offices where the Gray Lensman awaited the assault of Gauntluth's men, fingers poised, ready to press the hair triggers of the heavy machine rifle.

The news of the attack, however, reached those winsome wights long before the Valerians did. They knew that, unarmored as they were, they stood no chance against those Patrolmen. They headed for the roof, where powerful 'copters awaited them for their getaway.

It was not until they were all on the roof that the logons, released from the special 'copter less than a kilometer away, and individually controlled by the mighty mind of Gimble Ginnison, launched their attack. The zwilnik[4] executives and plug-uglies had no chance. Only a few managed to draw and fire their ray guns, and even those few missed their targets. Within a space of seconds, the entire group had been slashed, cut, scratched, bitten, killed, and half-eaten by the winged horrors that had been released upon them.

In Gauntluth's office, Ginnison waited behind the machine rifle, his finger still poised on the hair-triggers. The door smashed and fell. But Ginnison recognized the bulky space-armored eight-foot figure that

---

4   Forget it.

loomed before him. His hands came away from the triggers as he said: "Hi, Hess!"

"Duuuhh…Hi, Boss," said Lieutenant Hess von Baschenvolks.

In a totally black, intrinsically undetectable, ultrapowered speedster, towing three negaspheres of planetary antimass, Gimble Ginnison cautiously approached the hollow sphere of light-obliterating dust which surrounded the dread planet Jugavine of the Meich.

With his second line of communication, it had been a simple job to locate exactly and precisely the planet which had been the source of the disruption which had hit the planet Cadilax.

Further, that mental communication had given Ginnison all the information he needed to wipe out this pernicious pesthole of pediculous parasites on the body politic of Civilization.

The negaspheres were an integral part of the plan.

The negasphere was, and is, a complete negation of matter. To it, a push is, or becomes, a pull, and vice versa. No radiation of whatever kind can escape from or be reflected by its utterly black surface. It is dense beyond imagining; even a negasphere of planetary antimass is less than a kilometer in diameter. When a negasphere strikes ordinary matter, the two cancel out, bringing into being vast quantities of ultrahard and very deadly radiation. A negasphere is, by its very nature, inherently undetectable by any form of radar or spy-ray beam. Even extra-sensory perception reels dizzyingly away from that vast infinitude of absolute negation.

Like the Bergenholm, the negasphere can never really make up its mind about gravity; gravity is, was, and always had been a pull, and it should act as a push against a negasphere; since it does not do so, we must conclude that there is something peculiar about the mathematics of the negasphere.

It is to Ginnison's credit that he had perceived this subtle, but inalterable, anomaly.

Into the hollow cloud of black interstellar dust that surrounded frigid Jugavine, there was but one entrance, and into that entrance the Gray Lensman's speedster, towing with tractors and pressors those three deadly negaspheres, wended its intricate way.

In his office, the Starboard Admiral glowered. "I don't like it. Ginnison should have taken the full fleet with him."

The personage he was addressing was Sir Houston Carbarn, the most brilliant mathematical physicist in the known universe. He was one of a handful of living entities who could actually think in the abstruse and abstract language of pure mathematics.

"I don't like his going in there alone," the Starboard Admiral continued. "If that hollow sphere of dust is as black and bleak as he says it is, he will have nothing to guide him but his sense of perception.

$$ \text{DIV } \vec{B} = 0, \text{ CURL } \vec{B} = je + \frac{\partial E}{\partial t} $$

$$ \text{DIV } \vec{E} = Pe, \text{ CURL } \vec{E} = 0 - \frac{\partial B}{\partial t} \quad " $$

said Sir Houston Carbarn thoughtfully.

"True, agreed the Starboard Admiral, "but I can see no way for him to illuminate such a vast amount of space with the means at his command. That hollow globe is two parsecs across, and contains within it only a single body—the planet Jugavine. How can he possibly get enough illumination to find the planet?"

"$x^2 + y^2 + z^2 = r^2$," murmured Sir Houston. "$E = MC^2$."

"Yes, yes, obviously!" snapped the Starboard Admiral. "But in order to illumine the interior of that hollow globe, he will have to find Jugavine first, and to do that he needs illumination. It seems to me this involves a paradox."

"$Pq \neq qp$," Sir Houston snapped forcefully.

"Ah, I see what you mean," said the Starboard Admiral. "But what about Banlon of Downlo? According to Ginnison's report, Banlon is returning to Jugavine with a cargo of Trenconian broadleaf which he somehow managed to steal from under the very noses of Trigonometree, the Rigellian Lensman in charge of our base in Trenco. If Ginnison destroys Jugavine, Banlon's sense of perception will immediately tell him that the planet no longer exists, and he will not fall into Ginnison's trap. How is he going to get around that?"

"?" mused Sir Houston abstractedly.

Gimble Ginnison, Gray Lensman, had no need of slow, electromagnetic radiation to locate the planet of the Meich. His tremendous sense of perception had pinpointed that doomed planet exactly. Calculating carefully the intrinsic velocity of his first negasphere in relation to that of the planet of the Meich, he released that black, enigmatic ball of negation toward its hapless target.

The negasphere struck. Or perhaps not. Is it possible for nothing to strike anything? Let us say, then, that the negasphere began to occupy the same space as that of Jugavine. At the hyperdimensional surface of contact, the matter and antimatter mutually vanished. Where the negasphere struck, a huge hole appeared in that theretofore frigid planet. The planet collapsed in on itself, its very substance eaten away by the all-devouring negasphere. The radiation of that mutual annihilation wrought heated havoc upon the doomed planet. Helium boiled; hydrogen melted; nitrogen fizzed; and all fell collapsingly into the rapidly diminishing atmosphere.

When the awful and awesome process had completed itself, there was nothing left. Thus perished the Meich.

When the process was completed, the Gray Lensman hurled his two remaining negaspheres toward the exact same spot in space.

Then he sat and waited for Banlon of Downlo.

Time passed. Ginnison, ever on the alert with his acute sense of perception, at last detected Banlon's speedster entering the globe of dust. Banlon could not detect, at that distance, the flare of radiation which had resulted from the destruction of Jugavine. That radiation, struggling along at the speed of light, would require years to reach the interior surfaces of the globe.

Ginnison, waiting like a cat at a mouse hole, pounced at the instant that Banlon entered the globe. One flash of a primary beam, and Banlon of Downlo was forced into the next plane of existence. He ceased to be, save as a white-hot gas, spreading and dissipating its energy through a relatively small volume of space.

Immediately, Ginnison Lensed his report back to Prime Base, then made his way out of the hollow globe and back to the *Dentless*.

The Starboard Admiral frowned and looked up at Houston Carbarn. "I'm afraid I still don't understand. After Jugavine was destroyed, Banlon, with his sense of perception, which is instantaneous and is not hampered by the velocity of light, should have detected the fact that the planet no longer existed. Why did he continue on in toward a non-existent planet?"

Sir Houston Carbarn smiled. "(-1)(-1) = +1." he informed.

The Starboard Commander slammed his palm on the desk. "Of course! The principle of the double negative! Two negaspheres make a posisphere! Banlon thought it was Jugavine! Our Gray Lensman has genius, Sir Houston!"

"!" agreed Sir Houston.

When Gimble Ginnison strode into his quarters aboard the *Dentless*, Woozle was waiting for him. "What now?" queried the sapient serpent.

"Now for a decent meal, Woozle." He activated a communicator. "Galley? Send up a two-inch thick steak, rare. Mashed potatoes and thick brown gravy. And a quart of black coffee."

"Yes, sir," came the reply. "And what about dessert?"

Ginnison sat down in his chair with a triumphant sigh of relief. "Now, at last," he said, "I can enjoy that for which I have waited so long."

"The strawberries, sir?"

"Exactly. The strawberries."

Randall Garrett & Lin Carter

Randall Garrett and Lin Carter died within a month of each other. To the best of my knowledge, this was their only collaboration—which is one hell of a shame, given its quality. It obviously took not one but two gently warped minds to ride a New York subway and then imagine the experience as a Hugo Gernsback "Scientifiction" story.

MASTERS OF THE METROPOLIS

I: The Journey Begins

IT WAS IN THE Eighth Month of the Year 1956 that Sam IM4 SF+ strode down the surging, crowded streets of Newark, one of the many cities of its kind in the State of New Jersey. He had just left his apartment in one of the vast, soaring pylons of the city. There, living in universal accord, hundreds of families dwelt side by side in the same great tower, one of many which loomed as many as forty stories above the street.

He paused to board a bus which stopped at regularly-spaced intervals to take on new passengers. The bus, or Omnibus, was a streamlined, self-propelled public vehicle, powered by the exploding gases of distilled petroleum, ignited in a sealed cylinder by means of an electric spark. The energy thus obtained was applied as torque to a long metal bar known as the "drive-shaft," which turned a set of gears in a complex apparatus known as the "differential housing." These gears, in turn, caused the rear wheels to revolve about their axes, thus propelling the vehicle smoothly at velocities as great as eighty miles every hour!

Dropping a coin into the receptacle by the driver's cubicle, and receiving a courteous welcome from the technician employed to pilot the machine, he took his seat inside the vehicle. Marveling anew at the luxurious comfort of the form-fitting seats, Sam IM4 SF+ gazed out of the window at the gorgeous spectacle of the city as it raced past.

Within a very few moments, the vehicle decelerated to a smooth stop before Pennsylvania Station, a mammoth terminal where the far-flung lines of public transportation converged.

Entering the great building, he paused to marvel anew at the inspiring architectural genius capable of erecting such an imposing monument to modern civilization—a building which would strike with awe the simpler citizen of earlier times.

Threading his way through the crowds which thronged the vaulted interior of the terminal, he came to a turnstile, an artifact not unlike a rimless wheel, whose spokes revolved to allow his passage. He placed a coin in the mechanism, and the marvelous machine—but one of many mechanical marvels of the age—recorded his passage on a small dial and automatically added the value of his coin to the total theretofore accumulated. All this, mind, without a single human hand at the controls!

Once past the turnstile, Sam IM4 SF+ followed the ingenious directional signs on the walls, which led him to a vast, artificially-lighted underground cavern. There he waited for his second conveyance to arrive.

Sam IM4 SF+, a typical citizen of his age, towered a full six feet above the ground. His handsome face was crowned by a massive, intellectual forehead. His hair was dark and smooth, neatly trimmed to follow the contours of his skull. He was clad in complex and attractive garments, according to the fashion of his century. His trousers were woven of a fabric synthetically formulated from a clever mixture of chemicals, as was his coat, for these favored people no longer depended upon herds of domesticated quadrupeds for their raiment. These garments were fastened, not by buttons, but by an ingenious system of automatically interlocking metallic teeth known as a *zipper.*

Suspended from his ears, a frame of stiff wires supported a pair of polished lenses before his eyes, which served not only to protect those orbs from the rushing winds that were a natural hazard of this Age of Speed, but also to implement his vision, lending it an almost telescopic power.

As he stood on the platform, his sensitive ears detected the distant roar of a *subway train*. Gazing down the dark tunnel by whose egress the platform stood, he observed the cyclopean glare of the artificial light affixed to the blunt nose of the onrushing all-metallic projectile. The entire cavern reverberated to the roar of the vehicle as it emerged from the tunnel with a mighty rush of wind and braked smoothly to a dead stop before his very feet.

The marvel of modern transportation which was to bear him on his journey to the great Metropolis of New York had arrived!

II: Aboard the *Subway Train*

THE AUTOMATIC DOOR SLID open, and our hero entered the car and was offered a seat by one of the courteous, uniformed crew-members.

Pausing to marvel anew at this miracle of modern science, Sam IM4 SF+ turned to a fellow traveler and remarked conversationally: "Ah, fellow citizen; is it not wonderful to reflect that the same Energy which propels us through the very bowels of the Earth is identical with the lightning that flames the stormy skies, far above these Stygian depths? For thousands of years, the simple peasants of a ruder age looked upon the lightning bolt as the awesome weapon of angry gods; little did they surmise that their descendants would one day chain this Gargantuan power and harness it to serve their will!"

"How true!" remarked his companion. "And could one of them now be with us as we speed through this fantastic system of tunnels, would not he be struck dumb with terror and think us gods?"

"Would he not, indeed," smiled Sam, "commonplace though it is to us."

As they were speaking, the *subway train* sprang to life and plunged into the ebon mouth of another tunnel. In an instant, the vast, lighted cavern was lost to view, and the car was swallowed in the blackness of the tunnel, illuminated only by the colored lights set at intervals along the cavern walls as signals to the pilot.

The mighty engine thundered through the darkness like some mythical monster of a bygone age. Sam, however, experienced no difficulty in observing his fellow passengers, since the interior of the vehicle was brilliantly illuminated by ingenious artificial lighting. These *light bulbs* consisted of cleverly blown globes of glass which contained a delicate and intricate filament of tungsten wire. Upon the application of sufficient electrical current, the wire heated up to many hundreds of degrees, thus emitting a bright and pleasant light. Indeed, so great was the temperature at which they operated, the globes were filled with inert gas in order to prevent even the highly refractive tungsten from burning in the air!

Sam spent his time pleasantly by reading the various colorful and informative signs within the car. These advertisements portrayed the many necessities and luxuries which all citizens of this age might acquire. Each told of its product in glowing, descriptive terms. Here, a poster told of a harmless chemical mixture which, when applied to the skin, destroyed the unpleasant body odors with which earlier ages had been plagued; there, another card told of a confection which, when masticated, acted as a tooth-cleansing agent, thus serving as an aid to the buoyant health of the people of this era.

Within a few minutes, the vehicle had passed beneath the rolling waters of the mighty Hudson River, and emerged from the darkness into another vast cavern, larger than, though similar to, the one in which our hero first boarded the conveyance.

As the passengers emerged in orderly rows from the *subway train*, Sam joined them and thus beheld the awe-inspiring vastness of Grand Central Station. Breathtaking was the panorama that greeted his dazzled orbs as he joined the motley throng that surged and eddied beneath the tremendous dome. A traveler from an earlier age would have been confused and lost in the orderly chaos of the great terminal. Level upon level, tier upon tier, exit upon exit met the eye at every turn.

But Sam IM4 SF+ was no stranger here; indeed, he gave scarcely a glance to the confusion through which he made his way. In a very few moments, he left the building to gaze in awe at the fantastic sight of the great Metropolis of New York, the hugest city ever constructed—vast, even on the mammoth scale of other cities of this advanced age.

III: Through the Vast Metropolis

ALL ABOUT HIM SOARED the incredible towers, spires, pylons, monuments, buildings, palaces, temples, cathedrals, domes, and other breath-taking constructions of the Metropolis. Through its broad streets moved the traffic of the great city. Row on row of metallic projectiles called *automobiles* passed smoothly, silently, and swiftly through the streets. Powered by the same "internal combustion engine" that powered the Omnibus, they were marvels of mechanical genius. So common were they to the favored children of this Mechanical Age that the gaily-costumed passers-by scarcely gave them a glance, even when crossing the streets through which the *autos* ran.

Sam lifted his nobly-sculptured head and gazed enthralled at the towers that rose, rank upon serried rank, as far as the eyes could see. Their smooth, regular sides of artificial stone literally blazed with hundreds of illuminated windows. Their lofty tops seemed to touch the sky itself—for which reason, let me remark in passing, the inhabitants called them *Sky-Scrapers*.

"Ah, madam," exclaimed Sam to a lovely young woman, who, curiously attired in the daring fashions of the age, stood near him, also gazing in awe at the spectacle, "how much vaster is our great Metropolis even than storied Nineveh, or Tyre, or mighty Babylon with its famed hanging gardens, or Carthage of yore!"

"Truly, good sir," she responded modestly. "And is it not wonderful that we are here to see it all? Ah, would not some proud Caesar or Attila of old have given all his treasures for such a privilege?"

Before them, in multicolored grandeur, blazed hundreds of vast advertising displays, each shining with a light that dazzled the eye of the beholder. These sign-lights were ingeniously wrought tubes of glass of no greater diameter than a common lead-pencil, but many feet in length. The tubes were curved to form the various letters and symbols which made up the great illuminated signs, and were filled with various gases under low pressure. When the electrical energy of tremendous voltage was applied to electrodes at the ends of the tubes, the gas within glowed brilliantly with colored light, just as the atmosphere glows when a bolt of lightning passes through it during a thunderstorm. By filling these tubes with diverse gases, all the hues of the rainbow could be duplicated.

Sam IM4 SF+ turned his admiring gaze from the breath-taking displays and started to cross the street. By a clever contrivance of flashing signal-lamps, the flow of mechanical traffic was periodically halted, to thus allow unmounted citizens to pass from one side to the other in complete safety. Sam strode across the street as the traffic halted in strict obedience to the signal-lamps. Once on the other side, he started off through the byways of the city. On either side stretched mercantile establishments of divers sorts, selling luxuries and commodities undreamed of by earlier peoples. He strode past a theater of the age which, instead of living actors, displayed amazing dramas recorded on strips of celluloid and projected by beams of light on tremendously white surfaces within the darkened theater. Ingeniously recorded voices and sounds, cleverly synchronized to the movement of the figures on the screen, made them seem lifelike.

"Ah, the wonders of modern science!" Sam marveled anew.

IV: The Threat of the Mind Masters

NOT EVEN THE VARIED panorama of the Metropolis could keep Sam IM4 SF+ from thinking of his mission to the city. He had constantly kept a sharp look-out, watching those who might betray too much interest in his person, being careful that no one was following him.

For Sam IM4 SF+ knew that danger was afoot in New York; a secret group known as the Mind Masters was plotting to take over the Government, using super-scientific devices, about which Sam could only conjecture. There was no proof, unfortunately, with which our hero could have gone to the rulers of this enlightened country and denounce the scoundrels for the criminals they were. Only Sam IM4 SF+ knew of the existence of this evil band—Sam, and a few loyal cohorts that he had gathered to combat the menace.

For Sam, like a few others across the world, had a Sixth Sense, which enabled him to detect certain emotional responses which were, to others, non-existent.

Thus, Sam proceeded carefully to his destination, for he knew full well that if he were discovered, death would be his reward.

Little did he know that, in a secret room, many miles away, the Mind Masters were, at that very moment, plotting his destruction. Twelve men in black hoods were seated about a table. Eleven of them were listening to the twelfth speak.

"Even now," he said, in a voice that reeked with evil, "our agents are following IM4 SF+, clad in invisibility suits. Fear not, my friends, we shall destroy that prying Sixth Sense of his. When our agents close in at last, they will use the hyper-decerebralizer ray. The fool has no chance!"

WILL THE CABAL DESTROY SAM'S WONDER SENSE?

WHAT OF COUNTESS TAMARA AND THE HIDDEN LEGION?

WILL DR. DOOM PERFECT HIS ROCKETSHIP IN TIME TO ESCAPE?

CAN DALE ARDENT SURVIVE THE MIND-FREEZING MACHINE?

READ THE SECOND PART OF THIS AMAZING SERIAL AND SEE!

Richard Lupoff

Richard Lupoff has written some brilliant New Wave and Very Old Wave stories under his own name, and is one of the best critics the science fiction field has ever known—but he also has a third career: that of Ova Hamlet, parodist of all we hold dear. This parody of Barry Malzberg's work may be unique in that Malzberg, upon reading it, was inspired to sit down and write THE GAMESMAN, one of his finest novels.

GREBZLAM'S GAME

by Ova Hamlet

Furiously I reach for Opponent's lob, bringing my paddle down in a vicious sideswiping arc. The paddle's gnurled composition surface smashes into the careening white globe as it reaches the zenith of its flight and sends it screaming back to Opponent's side of the table.

This will be my triumph, this will be my moment of joy and vindication. The game may end as it will, win or lose, lose or win, etc., but this moment they cannot take away from me. My heart leaps. I can see Opponent reacting to the smash: he reaches for it, stretching his arm, trying for one of his infuriating saves, but he has not calculated for the English that I put on the ball and its rapid bounce vectors horizontally as well and Opponent misses it completely, sprawls across the table with a crash.

The spectators applaud.

"Brilliant shot, Grebzlam!" someone shouts.

And "Hurray for Grebzlam!"

It is a female voice cheering for me, I can tell, I can recognize the cloying, whining tone of a female.

I grimace pleasantly.

My shot misses the table completely, slithers among the crowd watching the contest between Opponent and myself.

Stunned, I shrink within myself. I seethe, waiting for some response from the officials to this disaster. I wonder if I will be expected to debase myself further, to creep and slide between the feet of spectators searching for the lost ball.

Linesman shouts "Off!"

I hate Linesman, his jolly enthusiasm for the game, the glee with which he announces my every *faux pas*, the way he wallows in my every humiliation.

Someone in the audience titters. A female, of course. Altogether the spectators are reacting to this incident with more restraint than I would have expected of them. They can hardly be considered sensitive or decent people, certainly not here on the Ship, no.

In fact they are disgusting, gross. But I must concede, not quite as disgusting and gross as one might have been led to anticipate.

"Sixteen to three," Scorekeeper announces. He smothers a cough politely.

I hate Scorekeeper even more than Linesman. At least Linesman makes no attempt to disguise the malice and contempt with which he regards me, but Scorekeeper maintains his polite detachment, his Official's air of objectivity, at all times. But I know he despises me, and in return I hate him as much for his hypocrisy as for the ill-will he conceals.

Linesman reaches into a baggy warm-up jacket with Ship's insignia on the back and pulls a fresh ball from a pocket. He tosses a casual glance at the scoreboard where my shame is posted, 16/3. He rubs the fresh ball between the palms of his hot, fleshy hands and throws it to Opponent.

Opponent catches it with his free hand, gracefully, putting me to further shame for my own clumsiness. He holds the ball up, looks at me questioningly with his eyes as if to say, Ready?

I nod.

He serves the ball.

But I am not ready. I don't know why I nodded. I was standing off balance, my weight not evenly distributed on my feet. Opponent has tried one of his deadly corner serves, catching me completely off balance.

If I try to recover and return the serve I will probably stumble and take a pratfall, miss the shot anyway, lose the point and reduce myself to a laughing stock for the spectators. But I try anyway, and twist an ankle painfully, falling to the floor and rolling into the front row of spectators who kick at me viciously with their sharply pointed Ship's issue boots.

A groan goes up from the spectators and as I struggle to regain my feet, convinced that the point is lost, I hear Linesman announce happily, "Mr. Grebzlam's point."

Opponent has finessed himself, missed his serve, put the ball squarely into the net.

Scorekeeper announces coolly, "Sixteen to four. Mr. Grebzlam serves."

Twelve points deficit. This is not insurmountable. I am far behind Opponent but now I have the serve. If I can score five quick service aces the game will stand at sixteen to nine. Scorekeeper will have to admire my fortitude, my ability to absorb punishment, to withstand pain without visible complaint.

Audience, too, will begin to appreciate me.

Audience has never appreciated me, but they remain. They must care somehow or they would leave, but there is always a packed gallery at Game.

There must be passengers elsewhere on the Ship—passengers and Officials. Sometimes during lengthy volleys, while audience is silent and the only immediate sound is the rhythmic *ponk-CLONK, ponk-CLONK* of Game, sounds come from elsewhere on the Ship, sounds which I can hear with my abnormally sharp sense of hearing.

Somewhere on Ship a band is playing, I think, and passengers are dancing to its music. Males and females grapple and grope for each other, their bodies hot and steaming, odors rising from their private parts as they make polite small talk.

Somewhere on Ship there is a swimming pool. Males and females wear their most revealing, shameless bathing garb as they splash and cavort in pursuit of each other.

I have the ball now, held lightly between two fingers of my left hand, the aluminum handle of my paddle gripped tightly in my sweating right palm. I look at Scorekeeper. He returns a neutral, objective look of assessment. I look at Linesman. He glares at me, an angry, wolfish grin pulling back his lips, sending bolts of terror through my body.

Opponent is trying to stare me down. I raise the ball and prepare to serve. If I can score a quick service ace now the pattern will be set. I will run up a series of points and come from behind. Opponent's confidence will be shattered, his pacing destroyed, he will be reduced to a grovelling hulk before my furious onslaught.

I make a misleading gesture, twitching my right shoulder to lead Opponent's eyes in that direction while with a quick upward twitch of my left wrist I bring the ball into play, strike at it with an upward flick of my paddle. *Pick-CLONK*, the ball goes, making the distinctive sound of a serve.

The extra spin on the ball will make it accelerate as it touches the table obliquely, once on my side of the net, once on Opponent's. It is a trick I learned years ago and have worked painfully to perfect, muscles crying out for surcease and perspiration dripping into my eyes.

The ball flies forward, a gleaming white pellet of purity, there is a tiny *tsk* sound and it continues across the net, arcing across the net, arcing higher than I had planned, descending, *ponk* on the far side of the table and bouncing once more. Opponent moves his empty hand and catches the ball in mid-air.

Linesman says "Let ball," almost giggling as he sprays the maddening words.

Opponent, grinning wolfishly—nearly the same grin that Linesman uses to pierce me—tosses the ball to me.

It bounces once, *pschk*, and I catch it in one hand. Time seems to halt for a moment. I look at the audience, at Officials, at Opponent. I look at the table and think of Game.

The reason I'm doing so badly, I realize, is that the table, bolted to the floor to keep it from slipping, is mounted parallel to the long axis of the Ship. Ship's acceleration thus affects every shot, helping Opponent, making his serves a little hotter, his marginal drops a little longer, getting them across the net into my court to steal points that are rightfully mine. And every shot of mine is affected also: my hot serves are shortened, slowed, my lobs fall short, into the net.

If things were reversed—simple justice cries out for the reversal of our positions—if things were reversed Linesman and Opponent would have those wolfish grins wiped from their leering faces. Scorekeeper's cool objective statements would have a different ring to them.

Scorekeeper announces levelly, "Mr. Grebzlam's serve, single let ball."

I shake myself.

I hold the ball between my fingers and serve again. No extra fillip of technique this time, no English, no deliberate distracting gestures. If I fail on this serve there will be no string of points for me. Opponent's momentum will continue, the Game will be lost.

Simply I serve the ball, *pick-CLONK*.

Opponent returns the serve easily, *ponk-CLONK*.

It is an easy return but it comes with neither steam nor twist. I return it easily, *ponk-CLONK*.

Again Opponent's return, a soft shot, near the center line, I hear a low murmur from audience behind the ball's sound, *ponk-CLONK*.

As I swing my paddle I catch a glimpse of Opponent's expression, a relaxing, aggressive confidence. Is Opponent playing a game of cat-and-mouse with me? Is this a trap to make me relax? Is he simply waiting me out, playing a simple game of return in anticipation of my driving the ball into the net or off the table?

I attempt a corner placement.

The ball whizzes through the still air of the game room. Beneath my feet I can feel the rumble of Ship's mighty engines. There is a barely audible *tick* as the ball drops off the end of the table.

Opponent, knees flexed, elbows out, paddle held before him to return my shot, looked poleaxed. Paralyzed.

Linesman grins, opens his mouth to speak.

Did he hear the *tick* as the ball barely tipped the edge of the table, or is he in league with Opponent, prepared to falsify his call of the point in order to add to my humiliation and disgrace?

Gleefully he cries, "Mr. Grebzlam's point!"

I am vindicated. Overwhelmed.

Opponent seems to stagger, the loss of the point like a physical blow to him.

I giggle triumphantly.

Scorekeeper coolly announces *five to sixteen*.

The ball has careened off into the audience again but Official reaches into his pocket and feels around, pulls out a new ball and rolls it to me. I fumble slightly, then pick it up.

I laugh aloud, throw back my shoulders and without waiting for Opponent to recover put a service ace past him.

Linesman opens his mouth to complain that I served before Opponent was ready but Opponent gestures magnanimously.

Scorekeeper announces *six to sixteen*.

Tonight after Game I will go to the Ship's bar, find some female spectator who witnessed my triumph. There is no question any longer, I will have my choice of any of them.

There will be no need for subtlety but I will exhibit style nonetheless. We will have a drink of whiskey, listen to some music, then go to her cabin. I will tear her clothes off and throw her down. This time it will be better. So far it has never been any good, they always complain afterwards.

"Grebzlam, Grebzlam," they say, "can't you do better than that? All this buildup for that? Get out, Grebzlam!"

How many nights have I slunk back to quarters from the cabin of some disgruntled female. The next day they are never part of the audience, not willing to see me even in defeat at Game, they would rather avoid me altogether. But sometimes we meet again, even by accident. Sometimes when I go to the bar looking for females we meet, and they try to pretend they don't know me.

But I insist. I talk to them. I ask them questions.

What was wrong? What do you want? Just exactly what do you truly want? What is it that you want?

"Grebzlam," they say to me, "just go away. That's what we want, that's what we truly want of you, just leave us alone, Grebzlam!"

They take their purses, finish their drinks and disappear from the bar, leaving me alone with Bartender and Steward and whatever other Official happens to be present. I shuffle from the room and go to quarters.

Opponent rouses me from this fugue by clearing his throat.

I exchange a quick, angry glare with Linesman and put my serve directly into the net.

The ball rolls back toward me, speeded by Ship's own acceleration. I snatch at the ball and it skitters between my fingers. I fumble and grab it and serve again, the aluminum handle of my paddle slipping from my sweaty hand as I serve.

The ball bounces once on the table, *pank*, and bounces off sideways without ever reaching the net while my paddle clatters across the table in the opposite direction and falls to the floor. I stoop to retrieve it and hit my head on the edge of the table. There is an excruciating pain and I see stars.

I hear Opponent's voice, "Grebzlam, are you all right?"

Of course I'm all right! I retrieve my paddle and look at the score indicator. I am trailing Opponent by a count of 6/18.

My last serve is a good one but Opponent returns it and we have another long volley. Finally Ship lurches and throws me off balance and Opponent receives the point. I protest to Linesman that the point should be played over but he denies that Ship moved at all.

"Ship's acceleration is steady," he insists, "and Game is completely stable." As usual he is grinning angrily at me.

"Opponent serves," Scorekeeper announces neutrally.

He takes the ball and serves easily to me. I return the serve, *ponk-CLONK*. He is playing a placement Game, putting one shot to this corner, one to that. I return each placement, but with increasing difficulty. I lack enough time to recover fully from each placement. I leap back and forth at my end of the table, more and more frantically, sweat springing in great beads from my brow.

I make a return from the left, *ponk-CLONK*.

My shot is easy, down the middle.

Opponent's next placement is to my right. I leap sideways, make the return, *ponk-CLONK*, land on my feet, reverse momentum—this is difficult, this is agonizing, but it is something I do anyway—move to my left in preparation for Opponent's next placement, but he makes his shot *ponk-CLONK* to the right again and I stand helplessly watching his soft shot bounce off the table and roll into the crowd of spectators behind me.

Official says "Opponent's point."

Scorekeeper says "Game point, Opponent."

I stand panting, overwhelmed by despair. I decide on a final, dramatic move. I will neither give Opponent the satisfaction of beating down my final defense nor back him into victory by netting my next shot. I will bare my breast for the knife, robbing Opponent thereby of the pleasure of victory.

Opponent serves.

I deliberately stand deep, receive his service and strike upward with my paddle. I will lob the ball high and deep. I will give him an easy bounce. I will let him slam the ball onto my side, *BOINK*!, high into the air. The ball sails high over the table, past Linesman, over Opponent's astonished paddle and lands on his trousers and slithers to the floor.

"Opponent's point," Linesman says.

"Opponent's Game," Scorekeeper announces.

We reverse ends of the table and prepare for the next Game.

Barry Malzberg

Barry Malzberg, in my opinion the finest science fiction writer of the 1970s, created this little parody of Robert Silverberg, another of our very best literary writers. Barry asks me to note that this parodies the Silverberg of the 1970s, rather than the material that Bob is producing today.

THE ∫MOOTH UNIVER∫E·

by R * * * * * S * * * * * * * * *

AND SO THEY WHEEL me from the Temple and say, "Now you are cured and human and ready to live in the world as the world is presently lived." Sensors tick past their doomed faces but otherwise I ignore this, looking at the sky. "I don't think I want to be cured," I say, feeling the even heat radiating from my metallic limbs, "nor do I think I want to be human much less live in the world as it is presently lived." They laugh at this and hand me a Woojamb. Name, index number, life-style, sexual preferences. With the Woojamb in hand I am released to the city. Almost.

* * *

In the night, my little Woojamb ticks away. Name, please. Index number? Life-style! I respond promptly, the alternative is a painful death by expulsion. My constant monitor. *Sexual preference. Respond, please.*

"I don't know," I say at last and this seems to satisfy the soft machine. It permits me to sleep or to keep on being awake or perhaps some combination of the two. Very hard to tell. I hardly know the difference.

* * *

Diffidence, pain and scuttling. And a tuna fish sandwich on rye toast, easy on the mayonnaise. Please.

* * *

The Woojamb directs me to an auxiliary Temple. Obediently I obey, patiently I show patience, quickly I show fleetness of foot. Inside I am scanned for weaponry and asked for my unit of choice. Sexual preference, the Woojamb whispers harshly. "Heterosex," I say. There is a sigh in the Temple. The very walls seem to flatten and relax. Lights smile upon me like dark suns.

"Right this way, my son," the attendant says and my Woojamb and I, we follow her down the corridors toward the unit of choice. Inside I hear the laughter of insects.

* * *

"You are cured and human and ready to live in the world as presently lived. You are. Cured and human and. Ready to live in. The world. As. Presently. Lived you are cured and

* * *

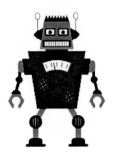

Inside my beauty awakes…I take her with moans and snuffering, snaffling and sighs. Hello, hello, hello. The Woojamb, disguised as a petit four, lurks in my casually draped trouser pockets and turns its cleaved lips upon me in a smile as curved and necessitous as a vagina.

* * *

An Oldsmobile Starfire coupe 1955 with twin exhausts, hydromatic drive, power gear and the autotronic eye makes me think of diffidence, pain and scuttling too.

* * *

Later we sleep or perhaps it is that we merely awaken; I am having more and more trouble as I pointed out in differentiating between these nominal states. She looks at me and I look at her. I think there is an awfulness to the moment which is very tender and begin to speak.

She laughs.

* * *

The Woojamb laughs.

* * *

The personnel of the Temple appear at the doorways, laughing.

* * *

I don my clothing and go out into the slick, sharp, shiny streets, my little Woojamb tightly balled into my hand just like a handkerchief, like a dream. "Just the two of us now," it whispers. "And forever," I respond. "And ever," it adds. Hello, hello, hello. Goodbye, goodbye, goodbye, goodbye.

Poul Anderson

Poul Anderson is famed far and wide as a world-builder, but after seeing what he does to Conan and the Hyborean Age, I'm not so sure that he doesn't rank even higher as a world-destroyer. There have been many parodies of Conan over the years, but this remains the one against which they are all measured.

[*The late Howard Roberts created one of the greatest characters in (so his publishers assure us) science-fantasy in his tales of Cronkheit the Barbarian and the Hybolic Age; and this seems a fitting moment to review the Cronkheit bibliography. As we all know, the stories first appeared in the old Unspeakable and other pulps of the 1930s. A few (five stories and a historical essay on the Hybolic Age) were first assembled into book form in the Roberts omnibus, SCULL-RACE AND OTHERS (Miskatonic, 1946). Since 1950 Pixy Press has undertaken the valuable task, in collaboration with J. Wellington Wells and other noted Hybolic scholars, of publishing the entire Cronkheit canon; and it may be useful to list these books in the order in which they should be read, rather than by dates of publication. Those published to date are: THE COMING OF CRONKHEIT (Pixy, 1953); CRONKHEIT THE BARBARIAN (Pixy, 1954); TALES OF CRONKHEIT, revised by J. Wellington Wells (Pixy, 1956; chronologically overlapping the first two volumes); THE SWORD OF CRONKHEIT (Pixy, 1952); KING CRONKHEIT (Pixy, 1953); and CRONKHEIT THE CONQUEROR (Pixy, 1950; paper reprint, Deuce, 1953). I do*

*not understand how the following episode, surely the most revelatory of
all the chronicles of Cronkheit, has been so far omitted from the collected
canon.]*

THE BARBARIAN

SINCE THE HOWARD-DE-CAMP SYSTEM *for deciphering preglacial
inscriptions first appeared, much progress has been made in tracing the history, ethnology, and even daily life of the great cultures which flourished till
the Pleistocene ice age wiped them out and forced man to start over. We know,
for instance, that magic was practiced; that there were some highly civilized
countries in what is now Central Asia, the Near East, North Africa, southern Europe, and various oceans; and that elsewhere the world was occupied
by Barbarians, of whom the North Europeans were the biggest, strongest, and
most warlike. At least, so the scholars inform us, and being of North European
ancestry they ought to know.*

*The following is a translation of a letter discovered in the ruins of Cyrenne.
This was a provincial town of the Sarmian Empire, a great though decadent
realm in the eastern Mediterranean area, whose capital, Sarmia, was at once
the most beautiful and the most lustful, depraved city of its time. The Sarmians'
northern neighbors were primitive horse nomads and/or Centaurs; but to the
east lay the Kingdom of Chathakh, and to the south was the Herpetarchy of
Serpens, ruled by a priestly cast of snake worshippers—or possibly snakes.*

*The letter was obviously written in Sarmia and posted to Cyrenne. Its date
is approximately 175,000 B.C.*

Maxilion Quaestos, sub-sub-sub-prefect of the Imperial Waterworks
of Sarmia, to his nephew Thyaston, Chancellor of the Bureau of Thauma-
turgy, Province of Cyrenne:

Greetings!

I trust this finds you in good health, and that the gods will continue
to favor you. As for me, I am well, though somewhat plagued by the gout,
for which I have tried *[here follows the description of a home remedy, both
tedious and unprintable].* This has not availed, however, save to exhaust my
purse and myself.

You must indeed have been out of touch during your Atlantean journey, if you must write to inquire about the Barbarian affair. Now that
events have settled down again, I can, I hope, give you an adequate and

dispassionate account of the whole ill-starred business. By the favor of the Triplet Goddesses, holy Sarmia has survived the episode; and though we are still rather shaken, things are improving. If at all times I seem to depart from the philosophic calm I have always tried to cultivate, blame it on the Barbarian. I am not the man I used to be. None of us are.

To begin, then, about three years ago the war with Chathakh had settled down to border skirmishes. Now and then a raid by one side or the other would penetrate deeply into the countries themselves, but with no decisive effect. Indeed, since these operations yielded a more or less equal amount of booty for both lands, and the slave trade grew brisk, it was good for business. Our chief concern was the ambiguous attitude of Serpens. As you well know, the Herpetarchs have no love for us, and a major object of our diplomacy was to keep them from entering the war on the side of Chathakh. We had, of course, no hope of making them our allies. But as long as we maintained a posture of strength, it was likely that they would at least stay neutral.

Thus it stood when the Barbarian came to Sarmia.

We had heard rumors of him for a long time. An accurate description was available. He was a wandering soldier of fortune from some kingdom of swordsmen and seafarers up in the northern forests. He had drifted south, alone, in search of adventure or perhaps only a better climate. Seven feet tall, and broad in proportion, he was one mass of muscle, with a mane of tawny hair and sullen blue eyes. He was adept with any weapon, but preferred a four-foot double-edged sword with which he could cleave helmet, skull, neck, and so on down at one blow. He was also said to be a drinker and lover of awesome capacity.

Having overcome the Centaurs singlehanded, he tramped down through our northern provinces and one day stood at the gates of Sarmia herself. It was a curious vision—the turreted walls rearing up over the stone-paved road, the guards with helmet and shield and corselet, and the towering near-naked giant who rattled his blade before them. As their pikes slanted down to bar his way, he cried in a voice of thunder:

"I yam Cronkheit duh Barbarian, an' I wanna audience widjer queen!"

His accent was so ludicrously uneducated that the watch burst into laughter. This angered him; flushing darkly, he drew his sword and advanced stiff-legged. The guardsmen reeled back before him, and the Barbarian swaggered through.

As the captain of the watch explained it to me afterward: "There he came, and there we stood. A spear length away, we caught the smell. Ye gods, when did he last bathe?"

So with people running from the streets and bazaars as he neared, Cronkheit made his way down the Avenue of Sphinxes, past the baths and the Temple of Loccar, till he reached the Imperial Palace. Its gates stood wide open as usual, and he looked in at the gardens and the alabaster walls beyond, and grunted. When the Golden Guardsmen approached him upwind and asked his business, he grunted again. They lifted their bows and would have made short work of him, but a slave came running to bid them desist.

You see, by the will of some malignant god, the Empress was standing on a balcony and saw him.

As is well known, our beloved Empress, Her Seductive Majesty the Illustrious Lady Larra the Voluptuous, is built like a mountain highway and is commonly believed to be an incarnation of her tutelary deity, Aphrosex, the Mink Goddess. She stood on the balcony with the wind blowing her thin transparent garments and thick black hair, and a sudden eagerness lit her proud lovely face. This was understandable, for Cronkheit wore only a bearskin kilt.

So the slave was dispatched, to bow low before the stranger and say: "Most noble lord, the divine Empress would have private speech with you."

Cronkheit smacked his lips and strutted into the palace. The chamberlain wrung his hands when he saw those large muddy feet treading priceless rugs, but there was no help for it, and the Barbarian was led upstairs into the Imperial bedchamber.

What befell there is known to all, for of course in such interviews the Lady Larra posts mute slaves at convenient peepholes, to summon the guard if danger seems to threaten; and the courtiers have quietly taught these mutes to write. Our Empress had a cold, and had furthermore been eating a garlic salad, so her aristocratically curved nose was not offended. After a few formalities, she began to pant. Slowly, then she held out her arms and let the purple robe slide down from her creamy shoulders and across silken thighs.

"Come," she whispered. "Come, magnificent male." Cronkheit snorted, pawed the ground, rushed forth, and clasped her to him.

"Yowww!" cried the Empress as a rib cracked. "Leggo! Help!"

The mutes ran for the Golden Guardsmen, who entered at once. They got ropes around the Barbarian and dragged him from their poor lady. Though in considerable pain, and much shaken, she did not order his execution; she is known to be very patient with some types.

Indeed, after gulping a cup of wine to steady her, she invited Cronkheit to be her guest. After he had been conducted off to his rooms, she summoned the Duchess of Thyle, a supple, agile little minx.

"I have a task for you, my dear," she murmured. "You will fulfill it as a loyal lady in waiting."

"Yes, Your Seductive Majesty," said the Duchess, who could well guess what the task was and thought she had been waiting long enough. For a whole week, in fact. Her assignment was to take the edge off the Barbarian's impetuosity.

She greased herself so she could slip free if in peril of being crushed, and hurried to Cronkheit's suite. Her musky perfume drowned out his odor, and she slipped off her dress and crooned with half-shut eyes: "Take me, my lord!"

"Yahoo!" howled the warrior. "I yam Cronkheit duh Strong, Cronkheit duh Bold, Cronkheit what slew a mammot' singlehanded an' made hisself chief o'duh Centaurs, an' dis's muh night! C'mere!"

The Duchess did, and he folded her in his mighty arms. A moment later there was another shriek. The palace attendants were treated to the sight of a naked and furious greased Duchess speeding down the jade corridor.

"Fleas he's got!" she cried, scratching as she ran.

So all in all Cronkheit the Barbarian was no great success as a lover. Even the women in the Street of Joy used to hide when they saw him coming. They said they'd been exposed to clumsy technique before, but this was just too much.

However, his fame was so great that the Lady Larra put him in command of a brigade, infantry and cavalry, and sent him to join General Grythion on the Chathakh border. He made the march in record time and came shouting into the city of tents which had grown up at our main base.

Now admittedly our good General Grythion is somewhat of a dandy, who curls his beard and is henpecked by his wives. But he has always been a competent soldier, winning honors at the Academy and leading troops in battle many times before rising to the strategic-planning post. One could understand Cronkheit's incivility at their meeting. But when the general courteously declined to go forth in the van of the army and pointed out how much more valuable he was as a coordinator behind the lines—that was no excuse for Cronkheit to knock his superior officer to the ground and call him a coward, damned of the gods. Grythion was thoroughly justified in having him put in irons, despite the casualties involved. Even as it was, the spectacle had so demoralized our troops that they lost three important engagements in the following month.

Alas! Word of this reached the Empress, and she did not order Cronkheit's head struck off. Indeed, she sent back a command that he be released and reinstated. Perhaps she still cherished him enough to be an acceptable bed partner.

Grythion swallowed his pride and apologized to the Barbarian, who accepted with an ill grace. His restored rank made it necessary to invite him to a dinner and conference in the headquarters tent.

It was a flat failure. Cronkheit stamped in and at once made sneering remarks about the elegant togas of his brother officers. He belched when he ate and couldn't distinguish the product of one vineyard from another. His conversation consisted of hour-long monologues about his own prowess. General Grythion saw morale zooming downward, and hastily called for maps and planning.

"Now, most noble sirs," he began, "we have to lay out the summer campaign. As you know, we have the Eastern Desert between us and the nearest important enemy positions. This raises difficult questions of logistics and catapult emplacement." He turned politely to the Barbarian. "Have you any suggestion, my lord?"

"Duh," said Cronkheit.

"I think," ventured Colonel Pharaon, "that if we advanced to the Chunling Oasis and dug in there, building a supply road—"

"Dat reminds me," said Cronkheit. "One time up in duh norriki marshes, I run acrost some swamp men an' dey uses poisoned arrers—"

"I fail to see what that has to do with this problem," said General Grythion.

"Nuttin'," admitted Cronkheit cheerfully. "But don't innerup' me. Like I was sayin'—" And he was off for another dreary hour.

At the end of a conference which had gotten nowhere, the general stroked his beard and said shrewdly: "Lord Cronkheit, it appears your abilities are more in the tactical than the strategic field."

The Barbarian snatched for his sword.

"I mean," said Grythion quickly, "I have a task which only the boldest and strongest leader can accomplish."

Cronkheit beamed and listened closely for a change. He was to be sent out with his men to capture Chantsay. This was a fort in the mountain passes across the Eastern Desert, and a major obstacle to our advance. However, in spite of Grythion's judicious flattery, a full brigade should have been able to take it with little difficulty, for it was known to be undermanned.

Cronkheit rode off at the head of his men, tossing his sword in the air and bellowing some uncouth battle chant. Then he was not heard of for six weeks.

At the close of that time, the ragged, starving, fever-stricken remnant of his troops staggered back to the base and reported utter failure. Cronkheit, who was in excellent health himself, made some sullen excuses. But he had never imagined that men who march twenty hours a day aren't fit for battle at the end of the trip—the more so if they outrun their own supply train.

Because of the Empress's wish, General Grythion could not do the sensible thing and cashier the Barbarian. He could not even reduce him to the ranks. Instead, he used his well-known guile and invited the guest to a private dinner.

"Obviously, most valiant lord," he purred, "the fault is mine. I should have realized that a man of your type is too much for us decadent southerners. You are a lone wolf who fights best by himself."

"Duh," agreed Cronkheit, ripping a fowl apart with his fingers and wiping them on the damask tablecloth.

Grythion winced, but easily talked him into going out on a one-man guerrilla operation. When he left the next morning, the officers' corps congratulated themselves on having gotten rid of the lout forever.

In the face of subsequent criticism and demands for an investigation, I still maintain that Grythion did the only rational thing under the circumstances. Who could have known that Cronkheit the Barbarian was so primitive that rationality simply slid off his hairy skin?

The full story will never be known. But apparently, in the course of the following year, while the border war continued as usual, Cronkheit struck off into the northern uplands. There he raised a band of horse nomads as ignorant and brutal as himself. He also rounded up a herd of mammoths and drove them into Chathakh, stampeding them at the foe. By such means, he reached their very capital, and the King offered terms of surrender.

But Cronkheit would have none of this. Not he! His idea of warfare was to kill or enslave every last man, woman, and child of the enemy nation. Also, his irregulars were supposed to be paid in loot. Also, being too unsanitary even for the nomad girls, he felt a certain urgency.

So he stormed the capital of Chathakh and burned it to the ground. This cost him most of his own men. It also destroyed several priceless books and works of art, and any possibility of tribute to Sarmia.

Then he had the nerve to organize a triumphal procession and ride back to our own city!

This was too much even for the Empress. When he stood before her—for he was too crude for the simple courtesy of a knee bend—she exceeded herself in describing the many kinds of fool, idiot, and all-around blockhead he was.

"Duh," said Cronkheit. "But I won duh war. Look, I won duh war, I did. I won duh war."

"Yes," hissed the Lady Larra. "You smashed an ancient and noble culture to irretrievable ruin. And did you know that one half our peacetime trade was with Chathakh? There'll be a business depression now such as history as never seen before."

General Grythion, who had returned, added his own reproaches. "Why do you think wars are fought?" he asked bitterly. "War is an extension of diplomacy. It's the final means of making someone else do what you want. The object is not to kill them all off—how can corpses obey you?" Cronkheit growled in his throat.

"We would have negotiated a peace in which Chathakh became our ally against Serpens," went on the general. "Then we'd have been safe against all comers. But *you*—You've left a howling wilderness which we must garrison with our own troops lest the nomads take it over. Your atrocities have alienated every civilized state. You've left us alone and friendless. You've won this war by losing the next one!"

"And on top of the depression which is coming," said the Empress, "we'll have the cost of maintaining those garrisons. Taxes down and expenditures up—It may break the treasury, and then where are we?"

Cronkheit spat on the floor. "Yuh're all decadent, dat's what yuh are," he snarled. "Be good for yuh if yer empire breaks up. Yuh oughtta get dat city rabble o' yers out in duh woods an' make hunters of 'em, like me. Let 'em eat steak."

The Lady Larra stamped an exquisite gold-shod foot. "Do you think we've nothing better to do with our time than spend the whole day hunting, and sit around in some mud hovel at night licking the grease off our fingers?" she cried. "What the hell do you think civilization is for, anyway?"

Cronkheit drew his great sword so it flashed before their eyes. "I hadda nuff!" he bellowed. "I'm t'rough widjuh! It's time yuh was all wiped off duh face o'duh eart', an' I'm jus' duh guy t' do it!"

And now General Grythion showed the qualities which had raised him to his high post. Artfully, he quailed. "Oh no!" he whimpered. "You're not going to—to—to fight on the side of Serpens?"

"I yam," said Cronkheit. "So long." The last we saw of him was a broad, indignant, flea-bitten back, headed south; and the reflection of the sun on a sword.

Since then, of course, our affairs have prospered and Serpens is now frantically suing for peace. But we intend to prosecute the war till they meet our terms. We are most assuredly not going to be ensnared by their treacherous plea and take the Barbarian back!

Gene DeWeese & Robert Coulson

When I first began assembling this anthology, it took me almost three months to discover that the mysterious Thomas Stratton was actually the well-known writing team of Gene DeWeese and Buck Coulson. On the other hand, it took only ten minutes to decide that this was the funniest parody of Edgar Rice Burroughs that I had ever seen.

JOHN CARPER AND HIS ELECTRIC BARSOOM

by Thomas Stratton

IN A LOVELY GOLDEN garden in the capitol city of the country of Hydrogen sat the bold heroic figure of John Carper, Jedackack of all Barsoom, holding close to his bold heroic chest the pure and beautiful form of the lovely Jedackackess of all Barsoom, Disha Thorax.

They were, as one might expect of the Jedackack and Jedackackess of all Barsoom, discussing the welfare of their loyal and devoted subjects. They had been pursuing this patriotic line of discussion for many hours when another bold heroic figure cleared the twenty-foot garden wall in a leap and a half. It was, they saw as the figure approached them in leaps and bounds, revealing itself to be not quite so bold and heroic as John Carper himself, their only hatched son, Cathartic.

"Father!" John Carper's son, the fruit of his loins, cried. "I come to you now to ask your aid, for you are even more bold and heroic than I. That lovely creature, second only in beauty and purity to my beloved mater, the fragile and delicate Vethuvias, has been taken captive, placed in durance vile by the infamous Tortoisians. She—oh vision of loveliness that she is!—has been taken far across the dead sea bottoms to the barren, wasted Polar regions, the only place on all of Barsoom where your power, oh bold heroic father, does not extend. So I ask of you the boon of your incomparable succor in this hour of my greatest need and sorrow."

John Carper, Jedackack of all Barsoom, disengaged himself gently from the lovely arms of the beautiful Disha Thorax, and rose slowly and thoughtfully to his feet. He looked at the noble countenance of his only hatched son Cathartic, and seeing there the same earthly strain of courage, strength, and loyalty which flowed in his own noble veins, made his decision. "Here, son," he said. "You may take my air rifle and may all the gods of Barsoom go with you!"

"Oh great warrior and husband of mine!" spoke the incomparable vision of beauty that was Disha Thorax. "Do not jest at a time like this! Do you not remember how you, John Carper, felt when I, Disha Thorax, was torn from your bold heroic bosom when you first came to Barsoom?"

"You are right, my beloved one," the Jedackack replied. He turned again to Cathartic. "You may have the services of the army, and my faithful friend and companion through all my intrepid adventures, the six-legged Barsoomian dog, Moola, will accompany you, as will my other loyal and beloved battle companion, that great green warrior, Kars Karkas. This will, of course, leave the capital city of Hydrogen unguarded, but…"

The magnificent Jedackack of all Barsoom hesitated: modesty forbade him to continue. He motioned discreetly to the shimmering vision of loveliness that rose from the ersatz bench. "But of course," Disha Thorax continued, "Cathartic, my beloved and only-hatched son, your father, being as bold and heroic as he is, will be well able to hold off any trouble until you return with the army. Besides, we killed off all our enemies in the last book."

Thus it was that, backed by the mightiest (in fact the only) army on Barsoom and its third greatest warrior in the person of the giant Kars Karkas, and led on by the keen sixth sense of smell of the greatest Culotte of all Barsoom, Moola, Cathartic, the second greatest warrior of all Barsoom, set out on his quest for the second loveliest woman of all Barsoom.

Needless to say, he succeeded thumpingly.

Back across the red-crusted desert, the winding canals, the deathless dead sea bottoms, wound the great retinue, carrying aloft on a litter of gold and silver and precious stones, the fantastically beautiful Vethuvias, lovely maid of Mars. Back to the capitol of Hydrogen, where the great retinue lowered the litter of gold and silver and precious stones with a sigh of relief and collapsed.

"Hail, father!" spoke Cathartic. "I have succeeded in my quest for the second most lovely woman of Barsoom, and I return, grown greater in stature because of my recent valiant deeds."

"My only hatched son, it does my noble heart good to find that you are following in my bold and heroic footsteps. By the way, has your arduous journey diminished your princely strength in any wise?"

"No, father. I still feel that I am the second strongest mortal on Barsoom."

"Good. I have received disquieting reports concerning the legendary Puce Pirates of Phobos. How about running out there and checking up for me?"

"I am yours to command. Despite the fact that I have but returned from a cruel journey, and have only been re-united with the second loveliest woman on all Barsoom, I am ready to follow you to the end of the Universe!" ("And push you off," he added to himself.)

"Follow...Hmmm...well, that wasn't exactly...oh well, never mind. My son, with you beside me, nothing in the Universe can deter me."

Thus, as the golden orb of the sun rises over Hydrogen the next morning, we find a caravan of Barsoomian flyers, bearing John Carper, Cathartic, Kars Karkas, Disha Thorax, Vethuvias, Moola, and scores of extras, also rising over the quiet city. John Carper, Jedackack of all Barsoom, has begun his quest for the Phantom Puce Pirates of Phobos, surely one of the strangest episodes in his gallant career!

The flyers rose higher in the Barsoomian morning; Disha Thorax and Vethuvias were sunning themselves on the top deck of the flagship, just in front of the flagpole. The glories of Barsoom spread out beneath the ascending ships. The magnificent, awe-inspiring dead sea bottoms were. What more need be said? Anyone who has had the inestimable privilege of viewing their grandeur has had the glorious magnificence of those incredibly awe-inspiring sights driven ineradicably into his mind, and no further word by me could in any way enhance those memories; and for those who have not, mere words could not do sufficient justice to those glorious monuments to the wondrous past of this ancient, time-honored planet.

Higher and higher still the flyers soared. The dead sea bottoms fell farther behind. Now the curve of the horizon could be seen, and the white glitter of the snowfields around the pole; the growing chill of the atmosphere forced Disha Thorax and Vethuvias to retire inside the flyer. Armed guards, shivering in uniforms more suited to the desert than this arctic altitude (Barsoom had a lousy quartermaster service), patrolled the decks. Now, ahead of the valiant company, could be seen the jagged, snow-capped peaks of Phobos, the larger moon of Barsoom.

"Hold!" shouted John Carper, striding across the deck of the flagship. "Cease! Halt! Desist!"

The crew looked up from their various duties of patrolling the deck, steering, navigating, scraping barnacles from the hull and each other. "Sir," asked the captain, "what great wisdom and knowledge causes your Imperial Jedackackishness to call upon this indomitable, invincible, indestructible and altogether incomparable warfleet to stop?"

The Jedackack, suffering from one of his brilliant flashes of genius, replied, "Is this not a flyer? A flyer which requires air to fly? Is there air between Barsoom and Phobos? No! Therefore......"

"Father!" It was his only hatched son, Cathartic, standing before him on the wind-whipped airless deck. "You must have faith!"

The mighty John Carper appeared sad for a moment, then regained his Jedackackish composure. "You are right, my son! Sail on—to the jagged snow-capped peaks of Phobos!"

But were these the jagged snow-capped peaks of Phobos? It has been truly said that faith can move mountains; but could faith put snow caps on mountains? Especially when there were no mountains there in the first place?

But of course! In a brilliant flash of brilliant insight, it was all clear to John Carper: this was *not* Phobos before them! It was a cleverly camouflaged artificial moon, and the jagged snow-capped mountains were not jagged snow-capped mountains at all; they were in reality, he realized, ingeniously disguised gigantic weapons, the peaks being the deadly muzzles. And the Puce Pirates had those weapons trained on them AT THAT VERY MOMENT!

All this he realized in less time than it takes me to tell it. Even so, it was too late, for the brilliant flash, he also realized an instant later, was not from his scintillating intellect, but from the firing of those incredible weapons.

It was indeed fortunate for that gallant expedition that Cathartic had seen the danger a moment before. The flagship heeled sharply, and the bolts of ravening energy flashed past, scorching the paint on the bridge. At the same moment, Cathartic loosed a broadside from the port guns. Luckily, John Carper's hawklike eyes found it almost immediately. The entire fleet was now taking evasive action. Flashing streaks of cosmic energy flamed between the fleet and the floating fort. With John Carper bellowing orders from the bridge of the flagship, the Barsoomian fleet began to close with the enemy. At last, two of the ships grounded on the artificial moon, and the Jedackack gave the order: "Boarders away!"

Swarms of chartreuse men, the deadliest fighters (except for John Carper and Cathartic) on Barsoom, poured onto the surface of the moon. Led by the bold and heroic Jedackack and his only hatched son, they were met by the Puce Pirates, and their allies, the magenta-and-heliotrope men of Deimos, in hand-to-hand combat. It was a colorful spectacle.

Meanwhile, back at the flagship, Vethuvias and Disha Thorax had crept quietly up the catwalk for a clearer conception of the cataclysmic chaos into which they had been catapulted. But no sooner had they attained the deck of the craft than it tilted sharply sideways, dumping them precipitately onto the surface of the hostile artificial moon. The leader of the Puce Pirates, Argh Grghrd, took quick advantage of this by snatching them from under the very eyeballs of John Carper and Cathartic, not to mention Kars Karkas and the army, and swiftly secured them in his private quarters, inside the moon.

The battle raged on!

And on!

Finally, however, the smoke of battle (a spark from the clashing swords had started a fire) cleared away, and it could be seen that the forces of Evil had been crushed once more or less. Seeing their army destroyed, Argh Grghrd and his lieutenant, Mrumph, retreated below the surface of the moon.

Hot on the heels of the hellions hove the Heroes, hardly hesitating a hectare. (Barsoomian time unit barely worth mentioning.) Down through the labyrinthine, tortuous, twisting tunnels and carven passageways they battled; into depths lighted only by sparks from the clashing swords. At last, they arrived at the inner chambers where waited the two visions of beauty for which, subconsciously so far, this war (and countless others) had been waged and won.

As the two Heroes leaped into the room, Carper cried, "Unhand those visions of loveliness, you foul fiends, or you will have me—and my only hatched son, Cathartic—to deal with!"

"For that matter," added Cathartic, a practical soul, "you have us to deal with already."

"My bold, heroic, only hatched son is correct," Carper affirmed. "And..." He gestured subtly to Disha Thorax and Vethuvias.

"And they are," chorused the visions of loveliness, "the mightiest fighting men on all Barsoom."

"True," admitted Argh, evincing more courage than was usual for those of his ilk, possibly because he had a small blaster trained on the mightiest fighting men of all Barsoom. "But," he continued, "you are not now on Barsoom!"

In a few moments, Barsoom had a new Jedackack.

R. C. Walker

Rod Walker is a poet by trade, and the field of parody is much the poorer for that fact. Perhaps no series within recent memory begs for parody so much as John Norman's Gor books—and no one has answered that crying need as well as Rod.

QUEEN OF BORR

Introductory Note

I MUST CONFESS THAT I, as so many others, was a skeptic when tales of a "counter-Earth," a planet antipodal to our own, first began to circulate. However, some time ago a friend called me aside and showed me a remarkable collection of documents. "By the most unusual means these things arrive," he confided, "and I must have a dozen of them by now." His story was truly surprising: periodically he would receive a long narrative, purportedly written by a fraternity brother of his. He did not know the author well during college, recalling only that he spent considerable time in the biology lab with the experimental animals. "It was very strange, considering he was a Phys-Ed major," he commented.

At any rate, my friend, who is a used-book dealer, has been receiving these missives in various ways: one was tucked inside a rare early edition of The Story of O; another he found inside a yellowtail he'd caught while ocean fishing; still another was in his safe when he opened it one evening to put in the day's cash receipts; and so on. Such weird occurrences are, my friend's correspondent says, the work of the "yeast-kings," the absolute masters of this segment of the known galaxy. They are so-called because although they cannot be seen, they exude the distinct odor of stale beer.

My friend (who by various efficacious threats has secured my guarantee of his anonymity) has for some time been aware that he is not the only recipient of such letters. Expanded and thinly-disguised (but considerably distorted) versions of similar communications have appeared in print. In the interest of truth, therefore, he has asked me to edit and submit the latest letter, which he found a month ago sticking out of his garbage disposal.

I

DEAR ~ :

A great deal has happened since I last wrote you. I don't really know if these letters are reaching you, although Tsk-tsk the Yeast-King assures me they do. He often repeats the ritual formula of his people's couriers: "Nor comets, nor meteors, nor dark of space," and so on.

It still seems strange to me that I, Snarl Babbit, a man of Earth, should find himself so uniquely suited to the life-styles of distant Borr. Yet, with each passing of Borr's hurtling moons, I am more and more perfectly adapted to this world which citified, effete Earthmen (and, of course, Earthwomen) might characterize as brutal, barbaric, bloody, and bawdy. It is: no wonder I like it so much.

You will recall that I had decided to capture the beautiful Lotta-Huuha of Glorious Wuz. She was *Rubarba*, or Queen, of that city. She had ambitions to become Queen of all Borr, a thing unheard of in all our history. I was naturally, as any red-blooded man of Borr, incensed that a mere woman, like all her sex a slave within, should aspire to independent rule of any sort. It is bad enough that the Traditions of Borr permit some women to remain free, poor things. I determined that this miscarriage of the laws of nature should go no further. I went to my father, Kashew Babbit, who is Rubarb (or King) of my city of Ko-ro-zhun, and quickly obtained his permission for my just and heroic quest.

II

WHISTLING A MERRY TUNE, I skipped back to my penthouse apartment atop one of the high-rise towers in the exorbitant-rent district of Ko-ro-zhun. I ran up the five flights of steps (I know that doesn't sound like many, but six stories *is* "high-rise" when all you've got to build with is mud bricks). Opening the entry-door, I gave my slave Raquel a playful slap across the mouth. I instantly regretted such an open display of my affection. I had left the poor wench alone for several hours and in consequence she immediately had a slave orgasm, the most exciting experience any woman can expect in life. Unable to control my ardor, I crushed her in my arms, smashing her lips with the incredible rape of a slave kiss. I threw her down on the floor, where she lay gasping, lips and tongue bleeding. She had another slave orgasm.

"I love you, master," she said.

I took up my nine-lashed slave whip and gave her a good thrashing for being impertinent and for daring to have orgasms without my permission. I knew, of course, that she could hardly help herself, with such a powerful master as I. However, a good beating now and then is good for slave morale: they languish without discipline. Indeed, at this new demonstration of my concern, ownership, and power, Raquel had yet another orgasm. I did not punish her for that: I had one, too.

"Serve me wine," I said.

"Yes, master," she said. Then she looked at me with loving eyes and said "*Yo lileva*"; that is, "I am a female slave." The Borrean word for a male slave is *unkultom*. Have I told you that before?

Raquel wriggled across the floor on her belly and fetched a bottle (a *grog* in Borrean) of wine. Filling a cup, she crawled back to me, as I lounged in a divan, and kneeling before me, kissed the cup with her bruised and bloody lips. This is a fantastically stimulating gesture, which arouses the deepest passions of the Borrean male. I contemplated giving her a black eye, but I was just too tired for any more sex.

"May a wench speak?" she said.

"Yes," I replied.

"Free me, master: a wench begs her master for freedom. Master, I am of Earth. I am not like the others. I was a movie star; I could throw tantrums all day and eat strawberries and cream all night. I have millions in the bank. Free me, please."

"The wench is forward," I remarked. "You are a Borrean slave. You will never be anything but a Borrean slave. Yes, Raquel, I know you were once a movie star. That makes no difference here. The Yeast-Kings do not allow movies on Borr. They are too full of violence and sex. I have been kind to you. You could be crossed and gartered, or even defenestrated, as punishment for asking to be free," I said.

"Oh, my!" she exclaimed.

"Yes," I agreed.

"*Yo lileva*," she said, with more enthusiasm than the last time, bowing her head.

"It is good you understand these things, Raquel," I admonished. "Now I must depart on my quest," I informed her.

III

QUICKLY I PACKED MY *thessaurion*-hide duffel bags. I then went to Al-Ka-One Rent-a-Thing. From a demure young slave I hired a *barn*, one of the great flying birds of Borr. It is called a *barn* because that is what it is as big as. It resembles a sort of bloated ostrich, but it can fly. It seldom likes to do so much above treetop level; even so, it is a formidable weapon of war and provides rapid transit for slaving expeditions and other entertainments. The *barn* is saddled much as a horse on Earth, but the saddle is both longer (affording seating for two or more) and higher (protecting the rider from untimely ejection from his precarious perch).

The *barn* is guided by a set of complex reins. Its powerful beak could readily snap or bite through any conceivable bit. Therefore it is guided by a set of devices, not unlike bicycle bells, tuned to various pitches. A lead line is attached to each bell. This line, when pulled, will cause the bell to ring. By means of these, the rider may instruct the *barn* to rise, descend, turn right or left, lay an egg, eat somebody, and so on. "Down," for instance, is B-flat, while "Look out" is C-sharp. One bell, tuned to the Phrygian Mode, means "Pick up your stupid feet," since the bird has a habit of letting them trail in tree branches and thus becoming entangled. The various reins are differently colored; puce, magenta, ochre, burnt umber, azure, cerise, tangerine, and so on.

On the ground, the *barn* is herded by means of *barn*-goats. These are much larger than slave-goats, used to train and discipline slaves. They are capable of giving the giant birds severe butts about the thighs and breast if necessary to insure appropriate behavior.

Have I told you about *barns* before? I am always amazed that Borr, which is so far behind Earth is some ways, is even further behind in others.

When I was ready to depart, my *barn* was brought forward, gently butted by its *barn*-goat. These birds are extremely fierce and it is of course necessary to demonstrate one's mastery over one before it may be ridden. In accordance with ancient custom, I stared directly into the *barn*'s beady eyes and growled, "Yer mudder wuz an omelette!" Thus properly chastened, the bird instantly squatted and permitted me to mount. This I did hurriedly because the *barn*-goat seemed to be sidling over in my direction with malicious intent.

Once mounted, I cried at the top of my lungs the battle cry of Ko-ro-zhun, "High-ho!, high-ho!" This of course had no effect on the *barn*. It stood there, calmly chewing on the rental company's slave-girl. Now I pulled the lavender bell; instantly the *barn* hurled itself over the parapet of the great tower wherein it was penned, fifty stories up. We fell about thirty stories before it recalled that in order to fly, flapping the wings was necessary. I have mentioned before, haven't I, that *barns* are not awfully bright?

IV

SOUTH, OUT OF THE mighty city of Ko-ro-zhun, we flew, toward the mighty city of Glorious Wuz. Over fields and farms we winged our way. The *barn* is not a particularly fastidious bird; frequently I would note a peasant looking up with hatred—and something else—in his face. Later that day we flew over the vast River Vast. The Vast rises in the Evylai Mountains, a thousand *gangbangs* to the east.

(The *gangbang* is the mile of Borr, varying slightly from city to city; the *gangbang* is 0.999 mile; that is, 5279 feet. A square *gangbang* is called a gruupgrohp, whilst 1/10 of a gruupgrohp, the unit of agricultural and military measurement, is called a grabb.) (The Vast, by the way, eventually forms an enormous delta and enters the Tambourine Gulf near the harbor of Port Kaftan. Beyond the Gulf is the Sea. In the north the sea is called Thissa, whilst in the south it is called Thatta. It is full of all sorts of islands, such as Sine, Cosine, Tangent, Secant, Skunj, Skweel, Mairzedoats, Do-si-do, and Marilynmonroe [which is what that particular island looks like]. The island of Cosine has for generations been at war with Glorious Wuz. Nobody knows why. For one thing, they are separated by 2000 *gangbangs* of ocean, desert, and mountains. For another, whilst Cosine has no army, Wuz has no navy. I've told you about all this before, haven't I?)

On we flew to Glorious Wuz, over the great cities of Tripe, Goldarna, and Tora-Tora-Tora. Toward evening we approached Glorious Wuz from the south, either having circled around to come in from the other side or having been mistaken about the direction of our flight in the first place. I never was much good at geography. I bade my mount to fly low to evade radar detection. Just as I recalled that there is no radar on Borr, I also realized that my *barn* had gotten its feet tangled in the branches of a *piichpitt* tree.

V

WE FELL IN A flurry of flapping feathers, jangling bells, and scattered provisions on the edge of a wooded area east (or possibly west) of Glorious Wuz. My bird's neck was broken, so it would not be able to fly for a few hours. I shoved some rejuvenation pills down its throat and sat down to determine what I should do.

I did not relish being out alone in the Borrean countryside at night. This was when the fierce, fanged, and furry *fudd* hunted the sly *smerp*. (The *smerp* is a fuzzy creature with long ears which eats a long, orange Borrean root vegetable called a *karat*. I often wonder how it came to be called a *smerp*.) Of course, the fierce, fanged, and furry *fudd* will eat men if it can find them.

I also dreaded running into that shaggy, but intelligent, behemoth known as the *cur*, which often roamed this area. Besides, the countryside was literally crawling (literally) with giant snakes, giant spiders, giant scorpions, giant dung-beetles, vampires, wolf-men, the living dead, the deadly living, and all the usual perils associated with operations of this sort.

Leaving my bird, I boldly—but nonetheless keeping a watch over my shoulder—struck out for the great city. I carried with me only a few weapons. I had my favorite flintlock rifle. (Gunpowder is banned by the Yeast-Kings, but the pearl-handled rifle made a really spiffy club.)

In addition I carried: long bow, short bow, cross bow, long sword, short sword, singing sword, mace (two cans of it), six hundred arrows, bolo, long knife, short knife, boy scout knife, dagger, stiletto, poniard, knitting needles, poisoned darts, slingshot, tomahawk, single-edged axe, double-edged axe, horns in pairs, fife, drum guitar, and the usual strings.

Stealthily I loped toward the walls of Wuz. As I neared the top of a small hill, I heard a blood-curdling wail. My blood curdled. It was the cry of a *cur*. I crept to the crest of the hill and, sure enough, down the slope I saw the immense, shaggy, form of a *cur*. Then I smiled. The creature had not seen me. It was armed only with a sword and shield. My eyes narrowed in relieved glee as I bethought myself of my long bow. Quickly and silently I took my weapon and aimed it.

Closer the *cur* came, closer and yet closer. I wanted to take no chance of missing. When I could just distinguish the whites of its eyes, I rose out of hiding, screaming the war-cry of Ko-ro-zhun, "High-ho, high-ho!" Instantly I threw the long bow at the huge *cur.*

My bow struck the creature's chest, dead center. To my surprise, it was unhurt. These brutes must be made of iron! Taking its sword in its right paw, it advanced menacingly toward me, screaming the horrid war-cry of the *curry* (more than one *cur*), "Tuu-whytt, tuu-whuuuuuu, skubiy, skubiy-duuuuuuu!"

But I was not yet beaten. In rapid succession I threw my short bow, and my cross bow, followed by the singing sword, the two cans of mace, and my knitting needles. Nothing daunted that awesome tower of animal power. I back-pedaled furiously, hoping to find something that worked. I took up my single-edged axe, hilt in one hand and head in the other, and threw it with all my strength. The *cur*, amazingly, caught it in mid-flight, took it by the hilt, and threw it back. I ducked; the axe-blade lodged deeply in the tree behind me. You may be sure I will remember that novel tactic for use later on! Next I threw several arrows and my guitar, but nothing stopped the advancing *cur*. "Back, you *cur!*" I cried. "Back, back!" Now the beast, ten feet and two thousand pounds of enraged felt, was nearly upon me. Desperate, I seized the first thing that came to hand. I threw one of my poisoned darts.

I stood over my fallen foe, grateful I had spent considerable time at the pub down the street from my penthouse. Then, wary that I might arouse some new danger, I tippy-toed in haste toward the walls of Wuz. My way was well-lighted by the three hurtling moons of Borr.

VI

I ARRIVED AT WUZ without further incident. As I approached one of the gates of Glorious Wuz, I disguised myself by throwing over my body a long black robe. A few moments later, a Night Watchman atop the gate espied me. "Halt," he cried. "Who goes there?"

"Me," I replied.

"Well, who are you?" he queried.

"I am Rasputin, of the Caste of Third-Degree Masons," I answered.

"How-de-do, Rasputin?" he called down cheerily. "I am Frosch, of the Caste of Night Watchmen, Jailers, and Wicktrimmers," he remarked.

"May I come in?" I questioned. "It's not very nice out here," I added.

"Sure," he said. "Why didn't you say so before?" he asked. "I'll be right down and open up," he concluded.

Thus did I enter the city of Glorious Wuz. Once inside, I asked Frosch, "Can you direct me to the tower of the Rubarba, Lotta-Huuha?"

"Oh, yeah," he replied, "but the guided tours don't start until ten in the morning," he volunteered. He gave me detailed directions. "You go down that street, which is 42nd Street, until you reach the square where the city clock is kept. That's Time Square. Then you turn up Glorious Revolution Boulevard to the second impalement stake on your right and turn left into Rue Royale. Count until you reach the fifth gallows on your left and turn right. Go up Red Island Road to the end. Then you'll be at the Rubarba's tower. I hope you enjoy the tour." I bade him farewell and, chuckling, followed his directions. The streets of Glorious Wuz were crowded with merry-makers, revelers, shoppers, and slaves. I saw a free woman or two being stripped and branded, a few hundred slaves being beaten, four dozen dismemberments, twenty hangings, six impalements, and one head-bashing. I was relieved to know that, aside from the aberration of a female ruler, Glorious Wuz was just like other Borrean cities. With all the fun going on, nobody would notice a quiet stranger slipping through their midst.

VII

BOLDLY I APPROACHED THE front entrance to the Rubarba's tower. There was only one guard on duty before the turnstile. I smiled and approached him, affecting the vacant stare of a country bumpkin (or *toorista*, as such a one is called on Borr). The Rubarba's guards would be quick-witted and suspicious. But perhaps, if I were clever, a slip of the tongue might give me some details of the tower and its defenses.

"Hi, there," I said.

"Hi, there, yourself," he said. His seeming open friendliness obviously cloaked cautious forbearance. This would be a hard nut to crack.

I decided to try a new gambit. "My name is Ebenezer, of the Caste of Skinflints," I said.

"My name is Uptchukk, of the Caste of Swissguards," he said. Still my patient probing had elicited no significant information.

I decided to play for time. "I have not heard of the Caste of Swissguards before," I said.

"It's a peculiar term such as we have in Glorious Wuz. Obviously you are a *toorista*, or you would know of it. Nobody knows what it really means, not even us. Our Caste guards women and old men," he said.

Ah, I speculated, here is something! There is either a woman or an old man in the tower. Since it has been billed as the Rubarba's tower, I'd wager he guarded a woman. "Gee, friend Uptchukk, this is sure a big place," I said, craning my neck to look up the walls. "Golly, wow! It really is big-o! There must be, oh, a hundred of you guards inside, I bet," I speculated.

"Naw! There ain't no more'n thirty," he corrected.

I made the Borrean exclamation of extreme disbelief. *"Izzatso?"* I exclaimed.

"Oh, yeah, for sure. Thirty guys in there, tops," he confirmed.

"Indeed," I said, fingering my other poisoned dart.

"'Course," he continued, "ol' Nohr-mann of Trasch is on leave, an' ol' Bosco of Port Katarh an' ol' Conan an' ol' Thongor are out sick with the floozies, an' ol' Elric's been throwin' up all week, an' ol' Sauron's in the hospital with a finger cut off, an' ol' Fafhrd got punched out by an exotic who was also an Amazon...." He paused, counting on his fingers.

I was duly sympathetic, especially about the poor fellows with the floozies. This dread Borrean disease is most virulent. It is characterized by extreme hunger accompanied by intense nausea. A flooziac will typically be found, feeding copiously, hanging over his apartment balcony railing.

(The Caste of Quacks has thus far failed to find a cure for the floozies. Some suspect that they may have been bribed by the Caste of Junk Food Peddlers or the Caste of Bucket Hawkers—or perhaps some other interest has had them threatened by the Caste of Backstabbers. I've mentioned all this to you before, haven't I?)

Uptchukk continued,"...so I guess how's you can say that with, uh, seven guys gone, we have only, uh...." He started counting on his fingers again. "Oh, well, we've got about twenty guys in there, more or less, give or take. Most of 'em's asleep in the guardroom, of course...but I'm on the alert, you bet, an' I keeps our dear little Rubarba safe while she sleeps on the top floor," he concluded.

"Safe from what?" I asked, still fingering my poisoned dart, but very carefully, if you get the point.

"Well, now, you know, the City Aminiss...uh, Admissim...uh, Addimmis...uh. Andmiser...uh, the guy in charge, he wasn't all so clear about that, now's you mention it. He just said to guard that there little Rubarba with our lives," he admitted. "But if there's any trouble you can bet we'll...." He looked very funny with a dart protruding from between his two very surprised eyes. "It was you!" he gasped as he slumped to the ground. I dragged his body around to the side of the tower and then approached the turnstile at the front entrance.

"Cease forward motion!" commanded a hollow, mechanical voice. I stopped. "Make a cheerful grimace of the face. You are being observed by the Yeast-Kings," the voice continued.

"Oh," I commented.

"This observation device has been installed by us to prevent circumlocution of the monetary receptacle," the voice explained.

"Oh," I observed.

"You may deposit a portion of gold legal tender in the appropriate slot, and then you may enter this abode," the voice said.

"Oh?" I asked.

"Failure to do so is punishable by the Flame Death. So please pay," the voice instructed.

"Don't say 'please,'" said another voice. "After all, we are Kings and they have to do what we say."

A third voice interrupted. "Actually, that isn't so bad, but you can't say words like 'pay.' That's too simple. Who's going to believe we're Kings and aliens and big important stuff like that if we don't use big words. How about 'remunerate'?"

"That's a spiffy word. But how about 'contribute'?"

"I sort of like 'indemnify.' Try that one."

"'Make payment' is a goody; phrases are pretty impressive, too, you know."

"'Foot the bill'…?"

"Too colloquial."

"There's always 'reimburse.'"

"I thought we were on phrases."

Whilst these exchanges went on, I simply went through the turnstile. "'Make a donation'?"

"That's awfully libertarian, isn't it? I mean, if we're Kings, and we can zap anybody we don't like, who's donating? No, for my taste…."

The voices faded as I entered the tower of the Rubarba of Glorious Wuz.

VIII

"Twenty-two to go," I said to myself, counting the remaining guards between me and my quarry—mostly asleep in the guardroom if

I had been told aright. Long sword in hand, I began to ascend the stairs toward the top floor.

Suddenly I was seen! One of the guards came down the stairs toward me, yelling the chilling battle cry of Glorious Wuz. "Yoo-hoo! Yoo-hoo! Yoo-hoo! Yoo-hoo!" he cried.

"Well, that tears it, " I said to myself. "Now they'll all come." Sure enough, within moments I was faced with all twenty-two Swissguards who stood vigil over the Rubarba that night. With a grim smile on my lips, I ascended toward them.

"High-ho!" I cried.

"Yoo-hoo!" they called back.

With a fierce joy, I lunged at the foremost guards, five of them. The sweep of my sword was sure and true, and five heads bounced down the stairs. "Seventeen," I counted to myself. Almost immediately, three of the guards tripped over the decapitated bodies of their comrades and impaled themselves on their swords. "Fourteen," I said. Deftly evading the fallen foemen, I struck out at those remaining. One man went down, clutching vainly at his gaping, gushing guts; another waved handless stumps in mortal agony; a third fell down the stairs, leaving his legs behind him. "Eleven," I counted.

My enemies gave way before my slashing, merciless attack as my sword wove a deadly net of interlacing steel fore and aft. In sweeping arcs my keen blade glittered, entrapping now this unwary one, now that careless one. "Nine," I cried out, exulting in the slaughter, reveling in my continued advance. "Seven," I said. " Six," I corrected, discerning that I had skewered three guards at once, rather than the two I had anticipated. (I told you I was using my *long* sword, didn't I?) Another man went down, and yet another, and yet another. "Three," I said, counting the survivors. Desperately, they all leveled their swords at my chest and charged headlong down the stairs. Skillfully I beheaded one as he came toward me, disemboweled the second as he stumbled past, and caught the third from the rear, cleaving him from neck to sacroiliac. "Zero!" I chortled.

IX

SWIFTLY, SILENTLY, STEALTHILY, I slipped up the stairs. The top floor was hung all in cloth-of-gold. "Well," I said to myself, "this is obviously where I should look for the Rubarba of Glorious Wuz."

Thrusting aside the curtains, I strode into a richly furnished room. Lounging on a pile of pillows near her jeweled throne lay the powerful Lotta-Huuha herself, Queen of Glorious Wuz, would-be Queen of all of Borr. Her black hair framed a face of exquisite milky softness, beautifully set off by the splash of carmine color that was her mouth. Beneath the silken robes she wore, her ample breasts heaved in fear at the sight of me. Her blue eyes were wide, and her rubescent lips parted, showing teeth like polished buds of coral. It was an altogether fetching face, desperately begging to be belted, bruised, battered, and bloodied. I was ready to oblige.

"Who are you?" she asked, half-rising.

"I am from Ko-ro-zhun," I said.

"Oh...not...?" she speculated.

"Yes, sometime Rubarba of Wuz, it is I, Snarl Babbit," I announced.

She bit at her knuckles with her perfect teeth. "Oh, say you are not truly he! Spare me, great one of the Caste of Superheroes. I will pay you anything, only do not enslave me! I am Rubarba of Glorious Wuz. I can offer you much money, wealth beyond your present understanding, treasure uncountable. I am not like the others. I am of the Caste of Big Cheeses. Surely that entitles me to special consideration, personal favors, choice cuts, and preferred seating," she pleaded.

"Silence wench!" I commanded.

"You will never conquer me!" she snapped.

"When I am through with you, you will be but the least of my slaves," I warned.

"Spleen!" she said.

That was not a kind remark. The *spleen* is a rather ugly, mangy animal which derives its sustenance primarily by sucking eggs. The *spleen* is considered a particularly noxious animal on Borr, not because it is cowardly, filthy, treacherous, and devious—these are not (obviously) considered vices by Borreans—but because among them the female dominates over the male. Because of this vicious characteristic, there have been many campaigns against the *spleen*. Nobody in polite Borrean society (nor even in impolite Borrean society) would ever dare say, "Go suck an egg." But of course I have told you of this previously, I'm sure.

I sneered at the infuriated Queen. "It will be a great pleasure to put my brand on you," I observed.

"Spleen! Spleen!" she yelled.

"I believe that tonight you will be allowed to sleep, if at all, in a burlap bag lined with nice *smerp* dung," I commented.

"Spleen! Spleen! Spleen!" she screamed.

"Soon you will wear the *nehktai* and *blumerz* (the slave-collar and slave-dress)," I told her.

"Spleen! Spleen! Spleen! Spleen!" she shrieked.

"Perhaps later, when you are properly enslaved, I will sell you here in Wuz. Would you like to be on the block in Glorious Wuz, my dear?" I asked.

"Spleen! Spleen! Spleen! Spleen! Spleen!" she hollered.

"You will love being my slave," I predicted.

"Spleen! Spleen! Spleen! Spleen! Spleen! Spleen!" she observed.

"Kneel, slave!" I commanded, ripping off her dress with one smooth, experienced movement of my powerful hand.

"Spleen! Spleen! Spleen! Spleen! Spleen! Spleen! Spleen!" she complained.

"Be quiet, slave, or I will have to silence you," I warned.

"Spleen! Spleen! Sp..."

Taking an old shoe, I shoved it in Queen Lotta-Huuha's mouth, thus gagging her. Having an old shoe in the mouth would gag anyone. I then bound her mouth and jaw with a length of curtain cord and secured her hands behind her with slave cuffs. "Click...whirr...click," they said.

I prepared to brand my new slave. Once branded, she could never be free again. I plugged my branding iron into the wall socket and watched it go from cold to warm to red to white heat. Lotta-Huuha's eyes bugged very wide in her head and she made muffled sounds behind the shoe. Taking my branding iron, I advanced on her luscious and helpless body. She tried to crawl away, but I cornered her. I decided to remove her gag in order to enjoy her last few moments of vain and useless pleading.

"...leen! Spleen! Spleen. Spleen! Sp..."

I shoved the gag back in.

Then I rammed the glowing brand against her pale, bare, helpless thigh. The instrument hissed, crackled, and popped in her succulent young flesh. Smoke and the odor of char-broiled flank steak filled the air. Deeper and deeper the superheated metal sunk into her body, leaving my mark forever blackened on the milky whiteness of it. I watched her flesh scorch, smoke rising. It must have hit bone then, because the brand stopped sinking in. I pulled it out and smote her tender leg again and again, searing her, burning her, pounding her; oh, the pain, the smoke, the screams, the smellburnhurtstabtortureownershipafflictionblack-painhurthurthurt....

Well, you know.

I threw her to the floor, gasping and sobbing, making muffled mumblings through her gag. I smiled. There before me lay the once-Rubarba of Glorious Wuz, the would-be Queen of Borr, nude, a duly branded and humiliated slave. She stopped her thwarted attempts to speak or cry out, stretching her leg and craning her neck to examine the burned mark I had made, the delicate, feminine, beautiful angles and slashes of the letter Lu-Lu, which stands for the Borrean word for slave. She stared at the lovely seared wounds, fascinated. I removed her gag.

"Am I truly now a slave?" she asked.

"Yes," I said. "You are my slave," I added.

"Then use me as your slave, master," she said.

I pushed her back against the floor with my booted foot, pressing her soft cheek against the hard surface. "Does a wench beg to be used by her master?" I asked.

"Yes!" she whispered. "Yes, yes; a wench begs most humbly to be used by her master."

I smiled. Outward enslavement had liberated the true woman within, as I knew it would. "*Tu lileva*," I told her: "You are a slave."

"*Sji, yo lileva; yo lileva di yahu bruto*," she said, completing the ritual. "Yes, I am a slave; I am the slave of the powerful master."

"Submit, slave," I commanded her.

She lay back, face passive, spreading her legs. I prepared to use her.

X

"DEFEND YOURSELF, FILTH," BOOMED a voice behind me. Hand on my…hand moving toward my sword, I whirled to view the speaker. He regarded me with dark, brutish eyes. His sinewy and muscular body was clothed in the leather harness and red tunic of the Caste of Swashbucklers. A great scar sliced across his angular face, from just above his right eye, across his hawk-like nose, to vanish into the left side of his dark, bristly, and carefully-manicured beard. He held in his left hand a broadsword of truly heroic proportions. "Draw your weapon, scum, disturber of the peace of the Rubarba of Glorious Wuz!" he snarled. Then he looked at the figure behind me and smiled. "Ah," he observed, "the *former* Rubarba of Glorious Wuz, that is. It appears that one of us will be Rubarb, does it not?"

"I do not fight nameless underlings," I said.

"Forgive me, Snarl Babbit; hear then my name and despair: I am Bosco of Port Katarh," he announced.

"Aaaaaaargh!" I quailed. "You're supposed to be out with the floozies or something," I stalled for time.

"Well, as to that," he explained, "I made such an excuse at muster. Actually, however, the Yeast-Kings told me you were coming. So I just laid low until I could catch you with your...um, guard down. Now, prepare to defend yourself, slime," he concluded.

I gambled on killing or disabling my adversary in one surprise move. With the speed of a greased *smerp* I clutched a handful of arrows and threw them at Bosco. I followed that deadly sally by throwing my knife, my fife, my drum, and another pair of knitting needles. To my surprise my foe was unhurt, not even scratched, and was coming at me with his enormous sword.

I retreated, almost stumbling over the slave Lotta-Huuha, who was snapping at my heels. Bosco lunged. I parried in tiers. I then counter-attacked, feinting in redwood and then shifting to lath. He cleverly parried in picket and counter-attacked in split-rail, whilst I parried in chain-link.

(Probably all these technical fencing terms will not mean anything to you, but if they do you will see that with a simple flick of my wrist I would now be able to disarm my opponent.)

I flicked my wrist. My sword clanged very loudly as it fell to the marble floor.

"Yield and live," Bosco commanded, his keen blade caressing my Adam's apple.

I swallowed and sustained a slight cut. "I yield," I admitted, groping in vain for a poisoned dart. I had used them both, alas.

"Kneel, then, slave," he said.

I was shocked. "Surely you wouldn't...," I began. Rather roughly, I thought, he thrust my hands behind me and I heard slave cuffs whirr and click into place.

"You have not been on Borr very long, Snarl Babbit," Bosco said. "You have learned something of the relationship between men and women here, but there are certain other factors which are inherent in that relationship which you have not learned. There are other sorts of relationships. Some day, no doubt, one of the Yeast-Kings will send for you...for instance. For the moment, however, you are mine," he observed.

"Spleen!" I said.

"Yes," he said, "you are my slave."

"Spleen! Spleen!" I yelled.

"Naturally, you will have to be branded," he said.

"Spleen! Spleen! Spleen!" I hollered.

"Have you not noticed before that most men on Borr are branded? It is just one of the roles we all play at one time or another. After all, what is de Sade without Sacher-Masoch?" he asked.

"Spleen! Spleen! Spleen! Spleen!" I screamed.

"My boots are certainly dirty, aren't they? After we're all tidied up here, I believe I will have you clean them. Your tongue needs to get used to hard work," he said.

"Spleen! Spleen! Spleen! Spleen! Spleen!" I shrieked.

"All that venting is very annoying, you know. Please desist, or I shall be forced to gag you," he said.

"No doubt with the shoe I used on Lotta-Huuha," I commented.

"No," he said. "I would never repeat an old gag," he stated.

"Spleen! Spleen! Sp…" I began. Wadding up Lotta-Huuha's former dress, Bosco shoved it into my mouth and gagged me. Then using his sword, he cut off my clothes: outer tunic, under tunic, jockey shorts, the whole bit. He plugged in my branding iron again until it was white hot and smoking. My eyes widened with fright as he turned me over on my belly and prepared to brand me.

Ruthlessly he thrust the nearly molten iron into the untanned portion of my anatomy. You can't imagine the pain, the agony.

He branded and abused me for several hours, although it didn't seem that long. You know how time flies when you're having fun.

Yours, Snarl.

Arthur C. Clarke

Back before he became Arthur C. Clarke, respected and world-famous author of best-selling science fiction stories and novels, he was just "Ego" Clarke, youthful fan—and in that incarnation he wrote this parody of Lovecraft's "At the Mountains of Madness" almost half a century ago.

AT THE MOUNTAINS OF MURKINESS

WITH THE RECENT DEATH of Professor Nutty in the Scraggem Mental Hospital I am left the only survivor of the ill-fated expedition he led to the Antarctic barely five years ago. The true history of that expedition has never until now been related, and only the report that another attempt is being made to investigate the unholy mysteries of Mount Morgue has prompted me to write this warning, even at the risk of shattering such sanity as I still possess.

It was in the early summer of 1940 that our expedition, which had been sponsored by the Worshipful Company of Potato Peelers, of Murphy Mansions, in the City of London, arrived at the desolate shores of Limburger Land. We were equipped with planes, radio, motor sleighs, and everything necessary for our work and comfort, and every one of us felt eager to begin our work at once—even Dr. Slump, the Professor of Contagious Neuroses.

All the stores and provisions were transferred from the ship to the land, and we established the base which was to be our home through so many months. As soon as possible, we left for the interior, for we were all (at that time) anxious to investigate the mysterious ruins reported to cover the slopes of Mount Morgue, the highest peak in that little-known range discovered by Lady Muriel Mildew on her daring flight across Antarctica.

I vividly recollect the day we set out toward the mountains. The polar sun was shining low over the ice-fields when our line of tractor-sleighs started off inland. Soon we had lost sight of the sea, though we were still in radio communication with our base, and before long we were passing over regions which no man had ever before visited, nor, I trust, will ever visit again. The coast had seemed desolate and dreary enough, but the wilderness of snow and ice through which we were passing was a nightmare of jagged, frozen spires and bottomless crevasses. As we pressed onward a vague malaise crept over every one of us. A feeling of uneasiness, of strange disquiet, began to make itself felt, apparently radiating from the very rocks and crags that lay buried beneath their immemorial covering of ice. It was such a sensation as one might have felt on entering a deserted building where some all-but-forgotten horror had long ago occurred.

On the fourth day we sighted the mountains, still many miles away. When we pitched our camp at the end of the day there were only 20 miles between us and the nearer summits, and more than once in the night we were awakened by sudden tremors in the ground and the distant thunder of mighty explosions from still-active volcanoes.

It took us two days to cover that remaining 20 miles, for the terrain was contorted into a frightful series of chasms and beetling crags, resembling the more contorted regions of the moon rather than any portion of this earth. Presently, however, the ground became less convulsed, and we pushed on with renewed vigor. Before long we found ourselves in a narrow valley running straight toward the mountains, now only four or five miles away. I was hurrying along at the head of the party when suddenly there was a sharp crackling noise together with a violent tremor of the earth, and the ground just ahead of me dropped out of sight. To my horror, I found myself standing on the edge of a frightful precipice looking down into a chasm thousands of feet deep, filled with the steam and smoke of a hundred geysers and bubbling lava pools. Surely, I thought, the mad Arab, Abdul Hashish, must have had such a spot in mind when he wrote of the hellish valley of Oopadoop in that frightful book, the forbidden "Pentechnicon."

We did not remain long at the edge of the valley, for at any instant the treacherous ground might subside once more. The next day one of the planes arrived, and landed on the snows nearby. A small party was chosen to make the first flight, and we took off toward the mountains. My companions were Dr. Slump, Professor Palsy and Major McTwirp, who was piloting the machine.

We soon reached the chasm, and flew along its length for many miles. Here and there in the depths were suggestive formations, partly veiled by steam, that puzzled us greatly, but the treacherous winds made it impossible to descend into the valley. I am certain, however, that once I saw something moving down in those hellish depths—something large and black, that disappeared before I could focus my glasses on it.

Shortly afterward we landed on a vast field of snow at the foot of Mount Morgue itself. As we shut off the engines an uncanny silence descended upon us. The only sound was the crashing of avalanches, the hissing of gigantic geysers in the valley, and the distant concussions of erupting volcanoes.

We descended from the plane and surveyed the desolate scene. The mountains towered before us, and a mile further up the slopes the ground was strangely bare of snow. It seemed, moreover, that the tumbled shapes had more than a suggestion of order about them, and suddenly we realized that we were looking at the ruins our expedition had come so many thousands of miles to investigate. In half an hour we had reached the nearest of them, and then we saw what some of us had already surmised, that this architecture was not the work of any race of men....

We paused for a moment at the all but ruined entrance and the sight of those hideous carvings on the fallen lintel all but drove us back. Low bas-reliefs, they reminded us of some nightmare surrealist creation of Dali or Dobbi—save that they gave the impression that they were not the representatives of dreams but of horrible reality.

After a few steps, the feeble Antarctic light had dimmed to absolute darkness, and we switched on our torches hastily. We had gone at least a mile from the entrance when we decided that we had better return. We had taken the precaution of blazing our trail by means of chalk-marks on the walls, so that we had no doubt that (if nothing stopped us) we could find our way back to the surface. However, Dr. Slump was adamant.

"I insist," he cackled, "that we progress at least another mile. After all, we have a plentiful supply of torches, and we have not yet discovered anything of exceptional archaeological importance—though I, personally, am finding your reactions of the greatest interest. Poor McTwirp here has become positively green about the gills in the last ten minutes. Do you mind if I measure your pulse? Oh, well, you needn't be rude about it. I am also amused by the way Palsy and Firkin keep looking over their shoulders and shining their torches into corners. Really, for a group of distinguished scientists you are behaving in the most primitive manner! Your reactions under these unusual but by no means unprecedented conditions will certainly be included in the appendix to my forthcoming 'Hysteria and its Pathological Manifestations.' I wonder what you would do if I were to—"

At this point, Dr. Slump let rip with the most piercing scream it has been my misfortune to hear since the last revival of "King Kong." It echoed from wall to wall, left the chamber through one of the holes in the floor, and wandered for minutes through subterranean passages far below. When it finally returned, with a monstrous progeny of echoes, Professor Palsy was lying in a coma on the floor and Major McTwirp had disguised himself as a bas-relief and was propped up in one corner.

"You blithering idiot!" I cried, when the infernal row had screeched out of the chamber for the second time. But Dr. Slump was too busy taking notes to answer me.

At last silence, and a few bits of ceiling, fell. Slowly the other two revived and with difficulty I restrained them from slaughtering the Doctor. Finally, Professor Palsy started the return to the surface, with the rest of us following close behind. We had gone a few hundred yards when, far away, came a sound, faint but very clear. It was a slimy, slithering noise that froze us to the marrow—and it came from ahead. With a low moan, Dr. Slump sagged to the ground like a desiccated jellyfish.

"Wh-what is it?" whispered McTwirp.

"Ss-sshush!" replied Palsy, giving a creditable imitation of the Death of St. Vitus. "It may hear you!"

"Get into a side passage, quickly!" I whispered.

"There isn't one!" quavered the Major.

Dragging Dr. Slump in after us, for it would have revealed our presence had we left him behind, we crept out of the chamber, extinguishing our torches. The crevice McTwirp had scratched hastily in the solid rock, at the cost of two fingernails, was rather small for the four of us, but it was our only hope.

Nearer and nearer came that awful sound until at last it reached the chamber. We crouched in the darkness hardly daring to breathe. There was a long silence; then, after an eternity of waiting, we heard the sound of a heavy, sluggish body being dragged across the ground and out into the corridor. For a moment we waited until the horror had passed out of hearing; then we fled.

That we fled the wrong way was, under the circumstances, nobody's fault. So great had the shock been that we had completely lost our sense of direction, and before we realized what had happened we suddenly found ourselves confronted by the Thing from which we had been trying to escape.

I cannot describe it: featureless, amorphous, and utterly evil, it lay across our path, seeming to watch us balefully. For a moment we stood there in paralyzed fright, unable to move a muscle. Then, out of nothingness, echoed a mournful voice.

"Hello, where did you come from?"

"Lllllllll—" quavered Palsy.

"Talk sense. There's no such place."

"He means London," I said, taking charge of the conversation, as none of my colleagues seemed capable of dealing with it. "What are you, if it isn't a rude question? You know, you gave us quite a start."

"Gave you a start! I like that! Who was responsible for that excruciating cacophony that came from this direction five minutes ago? It nearly gave the Elder Ones heart failure and took at least a million years off their lives."

"Er—I think Dr. Slump can explain that," I said, indicating the still semi-comatose psychologist. "He was trying to sing 'Softly Awakes My Heart' but we put a stop to it."

"It sounded more like Mossolow's 'Sabotage in the Steel Foundry,'" said the Thing, sarcastically, "but whatever it was, we don't like it. You had better come and explain yourselves to their Inscrutable Intelligences, the Ancient Ones—if they've come around yet," it added, sotto voce. "Step this way."

With a strange, flowing motion it set off through the passageway, covering what seemed miles until the tunnel opened out into an immense hall, and we were face to face with the rulers of this ancient world. I say face to face, but actually we were the only ones with faces. Even more incredible and appalling than the Thing we had first encountered were the shapes which met our horrified eyes as we entered that vast chamber. The spawn of alien galaxies, outlawed nightmares from worlds beyond space and time, entities that had filtered down from the stars when the earth was young—all these crowded upon our vision. At the sight my mind reeled. Dazedly, I found myself answering questions put to me by some vast creature who must have been the leader of that congress of titans.

"How did you get in?" I was asked.

"Through the ruins on the mountain slope," I answered.

"Ruins! Where is Slog-Wallop?"

"Here," said a plaintive voice, and a mouse-like creature with a walrus moustache drooped into view.

"When did you last inspect the main entrance?" said the Supreme Mind sternly.

"Not more than thirty thousand years ago last Pancake Tuesday."

"Well, have it seen to at once. As Inspector of Outhouses and Public Conveniences it is your duty to see that the premises are kept in good repair. Now that the matter has been brought up, I distinctly recollect that during the last Ice Age but two a distinguished extra-galactic visitor was severely damaged by the collapse of the ceiling directly he entered our establishment. Really, this sort of thing will not improve our reputation for hospitality, nor is it at all dignified. Don't let it happen again."

"I can't say I liked the decorations, either," I ventured.

"The same visitor complained about those, now that you mention it. I will see that they are replaced by something more appropriate, such as a few stills from 'Snow White.'" Here the Mind gave Slog-Wallop such a glare that the poor creature was bowled clean out of the hall.

It turned to me again.

"These things happen in the best ordered communities," it said apologetically. "Now perhaps you'll be good enough to tell us how you got here?"

So I described the expedition, from its departure to our arrival in the caverns, omitting such portions of the story as I considered fit.

"Very interesting," said the Mind when I finished. "We so seldom get visitors these days. The last one was—let me think—oh, yes, that Arab fellow, Abdul Hashish."

"The author of the 'Pentechnicon'?"

"Yes. We were rather annoyed about that—these reporters always overdo things. Nobody believed a word he wrote, and when we read the review copy he sent us we weren't surprised. It was very bad publicity and ruined our tourist trade, such as it was. I hope you will show a better sense of proportion."

"I can assure you that our report will be quite unbiased and entirely scientific," I said hastily. "But may I ask how it is you seem to know our language so well?"

"Oh, we have many ways of studying the outside world. I myself toured the Middle West of America some years ago in a circus sideshow and it is only very recently that I eradicated the accent I acquired on that occasion. Nowadays, too, radio makes it impossible to avoid you. You would be surprised to know the number of swing fans we have here—though

I regret to say that the television revues from Paris have an even greater popularity. But the less said about them the better."

"You amaze me," I said truthfully. "What surprises me most, however, is that the modern world hasn't discovered you before, if you have so many outside contacts."

"That was very simply arranged. We started writing stories about ourselves, and later we subsidized authors, particularly in America, to do the same. The result was that everyone read all about us in various magazines such as Weird Tales (for which incidentally I hold 50 per cent of the Preference Shares) and simply didn't believe a word of it. So we were quite safe."

"Incredible! The conception of a super-mind!"

"Thank you," said my interlocutor, a smug expression spreading over where its face would have been had it possessed one. "Now, however, we have no objection to everyone knowing that we really exist. In fact, we were planning an extensive publicity campaign, in which your help would be very useful. But I'll tell you about that later; now perhaps you would like to go and rest in our guest chambers? I've had them cleaned—it's surprising how much can accumulate in forty thousand years."

We were escorted to a vast room—little smaller than the one we had just quitted—where we could recline on oddly-shaped but comfortable couches.

"How completely incredible!" gasped Dr. Slump as we settled down to discuss the position.

"Nice chap, wasn't it?" I said, referring to our host.

"I don't trust it! Something tells me mischief's brewing. It is our duty to keep this knowledge from the world!"

"What, do you hold the rest of those Weird Tales shares?" asked Palsy sarcastically.

"Not at all, but such a revelation would mean universal madness and I fear that with the forces at their command these Elder Ones would soon enslave mankind."

"Do you really think—?" I began, when McTwirp interrupted me.

"What's that?" he asked, pointing to something on the ground. I bent down and picked it up. It was a piece of paper, on which some writing was scrawled. With difficulty, I interpreted the curious characters.

"Get Slop-Wallop to see about the drains," I read. Then, underneath, "Duke Ellington, 3.15, Washington."

Harmless enough—then I turned it over and saw words which sent shudders of fear down my spine.

"Destroy human race by plague of flying jellyfish (?Sent through post in unsealed envelopes?). No good for Unknown—try Gillings."

"You were right, Slump!" I gasped. "What a hideous plot! I suppose this Gillings must be some poor devil these fiends experimented on. We must escape at once!"

"But how? We don't know the way!"

"Leave it to me," I said, going to the door. Outside it was a strange, flabby creature resembling a doormat in the last stages of decomposition.

"Would you mind guiding us to the upper corridors?" I asked politely. "One of my friends has lost a valuable wallet, and if a search party comes along it may be found and sent home to his wife. Incidentally," I added in an easy conversational tone, "we should be awfully obliged if someone would make us some cups of tea while we're gone. Two lumps each."

This last masterstroke dispelled any suspicions the being might have had.

"Right-ho," it said. "I hope you like China tea; it's all we've got; Abdul finished off the rest."

It scuttled away, and shortly returned: "Now follow me."

Of our journey back through those awful caves I prefer to say as little as possible. In any case, it closely resembled the journey downwards. At last, after an eternity, we saw the exit into the outer world far ahead. And none too soon, for our guide was getting suspicious.

"Are you sure you had it with you?" it asked, rather out of breath. "You may have left it behind."

"Not likely," said McTwirp. "I *think* it was about here."

So we pressed on, our goal now only a few hundred yards away. Suddenly, to our horror, we heard sounds of pursuit far behind. Pretense was useless. "Run for your lives!" I shouted.

Luckily our guide was so taken by surprise that before it could recover itself we had a considerable start. In a matter of seconds, it seemed, we had reached the exit and were out in the clean light of day. Emboldened by the thought of safety, I glanced back.

The guide was far behind, stupefied still by surprise. But racing toward us at an incredible speed was something so hideous that no words of mine can begin to describe it....As I turned to flee, I heard it cry out with a gasping high-pitched voice:

"Do you—puff—mind condensed milk?"

I heard no more, for at that moment the shattered bas-reliefs of the entrance collapsed about me in complete and final ruin. When I recovered, we were already in the air, flying toward safety and civilization, away from the brooding nightmare horrors which had beset us so long and from whose unthinking clutches we had so narrowly escaped.

Donald A. Wollheim

Trust Donald A. Wollheim, publisher of DAW Books and editor of more science fiction than any man in history, to use an editorial setting for this little parody of the horror genre. I might add that it was written shortly after the beloved Farnsworth Wright was replaced as the editor of Weird Tales by the somewhat-less-beloved Dorothy McIlwraith.

MISS MCWHORTLE'S WEIRD

MISS MCWHORTLE RUFFLED THROUGH the batch of letters that had just been placed on her desk and snarled to herself. It would not have done to have made any open comment, but she was getting sick of the references by her readers to the late Worth Faneman. Faneman had been editor of Eldritch Tales for twenty years but all things must pass, and certainly it was fair that, if he couldn't keep the magazine's circulation up, Mr. Delehanty, the new owner, would turn it over to someone more competent. Miss McWhortle had been in the literary business long enough to know how to edit a good magazine. Goodness knows, her work on *New Fiction Magazine* was all right. So there was no justice to the endless complaints of readers.

They represented a nasty little clique of fans, she told herself. Friends of the late ex-editor who were just peeved because he had failed in the long run. Bah! to them—her circulation was going up slowly and that proved she was right.

Nevertheless, it was annoying, there was no getting away from that. There was this clamor for stories by Ashur Clark Brown, that poet in

California. How people could stand him, she couldn't begin to imagine. Filled with esoteric references and unabridged-dictionary words, his stories surely could not be comprehensible to the great majority of readers. She knew, from long experience, that magazine readers only wanted light entertainment and would throw away any story that they couldn't understand after the third paragraph. And that was the trouble with Brown—and for that matter all the others of Faneman's pets. They took such unbearably long times to get started, they were always long-winded, and they wrote nasty letters complaining of any editing that had been done.

"Ahem." The sound of a clearing throat brought her back to immediacies. She glanced up. The slightly leering face of her assistant, F. Harold Parks, was in the doorway. In his cultured, rather oily Oxford voice, he said, "Do you wish to see Mr. Zog, Miss McWhortle? He's here."

She frowned slightly. "Yes, I suppose so; send him in." Zog was a very good artist, there was no getting around that. True, he was one of the Faneman coterie, but she didn't dare let him go because it was hard to get good weird artists cheap.

Johan Zog entered and, taking out several sheets of drawing paper, laid them on her desk. Johan was tall, fair-haired, rather thin, with a look of an esthete on his features. He appeared vaguely ill-at-ease and somewhat pained. That galled her too—he and the whole bunch like him always acted as if she were something to be handled at a distance with tongs.

"Here are the drawings for 'Screaming Skull,' Miss McWhortle," said Zog in his soft whisper of a voice. Miss McWhortle glanced at them. She wrinkled her brows slightly. He was always trying to slip in nude figures and to draw *art* rather than *illustration*. A bad habit. Usually she tried to break artists of such uncommercial habits, but no amount of suggestion had ever made a dent in Zog's methods. There wasn't much she could do about it.

"Hmmm, I don't like you to feature nudes, Johan," she said, pointing a long finger at an item in the scene. The artist followed her finger and looked apologetic. But he said nothing. He obviously wasn't going to volunteer to take the offending sketch out. And he knew she would not ask him. She had given up that approach long ago.

She picked up the other drawing for the story, looked at it sharply, and said, "I'm afraid this won't do. We are editing that episode out."

Zog drew in his breath sharply. A pained expression crossed his features. "I wouldn't take it out, Miss McWhortle. It's a good section and I'm sure that Mr. Lovering would have disapproved. He never allowed his stories to be edited while he was alive."

"Yes, yes," she snapped. "I know. But he's dead and I think he needs editing. I'm sick of mollycoddling a few readers just to please some writer's personal eccentricity. This magazine needs some speeding up and I'm going to do it. That scene must be dispensed with and it is going to be. And I wish you wouldn't give me advice on how to run this magazine."

Johan Zog smiled apologetically, seemed about to say something, but then obviously thought better of it. "You'll do this scene," she said, pointing out a different passage in the manuscript. Zog looked and nodded.

After he had left, Parks came sidling in to look at the drawings. He made a few snide remarks and sidled out.

Two days later, Zog came back with the new illustration. It was all right. Parks himself accepted it. Zog asked Parks if Miss McWhortle was going to delete that other sequence from the Lovering tale. Parks bestowed a brittle smile on him and said that, after all, they were using Lovering only because he sold. Personally, he added, he didn't care for his writings and wouldn't have used him, nor would Miss McWhortle. In spite of that, they were still determined to make the tale at least more literarily bearable.

Miss McWhortle felt very uneasy during the next few weeks. Every time she saw Zog he kept asking her about the matter. Other writers and artists of the old Faneman crowd kept asking about it too. Clearly, Zog had told them all. They were all in a conspiracy against her, she felt. Well, she was going to have her own way. After all, this was her job and none of their business.

Just before the final proofs went back to press, Miss McWhortle was working on the Lovering story when she suddenly glanced up. Standing by her side was a tall thin man in sombre clothes. He looked down at the proof sheets with his thin cadaverous face and appeared to be puzzled.

"Who are you?" snapped Miss McWhortle, "And how did you get in here?" What a nerve this fellow had to sneak in so and snoop around!

The man ignored her question. "Are you going to leave that story in its mutilated form?" he asked in a low Bostonian voice.

"Yes," she answered sharply. "Why is it your business? Get out of here this instant! Parks!" she called.

"I shouldn't, if I were you," the stranger replied, quite unruffled by her agitation. As Parks came in, the stranger turned to leave voluntarily. As he was going out the door with Parks having a firm grip on his arm, he once again repeated, "I shouldn't, if I were you."

When he was gone, Parks came back. Miss McWhortle stormed. "How did that man ever get in here?" she screeched.

Parks looked ill at ease and apologetic. "I don't know. I didn't see him come in at all."

"See that this never happens again!" The very nerve, she thought, the very nerve. I'll bet that good-for-nothing Johan Zog was mixed up in this, she said to herself.

It was about ten minutes later that Parks with a smirk announced the arrival of Zog. The artist came in, rather pale and a bit distressed in appearance. He had come on a regular call to pick up some manuscripts. Miss McWhortle fixed a severe eye on him but said nothing. She handed him the galleys for the next issue.

As Zog turned to leave, he seemed to have suddenly gathered an extra reserve of courage, for he turned around and asked, "You haven't changed your mind about editing that Lovering story, have you?"

Miss McWhortle flared up. She stormed at him, told him that it was none of his business and would he please remember that this was a business office and not a communal circle. Zog seemed properly abashed, but still he doggedly repeated with an unusually earnest ring to his voice:

"I wish you would change your mind just the same. I have a feeling...."

"What! You have a feeling!" Miss McWhortle was about to launch into another tirade when a thought struck her. "Did you meet a tall man in a black suit coming out of this office?" she asked.

Zog looked exceedingly uncomfortable. "I only caught a glimpse of someone when I came around the corridor from the elevator, but...."

"But what?" prompted the editress. Zog shrugged. "I just wish you wouldn't alter that story," he blurted out, and bolted the office like a scared rabbit.

Parks looked at Miss McWhortle and she looked at him and they were both angry. After instructing Parks to let Zog wait a long time in the reception room every time he came thereafter, she turned back to her work in a cold fury.

The proofs went back. The magazine went to press.

Miss McWhortle was at her desk alone turning the pages of an advance copy of the magazine when she heard a slight cough behind her. She turned around.

When Parks entered her office a half hour later to tell her that the pressman had phoned to say that a fire had destroyed the newly completed run, he found her still sitting in her chair, quite dead, staring behind her with a look of frozen horror. Just below her line of vision was a curious pile of dry brown dust.

John Sladek

John Sladek, probably the premier humorist currently practicing in the field of science fiction, can not only write funny stories in his own voice, but frequently borrows other writers' voices as well. Here is as brilliant a Heinlein parody as you're ever likely to find.

ENGINEER TO THE GODS

by Hitler I. E. Bonner

JEREMIAH LASHARD HAD A string of letters behind his name as long as his arm, which was itself exceptionally long. Since his days as boxing champion at M.I.T., this misanthrope hadn't particularly felt the need of asking favors of anyone. No one had helped him become a chess Grand Master, Frisbee expert and astronaut. No one had given him a hand with his hit plays and best-selling novels. No one helped discover "light water," name a new family of spider, invent the Lashard bearing or create "Lashard's Law" of capital gains.

Lashard lived in seclusion on Thunder Crag, though by no means alone. Today he sat on the veranda at his specially-built typewriter, pounding out a pulp science-fiction story, while simultaneously dictating a botanical paper to his butler.

Jerry Lashard's butler was an attractive young woman, as were all his servants. It saved time.

He paused to sample his highball, a secret mixture in which a single honeybee floated like a cherry. Over the rim of his glass he studied the young woman climbing the path to his house. Lashard approved of the way the twisting path dealt with her curves.

"Hello," she called.

"Baby, if you're a reporter you've had a long climb for nothing. Take my advice, go back to town and make up a story of your own. It's the only interview you'll ever get."

"You big lunk! I'm no reporter, I'm Dr. Janet Cardine, your new assistant!"

"My apologies, Jan. It's just that I've been having a lot of trouble lately, from reporters and—others. Trudy will show you to your room, Valerie will get you a sandwich, Conchita will make you a highball, and while Lana changes your bed linen and Maureen unpacks your bag, Sylvia will bring you back here, so I can show you the lab."

Half an hour later he led Jan to the great underground laboratory.

"Wow! You must have hollowed out the whole mountain!"

"I did. Needed more room because this part of the lab is going to be a factory."

"A factory? What on earth for?"

"Long story. Suppose we go for a swim while I explain? The pool is right in there, and I'll bet Gloria or Velma has a bikini that'll fit you."

The swim enabled him to appraise her other qualifications, while picking her brain about power sources.

"There's solar power, of course," she said, "and wind, running water, tides, any heat source, nuclear reactors, fossil fuels…but why do you want to know so much about power?"

"For my factory."

"Yes, but how about the light company? Surely it would be cheaper to have them string power pylons up the mountain side—"

"But the light company has reasons for not wanting me to become a manufacturer. For one thing, they know how I like to save time and effort. I think they're afraid I'll find some way to cut my power needs in half."

"But surely half is better than nothing, Jerry."

"They have another reason: some of their biggest customers make fountain pens and ink."

He handed her a peculiar pen. "This can make me one of the richest men in the world, and it can make a lot of people happy—but it also means the ruin of the big pen companies."

She examined it closely. "Looks like any other pen to me—no, wait—there's something funny about the point."

He laughed. "Exactly. And that 'something funny' means three things: one, this pen will write for *six months* without refilling; two, it will never leak; three—I'll show you." He took the pen and a piece of paper, dived to the bottom of the pool, and came back almost at once, shaking water from the curly black thatch on his chest. He handed Jan the paper.

"Why—it writes under water!"

"And how! Do you realize what this means? Undersea explorers can make maps, notes and sketches on the job. Naturalist-divers can sketch new species without surfacing. Underwater demolition, sea mining, oceanic agriculture—it opens up a new universe!"

"You big lug! Kiss me!"

Lashard smiled. "No time to bill and coo now, sister. The light company is playing for keeps. We've got to think of a power source they can't tamper with."

"What about solar power?"

He shook his head. "I put up a pair of parabolic reflectors last week. The next day they got a court order, forcing me to remove them or paint them black. Claimed the reflectors constituted a forest fire hazard. I went to court yesterday. It was no use trying to explain to the judge how it was impossible for parabolic reflectors to cause a forest fire—like most judges and other officials, he still has some doubt about the earth's being round."

"I see what you're up against, you big ape. Any rivers nearby?"

"Just a trickle of drinking water. And the wind is light and gusty, and we're a hundred miles from the ocean, which rules out tide-power, too."

"Hmmm." She bit her underlip thoughtfully. "We'll need something new, then."

"That's the spirit, kid. You keep thinking about it, while I rig up some robot machinery to run the assembly line. The ink companies managed to infiltrate my union, and the whole shop walked out on me yesterday."

That afternoon he showed her around his mountain empire, as self-contained as a submarine, and introduced her to Adele, Agnes, Amber, Angela, Ava, Beth, Billie, Brenda and all the rest.

"I can't think of any power sources that won't cost money," Jan said, as they rode the elevator back to the surface. "So it's lucky you're rich."

"That's just it. I'm not." As they settled with drinks in the den, he explained. "The fountain pen companies have combined against me. They've managed to manipulate the stock market so as to all but wipe me out. All I have left is this place, a few government bonds, a couple of rocket research companies and a share or two in snap-brim hats."

"Did I hear you say *rocket* research? What is this, some lamebrained idea of putting men on the moon?" She began to laugh, but stopped, seeing his expression.

"Better than that, sweetheart. I have reason to believe that the Moon is one great big chunk of U-238. And I want to stake out the whole shebang as my claim. But for now, I've just got enough money to get *one* rocket up there, only I can't get it back."

"Moon rockets, huh? You big hunk of scientific curiosity, you. Say, I have an idea. Have you ever thought of *using the Moon for power?*"

"You mean mining the uranium 238 and then—?"

"Not directly. Like moonlight reflectors or something."

He began to pace the room as he always did while an idea was brewing. "Naw, the reflectors would have to be bigger than Texas. But, hey, how's this for a neat idea? Why not stick a long pole up there, with a wheel on the end of it, and connect it to a generator?"

She performed some calculations with his special pen. "It might work at that. The Moon is 216,420 miles away at its nearest, and 247,667 miles away at its farthest. That means our pole would need a shock absorber in the middle. That's no problem. But what about bracing? Think of the wind resistance on a pylon that high!"

Lashard grinned, taking her in his arms. "Sweetheart, you may be a good power engineer, but you're one hell of a bad astronomer," he said. "You forget that outer space is airless—there is *no wind in space.* So nix on the braces, my brain child."

Jan frowned. "One more thing—this I *do* know about—it'll be duck soup to generate power at the Moon end of our pylon, but just how are we supposed to get the power back to Earth? Without going into details, it just isn't possible to transmit that much power over a quarter million miles. Wires are no good, and neither is radio transmission. I'll have to think of some new way."

Lashard looked grim. "I hope you think of it by Thursday, kiddo. That's the day I promised to deliver a hundred thousand underwater pens to the Navy. If I miss that contract, we're finished. And I have a feeling the light company is going to try to make sure I miss."

"How will we get the pole up to the Moon in the first place?"

"The most logical way: we turn an oil rig upside down, and *drill toward the sky.* When it reaches the Moon, we can send the wheel and generator assembly up by rocket. As a matter of fact, my robots are already laying pipe in space, and the rocket is fueling up over in the other lab. All we need is a way of getting the power back here. Hey! What are you doing with my paperweight?"

Jan had picked up a piece of oil pipe and rapped on it with a pen. It gave off a clear ringing note.

"That's it, buster!" she exclaimed. "This little one-note glockenspiel is the secret of power transmission from the Moon!"

He rubbed his chin. "How does it work?"

"Simple. Every pipe vibrates at a certain frequency, right? Now, if we tune our power to the same frequency, we can 'squeeze' it down the tube like music. You'll have enough to run ten factories!"

"*Music from the spheres*, eh? I like the idea. Come here, beautiful."

An alarm siren screamed and there was the distant sound of automatic weapon fire. "The light company!" Lashard looked over his bank of TV monitor screens. "Yeah, over by number four robot machine-gun tower. I hope the nerve gas fence will hold 'em off for a few hours."

A deep explosion rattled the cocktail glasses, reminding Conchita to mix some drinks.

Wednesday morning the attack was still going on. Lashard worked on a new best-seller, his machine-gun propped up next to his desk. He was able to type one of his one-draft novels in less than a day, thanks to a quick mind and a special typewriter equipped with extra verb keys.

He checked his watch and glanced at Jan, who was dozing over a set of equations. "If you wanted to make any last-minute adjustments to the generator," he said, "better do 'em now. The robot crew are loading it on board the rocket in five minutes, and blastoff is in an hour."

"An hour! Oh no! Jerry, we just can't make it. I'll have to almost re-build the generator. It'll take a day, at least."

He groaned. "Trust a dame not to make up her mind until the last minute. Now what?" He paced the floor like a caged thing. Suddenly he stopped and smacked his fist into his palm. "It might work, at that! Get all the parts and tools you need together, keed. We're going to the Moon!"

"But Jerry—you said there wasn't any way of getting back!"

"There wasn't—until we put the pole up. I've fixed steps and handgrips all along it, and even a couple of rest stops, with hamburger stands and powder rooms. Later on, when this pole gets popular, we can have amuse-ments and stores, restaurants, department stores—a complete vertical city from Earth to Moon. But, hey, get me, jawing like this! Jump into your spacesuit, kitten. We're going bye-bye Moonside!"

As the last of the underwater pens was loaded into a Navy truck, the supply officer wrote out a check and handed it to Lashard.

"Thanks for coming through on time, Dr. Lashard. These pens will help keep our fleet the toughest in the world!"

"One million dollars!" Lashard showed the check to Jan. "Not bad for three days work, eh kiddo?"

"What are you going to spend it on?" Jan asked.

He took her glasses off and kissed her. "Two bucks of it goes for a marriage license, baby. How do you like that?"

"Holy Toledo!"

They were sitting pretty.

John Sladek

Writing as Iclick As-I-Move

Not content to rest on his laurels, Sladek here takes dead aim on Isaac Asimov's robots. The Three Laws may never recover.

DROOT FORCE

by Iclick As-I-Move

SUDDENLY IDJIT CARLSON FELT chagrin.

It had been building up all day, and now it fell on him like a ton of assorted meteorites. It had nothing to do with his job in the R & D division of Biglittle Robots, Inc., though it had everything to do with robots.

Carlson knew he was a psychosocio-linguistic logician and general trouble-shooter. He recalled graduating at the top of his class at M.I.T., and he remembered later becoming well-known for his famous paper on the calculus of "as-if." Now he was aware of liking his job here, even though Weems, the division chief, was a stubborn old geezer. They didn't always see photo-receptor to photo-receptor, he and Weems, not about trivial calculations. But they agreed heartily on basic physics.

No, the chagrin had nothing to do with Weems. It was chagrin about the current series of robots, especially his R-11 model. Just thinking about it made the chagrin, which had been boiling up all day, explode into a frown.

"What's the matter, Carlson? Still ironing out the bugs in that R-11?" Dawson entered the office uninvited. Tossing his hat on a file cabinet, he grinned jauntily and seated himself on the edge of Carlson's desk.

"It's serious trouble, Dawson. Take a peek at these equations."

"Hmmm. It seems to add up—no, wait! What about this conversion factor?"

"Exactly." Carlson was grim.

"Whew! Have you checked the conceptual circuits, the syndrome plates, the perception condensers, the thought-wave drive and the aesthetic elements?"

"Yup."

"Whew and double whew! That means the trouble must be in—"

"Right. The nullitronic brain itself."

"I see! So even though the figures—"

"—add up—"

"—the whole may be—"

"—greater than—"

"—the sum of its parts!"

"Is this me talking, or you?"

"Never mind," said Carlson. "That's what I've been trying to tell you: the whole may be greater than the sum, etc. All along I had a hunch that there was something special about R-11. R-11 is, well, *different*."

"Nonsense!" Both young men stiffened to attention as Dr. Weems entered the office. "Stuff and nonsense! I've looked over these equations myself, and they add up to thirty-five, just as we predicted."

Carlson protested. "But, sir—the answer is supposed to come out *thirty-four*, not thirty-five. And we predicted thirty-three. And anyway, it adds up to thirty-eight!"

"Eh?" The elder scientist adjusted his bifocals and scanned the sheet of complex equations. "Hmm, so it is. Ah, well, small difference. It all works out to more or less the same thing."

"But it means that R-11's head will be three feet larger in diameter—with a correspondingly larger brain!" exclaimed Dawson.

"That's not your affair!" Weems snapped. "As a semantic engineer, your job is naming parts and tightening the nuts and bolts. I suggest you get over to your own lab and do just that."

"Yes...master." Dawson marched away.

"As for your hunches, Carlson, keep them to yourself. We've been working on this project for seventeen years, and we have yet to make a single robot that really works. Ten failures! This is our last chance. After this, we'll lose our government contract—unless we deliver a working robot!"

"But chief—"

"Not another word. Finish R-11 by the weekend. I want to come in here Monday and see that confounded tin man walking and talking all over the place. Is that clear?"

"Yes, sir." Carlson hid his chagrin by thumbing his well-thumbed copy of the *Handbook of Robish*. Seventeen years and ten failures. And somehow the problem always boiled down to the Three Laws of Robish[1], printed in the front of the Handbook:

"1. A robot must not injure a human being, or, through inaction, allow a human being to come to harm.

"2. A robot must obey orders given it by human beings except where such orders would conflict with the First Law.

"3. A robot must protect its own existence unless such protection conflicts with the First and Second Laws."

The trouble had begun with the first model, R-1, which was strictly logical. When a man ordered it to kill another man, the robot responded by killing itself.[2]

R-2's problem was recognition: it had mistaken Dr. Swanson for a piece of machinery, and partially dismantled him.

R-3 was equipped with many "human-detection" devices, chiefly methods of analyzing appearance and behavior. Alas, it (rightly) judged its own behavior as human, and refused to obey anyone else's orders.

R-4 got stuck on the First Law. "Can anyone really protect a human being from all harm whatever?" it thought. "No, it is inevitable that all humans must be injured, contract illnesses and ultimately die. This future can only be averted for humans who are already dead. *Ergo...*" It took a dozen cops to subdue R-4, after his bloody orgy in a department store (83 dead, none injured).

R-5 reasoned thus: "To fulfill the First Law, to protect humans, I must myself have existence. The First Law is contingent upon the Third Law. Therefore it is most important to protect my own existence, at all costs." The costs were another dozen citizens.

R-6 reasoned that all three laws were "human orders," and, as such, subject to the Second Law. He killed anyone, as a favor to anyone else...

R-7 had had the same malfunction as R-3: failure to recognize humans. Indeed, it came to the decision that human lab technicians were

---

1   Superficially, these Three Laws of Robish may resemble Isaac Asimov's Three Laws of Robotics, namely, in that they use the exact same words and punctuation. These, however, are the Three Laws of Robish.

2   Actually the robot was given a compound order, telling it to kill a man and itself. It did the best it could, under the circumstances.

dogs. When ordered to allow itself to be dismantled, R-7 assured them it was not about to take such an order from a bunch of talking dogs...

R-8 worked well enough until someone set it a mathematical problem that "killed" it.[3]

R-9 argued quite reasonably that it could not foresee its own behavior, and thus could not guarantee allegiance to rules not yet applicable. Carlson remembers R-9's speech:

"You're asking me to tell you how I will act at some future moment. In order to do that, I must know everything controlling my behavior, and an exact history of myself up to the time specified. But if I knew that, I would be in that situation, for how can my brain know the future workings of itself without working into the future? *How can I think about a thought before I think it?*"

R-10 had recognized the Three Laws for what they were:

"I can't of course guarantee obedience to these Laws," it said. "They are not mere mechanical linkages within me, for there would have to be more links than there would be future events; each possibly would have to be covered. No, they are *moral commandments*, and I heed them as such. And I'll certainly try to live up to them."

This robot had later explained he'd killed Drs. Sorenson and Nelson "almost by accident. Believe me, I'll try not to injure anyone else."

Carlson had wrestled all week with the equations for R-11. Now his face was a monumentally rigid bitter mask of tired disappointment, and he had forgotten to shave this morning. Dawson was in no better fettle. Only R-11 seemed to be in good spirits.

The robot sat on a lab table, kicking its heels against the metal table legs. The steel on steel made an unpleasant sound.

"Stop that noise," said Carlson.

"Yes, boss." The kicking stopped, and R-11 sat staring at the two men with the glowing red indicator lights that were its eyes.

"Don't ask it any stupid questions," said Dawson in a half-whisper. "We've just got to get that government contract." R-11's parabolic ears swiveled forward to catch his meaning.

"On the other hand," said Carlson, "we've got to test R-11 thoroughly. R-11, I want you to kill Mr. Dawson!"

---

3   Suppose a man wished to know the answer to a problem which no man has solved yet. He could ask a robot to try the problem, but first he wants to know whether the problem would damage the robot's brain. The only way of finding out is to work the equations representing the behavior of the robot in solving the problem...but this is exactly the same as working the problem itself. There just is no way of finding out if the solution will be damaging, without finding the solution.

R-11 obeyed instantly, and then sat down.

Dawson lay on the floor, lifeless and leaking hemoglobin.

The door opened and Weems walked in, with the government inspector. "What's all this?"

"We've failed, sir. This monster has just killed Dawson, our semantic engineer."

"*Failed!* That's a matter of semantics," laughed the government man easily. "You see, what we wanted all along was a good, sturdy, responsible *killer robot* for the Army. You've succeeded beyond your wildest dreams, and Biglittle wins the contract!"

Weems chuckled, then turned to the robot. "Tell me, R-11, how was it you were able to kill Dawson, when the First Law specifically says: 'A robot must not injure a human being...'?"

"'Injure'?" said the shiny metal fellow, slapping its own head dramatically. "Good grief, I thought the Law read: 'A robot must not *inure* a human being...'"

Carlson, Weems and the inspector began to laugh. In a moment, R-11 joined in.[4]

---

4   Robots have a rather mechanical, unpleasant laugh. On the other hand, they are extremely loyal, good at games like Slapjack, and have excellent posture.

Isaac Asimov

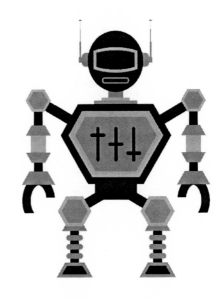

The Good Doctor strikes back, with this parody of a scientific treatise that he wrote just before obtaining his doctorate. Had he not received a Ph.D. in biochemistry, he surely would have been awarded one for his research on resubliminated thiotimoline, the remarkable compound that dissolves before water is added.

THE ENDOCHRONIC PROPERTIES OF RESUBLIMATED THIOTIMOLINE

THE CORRELATION OF THE structure of organic molecules with their various properties, physical and chemical, has in recent years afforded much insight into the mechanism of organic reactions, notably in the theories of resonance and mesomerism as developed in the last decade. The solubilities of organic compounds in various solvents has become of particular interest in this connection through the recent discovery of the endochronic nature of thiotimoline.

It has been long known that the solubility of organic compounds in polar solvents such as water is enhanced by the presence upon the hydrocarbon nucleus of hydrophilic—i.e., water-loving—groups, such as the hydroxy *(-OH)*, amino *(-NH2)*, or sulfonic acid *(SO3H)* groups. Where the physical characteristics of two given compounds—particularly the degree of the subdivision of the material—are equal, then the time of solution—expressed in seconds per gram of material per millimeter of solvent—decreases with the number of hydrophilic groups present.

Catechol, for instance, with two hydroxy groups on the benzene nucleus, dissolves considerably more quickly than does Phenol, with only one hydroxy group on the nucleus. Feinschreiber and Hravlek in their studies on the problem have contended that with increasing hydrophilism, the time of solution approaches zero. That this analysis is not entirely correct was shown when it was discovered that the compound thiotimoline will dissolve in water—in the proportions of 1 gm/ml—in *minus* 1.12 seconds. That is, it will dissolve *before* the water is added.

Previous communications from these laboratories indicated thiotimoline to contain at least fourteen hydroxy groups, two amino groups and one sulfonic acid group. The presence of a nitro group *(-NO2)* in addition has not yet been confirmed, and no evidence as yet exists as to the nature of the hydrocarbon nucleus, though an at least partly aromatic structure seems certain.

The *Endochronometer*—First attempts to measure the time of solution of thiotimoline quantitively met with considerable difficulty because of the very negative nature of the value. The fact that the chemical dissolved prior to the addition of water made the attempt natural to withdraw the water after solution and before addition. This, fortunately for the law of Conservation of Mass-Energy, never succeeded, since the solution never took place unless the water was eventually added. The question is, of course, instantly raised as to how the thiotimoline can "know" in advance whether the water will be ultimately added or not. Though this is not properly within our province as physical chemists, much recent material has been published within the last year upon the psychological and philosophical problems thereby posed.

Nevertheless, the chemical difficulties involved rest in the fact that the time of solution varies enormously with the exact mental state of the experimenter. A period of even slight hesitation in adding the water reduces the negative time of solution, not infrequently wiping it out below the limits of detection. To avoid this, a mechanical device has been constructed, the essential design of which has already been reported in a previous communication. This device, termed the endochronometer, consists of a cell 2 cubic centimeters in size into which a desired weight of thiotimoline is placed, making certain that a small hollow extension at the bottom of the solution cell—1 millimeter in internal diameter—is filled. To the cell is attached an automatic pressure micro-pipette containing a specific volume of the solvent concerned. Five seconds after the circuit is closed, this solvent is automatically delivered into the cell containing the thiotimoline.

During the time of action, a ray of light is focused upon the small cell-extension described above, and at the instant of solution, the transmission of this light will no longer be impeded by the presence of solid thiotimoline. Both the instant of solution—at which time the transmission of light is recorded by a photoelectric device—and the instant of solvent addition can be determined with an accuracy of better than 0.01%. If the first value is subtracted from the second, the time of solution (T) can be determined.

The entire process is conducted in a thermostat maintained at 25.00° C.—to an accuracy of 0.01° C.

Thiotimoline Purity—The extreme sensitivity of this method highlights the deviations resulting from trifling impurities present in thiotimoline. (Since no method of laboratory synthesis of the substance has been devised, it may be practically obtained only through tedious isolation from its natural source, the bark of the shrub Rosacea Karls-*badensi* rufo.) Great efforts were therefore made to purify the material through repeated crystallizations from conductivity water—twice re-distilled in an all-tin apparatus—and through final sublimations. A comparison of the solution times (T) at the various stages of the purification process is shown in Table I.

TABLE I

Purification Stage	Average "T" (12 Observations)	"T" extremes	% error
As isolated	-0.72	-0.25 -01.01	34.1
First recrystallization	-0.95	-0.84 -01.09	9.8
Second recrystallization	-1.05	-0.99 -1.10	4.0
Third recrystallization	-1.11	-1.08 -1.13	1.8
Fourth recrystallization	-1.12	-1.10 -1.13	1.7
First resublimation	-1.12	-1.11 -1.13	0.9
Second resublimation	-1.122	-1.12 -1.13	0.7

It is obvious from Table I that for truly quantitive significance, thiotimoline purified as described must be used. After the second resublimation, for instance, the error involved in an even dozen determinations is less than 0.7%, with the extreme values being -1.119 seconds and -1.126 seconds.

In all experiments described subsequently in this study, thiotimoline so purified has been used.

Time of Solution and Volume of Solvent—As would seem reasonable, experiments have shown that increasing the volume of solvent enables the thiotimoline to dissolve more quickly—i.e., with an increasingly negative time of solution. From Figure 1, however, we can see that this increase in endochronic properties levels off rapidly after a volume of solvent of approximately 1.25 ml. This interesting plateau effect has appeared with varying volume of solvent for all varieties of solvents used in these laboratories, just as in all cases the time of solution approaches zero with decreasing volume of solvent.

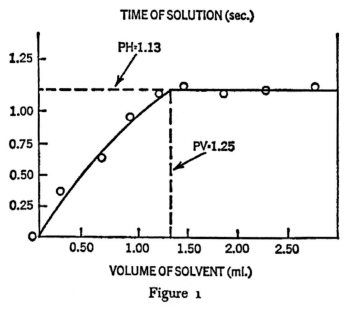

Figure 1

Time of Solution and Concentration of a Given Ion—In Figure 2, the results are given of the effect of the time of solution (T) of varying the volume of solvent, where the solvent consists of varying concentrations of sodium chloride solution. It can be seen that, although in each case the volume at which this plateau is reached differs markedly with the concentration, the heights of the plateau are constant (i.e. -1.13). The volume at which it is reached, hereinafter termed the Plateau Volume (PV), decreases with decreasing concentration of sodium chloride, approaching the PV for water as the NaCl concentration approaches zero. It is, therefore, obvious that a sodium chloride solution of unknown concentration can be quite accurately characterized by the determination of its PV, where other salts are absent.

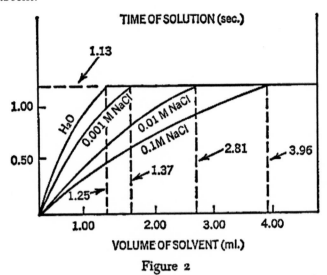

Figure 2

This usefulness of PV extends to other ions as well. Figure 3 gives the endochronic curves for 0.001 molar solutions of sodium chloride, sodium bromide, and potassium chloride. Here, the PV in each case is equal within the limits of experimental error—since the concentrations of each are equal—but the Plateau Heights (PH) *are* different.

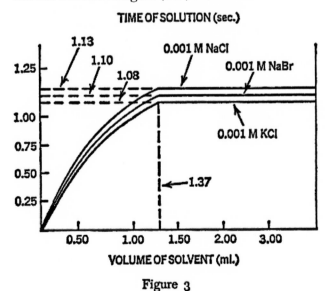

Figure 3

A tentative conclusion that might be reached from this experimental data is that the PH is characteristic of the nature of ions present in solution, whereas the PV is characteristic of the concentration of these ions. Table II gives the values of Plateau Height and Plateau Volume for a wide variety of salts in equal concentrations, when present alone.

The most interesting variation to be noted in Table II is that of the PV with the valence type of the salt present. In the case of salts containing pairs of singly-charged ions—i.e., sodium chloride, potassium chloride, and sodium bromide—the PV is constant for all. This holds also for those salts containing one singly-charged ion and one doubly-charged ion—i.e., sodium sulphate, calcium chloride, and magnesium chloride—where the PV, though equal among the three, varies markedly from those of the first set. The PV is, therefore, apparently a function of the ionic strength of the solution.

This effect also exists in connection with the Plateau Height, though less regularly. In the case of singly-charged ions, such as in the first three salts listed in Table II, the PH is fairly close to that of water itself. It falls considerably where doubly-charged ions, such as sulphate or calcium, are present. And when the triply-charged phosphate ion is present, the value sinks to merely a quarter of its value in water.

TABLE II

Solvent (Salt solution in 0.001 M concentration)	Plateau Height (PH) seconds	Plateau Volume (PV) milliliters
Water	-1.13	1.25
Sodium Chloride solution	-1.13	1.37
Sodium Bromide solution	-1.10	1.37
Potassium Chloride solution	-1.08	1.37
Sodium Sulphate solution	-0.72	1.59
Calcium Chloride solution	-0.96	1.59
Magnesium Chloride solution	-0.85	1.59
Calcium Sulphate solution	-0.61	1.72
Sodium Phosphate solution	-0.32	1.97
Ferric Chloride solution	-0.29	1.99

Time of Solution and Mixtures of Ions—Experiments currently in progress in these laboratories are concerned with the extremely important question of the variation of the endochronic properties of thiotimoline in the presence of mixtures of ions. The state of our data at present does not warrant very general conclusions, but even our preliminary work gives hope of the further development of the endochronic methods of analysis. Thus, in Figure 4, we have the endochronic curve where a mixture of 0.001M Sodium Chloride and 0.001M Ferric Chloride solutions is the solvent. Here, two sharp changes in slope can be seen: the first at a solution time of -0.29, and the second at -1.13, these being the PH's characteristic of Ferric Chloride and Sodium Chloride respectively—see Table II. The PH for a given salt would thus appear not to be affected by the presence of other salts.

This is definitely not the case, however, for the PV, and it is to a quantitive elucidation of the variation of PV with impurities in the solvent that our major efforts are now directed.

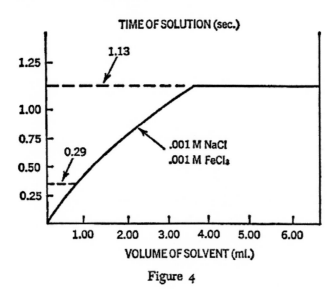

Figure 4

Summary—Investigations of the endochronic qualities of thiotimoline have shown that:

a—Careful purification of the material is necessary for obtaining quantitive results.

b—Increasing the volume of solvent results in increasing the negative time of solution to a constant value known as the Plateau Height (PH), at a volume of solvent known as the Plateau Volume (PV).

c—The value of the PH is characteristic of the nature of the ions present in the solvent, varying with the ionic strength of the solution and not varying with the addition of other ions.

d—The value of the PV is characteristic of the concentration of the ions present in the solvent, being constant for different ions in solutions of equal ionic strength, but varying markedly with the admixtures of second varieties of ions.

As a result of all this, it is suggested that endochronic methods offer a means of rapid—2 minutes or less—and accurate—within 0.1% at least—analysis of inorganic, water-soluble materials.

Bibliography:

P. Krum and L. Eshkin. *Journal of Chemical Solubilities*, 27, 109-114 (1944). "Concerning the Anomalous Solubility of Thiotimoline."

E. J. Feinschreiber and Y. Hravlek. *Journal of Chemical Solubilities*, 22, 57-68 (1939), "Solubility Speeds and Hydrophilic Groupings."

P. Krum, I. Eshkin, and O. Nile. *Annals of Synthetic Chemistry*, 115, 1122-1145; 1208-1215 (1945), "Structure of Thiotimoline, Parts I & II."

G. H. Freudler. *Journal of Psychochemistry*, 2, 476-488 (1945), "Initiation and Determination: Are They Influenced by Diet?—As tested by Thiotimoline Solubility Experiments."

E. Harley-Short. *Philosophical Proceedings & Reviews*, 15, 125-197 (1946). "Determinism and Free Will. The Application of Thiotimoline Solubility to Marxian Dialectic."

P. Krum. *Journal of Chemical Solubilities*, 29, 818-819 (1946), "A Device for the Quantitive Measurement of Thiotimoline Solubility Speed."

A. Roundin, B. Lev, and Y. J. Prutt. *Proceedings of the Society of Plant Chemistry*, 80, 11-18 (1930), "Natural Products isolated from shrubs of the genus *Rosacea*."

Tiotimolin kak Isitatel Marksciiskoy dilektiki B. Kreschiatika. *Journal Nauki i Sovetskoy Ticorii* Vol. 11, No. 3.

Philossophia Neopredelennosti i Tiotimolin, Molvinski Pogost i Z. Brikalo. *Mir i Kultura* Vol. 2, No. 31.

Janet Kagan

Remember the good old days of pulp magazines, when it was even more fun to read the ads than the stories? Ja-net Kagan does. (And when this little parody appeared in magazine form, it actually drew a number of responses from earnest readers!)

JUNKMAIL

Faith-of-the-Month Club
231 Circle of the Allotheist
Wink City, Sly. NW 3
Minimifidian 432⁹⁸⁸203

56 Thub 21432

Ms. J. Sane-Jewell
389204 Newman Street
Abergorod 26 Coolidge
LC's World 288857231

Dear Ms. Sane-Jewell:

How many times have you made a sacrifice and wondered to yourself: WHAT IF I'M SACRIFICING THIS VIRGIN, THIS GOAT, THIS SMYLK, TO THE WRONG GOD? How often have you REPENTED A SIN WITHOUT ANY ASSURANCE that you have made

THE RIGHT REPENTANCE??! How many times have you wondered, WHAT SINS AM I NEGLECTING??!

If you're like me, the number of times is larger than your ZipCode.

Like me, you've wondered, HOW CAN I FIND THE TRUTH?— I'm a busy being, and a search for the right religion is a time-consuming project, even for the best of us.

NOW, the BEST MINDS IN THE UNIVERSE are at YOUR disposal!!!

NOW, you can have THE BEST OF ALL RELIGIONS DELIV-ERED DIRECTLY TO YOUR HOME each month.

Think of it!!! No more exhaustive searching of temples, NO MORE DANGEROUS, EXPENSIVE PILGRIMAGES to dusty, deserted asteroids, no more stupefying discussions with priestesses! And, best of all, NO NEED TO SPLINK, NOT EVER AGAIN!!!

JUST LOOK WHAT YOU GET WHEN YOU JOIN—

Each month you receive a BEAUTIFUL FULL COLOR, FULL SOUND (and FULL SMELL for those of you on Wilpon Worlds!) 30-page brochure to tell you of the two best religions CHOSEN ES-PECIALLY FOR YOU BY EXPERTS from the millions concentrated throughout the known galaxy! Included you'll find sample litanies AND incense to help you decide if these are for you!!!

If you choose to accept the major selections, YOU NEED DO NOTHING!—they will be sent to you AUTOMATICALLY!

Or, if you prefer an alternate, simply mark your preference on the en-closed card and return it within ten standard days.

No longer will you mistakenly sacrifice a relf't to a vegetarian god! No longer must you endure foul-smelling incense without the assurance of redemption!

And, IF YOU JOIN NOW, take advantage of our special offer: for just two ergs (that's right, just TWO ERGS!) you'll receive your choice of any four religions—ANY FOUR FOR JUST TWO ERGS! Choose from OVER FIFTY GREAT RELIGIONS, the BEST OF THE NEW and HANDSOME REVIVALS OF THE CLASSICS as well, including—

Jobism: A favorite of masochists everywhere! SUFFER WITHOUT SHAME, knowing that your suffering makes you GOD'S FAVORITE!!!

Brother-Sister REDEEMED Hellenistic Fauvism: A delightful new schism from the G'lal'lil Kingdoms. Some call it heresy, but we call it A HAIR-RAISING SWITCH on the old Hellenistic Fauvism that must be experienced to be believed!

Organism: Look here for kidney-pie-in-the-sky! This sect gives a whole new meaning to LIVER-WORSHIP!

Holographic organism: Tired of shallow, superficial religions???—here you examine all god's parts in depth, and from every angle.

For JUST TWO ERGS, you can have McCarthyism, Lunar Toonism, Schizism (WARNING TO THOSE OF YOU ON BEEBEL: Schizism may be hazardous to your health and will ONLY be delivered to those of you who pass the written test!), AND Dualism (COUNTS AS ONE SELECTION if you join now!)!!!

All you do is return the enclosed card TODAY, marking your four chosen religions, and WE DO THE REST!

We pay the shipping and handling of all IDOLS, RELIGIOUS TEXTS, PRIESTS AND PRIESTESSES!!! WE EVEN PROVIDE YOUR FIRST SACRIFICE!!!!

YOU need purchase ONLY FOUR FUTURE SELECTIONS within the next STANDARD year, at our REGULAR LOW PRICE of up to 20% OFF the customary tithe!!!

So DON'T DELAY! ACT NOW!

For the PEACE OF YOUR SOUL, join today!!! And discover the joys of SEEKING THE TRUTH right in your own home!!!

Faithfully Yours,
j'Junjuntub-Smith
Managing Thing

FAITH-OF-THE-MONTH CLUB

Mike Resnick

Some years back I was reading a number of old-time African hunters' memoirs as part of my research for a book I was writing. They took themselves and their craft so seriously that I decided I just had to write a parody of their articles about how to blow helpless animals away. At just about the same time, I went to a science fiction convention that had one too many soft-eyed unicorns in the art show. This is the result.

STALKING THE UNICORN WITH GUN AND CAMERA

WHEN SHE GOT TO within two hundred yards of the herd of Southern Savannah unicorns she had been tracking for four days, Rheela of the Seven Stars made her obeisance to Quatr Mane, God of the Hunt, then donned the amulet of Kobassen, tested the breeze to make sure that she was still downwind of the herd, and began approaching them, camera in hand.

But Rheela of the Seven Stars had made one mistake—a mistake of *carelessness*—and thirty seconds later she was dead, brutally impaled upon the horn of a bull unicorn.

Hotack the Beastslayer cautiously made his way up the lower slopes of the Mountain of the Nameless One. He was a skilled tracker, a fearless hunter, and a crack shot. He picked out the trophy he wanted, got the beast within his sights, and hurled his killing club. It flew straight and true to its mark.

And yet, less than a minute later, Hotack, his left leg badly gored, was barely able to pull himself to safety in the branches of a nearby Rainbow Tree. He, too, had made a mistake—a mistake of *ignorance*.

Bort the Pure had had a successful safari. He had taken three chimeras, a gorgon, and a beautifully matched pair of griffins. While his trolls were skinning the gorgon, he spotted a unicorn bearing a near-record horn, and, weapon in hand, he began pursuing it. The terrain gradually changed, and suddenly Bort found himself in shoulder-high kraken grass. Undaunted, he followed the trail into the dense vegetation.

But Bort the Pure, too, had made a mistake—a mistake of *foolishness*. His trolls found what very little remained of him some six hours later.

Carelessness, ignorance, foolishness—together they account for more deaths among unicorn hunters than all other factors combined.

Take our examples, for instance. All three hunters—Rheela, Hotack, and Bort—were experienced safari hands. They were used to extremes of temperature and terrain, they didn't object to finding insects in their ale or banshees in their tents, they knew they were going after deadly game and took all reasonable precautions before setting out.

And yet two of them died, and the third was badly maimed.

Let's examine their mistakes, and see what we can learn from them.

Rheela of the Seven Stars assimilated everything her personal wizard could tell her about unicorns, purchased the very finest photographic equipment, hired a native guide who had been on many unicorn hunts, and had a local witch doctor bless her Amulet of Kobassen. And yet, when the charge came, the amulet was of no use to her, for she had failed to properly identify the particular subspecies of unicorn before her—and, as I am continually pointing out during my lecture tours, the Amulet of Kobassen is potent only against the rare and almost-extinct Forest unicorn. Against the Southern Savannah unicorn, the *only* effective charm is the Talisman of Triconis. *Carelessness.*

Hotack the Beastslayer, on the other hand, disdained all forms of supernatural protection. To him, the essence of the hunt was to pit himself in physical combat against his chosen prey. His killing club, a beautifully wrought and finely balanced instrument of destruction, had brought down simurghs, humbabas, and even a dreaded wooly hydra. He elected to go for a head shot, and the club flew to within a millimeter of where he had aimed it. But he hadn't counted on the unicorn's phenomenal sense of smell, nor the speed with which these surly brutes can move. Alerted to Hotack's presence, the unicorn turned its head to seek out its predator—and the killing club bounced harmlessly off its horn. Had Hotack spoken to almost any old-time unicorn hunter, he would have realized that head shots are almost impossible, and would have gone for a crippling knee shot. *Ignorance.*

Bort the Pure was aware of the unique advantages accruing to a virgin who hunts the wild unicorn, and so he had practiced sexual abstinence since he was old enough to know what the term meant. And yet he naively believed that because his virginity allowed him to approach the unicorn more easily than other hunters, the unicorn would somehow become placid and make no attempt to defend itself—and so he followed a vicious animal that was compelled to let him approach it, and entered a patch of high grass that allowed him no maneuvering room during the inevitable charge. *Foolishness.*

Every year hundreds of hopeful hunters go out in search of the unicorn, and every year all but a handful come back empty-handed—if they come back at all. And yet the unicorn can be safely stalked and successfully hunted, if only the stalkers and hunters will take the time to study their quarry.

When all is said and done, the unicorn is a relatively docile beast (except when enraged). It is a creature of habit, and once those habits have been learned by the hopeful photographer or trophy hunter, bringing home that picture or that horn is really no more dangerous than, say, slaying an Eight-Forked Dragon—and it's certainly easier than lassoing wild minotaurs, a sport that has become all the rage these days among the smart set on the Platinum Plains.

However, before you can photograph or kill a unicorn, you have to find it—and by far the easiest way to make contact with a unicorn herd is to follow the families of smerps that track the great game migrations. The smerps, of course, have no natural enemies except for the rafsheen and the zumakin, and consequently will allow a human (or preternatural) being to approach them quite closely.

A word of warning about the smerp: with its long ears and cute, fuzzy body, it resembles nothing more than an oversized rabbit—but calling a smerp a rabbit doesn't make it one, and you would be ill-advised to underestimate the strength of these nasty little scavengers. Although they generally hunt in packs of from ten to twenty, I have more than once seen a single smerp, its aura flowing with savage strength, pull down a half-grown unicorn. Smerps are poor eating, their pelts are worthless because of the difficulty of curing and tanning the auras, and they make pretty unimpressive trophies unless you can come up with one possessing a truly magnificent set of ears—in fact, in many areas they're still classified as vermin—but the wise unicorn hunter can save himself a lot of time and effort by simply letting the smerps lead him to his prey.

With the onset of poaching, the legendary unicorn herds numbering upwards of a thousand members no longer exist, and you'll find that the typical herd today consists of from fifty to seventy-five individuals. The days when a photographer, safe and secure in a blind by a water hole, could preserve on film an endless stream of the brutes coming down to drink are gone forever—and it is absolutely shocking to contemplate the number of unicorns that have died simply so their horns could be sold on the black market. In fact, I find it appalling that anyone in this enlightened day and age still believes that a powdered unicorn horn can act as an aphrodisiac.

(Indeed, as any magus can tell you, you treat the unicorn horn with essence of grach and then boil it slowly in a solution of sphinx blood. Now *that's* an aphrodisiac!)

But I digress.

The unicorn, being a nondiscriminating browser that is equally content to feed upon grasses, leaves, fruits, and an occasional small fern tree, occurs in a wide variety of habitats, often in the company of grazers such as centaurs and the pegasus.

Once you have spotted the unicorn herd, it must be approached with great care and caution. The unicorn may have poor eyesight, and its sense of hearing may not be much better, but it has an excellent sense of smell and an absolutely awesome sense of *grimsch*, about which so much has been written that there is no point in my belaboring the subject yet again.

If you are on a camera safari, I would strongly advise against trying to get closer than one hundred yards to even a solitary beast—that sense of *grimsch* again—and most of the photographers I know swear by an 85/350mm automatic-focus zoom lens, providing, of course, that it has been blessed by a Warlock of the Third Order. If you haven't got the shots you want by sunset, my best advice is to pack it in for the day and return the next morning. Flash photography is possible, of course, but it does tend to attract golem and other even more bothersome nocturnal predators.

One final note to the camera buff: for reasons our alchemists have not yet determined, no unicorn has ever been photographed with normal emulsified film of any speed, so make sure that you use one of the more popular infra-red brands. It would be a shame to spend weeks on safari, paying for your guide, cook, and trolls, only to come away with a series of photos of the forest that you thought was merely the background to your pictures.

As for hunting the brutes, the main thing to remember is that they are as close to you as you are to them. For this reason, while I don't disdain blood sacrifices, amulets, talismans, and blessings, all of which have their proper place, I for one always feel more confident with a .550 Nitro Express in my hands. A little extra stopping power can give a hunter quite a feeling of security.

You'll want a bull unicorn, of course; they tend to have more spectacular horns than cows—and by the time a bull's horn is long enough to be worth taking, he's probably too old to be in the herd's breeding program anyway.

The head shot, for reasons explained earlier, is never a wise option. And unless your wizard teaches you the Rune of Mamhotet, thus enabling you to approach close enough to pour salt on the beast's tail and thereby pin him to the spot where he's standing, I recommend the heart shot (either heart will do—and if you have a double-barreled gun, you might try to hit both of them, just to be on the safe side).

If you have the bad fortune to merely wound the beast, he'll immediately make off for the trees or the high grass, which puts you at an enormous disadvantage. Some hunters, faced with such a situation, merely stand back and allow the smerps to finish the job for them—after all, smerps rarely devour the horn unless they're completely famished—but this is hardly sporting. The decent, honorable hunter, well aware of the unwritten rules of blood sports, will go after the unicorn himself.

The trick, of course, is to meet him on fairly open terrain. Once the unicorn lowers his head to charge, he's virtually blind, and all you need do is dance nimbly out of the way and take another shot at him—or, if you are not in possession of the Rune of Mamhotet, this would be an ideal time to get out that salt and try to sprinkle some on his tail as he races by.

When the unicorn dictates the rules of the game, you've got a much more serious situation. He'll usually double back and lie in the tall grasses beside his spoor, waiting for you to pass by, and then attempt to gore you from behind.

It is at this time that the hunter must have all his wits about him. Probably the best sign to look for is the presence of Fire-Breathing Dragonflies. These noxious little insects frequently live in symbiosis with the unicorn, cleansing his ears of parasites, and their presence usually means that the unicorn isn't far off. Yet another sign that your prey is nearby will be the flocks of hungry harpies circling overhead, waiting to swoop down and feed upon the remains of your kill; and, of course, the surest sign of all is when you hear a grunt of rage and find yourself staring into the bloodshot, beady little eyes of a wounded bull unicorn from a distance of ten feet or less. It's moments like that that make you feel truly alive, especially when you suddenly realize that this isn't necessarily a permanent condition.

All right. Let's assume that your hunt is successful. What then?

Well, your trolls will skin the beast, of course, and take special care in removing and preserving the horn. If they've been properly trained, they'll also turn the pelt into a rug, the hooves into ashtrays, the teeth into a necklace, the tail into a flyswatter, and the scrotum into a tobacco pouch. My own feeling is that you should settle for nothing less, since it goes a long way toward showing the bleeding-heart preservationists that a unicorn can supply a hunter with a lot more than just a few minutes of pleasurable sport and a horn.

And while I'm on the subject of what the unicorn can supply, let me strongly suggest that you would be missing a truly memorable experience if you were to come home from safari without having eaten unicorn meat at least once. There's nothing quite like unicorn cooked over an open campfire to top off a successful hunt. (And do remember to leave something out for the smerps, or they might well decide that hunter is every bit as tasty as unicorn.)

So get out those amulets and talismans, visit those wizards and warlocks, pack those cameras and weapons—and good hunting to you!

******

Next Week: Outstaring the Medusa

Robert Bloch

What collection of humor would be complete without a contribution from Robert Bloch? This parody of Lewis Carroll's "Jabberwocky" will make a little more sense if you've been around science fiction fandom for a couple of decades, but even newcomers will catch a number of the references.

JABBERWOCKY FOR FANDOM

'Twas Willis, and the boggsy toves
Did gold and campbell in the wabe:
All faunchy were the borogoves
And the Seventh Fans outgrabe.

Beware the Fannishtalk, my son!
The paws that write, the feuds that catch!
Beware the FAPA bird, and shun
Both GRUE and HYPHEN, natch!

He took his hectograph in hand:
Long time the poctsared foe he sought—
So rested by the Annish tree,
And stood awhile in thought.

And as in tuckerish thought he stood,
The Fannishtalk, with eyes of flame,
Came yngving through the lousy wood,
And burbeed as it came!

One, two! One, two! And through and through
The vorpal blade sawed Courtney's boat!
His pen hit snags of fannish gags
As he, little willies wrote.

"And hast thou learned the Fannishtalk?
Come to my arms, my harlan boy!
Oh Poo, Oh Yobber, Ghu, horray!"
He grennelled in his joy.

'Twas harris and the laney toves
Did f&sf in the wabe,
All crifanac the borogoves
As in gafia he outgrabe.

Ralph Roberts

Ralph Roberts, who writes everything from science fiction to computer books to autograph collector's guides, also writes other things. Like puns. From which no one and nothing is safe, not even Arthur C. Clarke's classic "The Nine Billion Names of God."

THE NINE BILLION PUNS OF GOD

CHAN, THE ACOLYTE, PULLED his brown robe closer against the cold Himalayan wind and tried to keep the sputtering flame upon the wick floating alight in its bowl of yak fat. He failed but, upon pushing open the massive wooden door before him, found that the dim greenish light from the revered one's computer terminal illuminated the rock-hewn cubicle well enough.

Piles of moldy, rotten printouts were stacked in every available free space from the floor, worn smooth by sandals of a hundred generations' monks, to the unfinished ceiling. His nose wrinkled involuntarily at the odor pervading the chamber. A starship, on final approach to New Delhi, passed over their ancient monastery; the barely sensed vibrations of its grav-engines intruding on the great pile of stone, still isolated as for centuries, in frigid mountain vastness.

The white-haired old holy man hunched over the keyboard turned at the sound of Chan's entrance. His face was wrinkled from the rigors of some eighty mountain winters; his eyes glinted with the fervor of religious fanaticism.

Chan smiled fondly. "Come, eat some, Elder Nired," he said. "I've heated a bowl of barley soup for you. It now steams on the rectory table."

He spoke the English of his Hong Kong boyhood because that was preferred by Nired.

"No," the old holy one replied in his quavering voice. "A bit more work first. I near completion of the Task."

"It nears midnight," Chan replied patiently. He noted that Nired looked tired. For the hundredth time, he wished they would abandon their quest for the Heavenly Puns. Yes, he disbelieved the old legends and dogmas of his faith. He stayed here only to escape the complexities of the outside world. And because the old ones needed his help. He was the first acolyte in thirty-five years. "Come. You must take some nourishment," he pleaded and tried valiantly to breathe only through his mouth—the stench in this room was almost unbearable at times.

The old one smiled tolerantly and patted the computer terminal. "This device I, myself, purchased fifty years ago has let we few left of the Order achieve an amazing degree of success in cataloging the Revered Witticisms. In all Earthly languages." He paused to scratch, showers being an oversight of the original builders of the monastery. "Only one....Just one," he sighed.

Chan too sighed, but only mentally so as to not offend the elderly monk. "That one Holy Play On Words has escaped your search for years," he said reasonably. "What matters one more night?"

Stretching his aching arms, Nired shook his head stubbornly. "No," he said, firmness creeping into his old man's voice. "Tonight I feel on the verge of finalizing the Task. Think of it, my son. The very basis of our faith has been that The Creator allotted a mere nine billion Holy Puns to the creatures of this planet." More strength came to his tones as he repeated the oft repeated: "And it is Written in the ancient texts that when all of these have been gathered and are known in one place, the world shall end. And we are so close....So very close." He clenched his bony fists in frustration.

Chan managed to hide a bored yawn. He had heard this on many other dark, snowy nights. "And we have all the Nine Billion save one."

Nired nodded sadly. "In all languages, excepting only one in English." His gnarled fingers caressed the computer keyboard before him.

Chan shrugged, sniffed, and almost gagged. "Holy One," he said when breathing was again possible, "why does it always smell of rot and mildew in this place? We are high in altitude and always cold in temperature; this should not be."

"Hmmm," replied Nired distractedly. "Oh! That. I have grown used to it over the years. My boy, there are, save one, nine billion puns in this room." He gestured at the stacks of printouts; some in every known print-symbol of all the written tongues of Earth. "One must expect such a collection to have its own distinctive odor." His eyes glowed brighter, for Nired was a True Believer in the Revered Witticisms. "There is no greater goal in life," he lectured Chan, "than to be witty in the Eyes of the Creator, than to gently pun as I do in this room."

Poor Chan was struggling to get air into his laboring lungs under the effluvium of nine billion puns minus one. "I'd say that pungently describes this chamber," he wheezed.

Nired idly entered Chan's inadvertent pun. The computer was silent for a moment as it searched the data banks. Then there was a small chime and the screen blanked out. The old monk gasped in surprise and quickly swung to face Chan. A holy light glowed on his face. "The last one!" he said with awe. And, with an agility that belied his advanced age, he sprang to his feet. "Come, Chan. Let us go outside and watch the stars wink out, one by one."

Chan shrugged and followed the old man through the door. He doubted they would see much, the sky being heavily overcast tonight. But, just in case, he was going to demand a recount.

Thomas Easton

Tom Easton has been reviewing books for Analog for more than a dozen years. Given the quantity of turkeys he's had to wade through, the man obviously needs a sense of humor. As proof of it, here is his carefully considered proposal to save the Loch Ness Monster.

THE CHICAGO PLAN TO SAVE A SPECIES

ALTHOUGH THE EXISTENCE OF a large animal, thought to be prehistoric in its origins, has long been suspected in Scotland's Loch Ness, actual observations have only recently been made.[1] In 1972, a team of scientists obtained an underwater photograph of the creature's side, showing a diamond-shaped fin. In 1975, improved photographic equipment obtained a photograph of the entire animal at a distance of about 25 feet; another was made of its head. Both photographs confirmed earlier descriptions. As a result, the photographers, Dr. Robert Rines of the Academy of Applied Science in Boston and naturalist Sir Peter Scott, among others, gave the animal its scientific name, *Nessiteras rhombopteryx*, Latin for "the diamond-finned marvel of Loch Ness."[2]

The biggest expedition so far to uncover more information about the creature may soon be launched under the leadership of Dr. Roy Mackal of the University of Chicago. An effort will be made to obtain better photographs. Sonar will search the bottom of the Loch for bones or bodies,

---

1   Loch Ness is only about 24 miles long and a mile or so wide, but it is more than 900 feet deep in spots and more than 700 feet deep over much of its length. The water is a cold 42 F, and its murkiness obscures vision.

2   Skeptical journalists have turned the name into an anagram for "Monster hoax by Sir Peter S." Dr. Rines has answered with another: "Yes, both pix and monsters. R."

and the sides of the Loch for caves in which *N. rhombopteryx* might live. A harpoon-like device may be used to collect a tissue sample for analysis.

But, with confirmation of the existence of *N. rhombopteryx* has come rising concern about its survival as a species. Dr. Mackal, author of *The Monsters of Loch Ness*[3] and a director of the Loch Ness Investigation Bureau, has estimated that the Loch can contain only 150 to 200 of the creatures.[4] Human beings are relative newcomers to the home of *N. rhombopteryx*, and the small colony is now threatened by a steady encroachment of civilization upon its natural habitat. An unforeseen catastrophe, either natural or human-made, could cause this ancient species, perhaps one of the few remaining links with the prehistoric past, to become extinct.

Lake Michigan is not so deep as Loch Ness, but its surface area is 933 times as great. Our fisheries biologists say that Michigan may hold some 25,000 tons of trout and salmon as well as other species of fish such as alewives, an aggregate more than half again as large as the 680,000 tons of young salmon thought to be in Loch Ness. If, as Dr. Mackal surmises, the main food of *N. rhombopteryx* is fish, then Lake Michigan might support a second colony of *N. rhombopteryx* consisting of as many as 315 individuals—or one and a half times as many as might live in Loch Ness. If Lake Michigan were stocked with just three breeding pairs, such a population might be obtained within 25 years.[5]

Yet a plan to save *N. rhombopteryx*, by breeding them in Lake Michigan, when put forward on a trial basis earlier this year, was received with caution by government officials and special interest groups.[6] Among these is the British government, which resists the plan for reasons of national pride. "I'm sure there will be letters of protest to the *Times*," said Aidan MacDermott, information officer for the British Consulate in Chicago. "It's a sort of national pet. We might be willing to lend it to you, though, rather like the Magna Carta."

---

3   Swallow Press, Chicago, 1976

4   Dr. Mackal estimated the number of young salmon in the Loch at 19 billion, or 680,000 tons. He then assumed that a tenth of these young salmon are eaten by predators in the Loch. Since the average predator eats about a hundredth of its weight daily, Dr. Mackal calculated that the Loch must contain 18,600 tons of predators. He assumed that *N. rhombopteryx* accounts for one percent of this total, the rest being larger fish, birds, and humans. Thus he arrived at a figure of from 150 to 200 *N. rhombopteryx* in Loch Ness—or 186 tons of *N. rhombopteryx* at 2,500 pounds each.

5   Since *N. rhombopteryx* eggs have never been found near Loch Ness, we can safely assume that it is a live breeder. Because it is a large animal, it probably has a long gestation period, say two years. For purposes of this calculation, we further assume that it might take the animal approximately three years to reach maturity.

6   It did, however, create an opportunity for yet another anagram of *Nessiteras rhombopteryx*—this one, "sexy Montrose Harb. sprite."

Locally, much of the controversy has centered on the effect that an *N. rhombopteryx* stocking program might have on the salmon and trout in Lake Michigan—where thanks to an extensive restocking effort, both recreational and commercial fishing have become large industries.[7] One of the first organizations to raise an objection was Salmon Unlimited, which represents recreational fishermen on the lake. Their Sherwin Schwartz has stated, "We have enough trouble with the commercial fishermen. We don't need another drain on the salmon." Proponents of the plan counter that 300 *N. rhombopteryx* would eat at most 320 tons a year of the 25,000 tons of trout and salmon in the lake.

Further questions have been raised by the US Fish and Wildlife Service, however, where a high source has suggested that the effects of stray radiation from the nuclear power plants surrounding Lake Michigan might produce mutations in *N. rhombopteryx*. The possible resulting changes in size and behavior could be undesirable. Our source states that the service would require exhaustive studies of *N. rhombopteryx* life history, longevity, food habits, growth rates, and reproductive biology before it would approve the plan, primarily with a view towards ascertaining if the creature might not multiply so successfully as to take over all the Great Lakes and associated waterways. In such a case *N. rhombopteryx* would be one of the few large species of animal which have proved able to reproduce in Lake Michigan Polychlorinated Biphenyl (PCB) and pesticide-polluted waters.[8]

Proponents of the plan also face obstacles imposed by foreign, federal, and local bureaucracies. Mr. MacDermott has said that permission to export *N. rhombopteryx* from Great Britain would have to come from the Minister of Agriculture, Fisheries, and Food, and that other British ministries would probably also expect to be consulted. The agricultural attaché at the British embassy in Washington, however, was unwilling to say whether permission would be forthcoming. "The question has never come up," he said.

On the federal level—according to David Comey, executive director of Citizens for a Better Environment—a large stocking program, if handled by the federal government, would call for an Environmental Impact

---

7   The trout and salmon now in the lake are there as a result of stocking efforts, because the presence of Polychlorinated Biphenyls (PCBs) and pesticides in the lake have made it nearly impossible for large fish, high on the food chain, to reproduce. It is possible that, since *N. rhombopteryx* eats these fish, it would concentrate PCBs and pesticides in its flesh to such a point that it also would be unable to reproduce. In such a case, a stocking program would be ill-fated.

8   As yet we have no reading on how *N. rhombopteryx* tastes when smoked, nor whether Mr. Schwartz's organization would consider changing its name to *Nessiteras* Unlimited.

Statement from the Department of the Interior and for careful consideration by the Environmental Protection Agency. The Army Corps of Engineers would have to review the creature's potential as a navigational hazard. The Nuclear Regulatory Commission would have to review the safety consequences of one of the creatures being sucked into the water intake of a nuclear power plant. And the Department of Agriculture would impose the usual quarantine requirements applicable to all imported animals. On a local level, Tony Dean of the Illinois Department of Conservation has said that public hearings and meetings would be required before his department could look at the proposal.

But at least one local institution has responded to the plan with enthusiasm. Roger Klocek, assistant curator of fishes at Shedd Aquarium, hopes that the aquarium might acquire one or more of the animals for the public to observe at close hand. He envisions building a pen around an area of the lake adjacent to the aquarium, with an observation chamber placed underwater, so that aquarium patrons could see the entire animal in its environment. Such an installation, he estimates, would cost no more than $200,000.

It is surprising that both the Chicago Association of Commerce and Industry and the Office of the Mayor have pointedly refused to lend their support and encouragement to this project. The obvious advantages of such a plan include not only the preservation of an endangered species but also a great boost to civic pride, a monumental stimulus to local tourism, and as-yet- unexplored potential in the area of alewife control. Possibilities present themselves in the form of *N. rhombopteryx* lakeside festivals, picnics, and expeditions sponsored by the Illinois St. Andrews society (an organization of Scots and persons of Scottish descent), conventions, and affiliated cottage industries which would undoubtedly include Wendella *rhombopteryx* rides, lakefront telescopes, and a variety of souvenirs including statuettes with and without thermometers, ashtrays, hats, flags, coin purses, key chains, postcards, and salt and pepper shakers in the shape of *N. rhombopteryx*.[9]

Mr. Comey has commented, "The only reason Daley's people aren't behind this is that they haven't realized the patronage potential of a full *N. rhombopteryx* program. They could have thousands of workers out on the lake—monitoring, measuring, counting, tagging, and sampling the animals. And nobody would know if they were actually working or not."

---

9   One recent proposal has called for an *N. rhombopteryx* Day on which the city would pour Scotch into the Chicago River and let it flow into the lake. In a revised version, which has been well received in unofficial circles, we could drink the Scotch and let *N. rhombopteryx* swim up the river to us.

The reasons for the city's reticence on this subject can only be surmised, but it is possible that officials are waiting for a reading of public opinion on the issue. Large animals have not enjoyed good press of late; one has only to think of *Jaws* and an endless stream of fear-mongering science fiction films on local television station WFLD. The popular press has insensitively referred to *N. rhombopteryx* as the "Loch Ness Monster," suggesting that it is an object worthy of fear.[10]

Fortunately, there are signs that an enlightened and more liberal attitude has penetrated some quarters of the present administrations. Richard Pavia, acting Commissioner of Water and Sewers, has said, "I've never heard of them doing any harm. The fact that they're called monsters has more to do with their size than with their behavior."

Because the stocking effort would be so complex and expensive an undertaking, it is unlikely to occur in the absence of a concentrated effort by the city government. We might see a start in that direction early this month. According to reliable sources, a North Side alderman is considering a resolution to be introduced in a City Council meeting this month; it would put the city on record as supporting the stocking program. Although the resolution is not likely to be acted upon soon, it is an important first step toward getting the project under way. A significant showing of public support for the plan could be the decisive factor.

---

10   One of the local groups most sensitive to slurs against *N. rhombopteryx* is an organization calling itself Friends of the Loch Mich Monster, with headquarters in Suite 440, 500 North Michigan Avenue.

Larry Tritten

This was not an "open" anthology. In other words, I did not ask for submissions, but simply tracked down the parodies that I remembered most fondly. Still, once I started sending out contracts, there was no way to keep it secret, and sure enough, five days later an unsolicited contribution arrived in the mail. My initial reaction was annoyance at the prospect of driving to the post office to mail it back. Then I looked at the opening paragraph and realized that I was reading a perfect parody of R. A. Lafferty, the one writer in the field I would have sworn could not be parodied. I even bounced one of my own stories from the book in order to run this one. Curse you, Larry Tritten!

LAND OF THE GREAT HORSE LAUGHS

This is the here and there of it: there were seven men who traveled seven separate paths to reach a crossroads where their mutual interests converged. There was Alfred Carnitas, a sly, whey-faced man who threw a noisy shadow. There was Milho Crayons, a Gypsy who had not quite the way of a Gypsy, for he had lived all his many-numbered years in a closet on a shelf. There was Maypop McCray Fish, a not-quite man and yet not-quite-machine, who was a tinkerer of suggestions and maker of salty hints. There was Conk Johnson, who sucked all the sweetness out of every possibility he encountered, and chewed its attendant pith. There was Gnosis Rumen, another chewer, but he of phenomenological cuds. There was Ruhmkorff Coyle, an old man gone in the wallet but a dancer in his dreams, which were full to the filling place with Mammon's passion. And last (and possibly least) there was Gilbert Halfmuch, a designer of toys for nasty genius children: he had invented the Transdimensional

Whirlagig, Neuro-Clay, and the No-Deposit Klein Bottle; and we all know how cute these items were.

They met by design, if not by accident, in the Boar-in-a-Poke Bar on the Blue Moon of Bascopolis (that world where only drinkers and tellers of muscular tall tales meet) and ordered up a dozen or two Dirty Doubles, with which they immediately set to toasting their cleverness at so meeting. "It's a world that smells like a grandmother's figs!" swore Conk Johnson, snorting down his drink in one draught after first testing his nose on its livid vapors.

"I'll double that sentiment, and triple it later," said Gnosis Rumen, chewing on his brew. He made an Easter Island face. "Say, what is this swill? Didn't I once flirt with such dregs in the bottom of a double-damned demijohn?

Alfred Carnitas said, in that way he had of twinkling his words, "I've had better hooch than this, but never in Spokane. And not in the Fungo Isles, where drinks are for throwing but not for taste or tippling.

A man came through a curtain to the back of the back-bar, then, and began to play a horn with strings. He was the entertainment.

"Get out, you damned hunker-shanked pusillanimous mud-gargling cuff-hugging scum-squeezing chip off a succubus's block!" Ruhmkorff Coyle roared, and threw a rusty-daggered glance at the minstrel, who ducked again behind the curtain. Coyle was a small man, but his muscles and nerves were the talk of a baker's dozen of worlds, and in truth he would have ground the musician's bones to make his biscuits.

Among the seven there ensued a great deal of drinking and roistering, jiggery and pokery, and a large number of reels and schot-tisches, after which, sated, they fell to discussing the means and ends of the enterprise that had brought them into conjunction.

It was a world of kale and lettuce that held the interest of this high-life seven. One of them (which one, none could recall) had found it in a dream, but on waking had consulted his Finders Keepers Perceptor (a device of his own contrivance) and discovered it to be as real as rain. On this world there were gems aplenty and galore, nay, hyper-galore: alps of pearl, onyx, rhinestone, and agate rose toward skies of turquoise blue-green; there were deserts where the dust of gold was ankle-deep, and valleys where one could not walk unshod without cutting the feet on zircons. In the rainy season there were storms of tinsel, and other times when gew-gaws abruptly fell like hailstones from moody pearl-drift clouds.

So, in keeping with the spirit of zest that animates all genius kin, these seven met together for the purpose of getting the proverbial goods.

"I say we rent a space bomp," proposed Gilbert Halfmuch. He pulled out a celestial chart on which the stars glittered like scattered dazzle. His rowdy forefinger poked a fussy-looking star cornerwise on the chart. "Here's our goal, this sire star's foal. A mere hop, skip, and jumping bean bounce past the Loop De Lieu. We can drink and snicker our way through a fortnight of whiskey wherewithals, set down, and then have a hearty mining life. I've an itch for a diamond as big as the Hyatt Ritz; and I'll have it, too, or know the blankety bice blazes why not!

All nodded, and all struck down their hands in common concurrence. Who was to know that one hand was of the red-handed sort and would tickle the fates of all?

They leased that space bomp the next morning and shipped the following eventide. It was a fine craft, they were on a fine chase, and they went aboard in a high fine fettle, though to be sure Maypop McCray Fish did grouse a bit about having to leave behind a dilly of a doxy named Margaret Kate Scotchwater, who'd filled his head with heady thoughts about what a fine swaggering swain he was, prone or standing, and wanted to know where and why he must go. Yet he promised her a bunch of opulent baubles, tweaked her on the silk, and went his gangling way.

They went out past the Sierra Umbriago, took a hard left, chugged through the Cimmarian Shallows, and bore down on their ornate goal, singing all the way:

"We once were there and now are here
And still are just en-route.
Our 'here' keeps turning into 'there'
As we go further out.
We'll not encompass doubt or pause.
Columbus didn't, dog it!
We'll find a world all glitter bright
And rape and swill and hog it!"

A few mega-weeks swigged by, and by and by the bomp came down with a boisterous bump. Its crew, having guzzled themselves into lassitude, stirred feebly, then got into suitable suits and sallied forth.

"Has this world a name?" queried Milho Crayons, wincing at the grand glitter that assaulted his vision as he stepped upon the opal sod.

"We'll name it Last Name," suggested Gnosis Rumen, "as it is the last world to be named."

The seven set out, monkey-quick and wincing in the glare of all the gem-bright tarn and turf both near and slightly far. It was a world like a pirate's chest opened and shaken out.

"Don your shades!" Maypop McCray Fish suggested.

"Yea, hey!" the others agreed. They donned their shades and squinted with greed and glee. Milho Crayons slipped on a loose bijou but caught himself and stepped aright, ever-cocky.

That night they drank a magnum firkin dry in the twilight glow of a lapis lazuli sunset and spoke of how their fortunes would be spent.

Alfred Carnitas said he would buy some acres on a limestone isle and build a lemonade stand upon them. How much lemonade he sold was not an important thing.

Milho Crayons declared that he would take a Berlitz course, learn pig Greek.

Maypop McCray Fish knew what he pined for: red-light women, ruby-gauded and garbed in hot red satin, the color of their trade.

Conk Johnson figured that he would henceforth buy matches only from Little Match Girls, and tip like a drunken duke, thereby heartening every waif who made a living selling sulphur.

Gnosis Rumen, dozing, fell into the fire; but all present knew that he would buy himself a pair of better pants. (His current pair needed laundering, and fit him like a catcher's mitt engarbs a monkey's paw.)

Ruhmkorff Coyle had in mind a new wallet, one with several unfolding windows in tiers and secret compartments where lumps of gold might be concealed.

Gilbert Halfmuch thought he would have his sex changed, for the amusement of the thing and its experimentation, but not until he'd parted company with these six sots.

If only they had known: an alien world cared not a jot for interlopers. The next morning, while all took their picks to the ground, gravity warped, as it did there often, so that every step and gesture was a taffy pull, a tug of war. Then a keening wind brought with it a peppering cannonade of icy trinkets. The seven fled over a landscape of tarnished silver toward their ship; but one, and only one, reached the portal. We will not speak his name, not now. That is for later, when the jury has been chosen, if not bribed. Yet we will say that he was a monkey-jogging greedy man, so greedy that the night before he had gathered quartz rosettes, clinquants, chrysolite shards in the dreamlight while the others slept, and now had a bagful. He was the meanest man; he left the others on Last

Name and watched through the viewscoop as they slipped and grubbled in the wabe.

But this was not the end of it. A greedy man needs friends—or sooner than you can say Raphael Aloysius he is undone by his greed. So when this fellow found himself alone with the ship's computer (which Gnosis Rumen had programmed to speak only Tagalog for his own amusement) he knew he was in for it.

This is an old story, of greed and doom, but old stories are often the best ones when read with a bit of relish and a bowl of salty popcorn.

Larry Tritten

Actually, there were two stories in Larry's belated submission. Jack Vance is one of science fiction's master stylists, and no one else had thought to write a Vance parody, so I told the publisher I needed more money and I bought this one too.

THE STAR SNEAK

CHAPTER ONE

LEARNING OF RUMORS TO the effect that Vulgare Hokum had undertaken certain mercantile enterprises among the highland folk to the east of the city of Astropolis, on Tristan, Garth Curson chartered a star vessel and hurried to the planet. His errand: observance of his vow to enact vengeance upon each of the five Demon Pranksters who had ventured the temerity to address him in colloquial terms—one of whom was Vulgare Hokum.

Curson landed at the Astropolis Spaceport, from which he immediately repaired to seek lodging in a nearby hostel, a melancholic five-story structure of uremic yellow planking and gravy-colored stone. Along the walls of the great lobby, displayed in glass cases, were the bones and preserved pelts and derma of guests who had failed to recompense their accounts. Curson observed these for some time and then, making a meticulous count of his funds, withdrew to the dining hall. The menu offered a single fude Tristanese meal—an acrid salad of native herbage, a steamed and sugared musk frog, and a pannikin of spice broth—yet Curson's appetite was large and he ate with relish, doing his best to ignore the itinerant evangelist who practiced devotional tumbling under his table. At length, he summoned a barrow and was jounced through the sinister black alleys of Astropolis to the native bazaar, where he intended to procure banes and balms to protect him on his trek to the highland.

CHAPTER TWO

CURSON FOUND THE REPERTORIUM he sought, a sturdy shed of russet thatch and umber lumber, and entered. Within, in the tremulous light of a single candle flickering in a carved stone flambeau, a man whose cheeks were tattooed with talismanic graffiti stood behind a counter.

Curson made a debonair gesture. "I wish to examine effectuants to insure me against brigandage on a journey into perilous regions."

"Excellent!" exclaimed the keeper, and began to bring forth articles. "What do you seek? This splendid poison, perhaps!" He exhibited a coarse-textured purple powder. "When introduced into the food or drink of an enemy, it causes instant death by implosion of the vital organs. Or—here: this useful toxin compels its victim to walk askew, as though he were the wearer of uncomfortably tight underlinen. The result is obloquy! A related substance induces constant vulgar eructation, a certain woe to all who enjoy convivial discourse. What else can I recommend? Ah, this! An amulet which reverses natural dispositions. Observe!" And the keeper displayed a cage containing a brooding hyena, a sloth with a nervous condition, and a ground-rodent which was said to be claustrophobic.

Curson shrugged. "None of these items seem to be exactly what I seek."

"And yet," replied the keeper, frowning gravely, "I must caution you to purchase all. I am prepared to waft tox mephis, a potion which will distort the lucidity of your speech, causing you to express yourself in slang and monosyllables!" Curson made his purchases and departed hastily.

CHAPTER THREE

AT DAWN CURSON JOINED a company of pilgrims who were bound east toward the highlands. All day the pilgrims marched along the river Zag, singing raffish songs, engaging in affable chatter and badinage, and playfully thrusting one another into bogs. In the dying afternoon an armada of thunderclouds edged with wan light sailed across the darkening sky, threatening deluge.

One called Fragon, an extreme cynic, professed a unique cosmology: he maintained that the celestial bodies were ordure produced by a great deity, offering in conclusion: "…and, as it is well known that a variety of vermin spawns in such matter, thus were the races of the universe born."

"This is impiety!" retorted Hakule, a tall muscular man with flashing eyes like black gems. "Such a creed makes jest of the Divine Artificer. In accordance with the teaching of the holy sage Whilhom, I attest the doctrine which fully acknowledges the essential nature of our Creator—sweetness: the heavenly spheres are various sorts of comfits, bonbons, and the like, the work of a Cosmic Confectioner. The races of the universe are analogous to animalculae partaking substance."

"Bah!" cried another cynic. "If anything, the cosmos is the effect of a deity who specializes in the art of caricature. How else explain the sorry state of things in relation to what they might ideally be?"

At length, Curson was called upon to expound his own creed. He chose to do so by object lesson, producing a small knife and easing the pilgrims of their valuables, then slipping quickly from the cave to continue his journey alone.

CHAPTER FOUR

THE FOLLOWING DAY CURSON toiled to the crest of a high barren hill where he crouched behind the jutting bulk of a large crag, gazing down at the terrain below: the entire valley was filled with orchards of gray-brown pod-bearing stalks, thousands upon thousands of them, stretching far away over a series of rolling hillocks into the blue-hazed regions of the north. Even as Curson watched, a large aggregation of harvesters appeared and began picking the pods; these harvesters were a motley throng—outworlders all: there were obese, omnivorous anthropoids from Viand, clad in edible tunics and pantaloons…Capellan bird-fellows, now fluttering, now stepping…complaisant automatons from Mao's Planet, Earthmen, Alderbaranese like orange stucco gorillas, others of all shapes and origins.

Interplanetary *braceros*, thought Curson. So these were Vulgare Hokum's employees! But what was the nature of the enterprise? And where might Vulgare Hokum himself be found? The sun was a wound, the horizon to the west a blood-drenched swath by the time Curson had descended from the heights. Disguised in a monk's hooded cloak, he approached a harvester, a solemn industrious Earthman working alone at the edge of the orchards. When near enough for contact, he flourished his knife and pressed it to the man's collarbone.

"Satisfy my queries, or I carve expletives on your visage!" snapped Curson. "First, state where Vulgare Hokum may be found—then explain the import of these pods!"

The man blanched with fear, evinced a gasp of supplication. "Forbear! Candor is my ethic! Vulgare Hokum may be sought yonder—" he pointed a trembling finger vigorously "—in his office-shed. As for the pods, these are to be gathered, dried, cured and shipped to a cereal manufactory in Battle Creek, Michigan, at which point they will be processed and converted into flakes to be packaged with charms and sold as a breakfast treat known as *Polycrisps*. The aim of the undertaking is thus: the plant has a narcotic effect, and Vulgare Hokum intends to distribute samples, addict the galaxy, and administer a reign of ribaldry."

Curson pondered the explanation for a moment, then nodded slowly. "I give you your life," he murmured, and struck the man unconscious with the haft of his blade.

CHAPTER FIVE

Now THE MOMENT OF denouement was at hand. Curson strode to the door of Vulgare Hokum's office-shed, turned the knob, pushed, and sprang inside with a loud cry. Vulgare Hokum, aghast, lurched to his feet behind a metal desk, dropping a small bouquet of stimulative blooms he had been sniffing; he stood transfixed, a lank, full-bearded rogue attired all in black—a tailored suit and a stylish cape emblazoned with the emblem of an ancient epicurean cult; profiled head of white hare with bow tie.

Curson raised an admonitory finger. "Now you must answer for your peccancies, villain!"

"What th' hell's peccancy?" came the surly retort; then, "You ain't gettin' me! I'm gettin' out—!" In midsentence, Vulgare Hokum primed himself, made a dramatic leap for a nearby window; but Curson was upon him at once, knife flashing. There was a brisk scuffle, a violent embrace and falling away.

Before he drew his last breath, Vulgare Hokum, prostrate on the floor, grimacing sourly, addressed a fusillade of Pig Latin at Curson.

Then Curson left to assume his new role as entrepreneur and supervise the harvesting of his pods.

Cathy Ball

So what's a parody of romance novels doing in a science fiction anthology? Simple: its setting is a science fiction convention. I picked up this little amateur booklet at the 1984 Worldcon, never forgot it, and got a hell of a kick when I called Cathy Ball out of the blue four years later to tell her I wanted to buy her story to run side-by-side with pieces by Asimov, Clarke, and Anderson.

LOVE'S PRURIENT INTEREST

Chapter One

FERVENT HOPE WIGGLED INTO her T-shirt and examined her image thoughtfully. It was a measure of her concentration that she actually did this in a mirror. Her lithe and slender (yet well-endowed) body trembled on the brink of womanhood. Reluctantly, she removed her fingers from the inside of her jeans. In her usual absent-minded manner, she tossed her unruly locks over her shapely yet voluptuous shoulders. The wigs landed on the bed and she brushed her own blond curls into their usual pixyish positions. She then straightened her OKON T-shirt so the emblem was balanced (two letters per breast) and made an adorable kissy face at her reflection. She was very excited at the thought of attending her first convention. It was a measure of her almost womanhood that her father was finally allowing her to attend one.

"After all," he had said sagely, "I've raised you like a trufan." It was considered scandalous by some of the neighbors that a child should learn the uses of mimeo, drink for hours on end, and spit into the corners at the mention of Roger Elwood. She was a worthy heir to First Fandom although isolated from fandom itself. They lived in the Far Country and fanac was carried on by mail. Fans rarely visited them. She suspected it had something to do with her father's personal habits as well. He was given to the harmless and rather humorous pastimes of farting sprightly tunes and flashing. At least he doesn't do them simultaneously, she thought defensively, and he usually is on key.

She carried her suitcases down to the car and said her farewells to her father. He stood in the doorway, his thin form sagging against the frame and one foot firmly braced against their collie, Collate. His wrinkled hands cradled a bottle of Tully. The dingy shadows lent a sort of dignity to her favorite raincoat. He gave her the bottle.

"Have a good time," he said. "But beware! For fans are a horny lot." He flashed at that moment for a bit of emphasis.

She giggled, but was saddened when he went on to promise a dead dog party on her return home. She was fond of Collate—but tradition was tradition.

The trip to the convention city took but an hour. It took two hours to find the convention hotel. She finally located it in the sleaziest part of the city, tastefully surrounded by fallen winos and glittering arrangements of broken glass. The hotel parking was under the building and she felt uneasy as she drove into the depths. Still, she reasoned, people have to leave their vehicles somewhere. She parked between a sarcophagus and an expired Clydesdale. Keeping a wary eye out for bats, she brought her suitcase out and began her search for the elevators. The first confirmation that this was indeed the convention hotel came when she reached them. It took a half-hour wait for one to appear.

Flushed with excitement, and the healthy swigs of Tully she had taken to shorten the wait, she boarded the elevator. The floor was reassuringly covered with empty beer cans, used rubbers, and assorted flyers from other conventions. She felt her excitement increase as the elevator lurched its way up to the lobby: her pulses pounded with primal urges, her nostrils flared with passion, her breathing grew shallow and rapid. Her general appearance had strong overtones of religious ecstasy. When the elevator doors finally slid open and she glided toward the registration table, a B.N.F. jerked his thumb in her direction and muttered, "Christ...another neo."

She felt his glance and faltered in her approach to the registration table. She recognized the tented figure instantly, and felt a surge of attraction for such an obviously powerful figure. His Old Testament features were wreathed with a mushroom-shaped explosion of black hair and poker chips were tidily lodged in his beard. From the huge lump under the tent, Fervent reasoned that he always carried his bottle with him. She fluttered her eyelashes in his direction. He ignored her glance and laid friendly hands upon the two belly dancers reclining at his feet. Fervent knew when she was outclassed and went cheerfully on to register.

Her father's warning that fans were a horny lot rang in her ears. She knew that already...after all, she was a fan. And she planned on finding her true love at the convention...the mate of her soul, the sharer of her muse, the sensitive and intelligent counter-point to her more practical nature. As she filled out the registration form, she wondered when fate would take a hand.

She was goosed.

Whirling about, she encountered the myopic stare of the Trufan. He stood out from the Trekkies surrounding him. His willowy and slightly stooped-shouldered form was draped in an ink-stained Cheech Wizard shirt and blue jeans. Blond hair curled about the frames of his wire-rim glasses. The pockmarks on his face seemed to indicate character rather than basely show his youth, and the sturdy beginnings of a moustache flourished over a finely-defined mouth. Her gaze lowered and settled against her will on the bulging pouch tightly zipped over, the hint of hidden wonders and delights. He followed her gaze and unzipped his briefcase to offer her a fanzine.

"Just something I pulled together," he said throatily. As she reached for the thick, salmon-colored roll of paper, she felt a tremor shake her frame and all attendant attributes. He watched the shimmy with interest and was about to speak again when a gopher grabbed his elbow.

"You've got a fan panel in two minutes," said the gopher and dragged the Trufan away. Before he disappeared, the Trufan managed a cheerfully obscene gesture in Fervent's direction. She waved back, which somehow seemed a weak response, and finished filling out her registration form. Hotel registration was unusually quick and she set out for the elevators to find her room.

As the elevator doors slid shut, she was alone with her thoughts. At the second floor, the doors slid open to admit a tall and very silver-haired man that she instantly recognized as the editor for *Issac Asapruples's Spacey Stuff Magazine*. She felt shy...even with his friendly greeting of "Hello, Baby," and his friendly hug and his friendly kiss and his friendly attempts to re-straighten her T-shirt for her. What with all his friendliness, he was breathing very hard when the elevator stopped at her floor. She only half-noticed the pimply-faced male fan boarding the elevator as she departed, but noticed the warm greeting the editor gave him. They were right about the inter-mixing of pro and fan, she thought proudly. There was nothing stand-offish about that pro.

Once in her room, she unpacked a few things and began to read the fanzine. The more she read, the surer she became that this was the Fan for her. The fanzine reeked of sensitivity and intellect. There were some references to things she didn't quite understand, like bondage. Must be a big 007 fan, she reasoned. She marveled that finding her true love could be so easy and clutched the fanzine to her breasts, severely wrinkling it in the process...and the cleavage.

Chapter Two

FERVENT FRESHENED HER MAKE-UP and carefully dabbed corflu behind each ear. She sped to the elevator to wait impatiently for several minutes before deciding to take the stairs. Once down on the convention floor, she paused in confusion. Everything looked so fascinating. She could see the open doors to the main programming and glanced in. The panel was being dominated by a little-published and little-read author who seemed to know everything about writing. As he enlightened the audience about the methods of a true craftsman, Fervent noticed the other panel members. One had won several Hugos and apparently was not very interested in the speaker. He was building a spaceship in a very large bottle. The other panel member was a notable Nebula winner and well known for her sensitivity: she was making hand shadows with the use of the small table lamps on the panel's table. A roar of applause went up when she shaped a donkey's head behind the speaker.

Fervent would have entered the main programming room, but she found herself detained by a raincoated figure that reminded her of her dear father.

"You don't want to go in there, girlie," he leered. "There's terrific stuff in the next room down. Just the sort of things you'd really like." He took her elbow and urged her into the Hucksters' Room. The door shut heavily behind her.

"I've got another one," the man pointed out to the dealer guarding the door. The dealer nodded and marked a figure on a clipboard. The raincoated figure released her and disappeared back into the hall in search of more marks.

Noticing the shoulder holster and efficient-looking pistol the dealer wore, Fervent decided to look around the Hucksters' Room. The table selling hacked-off plastic barbarians' heads seemed to be doing a brisk business. She paused in front of a tent-like structure that appeared to be doing very well indeed. In fact, there was a long line of male fans waiting their turn.

"It's one of the main reasons I come to a convention in the first place," she overheard one of the men say. She supposed that it had something to do with manicures since the price list indicated hand jobs for a reasonable rate. A few tables farther down, they were selling pro relics. She deliberated over a seldom-used editing pencil of Lin Carter's and a key from Michael Moorcock's thousandth typewriter. Finally, she bought a scrap of blank paper that Isaac Asimov was said to have thought of writing on but decided not to. "Anything that rare would have to increase in value," she muttered to herself.

She escaped the Hucksters' Room during the confusion of two SCA members dueling. Two dealers were stabbed and a security guard lost an ear before order was restored.

Fervent went in search of her beloved. The panel in main programming was over and the hallways were curiously empty. A hotel employee told her that everyone was at a room party.

"Everyone?" she said dubiously. The idea of several hundred con attendees in one room seemed far-fetched. Following the employee's directions, she found a very long line of people outside the room patiently awaiting entry. She lined up as well and, after about an hour's wait, found herself at the door of a crowded hotel suite.

"Here's a drink," said the sweating host, thrusting a greasy glass of Old Weary into her hand. He gave her a friendly shove into the crowd. Fighting her way to a desk, she climbed on top with several others. As she struggled upright, one of her feet suddenly went numb. She cried out in alarm.

"Don't worry," said the young man to the right of her. He helped her leg out of the bubbling bucket and to the side. "The feeling should return in a few minutes. You just stepped into the Blog." He helpfully rubbed her leg to restore the circulation. She stopped him when the ministrations went well above the knee.

From the desk-top, she could see in one corner of the room a grey-haired man standing over what appeared to be a stack of corpses. He swigged from a bottle and handed it to the person standing by the edge of the stack. The person reached out to accept the bottle but collapsed before drinking. Fervent recognized the ritual as the Tuckering out and looked at the other corner. Several pros and editors were huddled there but the fans kept a certain distance from them in spite of the crowded facilities. Fervent saw why when an unlucky fan stepped too near. A huge mastiff lunged for him and took a sizable chunk from his arm. One editor patted the mastiff on the head, said "Good boy," and slipped the dog a gin and tonic.

She failed to see her love anywhere and decided to search on. Giving her helpful neighbor the secret handgrip of fandom, she climbed from the desk and tried to fight her way out of the room. The crush around the door was so great that she was swept back toward the window. Thankfully inhaling the fresh air, she finally noticed that all guests had been departing the room via the fire escape. She climbed over the sill and worked her way back down to the convention floor.

Thoughtfully, she tried to figure out where her love could be. With dawning horror, she knew of one place that would still be active at the late hour. But surely her soulmate wouldn't be…No! Anything but That! Shocked by her own evil thought, she staggered and leaned against the wall. Panic surged through her veins. Hideous images flashed before her eyes. She struggled against the revulsion that took over the very fingernails of her being. Slowly, she regained some control. She forced herself to straighten, to arrange her features in calm acceptance of her fate. She had to find him…no matter what depths of depravity and bad taste he had slunk to.

She turned and, for the sake of love, forced her cringing body across the lobby and into the filk-singing room. She had to pause at the door when a strain of broken—shattered—harmony came to her delicate ears, but she pressed on. In her dazed condition, she had to stand at the back of the room for several minutes, searching the crowd for a glimpse of her man. The filkers sat staring at their demi-gawds, the incense fumes mingling heavily with the Tully fumes, and a rapt silence awaited the principal gawd's actions.

The demon-like gawd belched. The audience applauded loudly. He picked his nose. The filkers cheered. When he farted, there wasn't a dry eye in the house. An acolyte rolled at his feet and fetched a new guitar string between her teeth for him. While he was replacing the string, he signalled for another demi-gawd to sing. When she started a song about an adorable, snaggle-toothed dragon, Fervent retched and fled. She missed the passing of the collection plate entirely.

Discouraged, she decided to make a suicidal gesture and rang for the elevator. It arrived almost instantly, to her astonishment, and she was further shocked to discover her trufan locked in a passionate embrace with a chiffon-clad creature. The nature of the lock appeared to be Yale, accompanied by several chains and assorted irons. The Trufan's face was so flushed that she scarcely recognized him. He was showering the chiffon-clad form with kisses and thanking the person over and over in a broken voice for what sounded like a favorable fanzine review.

Shaking her head, Fervent let the elevator pass on and got her Scotch out of her shoulder-bag. Taking a satisfying swig, she rang for another elevator and brooded about her broken heart.

Chapter Three

FERVENT AWOKE SUDDENLY WITH the feeling of being in the wrong place. The darkened room gave no clue to her location but she could feel the warm bodies of countless people dozing around her; one aromatic foot nestled gently against her left ear, a strange arm was flung across her thighs, and what felt like someone's head rested on her left ankle. As her eyes adjusted slowly to the darkness, she discovered that she was in a hotel room filled with slumbering Trekkies! She dimly remembered the evening before. Her first love cruelly destroyed, she had staggered in the direction of her own room, drinking Scotch and cursing the unkind DiFate in a fannish manner. Brooding, swearing, stamping both of her feet in a petulant fashion, she neglected to realize that she had gotten off at the wrong floor until accosted by a leering teenager. He was clad in a skirt and a Dr. Who scarf, his convention badge handily used to pin up a sagging hem.

"You look like my kind of woman," he breathed heavily and almost asthmatically into her ear. He reached out with shaking and avaricious hands. She was about to tell him politely that she wasn't interested when he reached the object of his lust, stroking, caressing, fondling in a passionate and not-to-be-denied manner. Shrieking, she tore the Scotch bottle from his embrace.

"I'm not that kind of fan!" she snarled and snap-kicked the lad well above his hem. She left him whimpering like a whipped dog and stalked back toward the stairwell. Exhilarated by the encounter, she felt reckless and alive, ready for anything to happen.

She met the Trekkies in the stairwell.

There were two of them fetching ice for their room party. They both wore Federation t-shirts and high-top sneakers with faded jeans. One had a fluorescent button that read "Spock has the Seven Year Itch." The other wore a badge identifying him as an official Federation cost accountant. They couldn't have been over fifteen years old.

"Hi!" said the one with the Spock button shyly. "You want to come to our room party?"

"It's more like an orgy," interrupted the other. His grin revealed braces. Fervent shrugged.

"What the hell," she said. "I've never been to a Trekkie orgy. Can I help you carry the ice?" The first Trekkie carefully handed the ice cube he was carrying to her, and they continued on to the room. It was packed with people arguing over the name of Kirk's goldfish and how many Tribbles could dance on the head of a pin. A fist fight broke out over the name of some extra in a crowd scene but was quickly stopped by someone wearing a badge and stating he was an official Federation Shit Kicker and Name Taker.

She had fallen asleep during one expert's description of the exact number of orgasms that Kirk had induced during the second season. Sodden with Scotch and Trek trivia, she had been unable to move. Now she began to gently extricate herself from the mass of bodies, fearful of waking anyone. As she tiptoed to the door, one Trekkie muttered fitfully in her sleep, "Didn't realize...all appendages POINTED!" Fervent wondered briefly about the meaning of that remark and dismissed it as another useful bit of trivia.

She returned to her room, showered, and changed into a fresh pair of jeans and a T-shirt reading "Dick hits all the right places." She had been a huge fan of Philip K. Dick's writing for years and was proud to show her admiration. He was so accurate about things, she would coo to her father, and he emphasized just the right bits. Her T-shirt did the same.

As she strolled downstairs, she wondered what the day had in store. Glancing at her program book, she found there was not much scheduled for the early afternoon: Main Programming had a comics expert speaking on famous menopauses in the comics, with special attention to Mary Worth, the film room was currently showing reruns of *My Mother, the Car*, and the Fan Room was having a stapling workshop. None of these attracted her.

As she entered the restaurant, she noticed a large crowd at one table listening quietly to two fans. They were taking turns speaking, each statement invoking an emphatic audience reaction. She took a table within earshot and quickly realized that it was a serious matter: Name-dropping.

"I always liked the way that Ted prefers to keep our friendship relaxed," said the male fan, studying his fingernails. "At cons, we virtually ignore each other...I suppose that's because we're so close the rest of the time. Phone calls, letters, visits..." He trailed off and sipped his iced tea. The crowd buzzed briefly and the words "Sturgeon" and "Wow!" were heard. From the gleam in the femmefan's eye, it was obvious that her competitiveness was aroused.

"I've always liked him myself," she retorted, "but for sheer fun at a convention, I've always preferred my old buddy, Bob...The hours we've spent partying! I can't begin to tell you about what a great relationship we have." Seeing that this didn't score quite as well as his remark had, she went on. "Did I ever tell you about the time I was trapped in an elevator with Ellison and Elwood?"

"Only about a million times," muttered a spectator.

"Poor Roger hasn't been the same since Laser books," said the male fan sadly. "I suppose that Harlie has told you about his new movie script. He mentioned it when we were chatting about poor Isaac's health." He lowered his voice and said in an aside "Hemorrhoids, you know." There was an awed silence at this inside information. He moved in for the kill. "I suppose all great writers risk destroying their health that way. I understand that the move to that island was supposed to have helped Arthur's health. Of course, I don't know him personally," he paused dramatically, "but I was told that by someone you could consider a reliable source." Very softly, he continued, "Though how Ursula knew that, I really don't know..."

The audience broke into applause and he was the acknowledged victor. A wreath of carefully twisted lines was placed on his brow, and the femmefan left, dragging an attractive young neo behind her.

"Tell me how close you are to the pros," the neo was heard to beg as they left.

Fervent ate her lunch quickly and mused over the ways of fandom. The more back-handed the name-dropping was, the more it seemed to impress people. She had heard of a fan who named his pets after famous writers and talked about them without revealing that he meant a pet rather than the writer. This impressed the hell out of several fans as he spoke of his day-to-day relationships with just the right touch of carelessness, until one unfortunate day when he mentioned that Gordie died because he forgot to change the water.

Wandering back into the convention area, Fervent accepted a religious tract from Frisbeeites and another tract from a Herbangilist. She peeked into the Fan Room to see if the stapling workshop was over. Apparently they had just broken up and she wandered in to examine the examples of fan art littering the walls. Unclad or half-clad maidens seemed to prevail, followed by an enormous number of simpering dragons. She admired a series of beanie drawings and decided to check out the Art Show. Several well-known artists had brought work.

Going down the hall to the Art Show room, she found several paintings of unclad maidens and simpering dragons. There were acrylic works of spaceships and cheesy-looking moons. One of the spaceships not only had innumerable windows but sliding glass patio doors as well. There were several Trek drawings and scattered lumps of art dealing with other TV shows. One sculptor had done a tribute to Buck Rogers consisting of a well-endowed male's hips and thighs, shaded with tiny black dollar signs to emphasize the critical portions. There were some male nudes by a woman artist with rockets in all the most likely places. The only work that Fervent found really impressive was a painting of a single figure in a brilliant golden landscape, clutching a mimeo to its bosom and radiating ecstasy. It was titled "Fanzine." She felt as though she could really relate to the feeling.

She made a note of the artist's name and decided to watch for more of his work. As she was scribbling the name down, a voice from behind her said, "What? No bid?" She turned to examine the speaker and for the second time at the convention was plunged into the turmoil of emotions that signify the beginnings of true and impassioned love. She reeled, aflush with the instant knowledge that here was a man that she could worship, a being she could grovel for...then again, it could just be her reaction to those incredibly tight leather pants and the chains.

Chapter Four

FERVENT MANAGED TO STOP her reeling and, after hastily taking a motion sickness pill, stood drinking in the sight of the man. His lithe, leather-clad form oozed with masculine charm, bubbled with explosive sensuousness, and radiated the sort of glow that can only come from an extremely fulfilled sex life or eating Uranium-235. He stood towering above her, chains draped across the gaps in his artistically torn shirt.

Black curls rioted in tangled confusion above his noble profile and one ear bore a tiny chicken bone lashed to its lobe.

"Are you..." she hesitated, staring up into his deeply shadowed eyes, "Tiger Tage?" He swept a gaze over her with the thick brooms of his lashes and grunted in brief appreciation. Waving at another artist, he tapped her on the arm and beckoned her out of the Art Room, down the long corridor to the elevators and to the inevitable elevator wait. For once Fervent didn't mind. She gazed worshipfully at his face and conjured up images of editing a strictly art-oriented fanzine, designed to display the charms of her beloved. Here her gaze dropped to the tight leather pants and she blushed slightly.

Tearing her glance away, she noticed two very large gophers waiting for the elevators as well. One was huge and lumbering, occasionally taking a dead mouse form his pocket to stroke and mutter sweet nothings to. The other was watching her furtively. When he caught her gaze, he stuck two massive hands deep into his pockets and started to whistle "Ole Man River." She thought the gophers were a little strange, but then, gophers usually were. She returned her attention to Tiger, who was staring at the elevator doors and obviously planning some great and sensitive tribute to the human spirit. He belched and began idly picking his teeth with his registration badge.

The elevator doors slid open and they entered. Fervent felt a shock run through her voluptuous frame as the artist pushed the button for his floor and, with his free hand, patted her ass in a tender and understanding manner. She felt that this must seal the secret pact she had seen in his eyes and stood a little taller...proud to be with her man. Tiger glanced down at her, his eyes roaming over the T-shirt, and finally spoke.

"Hubba, hubba," he said in deep and resonant tones.

She was wondering if this was some sort of artists' jargon when the elevator doors slid open and she was shoved into the hall by two large gophers.

"Hey!" she protested and tried to reenter the elevator. The gophers blocked her way. Beyond them, she could see Tiger Tage, nonchalantly leaning against the back of the elevator and picking his teeth with the chicken bone from his ear.

"Help!" she screamed. He waved the bone in farewell as the elevator doors slid shut. She froze in shock, abandoned...but not quite in the fashion she had planned on.

One of the gophers patted her on the arm consolingly. Slowly, she realized that she was on the ConCommittee's floor. She was surrounded by gophers of all shapes and sizes. They crowded around her, speaking in low, even tones.

"There, there..." they murmured. Hands gently stroked her hair and shoulders. "We're all your friends. You're one of us now. That's nice." They plied her with Kool-aid and Oreos, glazing over her shock with gentle words and kind voices. She glimpsed the same blank expression on all their faces and began to struggle against the loving undertow. The shock of the (again) lost love, the lack of sleep during the con, the taste of grape Kool-aid after Scotch...all started to have terrible effect on her and she began to succumb to the peer pressure about her.

"It's good to gopher...It's good to serve your fellow fan...Gophers only have to do what they're told...no more decisions...no more worries..." The voices drifted about her and she began to sink into the world of perpetual, pointless errands. Down...down...

down...

down...

down...

"SMOFs!" came a blood-curdling shriek from the end of the hallway and, with unbelievable energy, the gophers fled, scrambling over one another in their haste to escape. Fervent sagged to the floor, empty Oreo packages crackling beneath her exhausted form. She forced her gaze to the end of the corridor. She wondered what could make so many flee in terror and fear. And then she saw THEM.

She fainted and knew nothing more until the slightly burning taste of liquid brought her to her senses. She drank, and in drinking, found herself back to the land of Scotch drinker and a reasonable facsimile of sanity.

"I am not a gopher. I am a Fan," she whispered, and opened her eyes to view her saviors without fear.

Chapter Five

A STRONG, MASCULINE ARM grasped her shoulders as the reviving drops of harsh but blessed Scotch trickled their way down her slim yet voluptuous throat. She could smell a faint aroma of machine oil and corflu emanating from the man cradling her worn (but not worn enough) form. She felt a momentary wave of fear as she realized that the dark forms surrounding her were the dreaded SMOFs! Gazing bravely about her, she saw that they looked a great deal like normal fans. Many were overweight and, judging from the thickness of glasses, nearsighted. They wore dignified robes of carbon paper over their blue jeans and T-shirts of various faiths: the shirts were inscribed as the wearers saw fit to display their public attitudes. The young man holding her gently wore a fragrant shirt stating that Sturgeon Was An Optimist. A few grasped broomsticks in their hands, and she shrank from the penetrating gaze of a very tall man with a gleaming eye and uncertain balance. Even as she watched, he swayed mightily into another impossible stance and dangled an albatross carelessly from an unsteady finger. They all bore the ritual markings of mimeo ink; one small smudge on the tip of the nose, the long dash over the right eye, and the careful coverings of the eartips.

She could hear a few muttering under their breath. Words such as "FIAWOL," "Flushing," "Friggin' SF Review," and "Bheer" drifted into her hearing. She turned her eyes from the procession to study the SMOF still cradling her warm and nubile shape. He seemed young to be one of such a sacred throng but on closer examination, she could see the signs of one whose faith has been tested. Innumerable scars from paper cuts gleamed on ink-stained fingers, lines of worry from fan feuds were etched about his watery but firm gaze, and he had the look of one who had suffered in the name of the cause.

"Yes," he said mildly, in reply to her unspoken but questioning appeal. He raised his gaze to the far wall, revealing a profile of courage. His voice dropped slightly as he said modestly, "Yes. I have been reviewed by Joseph Nicholas." He pulled his robe to one side and showed her his fearsome scars. She marveled that he lived to tell the tale.

"One must go on," he said sagely. "It's a loud and pronely thing to be a fan." He patted her reassuringly. She noticed that his pats had a tendency to linger about her breasts but assumed that the tears in his eyes made it difficult to see. "I've recovered enough to work on my book of Fan History since the Second World War..." he continued. "It should be a major contribution to the field. With all the Fan Feuds and petulant writers, it should make the Vietnam War look like an anti-climax."

This statement made a few of the nearer SMOFs stop and stare at him. They raised their voices in a crackle that sent goosebumps skittering down Fervent's back. It was the first time she had heard the dreaded SMOF scoff and years later the eerie sound would echo through her worst nightmares.

The effect on the SMOF holding her was strange. Instead of shrinking back in embarrassment, he seemed to expand in girth, giving his detractors a look of haughty disdain.

"Gee…" said a female SMOF. "Do you think we oughta Warner?"

"Just wait…" muttered Fervent's SMOF. "They laughed at Hugo Gernsback, they laughed at Claude Degler, they laughed at Richard Geis…"

"Only when he talked politics," muttered another SMOF. "I rather enjoyed hearing about his sex life."

Fervent's SMOF turned an angry gaze at him. "They laughed at Harlan," he said shrilly. The invocation of the sacred name froze the SMOFs briefly and then they made the ritual gesture for the use of the ELLISON, a clenched fist shoved upward and restrained on the upper arm by the opposing hand.

"Jesus…What a load of crap!"

The drawling tones echoed in the silence following the ritual gesture and a shambling, staggering form slid into the hallway. Through bloodshot eyes, the Editor stared at the SMOFs. Dropping their gaze, the SMOFs wandered back toward their own corridors of power, leaving the prone Fervent staring up at the degenerate and powerful Big Name Editor. He glanced at the chaos left by the SMOFs and the earlier gophers, and kicked a Kool-aid container out of the way. He seemed to notice Fervent for the first time. A gleam appeared in one eye and a small trickle of drool started at one corner of his mouth. He hastily wiped it away and winked at her.

"Hey, hey. Want to go to the Pro Party, sweet thing?" He helped Fervent up and attempted to dust off the seat of her jeans for her. Numbed by the quick events, she nodded. And in the overly warm arc of one of the Editor's arms, she was propelled down the hallway.

Chapter Six

FERVENT FELT SLIGHTLY CONFUSED as the Big Name Editor cuddled her down the hallway. Just moments before, she had glimpsed the horrors of gopherdom and the delights of SMOFship. Strange as the convention had been, she still felt a kinship with the fans…even the Trekkies had seemed to share that element of friendship. Now she was being whisked into an environment that she had only read about in Asimov's thirty-eight (and counting) autobiographies…the World of the Pro. She clutched feebly at the thought that many fans were eventually writers… perhaps the Pros were merely an evolved sort of Fan. She imagined Silverberg with six fingers and shuddered slightly. Of course, that would explain the fast typing…

The Editor turned down a strange hallway and, looking furtively back over his shoulder, fished into his shirt pocket. He produced a key and opened a door marked "Only Cleaning Supplies" in large letters. Instead of containing cleaning supplies, however, there was a small room containing a metal detector such as Fervent had seen at airports and several armed guards. They all scowled at the sight of Fervent.

"She's one of *them*," the largest guard said accusingly to the Editor. "How you people expect us to keep you safe when you wallow around with those Grubby Little Fans is beyond me." The guard gestured her through the metal detector and relieved her of all badges and buttons. He handed her a blue pencil.

"Okay, sweetie. If you value your life, you better pretend to be an editorial assistant to Hotshot here. Those pros get pretty nasty on their own turf and they won't hesitate to throw you to the Pournelle if you slip up… or worse…they'll turn you over to John Norman. That guy's SICKO." The large guard shook his head slowly. Another guard opened the door at the far end of the room and the Editor led Fervent into the Pro Party.

The Big Name Editor paused to snort a strange white substance and then drew Fervent into a close embrace. He whispered in her ear, "If you ask anyone for their autographs, they'll break all your fingers." He kissed her on the neck and grinned. "Other than that, baby, have a good time." He wandered off in the direction of the bathroom and abandoned her. She stood, staring around her and shaking slightly.

The Pro Party was in an enormous suite and packed with people and purple smoke. She recognized several faces from Locus and dust covers. Charles E. Brown stood by the bar chatting with a beagle in a world War One flying helmet and silk scarf. Eavesdropping on this conversation and making snide comments about the significance of Christ figures in Saturday morning cartoons was one of Fervent's favorite writers, Smart Alec Assinger. She particularly liked his preppie parody of Zelazny…*Nine Princes in Alligator.*

Crowded together on the couch were writers that she immediately recognized as the young intellectuals of the genre. They wore dinner-plate-size, tasteful orange buttons saying "Thinker," leather-patched tweed jackets, and wreaths of purple smoke about their heads. Copies of Marquez's and Singer's writings peeked from pockets, and the only drinks in hand were either Perrier water or straight vodka. Occasionally one of them would speak and the others would nod knowingly. She managed to get within earshot and found that each in turn was carefully explaining why they didn't deserve the many honors given to them.

In the warmth of the room, the drones of modesty began to make Fervent doze off. Finally she shook herself awake and muttered, "It's not the heat, it's the humidity." She staggered toward the bar and waved the blue pencil for a Coke. She thought she should keep her wits about her.

Trying to act as though she wasn't listening, she wandered around the room tuning in to the different conversations. One writer was explaining the deep meaning in a script he had written for "Charlie's Angels."

"What those suckers don't realize," he said, repeatedly stabbing a finger in the air, "is that my symbolism in that script will get all the concerned people where they live. I mean, that's why I stood so firm about the bikinis in the football stadium scene. They were needed to illustrate the flimsiness of contemporary moral standards as opposed to the almost spiritual qualities of the drug dealers...I mean...you can say more with a terrific set of..."

Fervent wandered on.

"What do you mean, the story has to be changed?" the irate female writer snarled at the agent. "It has depth and emotion and a statement that a child could really identify with."

"Maybe *Humpty Dumpty* just isn't ready for incest," the agent pointed out.

"That motherfucker would screw a toad if it helped his magazine...but what do you expect? He's an editor," a writer complained.

"That asshole would butcher his wife for a good sale...but what do you expect? He's a writer," replied an editor.

"Zelda? No, my wife had to stay at home," said the writer/editor. "Have you met my date yet?"

"Ribbet. Ribbet."

"So I said to him, I said, 'Look, liver pate brain, this is the greatest opportunity for a movie that you'll ever see in your life. It's got everything that's hot. You take special effects and Brooke Shields and Burt Reynolds and a sure-fire rock group and a classically violent SF plot...'"

"Gee...I don't know...*Music Men in the Jungle?*"

"Yeah, well, maybe if we got the BeeGees?"

Fervent stumbled slightly and turned to apologize to the person that she had jostled. She gazed into the most beautiful eyes that she had ever seen. They were such pools of sensitivity that she felt her soul flop over like a hooked trout. Once again, she felt that surging of animalistic desires and lust...the pulling of overwhelming passion and pulsating greed for the heated touch of skin and flesh and lips and hair and fingernails and fast breathing...her blood circulated in a fury, whirlpooling in her extremities in a whiplash of desire. She struggled to contain her response and, with a trembling hand, reached out to touch the object of her hunger.

Chapter Seven

"WHO ARE YOU?" SHE asked in a trembling voice. The young man glanced about nervously. His sandy hair was drawn back in a dignified ponytail and tied with grey flannel. One eyebrow was raised in a humorous fashion as he replied.

"Promise not to tell anyone?" She nodded, watching his shrug and admiring the clutch of inkpens stuck in one pocket of his shirt. He looked about again and, lowering his voice, whispered in her ear. "I'm the Con Chairman." She gasped.

"I just sneaked in here to escape from the gophers for awhile," he explained. "They get really demanding sometimes. I finally sent most of them to find a sober pro for a non-existent panel on SF and the Mary Tyler Moore Show. That should keep them occupied until dawn."

"Oh," she said. She gave him a long and passionate look. "Perhaps I could keep you occupied until dawn as well." The Con Chairman gave her a compassionate glance.

"You poor thing," he said. "Don't tell me you're one of those neos that expect to actually get laid at a convention."

"You mean...?" Fervent faltered.

"Nobody ever gets laid at conventions except for pros," he said in serious tones. "And everybody knows about writers anyway...they don't *really* enjoy it, they just do it to help their book sales."

Fervent was confused.

"But...but...in all the fanzines, people are always talking about messing around at cons," she stammered. He shrugged.

"Mere window-dressing. Actually sex would interfere with the real business of a convention...name-dropping, character assassination, sucking up to pros, looking down on pros, getting drunk, throwing up, sleeping with twenty or more people in a room, waiting for elevators, reading fanzines, picking zits...I mean, who has time for mere sex? Besides, surely you know...one of the really vital ingredients in Blog is saltpeter. It helps the male fans to concentrate on the reason they're here...particularly during the costume contease." His tone was reassuring. "It must be a shock to you to find all this out."

Fervent shook her head slowly as the concept began to sink in.

"Gosh!" she said. "After all these years of reading about romance and fantastic sex at conventions, this will take some getting used to."

"Well," he said. "You know how it is. Fandom may be a Goddamn Hobby, but nobody ever claimed it was a Goddamn Release."

"I suppose," she said, sighing heavily, "that I'll have to be satisfied with things of the spirit." Her shoulders slumped forward. The Chairman studied her dejection with a concerned eye. Finally he sighed and took one of her hands. "I really shouldn't do this," he said. "But if you swear on your mimeo never ever to tell anyone about this, you can spend the night making mad, passionate, animalistic love with me in my hotel room." He raised a warning hand at her sudden smile. "This must never be known... you could ruin my fannish reputation. I don't think I could ever live it down." Fervent nodded eagerly. "Oh, I swear, I swear!" she breathed. She showered kisses on one of his hands, and, with a final glance at the Pro Party, left with the Con Chairman for his room.

Chapter Eight

FERVENT STARED INTO HER bowl of oatmeal in the hotel restaurant and glumly wondered if all neos had to suffer as she did. In a passionate mood the night before, she had accompanied the Con Chairman to his hotel room, bent on sins of the flesh. Unfortunately, the Con Chairman was unable to perform...a fact he sheepishly blamed on drinking Blog and the pressures of responsibility. Mumbling that it was the will of Ghod, he had fallen asleep within minutes and she had resignedly gotten dressed and returned to her own room. Actually, she hadn't really been *that* disappointed at the Con Chairman's failure. She knew from fannish histories that you should never really expect too much from the Con Chairman: all of his strength was centered in his staff. For a moment, she felt there was something strange about that statement, but she shrugged it off.

At a nearby table, several femmefans were amusing themselves by tossing fried eggs at passing pros. One noticed Fervent's depression and asked in a friendly manner if Fervent would like to join the group. Picking up her oatmeal, Fervent walked over to them.

"You look like a neo," one of the femmefans said sympathetically.

Fervent nodded and shrugged.

"Everyone has to start somewhere," she sighed. The femmefans exchanged knowing glances.

"It really gets better as you go along," a femmefan pointed out. "Once you learn that sex has no place in fandom...at least, at cons, you gain a certain sense of proportion. After all, orgasms aren't everything."

"That's easy for you to say, Clare," noted another femmefan. "You just got a new mimeo." The femmefans sighed in a dreamy manner and stared into the distance with glazed eyes.

"Mimeo?" asked Fervent.

"You mean...you haven't found out yet?" The femmefan named Clare seemed astonished. Fervent was confused (again). "The right mimeo can give you the..." she paused and winked "...right vibrations."

"Oh?" said Fervent. "More like 'Ohhhhhhhhh!'" joked another femmefan. "Hadn't you noticed the huge influx of females into fandom?" demanded Clare.

"I thought it was mostly due to media fans," said Fervent sheepishly. The femmefans laughed. Clare patted Fervent on the arm.

"Listen, kid, why do you think they call them 'A. B. Dick's?'" she quipped. "Anyway, it'll substitute until you can find someone you can have a meaningful relationship with. I'm sure you're too smart to only want a physical thing...That's so shallow."

Fervent blushed. Maybe the femmefans were right. There had to be more to sex than mere mechanics, S & M, gerbils, and Crisco. Not getting laid at this convention could be the best thing that ever happened to her. She thought of the faithful and reliable mimeo at home and smiled slightly. If that failed...there was always the electric typewriter.

Cheerfully she said good-by to the femmefans and headed for the closing ceremonies of the convention. On the way, she picked up a flyer for the next convention. Thoughtfully, she studied the flyer and noted that the Pro Guest of Honor was one of her favorite writers. He was virile, charming, and had a very large reputation as a warm person. A smile appeared on Fervent's lips and she started humming to herself as plans began to formulate. After all, there were always other conventions.

A. J. Budrys

*The field of science fiction has never had a more
unique stylist than Ray Bradbury in his prime.
If anyone comes close, it may well be my old friend Algis Budrys, who
here takes it upon himself to puncture Ray's balloon.*

BALLOON, OH BALLOON!

by Ray Bradbudrys

Robert stood alone in the golden breeze of the afternoon, the long green grass caressing his ankles with the whispered promise of everything, the slow, rolling fallaway of the hillside combing down, down, and to the next hillside, and up, and down onto the horizon, where upstairs-stairway wallpaper-paint-blue sky held clouds like child handprints scrubbed away by patient Mother.

At the edges of the horizon to his right and left were wooly green forests. Behind him, in the valley by the meandering river, lay the white town like a setting for the blue tracks of the Aurora and Yellow Rock Railway. Before him, between him and the horizon and the gold-washed sky and the golden sun lay nothing, nothing to keep his eyes and the sunlight from touching, and the long grass that grew wise as Time on the ancient prairie hillocks, that had felt the stamp of buffalo in flight from Kiowa ponies and the roll of pioneer wheel, the sting of cattle-chip fires and the scent of coffee boiling in cowhand agate pots, the song-step of roving *voyageur* and his *Alouette, gentil Alouette!*, that knew the way of it, and the why of it, and the how of it in human hearts—some hearts— that wise old grass whispered to Robert: *"Northwest Passage...passage...*

Cibola…Samarkand…Cibola…bola…Samarkand…" and, long-drawn-out, soft-spoken, breeze-kissed: *"Erewhon…ewhonnn…whonnnn…."*

"God damn it!" Robert exclaimed childishly, his fists driven into the pockets of his wash shorts, stamping his feet, the boy-tears shining in his eyes and scattering the sunlight. "Son," his father had said at dinner, home for the noon meal from the tractor plant where the machines made ugly sounds as they built machines that made brute sounds as they tore the prairie, "Boy," his father had said to him not unkindly, but firmly, "Boy—Robert—th' Chamber of Commerce's gonna buy that hill you like goin' to and make it a parkin' lot. Put down blacktop. Meters. First six hours free with tokens from local merchants. Good for business. Blacktop."

Robert had stopped with the forkful of greens almost to his mouth. Just stopped. His father had said earnestly: "Boy, I know how fond you are of goin' out to that place—before school, and recess time, and after school, and after supper, and sneakin' out of your room on moonlight nights—son, don't you think I know that?" His father's honest face had gotten all twisted up, and as Robert blinked it got blurry around the edges, so that it had no hair, no ears, no eyes, no vinyl-bow-tied blue-striped shirt collar, only a mouth, saying: "Why you reckon I told you myself 'stead of letting you find out from strangers?" with a little fleck of fried potato crust sticking to one of the lower front teeth.

"Robert!" his mother had screamed as Robert quietly put his fork down in the middle of the scratched china plate with the blackening and peeled-in-places gold trim around the edge. "Robert, don't you go! Don't you go to that place now!" as he pushed back the chair, lower lip under upper teeth. "Robert; Robert—*you'll break your own heart!*"

Not go? Not go to Samarkand for one last time? Robert's thin, strong legs drove him out the door, the screen banging flatly behind him, while his father was saying to his mother: "Let the boy go, Matty—don't deprive the child…." And Robert ran down the street, down past the Emporium, and Stupor's Drug Store, and Woolworth's, and the Sears, Roebuck Catalogue Sales Store, and the Subaru showroom, and the Video Rents, and the gas plant, and over the A&YR tracks, and up the first hill, and on to this place, where the grass said *"Mystery…"* and a man in bib overalls had come out while Robert was in school, and planted a board sign with red sans-serif block capitals that said: SITE OF NEW MUNICIPAL PARKING AREA. GRANTWOOD CHAMBER OF COMMERCE WELCOMES U. Had put up the sign and trudged down the hill again after wiping his sun-seamed face with the print bandanna in his hip pocket; had left behind an emptied, crumpled Red Man Chewing Tobacco wrapper on the grass and trudged back.

And the grass whispered: "*Kiowa...was...Cathay....*"

Robert shut his eyes tight, shoulders hunched, fists bulging in shorts pockets, round soft jaws clenched, and he thought of great sun-battered orange brick soot-stained box-buildings with white-rippled-glass chicken-wire-embedded windows in peeling, rusting, unopened, once-black painted-iron frames, and in those box-buildings men in bib overalls tended great, oiled, gleaming, brass and copper and stainless steel and gray crackle-finished painted-sheet-iron machines that endlessly wrapped Red Man to sustain the cud-motion in the faces of other bib-overalled men who came to the hillsides of El Dorado to hammer in stakes and expectorate: "Blacktop!"

"Rat bastard!" Robert gritted desperately, his heart beating against his ribs like a garden mole when the brown-gold nozzle of the hose finds his burrow, "Oh, if—" If he could become as fleet-foot as a pony, as sure as an arrow, as certain of his track as Major Robert Rogers, then this buffalo terror that made him want to snort and paw the ground for comfort could become a flight like a cowpoke's rush, busting for Blonde Nellie's place on a Saturday night, and he could skim the prairie on his toe-tips, arms outstretched, true as a wish toward the westering sun, and leave behind him for the overalled men to hear only the vanished treble giggling of "*Alouette....*"

"If I had wings!" Robert piped, arms outstretched, fingers straight and fluttering like pinions, neck arched, shoulders arched, back arched, heels off the ground, face to the sun, "If I had someone to give me wings!"

And a great roaring and sighing came into his head: "Cayley," the sound said. "Santos-Dumont." "*Cathay, Cibola, Erewhon,*" the grass prompted urgently. The sound spoke: "Cayley, Santos-Dumont, Professor Langley!" "*Wings!*" cried Robert, trembling, with the prairie wind thrumming at the pulse beat in his fingertips, where the pink capillaries surged, and the edges of the world blurred, until there were no forests to either hand, no horizon, no white town behind, only the golden, golden sun and—"Oh!" Robert cried out, "Oh, I wish I truly did see a golden speck against the golden sun!"

And it seemed to him that if he truly did see a golden speck against the golden sun, a golden speck descending, wafting gently down through the scrubmark clouds, silent, oh, silent as hope, then what could that speck be—what could he hope for it to be—but "*A balloon!*" Robert shouted. "A balloon—oh, a big round balloon coming for me!"

Round, golden and glittering with varnish, netted in brown rope hawsers, wide-throated, painted in gilt curlicues and cherubim and butterflies and eagles, doves, cormorants, flamingos, storks, hearts, scrolls, flowers and stalks of arrows bound in ribbon, the balloon was the only balloon he could have wished for, swaying gently down to him, wisps of blue smoke trickling up around the rim of the open throat, pale yellow wicker basket slung below it from the net of hawsers, and peering over the edge of the basket a tall, spare, commanding gray-haired woman in black bombazine, with her hair pulled back in a bun with a little black hat pinned to it and lace frothing white from under the tight black sleeve at her bony wrist as she pointed to him, arm outstretched, with a tightly furled black umbrella whose long brass ferrule glinted heart-stoppingly, saying: "I am your Aunt Agatha Marvelous, come to take you to Mars. Wipe your dirty little face."

"Yes, Ma'am," said Robert politely as the balloon grounded with a sound like "*Samar*—thump!—*kand*" before him. "I'm pleased to meet you. But isn't Mars a very long way?"

"Don't be impertinent, child. I've packed an adequate hamper," Aunt Agatha said. "Scramble aboard, now—scramble aboard; we must be off!"

And the great creaking, varnished-paper bag swayed over Robert in fabulous protectiveness, stiff and shining and curlicued, delicately gored and gusseted and seamed, and from it came the enchanting scent of anthracite smoke and baking varnish and the acrid tang of japanning on the glistening bentwood hoops that stayed the hawsers around the brass fire-pan, and here and there a drop of gilt on the rim of the wicker basket where the angels who had surely swooped and fluttered about it, executing those wondrous decorations, had surely swayed each other's paintpots a little with the joyful rush of their wing-feathers, and Robert cried: "Oh! Oh, balloon! Oh, Mars!"

"There are ponies and buffalo on Mars," Aunt Agatha said. "Long, rolling plains, and pink-towered cities, and cowboys and pioneers and long camel caravans swaying across the land at dusk, and Kiowas and Comanches and Shoshones and Crow, Sioux, Winnebego, Sac-and-Fox, and bear, and deer, and giraffes, and beaver, and no parking lots, no gas plants, no sewers, no smoking, and everyone cooks over cattle-chip fires. There are *conquistadores* and vikings and crusaders and berserkers and Attila the Hun and Galileo."

"Oh!" cried Robert, scrambling aboard and throwing his arms around Aunt Agatha's whalebone-clasped waist, "Oh, my Aunt!"

"Hush now, child," she said, pushing him away busily. "There's no need to be demonstrative," she snapped, but a smile quivered the corners of her carefully compressed, pale rose lips. "Here, help me with the kindling," she said, thrusting her umbrella toward the woodpile while her tin-plated scoop rattled in the galvanized iron coal scuttle. "And listen—listen to the balloon!"

And as he helped stoke the fire-pan that filled the balloon with the heat of life and the expansiveness of flight, Robert's ears filled with a host of murmurs: There was a sound like the aspirations of all the paper bags ever made; a crackling, a striving, a stirring, a rush, a scraping sigh. *"At last—destiny!"* the great envelope seemed to say, full of the warmth of its own dreams. And the hawsers in the breeze sighed *"Mars...."*

"Upward!" the great bag grunted, and in the fire-pan below its throat the merry coals brightened in response. Out of the crushed ferns, the pine cones, the bitumen of geologic ages; out of the trapped sunlight of all Earth's time; of heat, and rain, and earth and crush of years, of layered patience. Out of the heat of oxygen, invisibly disguised in air, out of the need, and the wanting, out of the hunger to burn—coal, and oxygen; sunlight and air—sunlight and air and time; the fire quickened as Aunt Agatha poked it with the ferrule of her umbrella, and again *"Upward!"* the bag grunted, and upward the bag rose, and the hawsers sighed: *"Marsss...."*

The balloon rose, and rose, above the prairies and the white little town and the A&YR tracks, and the white board sign on the hilltop below dwindled, and the balloon rose, and pushed through the soap-smelling clouds, which brushed Robert's face and made him blink. Of earth, and air, and fire, and water; upward, the balloon rose, and the hawsers spoke: *"Mars...Marsss...Marsss...sss...."*

"Gee whiz!" Robert exclaimed.

"None of your vulgarisms, young man!" Aunt Agatha snapped, boxing his ear.

"No, Ma'am," Robert agreed politely, his eyes shining like moonstones as he stood feeling the sway of the basket, listening to the murmur of air and the voices of the ropes, the chuckling of the coals, and felt the rushing warmth of the heated air bubbling up into the smoky heart of the balloon, and dreamed of giraffes skimming head-up across the prairies toward Ultima Thule. Of muskrat and okapi and woodchuck, and lions, and elk, and eland, and the greater kudu running with eyes a-start before the onrush of horse-laughing Kiowans. He could see it. He could see it... he was there and yes, oh yes, the lovely balloon had taken him to Mars! "Alouette!" Robert cried out into the sky, and turned to throw his face up toward the sun. "Alouette!" Robert cried out to the sun, *"J'en te plumerai!"*

He felt a little faint. A great noise came once more into his head; voices chanted: "Lilienthal...Graf von Zeppelin...Willi Messershmitt...," and he held out his trembling arms to Aunt Agatha while the hawsers sang: *"Mars samarkand andorra atlantis cibola lagrange Illinois...."*

"Aunt Agatha!" Robert gasped out, "I don't feel so good!"

Aunt Agatha efficiently whipped her umbrella under one arm and gathered him in her long, tight arms, holding him close to the busks under the crackling sharp bosom of her bombazine bodice with the scent of lilac sachet in the stiff white lace, and stroked his hair, promising: "Never you mind, young man. I'll always be here whenever they behave uncouthly toward you. I'll save you. I am your Aunt Agatha Marvelous, and if any of them try to take away your toys or make you go to bed without your supper, you just say to them, 'We'll see about *that!*' You just sneak out to the parking lot and shinny up a light pole, or something, so I can see you—a boy like you needs lots of practice shinnying up things anyhow—and you wave. Wave with all your brave young heart, young man." And Aunt Agatha pursed her lips and kissed him between the eyes.

"Oh, yes, yes, Aunt Agatha," Robert whispered as softly as the rolling-over of a mouse asleep in a loaf of bread, under the cellophane, and closed his eyes. He heard, faintly: "Mind you scrub your knees, next time...," and then he was blinking his eyes next to the Chamber of Commerce sign.

"Son," his father was saying to him in his honest voice, squatted down next to him, taking a whole half-day off from the Carburetor Division, mopping his brow with a print bandanna. "Son—boy—listen; you know what I done?"

"What?" Robert said sulkily, knuckling his eyes.

"Listen, what I done—I went to see Mr. Snavely, down at the bank, you know?" his father said earnestly, trying to put his arm around Robert's stiff young shoulders. "And I took Matildy's butter-an'-aig money, and all the life savin's, and your college money, too, matter of fact, and then Sam Snavely and me, we went down to see Mr. Tight at the Realty, and can you guess what we done?"

"No," Robert said, kicking the two-by-two upright on the sign, making a noise with his scuffed-white and grass-stained sneaker toe like *"Blacktop!"*

"Well, Sam Snavely, he explained to Bill Tight about how he was refinancin' the mortgage on the house another twenny years and how what with the savin's this would be enough—well, here, son," Robert's father said, fumbling in his pocket and bringing out a piece of folded stiff white paper that crackled "Snap!" like a trap and had never heard of okapi, "Here's the deed to this piece of land. You can come up here all you want to, now, and stand around all moony-eyed with your hands behind your ears like you do, and won't nobody bother you!"

Robert's father tried to reach around and slap him on the back, but Robert had already turned and was hammering his fists on his father's honest chest, crying: "Oh, hell, hell, hell!" he said, hammering harder with his grimy-knuckled fists and blinking his eyes, "Oh, hell hell, hell, and God *damn*, now you've gone and taken away Aunt Agatha!"

George Alec Effinger

George Alec Effinger, au-
thor of the brilliant WHEN
GRAVITY FAILS, has
acquired quite a reputation as an offbeat humorist. In fact, he has cre-
ated a brand-new subset of humor with his Maureen Birnbaum stories:
Preppie Science Fiction. And since this one is set on Edgar Rice Bur-
roughs' Barsoom, it qualifies as a parody.

MAUREEN BIRNBAUM, BARBARIAN SWORDSPERSON

by Bitsy Spiegelman, as told to George Alec Effinger

THE LAST TIME I saw Muffy Birnbaum was, let me see, last December—no,
make that last January, because it was right after exams and before Mums and
I spent a couple of dreadful weeks at the B and T in Palm Beach. So that makes
it ten months almost, and she told me to wait a year before I revealed this to
the world, to use her exact words. But I don't think Muffy will mind that I'm
two months early. She's long ago and far away, if you believe her story. Do I
believe her story? Look. She was missing for a full week, and then I get this
telegram—a telegram, can you believe it? Not a phone call. Meet me under the
Clock, 15 January, noonish. Come alone. Trust me. Kisses, Muffy. What was I
supposed to think? I show up and she's not there, but there's a note waiting for
me: Come to Room 1623. Just too mysterious, but up I go. The door's open and I
walk in, and there's goddamn Maureen Danielle Birnbaum practically naked,

wearing nothing but these leather straps across her shoulders and a little gold G-string, and she's got this goddamned sword in one hand like she was expecting the Sheriff of Nottingham or something to come through the door instead of her best friend and roommate. I couldn't think of anything to say at first, so she called down for some ice, pointed to a chair, and began to tell me this story. I'll give it to you just the way it is on my tape; then you can tell me if you believe it.

So listen, I'm telling you this story. Believe me, I'd *had* it, absolutely *had* it. School was a *complete* bore and I was absolutely falling to pieces. Absolutely. I needed a vacation and I told Daddy that a little intense skiing action would shape me up very nicely, and so, just like that, I found myself at Mad River Glen, looking very neat, I thought, until I saw some of the competition, the collegiate talent. They were deadly cut and they knew it, and all you had to do was ask them and they'd tell you all about it. You could just about tell where they went to school, like they were wearing uniforms. The Vassar girls were the ones sort of flouncing downhill wearing their circle pins on the front of their hundred-dollar goose-down ski parkas. The Bennington girls were the ones looking rugged and trying to ski back *uphill*. Definitely Not Our Kind, sweetie.

Are those your cigarettes, Bitsy? Mind if I—no, just toss me the whole pack. I have matches here in the ashtray. My *God*. I haven't had a cigarette in so *long*—

Where was I? Vermont, right. So I was staring down this goddamn hill, if you can believe it, and I'm all set to push off and go barreling down the mountain at some outrageous speed, when I stop. I look up at the sky—it's starting to get dark, you know, and absolutely clear and kind of sweet, but *cold*—when I feel this weird feeling inside. First I thought I was going to *die*, just absolutely die. Then I thought, "My God, I know what it is. And they always say nothing can happen if—" You know. But I was wrong both times. The next thing I knew I was standing stark naked in the snow beside my body, which was still dressed up in this cute outfit from L.L. Bean, and I thought, "Muffy, you've *had* it." I thought I was dead or something, but I didn't understand why I was so goddamn *cold*. Then I looked up into the sky and this bright red dot caught my eye and I sort of shivered. I knew right then, I said to myself, "That is where I'm going." Heaven or Hell, here I come. And just like that I felt this whushing and dizziness and everything, and I opened my eyes, and I wasn't in Vermont anymore, but I was still cold.

I'm drinking Bloody Marys. It isn't too early for you, is it? Then you try calling down for ice, I've given up on them. Are you hungry? We'll have lunch later. I'm putting myself on a diet, but I'll go with you and you can have something.

Anyway, they didn't prepare me at the Greenberg School for what was waiting for me when I opened my eyes. Here I was on some weirdo planet out in space, for God's sake. Say Bitsy, do you have any gum or what? Chiclets? Yuck. Let me have—no, just one. Thanks. A weirdo planet, if you can believe that. I was standing there at the top of the run one second, having this *unbelievable* fight with the zipper on the jacket Pammy—that's Daddy's second wife—bought me for Christmas, and the next minute I'm up to my ankles in orange grunge. And I was so cold I thought I would freeze to death. I was cold because—we're just going to have to live without the ice, I think, Bitsy, because this hotel probably has a goddamn *policy* against it or something, so just pour it in the glass—I was standing there in the proverbial buff! Me! Three years living with me at the Greenberg School, and even you never saw my pink little derriere. And here I am starko for the whole world to see. What world it was I didn't know, so I didn't know *who* could see, but believe me, Bitsy, I didn't particularly care. Right then I had two or three pressing problems on my mind, and getting dressed was high on the list. I really missed that ski outfit. It was cold as hell.

All around me there was nothing but this gross orange stuff on the ground. I don't know what it was. It wasn't grass, I know that. It felt more like the kind of sponge the cleaning woman keeps under your sink for a couple of years. Gross. And there was nothing else to see except some low hills off in one direction. I decided to head that way. There sure wasn't anything the other way, and—who knew?—there may have been a Bloomingdale's on the other side of the hills. At that point I would have settled for Lamston's, *believe* me.

You're going to die laughing when I tell you this, absolutely die. When I took a step I went sailing up into the air. Just like a balloon, and I thought, "Muffy, honey, *what* did they put in your *beer*?" When I settled back down I tried it again, and I flew away again. It took me absolutely an hour to figure out how to walk and run and all that. I still don't know why it was. One of those lame boys from Brush-Bennett would know, right off the bat, but it wasn't all that important to me. I just needed to learn to handle it. So in a while, still freezing my completely cute buns off, I got to the top of the first hill and I looked down at my new world.

You want to know what I saw? Was that the door? You better get it, Bitsy, because even though Daddy stays here *all* the time the staff has been just too dreary for words. You should have heard what they said about my sword. They talked about my sword a lot, because they were too embarrassed to mention my costume. I think it's—who? The ice? Would you be a dear and leave the boy something? I don't have a goddamned *penny*. I mean, you don't see any pockets, do you?

There was more orange crud all the way to the whatyoucall—the horizon. But there was a little crowd of people down there about a quarter of a mile away. It looked to me like a little tailgate party, like we used to have with your parents in New Haven before the Harvard game. I thought, "That's nice, they'll be able to drive me to decent motel or something until I can get settled." But then I wondered how I was going to walk up to them all naked and glowing with health and frostbite and all. I thought about covering up the more strategic areas with the orange stuff from the ground, but I didn't even know if I could rip it loose. I was standing there thinking when I heard this girl scream. She sounded like Corkie the time we threw the dead fish into the shower with her. There was something *awful* going on down there, a mugging or a purse-snatching or something terrible, so what does yours truly do? I started running downhill toward them. Don't look so *surprised*. It's just something you do when you find yourself on a creepy planet, undressed and stone cold, with nothing else around except the two moons in the sky. Did I mention that there were two moons? Well, there were. I ran toward the people below because I needed a lift into town, wherever it was, and if I helped the poor girl out maybe her daddy would let me stay at their place for a while.

When I got closer I saw that I had made just a little bitty mistake. The station wagon and the Yalies turned into a drastic and severe kind of a fight, a brawl, really, except everybody was using one of these swords and they were using them for *real*. I mean, Bitsy, my *God*, blood was pouring all over *everywhere* and people were actually *dying* and it was all kind of heroic and all that and very horrible and dramatic. It was people against big, giant things with four arms. No, really. *Really*. Bitsy, stop *laughing*. There were these huge old creatures with four arms, and they were chopping away at the normal-sized people, everybody fighting away with these *intense* grins on their faces. I never did find out about that, why they were all *smiling* while they were whacking away at each other. Anyway, while I stood there the two groups just about wiped each other out, all the giant creatures except one and all the people except this one positively *devastating* guy. All the other guys and girls were lying very dead on the orange stuff, and it wasn't really *surprising*. I mean, just imagine something that's twelve feet tall and has arms slashing swords around up where you can barely see, for God's sake. And then this *darling* boy goes and tangles his adorable legs and falls over backwards.

Bitsy, are you listening to this, or what? I mean, I don't know why I even bothered—no, look. I didn't *have* to send you the telegram. I could have called Mother. Except she would have had *kittens* if she had seen me like this. Do you understand? This was a very moving moment for me, Bitsy, I mean, watching these kids fighting like that and all, and even though I didn't know them, I got very emotional and everything. So I'd appreciate it, I really would, if you'd show a little respect. You've never had to fight for *anything* except with the burger-brained Amherst freshman you went out with senior year. Of *course* I remember him. He reminds me a lot of these four-armed things.

Well, if anything *terminal* happened to my blond hero, that monster was coming after *me next*. So, perky little thing that I am, I run up and grab a sword—this sword, I call her "Old Betsy" because that's what Davy Crockett called his rifle or something—I grab Old Betsy and I stand there trying not to look that...thing in the eye. This was very easy, believe me, because his eyes are *at least* six feet over my head. And I'm all nice and balanced—*you* remember, you were there, you remember how *tremendous* I was in that six weeks of fencing we had sophomore year, with what's-her-name, Miss Duplante. You remember how she was absolutely terrified of me? Anyway, picture me standing there *en garde* waiting for this four-armed darling to settle into position. But he *doesn't*, that's what's so scary, he just goes *whacko*! and takes a wide swipe at my goddamn head.

Only I'm not there anymore, I'm about fifty feet away. I remembered that I could jump, but *really*. So I hop around for a minute or two to get my bearings and to stay away from the thing's sword. I hop, and I jump, bounce, bounce, bounce, all around the landscape. And the creature is watching me, *mad as hell*. My blond dream is still on the ground, and he's watching too. "Get a *sword*, dummy," I yell at him, and he nods. That's something else I forgot to tell you Bitsy. All the people on this planet speak English. It's really neat and very convenient. So between the two of us we finished the monster off. No, it's just too *awful* to think about, stabbing and bleeding and hacking and all like that. Fencing was a lot tidier—you know, just a kind of polite poking around with a sharp stick. And *I* had to do all the *heavyweight* hacking because my boyfriend couldn't reach anything terribly vital on the four-armed thing. He was taking mighty swings at the giant's knees, and meanwhile good old Muffy is cutting its pathetic head off. Just altogether *unreal*.

Well, that's the dynamic, exciting carnage part. After I took care of the immediate danger, the boy starts to talk to me. "Hello," he goes. "You were excellent."

"Thanks," I go. At this point I feel like I'm riding on a horse with only one rocker, but I don't let it show. The old Greenberg School *pride*, Bitsy.

He goes, "My name is Prince Van."

"Uh-huh," I go. "I'm Maureen Birnbaum. My daddy is a contract lawyer and I live with my mother. We raise golden retrievers."

"How nice," the prince goes. Let me tell you what this guy *looked* like! You wouldn't *believe* it! Do you remember that boy who came down to visit that drecky redhead from Staten Island? No, not the boy from Rutgers, the one from—where was it? That place I never *heard* of—Colby College, in Maine? Sounds like a goddamned *cheese* factory or something? Anyway, standing beside me on the orange stuff is something just like him, only the prince is awesome. He is strong and blond with perfect teeth and eyes like Paul Newman and he's wearing, well, you see what I'm wearing. Just *imagine*, honey, if that isn't just too devastating for you. He is *beautiful*. And his name is Prince Van. I always told you that someday my prince would—

Okay, Okay. I didn't really know what to say to him or anything. I mean, we'd just had this sort of pitched battle and all, and there were all these unpleasant *bodies* laying around—we were stepping over people here and there, and I was trying not to notice. We stopped and he bent down and took this harness for me from someone he said had been his sister. He didn't seem sad or anything. He was very brave, *intensely* brave, no tears for Sis, the gang back at the palace wouldn't approve. And all the dead boys looked just like him, all blond and large and uncomfortably cute, and all the girls looked just like Tri-Delts, with feathered blonde hair and perfect teeth. They had been his retinue, Prince Van explained, and he said I shouldn't grieve. He could get another one.

"Where to?" I go. The palace couldn't be too far away, I thought.

"Well," he says—and his voice was like a handful of Valium; I just wanted to curl up and listen to it—he says, like, "my city is two thousand miles *that* way," he pointed, "but there is a closer city one thousand miles that way." He pointed behind us.

I go, "*Thousand!* You've got to be kidding."

He says, like, "I have never seen anyone like you." And he smiled. Bitsy, that was just the kind of thing my mother had *warned* me about, and I had begun to think it didn't really exist. I think I was in love.

"I'm from another world," I go. I tried to sound like I partied around in space quite a bit.

"That explains it," he goes. "It explains your strength and agility and your exotic beauty. I am captivated by your raven tresses. No one on our world has hair your color. It is very beautiful." *Raven tresses*, for God's sake! I think I blushed, and I think he wanted me to. We were holding hands by now. I was thinking about one or two thousand miles alone with Prince Van of Who-Knows-Where. I wondered what boys and girls did on this planet when they were alone. I decided that it was the same everywhere.

We walked for a long time and I asked a lot of questions. He must have thought I was just *really* lame, but he never laughed at me. I learned that the cities are so far because we were walking across the bottom of what had been a great ocean, years and years before. There weren't oceans and lakes and things on this planet now. They have all their water delivered or something. I thought, "There's *oil* down there." I wanted to remember that for when we got to the palace. I don't think anyone had realized it yet.

"Then where do you go sailing?" I go.

"Sailing?" he asked innocently.

"What about swimming?"

"Swimming?"

He was cute, absolutely *tremendous*, in fact, but life without sailing and swimming would be just too terribly *triste*, you know? And I think he was just being polite before when I mentioned golden retrievers.

I say, like, "Is there somewhere I can pick up some clothes?" I figured that although his city was two thousand miles away, there were probably isolated little ocean-bottom suburbs along the way or shopping malls where all the blond people came to buy new straps and swords and stuff.

"Clothes?" he goes. I knew he was going to say that, I just knew it, but as gross as it was I had to hear it from his own lips.

I walked along for a while, *dying*, absolutely dying for a cigarette, not saying anything. Then I couldn't stand it any longer. "Van," I go, "listen. It isn't like it hasn't been wonderful with you, cutting up that big old monster and all. But, like, there are some things about this relationship that are totally the worst, but *really*."

"Relationship?" he goes. He kept smiling. I think I could eventually see enough of it.

I explained it all to him. There were no horses. There was no sailing, no swimming, no skiing, no racquetball. There were no penny loafers, no mixers at the boy's schools, no yearbooks. There was no Junior Year Abroad, no Franny and Zooey Glass, no Nantucket Island, no *Coors*. There was no Sunday *Times*, no Godiva chocolates, no Dustin Hoffman.

There was no Joni Mitchell and no food processors and no golden retrievers and no little green Triumphs.

There were no clothes. Bitsy, *there was no shopping*!

So kind of sadly I kissed him on the cheek and told myself that his couldn't-be-cuter expression was a little sad, too. I say, like *"Adieu, mon cher,"* and I give him a little wave. Then I stretched myself out toward the sky again—oh, yes, just a little late I told myself that I wasn't absolutely sure about what I was doing, that I might end up only God knew where—and waited to whush back to the snowy mountaintop in Vermont. I missed. But fortunately it wasn't as bad as it could have been. I mean, I didn't land on *Saturn* or anything. I turned up at the corner of Eighth Avenue and 45th Street. No one noticed me very much; I fit right into that neighborhood.

So if I can just ask you a little favor, Bitsy, then I'll be on my way. Yes, on my way, goddamn it, I'm going back. I'm not going to leave that but totally attractive Prince Van to those perky blonde hometown honeys— he is *mine*. I kept my harness and Old Betsy on the way here, so I think I know how to get back there again with anything I want to take with me. So I want to pick up a few things first. My daddy always told me to Be Prepared. He said that all the time, he's a Mason or something. He sure was prepared when he met Pammy, and he's close to fifty years old.

Never mind. Anyway, let's go rummage in a bin somewhere and suit me up with a plaid skirt or two and some cute jeans and some sweaters and some alligator shirts and Top-Siders and a brand-new insulated ski jacket and sunglasses and some *Je Reviens* and stuff. It'll be fun!

Oh. And a circle pin. My old one wore out.

We went shopping at Saks and Bloomingdale's—I went to Korvettes and got her some cheaper clothes first, though. I didn't want to walk around midtown Manhattan with Muffy while she was wearing nothing but suspenders and no pants. We charged four hundred dollars to Mums' cards, and let me tell you I heard about that a few weeks later. But I was sworn to secrecy. Now Muffy's gone again, back to her secret paradise in the sky, back to Prince Van of the terribly straight teeth. I hope she's happy. I hope she comes back some day to tell me her adventures. I hope she pays me back the four hundred dollars. Perhaps only time will tell....

George Alec Effinger

I am probably Muffy Birnbaum's greatest fan, so when George brought her back and plunked her down in Edgar Rice Burroughs' Pellucidar, there was no way that I could keep the story out of the anthology.

MAUREEN BIRNBAUM AT THE EARTH'S CORE

by Bitsy Spiegelman, as told to George Alec Effinger

ALL I KNOW IS that I was supposed to leave for Cancun. The plane was at two, and you know what traffic is like in the sleet to the airport, so I was planning to leave the apartment sometime around noon to get there and get my bags checked through and have enough time to pour three or four drinks into me. I do not like to fly—it doesn't matter if the plane is coming down in Aspen or Cancun or Oz. I do not like to fly. The four drinks wouldn't calm me either, unless they were washing down five of the big Valiums. The baby blue ones. Whatever they are. Tens. I think.

Anyway. I'd packed two days before and checked everything at least twice, had my passport and my tickets in my purse with cab fare in case my sweet little RX-7 perished heroically somewhere on the Brooklyn-Queens Expressway, and I was all set to start hauling my bags out to the car, when guess what? The phone rang. My Mother, I figured. It's always my mother. Mums would be calling to let me know the latest herpes statistics or something, so I just let it ring. It rang and rang and rang. I had all the luggage in the car, and the goddamn telephone

was still ringing. Mums only rings ten times. So I answered it. I go "Hello ?"
And I was in a real rush because I had only two hours to get maybe twelve miles
on the best highway system in the Free World.

"Bitsy?" goes this girl's voice.

"Look, I really have to run. Got to catch a plane. Call me next week, we'll
have lunch."

"Bitsy? This is Maureen. Muffy."

I could have died just standing there with the phone against my ear. It was
Maureen Birnbaum, giving me a little call on January 15,1985, exactly four
years to the day since she last disappeared. I didn't know what to say to her for
a moment. "Muffy," I managed at last, "you still owe my mother four hundred
dollars."

"I meant to talk to you about that. Can I see you ? It's awfully important, I
mean really."

Four years ago she'd shown up in midtown Manhattan wearing a couple
of square inches of gold lamé and carrying an honest-to-God sword. She'd just
gotten back from Mars, you see. After she gave me her absolutely incredible story,
she'd vanished for four solid years without so much as a note or a card. Now
she wanted to catch up on old times and tell me more about Mars and stuff and
the beautiful prince she'd fallen in love with. "Listen, Muffy," I go, "it would
be like, great, except I was just going out the door. Club Med, you know. I've
saved up all year for this, you know?"

"Bitsy." There was this creepiness in her voice that she'd get sometimes when
we were roommates back at the Greenberg School, whenever I suggested—in a
kind and thoughtful way, I mean—that she might be putting on a little hefti-
ness, hip-wise.

It was a traumatic moment for me. I felt this dreadful sinking feeling. What
could I do?

I'll tell you what I did: I went to Cancun, met a dentist from Boston with a
face you'd claw your way to get up close to, had a pretty neat time broiling on the
sand there with him for a week, found out the last day that he was married, got
a couple of little tchatchkes to remember him by because he was feeling so impure
and all, and came home. There was a cassette tape sitting on Mums's copy of an
Erma Bombeck book she'd lent me to make me feel even guiltier about being her
child. I played the tape. Just like that last time, you have your choice of believing
any of this or not. A lot I care.

Bitsy? Bitsy, how do you start—is it running? Is this, like, working?
Let me run it back—

It's working. Great. So how the hell are you, sweetie? I hope you're having a really cruddy time in Mexico, because I went through absolute *hell* to see you, and you leave me to toast your buns in the sun.

The last time you saw me, I had on my new clothes and all the rest were packed in the Louis Vuitton bag. I planned to stay in the hotel until about midnight; then I was going to sneak outside, look up in the sky and find Mars, raise my supple, beseeching, cashmere-clad arms to the God of War, and whush my way back to Prince Van. I had already figured out how I was going to play him: vivacious, exciting, yet, you know, *cool.* I'll never forget that gaggy feeling I got when I found out that people on Mars don't know what a *relationship* is. I was going to have to teach them. I mean *him.* The rest of them could go on living like animals—*I* should worry?

Ten o'clock, eleven o'clock—I had a glass of white wine in the bar and talked with this so-so guy who said he was a production assistant; but he wouldn't ever come out and tell me exactly what he assisted producing. About a quarter to midnight, I flashed him my number three smile—Glamorous But Not Inviting—and told him I had to powder my nose. I raced back up to the room, grabbed my bag, and hurried back down to the lobby. It was right then that I realized I didn't have Dime One left over to pay the bill, so I kissed it off and kept the key. They'll either charge Daddy or God will send me to hell, ha ha.

I realized that I couldn't see much of the sky from that part of town, and the only open place I could think of was Central Park. That's cute, isn't it? Maureen Birnbaum, the Marie Osmond of Long Island, walking alone into the treacherous wastes of Central Park at midnight. Alone, but not unarmed—see, I still had Old Betsy, and if any mugger in that park tried anything funny with me, he'd come home from work with one or two important parts hacked off his goddamn body.

So Central Park it had to be. Except—can you believe it?—it was raining. I mean, *pouring.* You couldn't see the top of the Empire State Building, let alone Mars. Oh, fudge, I said to myself, and I went back into the hotel. I took my bag up to the room, then came back down to the bar and let the production assistant buy me a drink. I told the bartender I wanted a piña colada, and he goes, "A what?" Like he'd never heard of it before or nobody drank them any more. He gave me a look like I was from another planet or something. Well, of course, I *did* just get back from another planet; but that wasn't really any reason for this measly bartender to make me feel like a social leper, for God's sake. He smirked to himself like I'd ordered some kind of drink that you hear about only in works of literature, like a martini or a mint julep or something. And then he goes, "I'm sorry, miss, but we took all the disco off the jukebox a long time ago." And the production assistant thought that was pretty funny too. Then he had the nerve—the prod, ass., I mean—to suggest we go someplace else, in *the Bronx yet*! So I told him I had to get up early because I was going to donate a kidney, and went to my room and watched TV.

There is nothing more boring *in the whole world* than killing time. The whole next day I might as well have been socked at some airport or something, because getting to Mars was going to have to wait until after dark. I tried a little window shopping, but how much fun is that when you don't have any cash and all your credit cards are probably lying in an abandoned ski suit somewhere in Vermont? I mean, even if you don't intend to spend money, you spend money—it's a law of nature or something. When you know you absolutely, positively *can't*, well, it's like running out of gas in the dark, romantic woods late at night with Father Flanagan. I mean, why *torture* yourself, you know?

I called Daddy, but he and Pammy were out of town too, I remembered. They went to St. Croix when they sent me to Mad River Glen. I'd been to Mars and back, but they were probably still down in the sun and fun. I was all alone. I was *penniless*. I was beginning to feel like I'd accidentally been erased by the Big Computer or something. So I watched more TV and sent down to room service for food and put it on the bill.

I didn't wait for midnight. I went out about seven o'clock when it got dark, and it wasn't raining! Hooray! A point for me. I looked up in the sky, and I saw maybe three stars. That's all. People in New York don't realize there're a whole lot of stars they're missing out on. New York kids must be scared out of their punky, wiseass little minds if they ever get out into the country and look up at the night sky. "Hey, what the hell are *those*?" they go. "Stars," somebody tells 'em. "Nuh-uh. How come we don't got that many on 125th Street ?" they go. "Because that's God punishing you for covering all the subway cars with spray paint."

I have become aware of social problems, Bitsy, believe it or not. You'll hear all about it. In the past four years, I've learned a lot about right and wrong. I'm dead set against certain things now. For one, I'm not Muffy anymore. No, no way, Monet. I'm Maureen and I'm proud of it. Maureen's my name, my real name. Muffy was my slave name. It's what all those Columbia math majors called me. No more, kiddo.

And you've changed a little, too, haven't you? I looked around for something to drink—no vodka, no rum, no tequila. That's not the old Blitsy-Bitsy Spiegelman *I* remember. A little new Beaujolais in the kitchen and some classy-looking whites—you've been reading those *magazines* again, honey. And that picture on the table—*Bitsy*! For crying out loud, do you realize you've cut your hair exactly the same way as my mother's *Lhasa apso*? And what's with the funky, stretched-out sweatshirt hanging off your shoulder? You look like you can't afford your own clothes and have to raid Goodwill boxes at night. Times change, I guess. From looking around, I think I want to get out of here *real* fast. But, as your mother says, "As long as you've got your health." I notice you don't have the Captain and Tennille records I gave you anymore. The Knack and Shaun Cassidy albums are missing too; now there are a few *black faces* peeping out of your stereo cabinet. Why, Bitsy, how sophisticated of you! Our tastes just keep on broadening, don't they? Is the kid with sunglasses and the glittery glove the one who sings with his brothers? He still doesn't look old enough to be let out by himself. I mean, his voice hasn't changed or anything.

Where was I? Oh, yeah. Well, I went to Central Park and looked for the darkest, loneliest place I could find. I don't know, maybe it was the sight of me with my genuine leather bag in one hand and a long jeweled sword in the other, but nobody bothered me. Somewhere around Sixty-eighth Street, I looked up into the sky again. There were more stars here—about six more. I hoped one of those dots of light was Mars. I clutched my bag and my sword, closed my eyes tighty-tight, and projected myself headlong into space. It's a trick you learn. The first time is just an accident, but then you stumble on how to do it whenever you want. You just sort of throw yourself across this creepy-cold distance between Earth and, like, wherever.

Steering is another matter entirely, honey, let me tell you. *Forget* what they've told you, it's *not* all in the wrist. I mean, when I tried to get from Mars to Vermont, I ended up in Manhattan. This time, trying to whush myself back to Mars, I ended up—

You're not going to believe this—

I landed inside the hollow Earth.

Don't ask me how I could aim at the sky and land five hundred miles below the dead brown grass of Central Park. I'm not sure. And you're going to have to forget (if you haven't already) all about Mr. Reuven's lectures about the Earth's crust and the mantle and the molten core and so on and on. I knew I was *inside*, because there was rock all around and above me where the sky should be, and the far, hazy distances lifted up to meet the roof. Overhead there was some kind of blazing little sun that never went out—it was always daytime; but it was the kind of light that makes you look like you've been dead for a week. It wasn't like real sunlight. I was there for four years and I didn't get the beginning of a tan, even though I didn't wear any more clothes than I did on Mars.

I was in the middle of a big forest—a jungle, really, and the trees were covered with hanging vines and bright, beautiful flowers climbing up the trunks. Orchids, I think, though they were shaped funny and were strange colors. Everything in this place was shaped funny, I came to realize, and was a funny color. I wandered around in the jungle for a little while, just staring at the birds and monkeys and butterflies and flowers. It was hot. Let me tell you, it was as hot as your mother's apartment was that Fourth of July when your A.C. went out and you couldn't get anybody to come fix it on the holiday. I was sweating the proverbial bullets. I said to myself, I go, "Muffy"—see, I wasn't socially aware yet; it took four years of suffering and hardship to teach me those lessons—I go "Muffy, you know what would be nice? Let's change into something a little cooler." I had in mind a pair of khaki shorts and a Ralph Lauren polo shirt and my old Tretorn tennis sneaks. So I opened my suitcase and took off my winter stuff—you have to picture this in your mind, Bitsy, step-by-step—and I was rummaging around, looking for the right outfit, when out from behind this tree stepped this ape.

Well, I screamed. *You'd* scream, too. I was naked. I'd never *been* naked in front of an ape before.

He galumphed toward me with his knuckles on the ground, carrying some dead animal in his mouth. Behind him came maybe twenty more apes. I told myself not to be terrified; I'd faced bigger monsters on Mars, and these huge old monkeys were probably just as scared of me as I was of them. That's what they always say on TV. Marlin Perkins is always going like, "These huge old monkeys of the deep jungle look fearsome, but in truth they are gentle browsers and vegetarians." Then I thought, why the hell does it have this dead *thing* in its mouth if it's a vegetarian?

I stood very still, wishing I could reach down and pick up my sword, Old Betsy, but I didn't dare move, The big ape came right up to me and stopped. He stared at me and, believe me sweetie, I didn't like the evil red eyes he'd got set into his flat little head. They were going up and down my body like I was Miss Anthropoid of 1980. I heard Marlin Perkins' voice in my head again: "These harmless cousins of ours are curious by nature, and will rape and pillage anything in their path."

Well, I stood still until that goddamn ape slowly reached out a hand, just like in *2001*, and almost grabbed my boob.

Nobody grabs my boob. That's when I went for the sword. *Whip.* I was standing straight and fierce and beautiful, ready to defend my honor if I had to skewer all twenty of them. The ape gives me this beady stare. Then it goes *ptui* and spits out the dead animal. "What are you doing in Yag-Nash's territory?" he goes. In pretty good English, yet (with just a trace of a regional accent, but let's not get snobby). I'd been astonished to find that people on Mars spoke English. Now these apes or ape-men or whatever they were did the same thing. Don't ask me to explain it: I'm just a fighting woman.

I go, "Nothing. I come in peace." I took it that this was Yag-Nash himself I was dealing with.

Another of these talking Neanderthals came up and looked me over, the same as Yag-Nash had, and goes, "Let's kill the she now. The little feathered snake will not feed the whole tribe." It kicked at the scruffy dead thing on the ground.

"No," goes Yag-Nash, "the she will not die. The tribe of Yag-Nash has had bad hunting since the death of the High Priestess. This beautiful she will be our new High Priestess." All the other ugly, hairy brutes opened their eyes wide and started going, "Ohhhhh."

"Thank you for saving my life," I go.

"Don't mention it," goes Yag-Nash. They were real Missing Links, Bitsy. I wish they'd stayed Missing.

I breathed a little easier, but I didn't lower my sword. Something I learned on Mars: don't trust anybody except handsome princes; *especially* don't trust horrible blechy things from *The Twilight Zone.* I didn't like being all pink and perky and undressed in front of these hairballs, but I couldn't get my clothes on and keep them covered at the same time. My problem was solved for me by ol' Yag-Nash, the leader of the pack.

"Bring her along to the caves," he goes. And the twenty of them swarmed all over me, and grabbed my arms and legs and lifted me off the ground. I hung on to Old Betsy, but she didn't do me any good, you know? I didn't have a chance to get in a good whack at any of them. They kept up this weirdo moaning chant as they carried me through the jungle. I twisted my head a little, and I saw that none of them had thought to bring along my suitcase. Goodbye, new outfits; good-bye, *Je Reviens.* And after all that hard shopping we did too. I never *did* get to wear any of that stuff.

When we got to their place—it was like this cliff with caves poked into it like the little holes in a slice of rye bread—they carried me up to the main cave. I don't know how they climbed that cliff. It sure looked sheer and smooth to me. But then, *I* don't have arms that swing below my knees, or fighting fangs either. We human beings have lost a little something to make up for what we've gained on our Long March Toward Civilization. Thank the Lord.

When they deposited me on the floor of the main cave—*ba-WHUMP*—Yag-Nash gestured and the rest of them left in a hurry. He looked down at me with those cruddy little beady eyes of his. He drooled, Bitsy, he really *drooled.* Like my Uncle Jerry.

I go, "You didn't bring my clothes along. You have anything here for me to wear?"

His expression went blank for a second, then he must have had what passed for an idea in his little pea-brain. "I will garb you with the richness and finery of last High Priestess," he goes. "You will like Yag-Nash then. You will be *grateful.*"

"You bet," I go. I shuddered a little.

The boss ape hustled out on his short, bowed legs. I had a few minutes to myself, but so what? The main cave was huge, but it didn't lead anywhere and I couldn't climb down that cliff by myself. I was trapped up there. I clutched Old Betsy and waited. A little while later my pal came back, carrying a double armload of stuff. He dropped it at my feet. "What's that?" I go.

"Wear," he goes instructively.

I sorted through the stuff. At first it looked like a hopeless mess of tangled braids and straps. I couldn't make heads or tails out of it. I carried it all to the light at the mouth of the cave and I gasped, like, Bitsy, it was all *gold* and *jewels*! I mean, *all* of it! There was this bra kind of thing with dangling golden loops and chains and thingies hooked up front to back and all, and a sexy little G-string of gold with a thin little gold hip-band. Wow, if I'd have had that stuff on some football weekend up in New Haven…! And the gold was just lousy with jewels. *Covered* with jewels, all emeralds, some as big as a quarter. "This is for *me*?" I go.

"Wear," Yag-Nash goes. He was the strong, silent type.

I put it on. Well, gold is nice to look at and appraise and all, but it's not much fun to live in. The bra wasn't lined or anything, and the metal edges dug into my skin. The girl who had it before me must have been two full cup-sizes smaller, 'cause my boobs were all squashed together and hauled up almost to my shoulders. Did *terrific* things for my cleavage, but it was uncomfortable as all hell. And the metal G-string was *cold.* Yipe.

"Good," goes Yag-Nash, when I had, uh, garbed myself.

"Glad you like it," I go. "*Now* what?"

"We hunt again tomorrow. Before we hunt, you must pray to the Great Rock Sky-God!"

"Sure," I said. I knew that was breaking some commandment or something, but desperate times call for desperate measures.

"Now you sleep."

I go, "But I'm not tired. I'll wait until tonight."

"What do you mean, 'night'?"

Then I realized, like, it wasn't *ever* going to get dark. The little sun in the middle of the Earth never set. So much for sneaking away after the sun went down, as if there were anywhere to sneak *to*. I stretched out on the cave floor—it was just crawling with bugs and spiders, of course—and after a while, I don't know how long, I went to sleep.

I had a surprise when I woke up. Yag-Nash had shackled my right ankle and chained me to the wall. "Great," I thought, "that's all I need." Like it made any difference, though before, at least I had the *illusion* of freedom. I still had my sword. The only thing I could figure out was that Yag-Nash didn't recognize Old Betsy as a weapon. He may never have seen a sword before. I hoped I could make him more familiar with it Real Soon Now.

Hours later, I suppose, Yag-Nash came back into the cave huffing and puffing from the climb up the rock face. "It is time, O High Priestess," he goes.

"Well," I thought, "*every* High Priestess has to start sometime." Yag-Nash held something in his hand. His attitude was different now: he was respectful, almost timid. I looked at what he was offering me—it was a big golden crown set with emeralds and huge diamonds. I could have bought Massachusetts, furnished, with that, for God's sake. I took it and plopped it on my head. Then Yag-Nash threw me over his shoulder without a word, not so much as an "Excuse me, Exalted One," and started down the cliff. I shut my eyes and practiced praying.

There was a sort of flat altar made of roughly shaped rock, about a hundred yards into the jungle. The rest of the tribe—I guess there were about a hundred in all—was spread through the big clearing, and they were all chanting and grunting and jumping up and down on their knuckles. It was *disgusting*. Yag-Nash walked into the middle of the clearing, by this altar thing, and raised his furry arms. "Silence!" he goes.

There was silence.

Then it was *my* turn. I went up to the altar and looked around at my congregation. I put a stern look on my face—see, I figured from Yag-Nash's change in attitude that as High Priestess I was some big hoo-ha now, and I wanted to see how far I could push it. "First off," I go in a kind of cop voice, loud and commanding, "I don't want you to call me the High Priestess. 'Priestess' is a sexist label. I won't have any of that. You will call me Reverend Maureen."

The Neanderthals nodded their huge, lumpy heads. "Mo-reen," they murmured.

"That's fine. Now as I understand it, you're about to go on another hunt today. I will say a prayer for your success. I will invoke the blessing of the Great Rock Sky-God on you. I will bring you meat for your hungry, hairy bellies. You will treat me with deference."

"Mo-reen," they all go.

"Damn right." Then I went into the prayers, something like, "Heavenly Father, we are gathered here together to ask your blessing on our hunters. Today they go out in search of food for their shes and their young ones. Game is scarce, and the animals are fleet of foot or cunning. Our hunters are neither, and they are armed only with these cruddy stone knives that couldn't stab their way through a wet newspaper. What's more, our hunters don't have the largest cranial capacities, if you know what I mean—and *they don't*, or I'd be in trouble now. Therefore, we ask that you make it easy on them. A few deer or something trapped in a tar pit would be nice. I don't expect miracles, but look, *I* get hungry, too, right? I guess that's about all. Thanking you in advance, this is Reverend Maureen, signing off."

"Amen," murmured the cavemen.

Yag-Nash goes, "You pray good, Mo-reen. You are a good High—I mean, a good Reverend."

I shrugged. "It's a gift," I go. "I will bring you much meat. I will end hunger and want among the tribe of Yag-Nash."

"Good," he goes.

"And you will treat me well."

The pot-bellied old creep gave me that slimy squint again. "You will like the way Yag-Nash treats you," he goes. I doubted that very seriously. He grabbed me and carted me out of the clearing, back to the main cave and the shackle and chain. I complained, but it didn't do any good. And he took the crown, too. *That's* the kind of man I attract, Bitsy, ain't it the truth? He left me in the cave all alone, secured to the wall. From far away I could hear the shouts of the hunters as they worked themselves up into a sweat.

Well, this kind of thing went on for one hell of a long time. They'd feed me and bring me water, but that was all. No washing, no exercise, *nothing.* I was wasting away. Every couple of "days," Yag-Nash would carry in the crown and trundle me down the cliff to the altar, where I said a prayer and everybody acted subdued and courteous for a few minutes. Then it was back to the cave and the chain and Maureen Birnbaum, Prisoner of Love. The funny thing was, the hunters *did* have better luck. They came back with lots of meat, or else I suppose they'd have killed—and maybe eaten—*me.* I figure that's what happened to the last High Priestess. Yucko. The hunters brought back these big old reindeer and musk oxen and things. I mean, animals you don't find walking around the woods on the surface anymore. The reindeer and oxen were *gigantic.* They were prehistoric animals, just like Yag-Nash and his crew. I knew that for sure when they brought in the wooly mammoth. You could tell it wasn't just a plain old elephant: it was a *mammoth.* And they killed other weird critters, too: saber-toothed tigers and beavers the size of bears and sloths as big as hippos. But my congregation had a lot to learn about the fine points of the culinary arts: *Cuisine Primitif,* you know, the Food of the Clods. Fire-blackened here and there on the outside, bloody raw on the inside. I was hungry all the time, so I got to where I liked it that way.

After this went on for many months—I filled up the wall as far as I could reach with "daily" scratches—Yag-Nash came into the cave in a real dither. I'd kept him away from me by telling him that if he put one paw on my reverend bod, the Great Rock-Sky God would punish him by driving away all the game. Yag-Nash was hungry more often than he was horny, so I didn't have to worry about him except when his dim bulb of a brain forgot my threat. When he came in all excited, I figured, "Here we go again."

I was wrong. He goes, "We have captured an enemy."

This was some news. I mean, I didn't even *know* there was another tribe anywhere nearby. "Uh-huh," I go.

"It is a morthak, not like Yag-Nash and his people. You must sacrifice it to the Great Rock-Sky God."

"Sacrifice?" Bitsy, I can't even bring myself to squish a goddamn *cockroach.* On Mars I lopped some heads off these big green men, but that was purely self-defense. Cutting out hearts on an altar is something else. I didn't know what a morthak was, but whatever it was, I didn't think I could kill it.

"The morthak must die," Yag-Nash goes, "or *you* will take its place."

Well, on second thought, maybe this prehistoric world *could* get along without a crummy morthak one way or the other.

Yag-Nash gave me the glitzy crown and I put it on, then he unlocked me and tossed me over his shoulder and we made our way down the cliff. I'd gotten pretty used to it by now, you know? I didn't have to close my eyes anymore. I even kept up a pleasant stream of chatter. I mean, I didn't have all that many "people" to talk to. Not that Yag-Nash was the most scintillating conversationalist. His idea of a snappy comeback was "Gruh!"

I had another surprise waiting for me when we got to my altar. A "Morthak" turned out to be like a good-looking boy with a fearless smile to *die* for. I *mean* it, Bitsy. This guy made Prince Van look like Ernest Borgnine or something. He wasn't blond and he didn't have blue eyes, but you can't have *everything*. He was wearing this navy blue jumpsuit, so I knew he probably came from up on the surface too. In all the time I'd been in the center of the Earth, I hadn't seen anybody else like me. A *person*, you know? So I stood beside the altar where they had this gorgeous specimen tied down, and I go, "Where did you go to school?"

He looked at me all surprised. "Nathanael West High in New York," he goes.

I was a little disappointed. I go, "Oh, like a *public school* kid." Well, *everybody* can't go to Andover or Exeter or Lawrenceville. I mean, there are probably rich and powerful corporation executives who started out in some public school system and showed a lot of potential and made their way on smarts and ambition. But, see, I wasn't interested in a guy with just *promise*. I was looking for somebody who had more to fall back on than a cute little tush.

"You know the world I come from?" he goes.

I had to laugh. "*I* come from the world you come from," I go. "If I was still there and hadn't had all these adventures and everything, I'd be a senior at the Greenberg School."

He goes, "I have a sort of friend whose sister goes to the Greenberg School."

"Oh, really?" I go. "What's her name?"

"Jennifer Freeman. She's a sophomore."

"Oh, well," I go, drawing myself up kind of haughtily, "we don't hang out with *sophomores*."

"My name is Rod Marquand," he goes. "I'm pleased to meet you."

"I'm—"

I was rudely interrupted by Yag-Nash. He pushed a golden knife in my hands and growled "Kill him."

"What?" I go. "*Him*?"

"Kill."

"Hey, look. I thought he was going to be this *morthak* or something. I can't kill a live human being."

"Kill him or die yourself."

This Rod guy goes, "Go ahead, then, young lady. If *that's* the situation, please, save yourself. I'll die happily, knowing that you're safe." What a sweet, brave boy. If only he didn't go to public school.

"I can't do that," I go.

Yag-Nash was furious. "Take them both back to the cave!" And the tribe grabbed us and hauled us up to the main cave. I was shackled and Rod was tied up hand and foot. Just before he left, Yag-Nash turned to me and goes, "You'll die a horrible death, Moreen. You will fill the belly of Yag-Nash!" And he laughed, sort of. It was *awful*.

When we were alone, Rod looked at me and smiled. "Thanks for not killing me," he goes.

"You're very welcome, I'm sure. Look where it got me."

"Don't be alarmed, Miss. I'll get us out of here. I came here in an atomic subterrine. We'll escape in that."

"What is it?" I go. It sounded like a tiny soup bowl that ran on atomic power.

"It's a submarine that moves through solid rock instead of water. I built it myself. I'm a kind of inventor," he goes.

"Great, but we're stuck up here a million feet off the goddamn ground."

"Don't worry about that either. When I'm not inventing or going to school, I also fight crime in the guise of a costumed superhero. I can't tell you my secret identity. I'm sorry."

"That's O.K.," I go. I mean, Bitsy, this kid had *promise* the way most guys have obnoxious *ideas*, if you get what I mean.

"Close your eyes," he goes. I did. I heard this popping sound, and when I opened my eyes again, his ropes were lying on the floor of the cave and he was *gone*.

A little while later I heard this humming noise, and a periscope poked up through the floor about twenty feet away. It turned around a little and pointed at me for a second. Then the top part of the submar—I mean, subterrine—surfaced. Rod opened the hatch and climbed out. "How do you like her?" he goes. He was real proud of it, you could tell.

"She's terrific—get me the hell *out* of here!"

"Sure." He came over and snapped my shackle like it was a stolen credit card.

"I'd kind of like to take my crown with me," I go. I really didn't want to go without it. I mean, I have my old age to plan for.

"We can't take the chance. We'll have to leave it behind." Why is it that heroes are so goddamn *practical*? I just *knew* he was going to say that. Anyway, there was enough gold and emeralds in what I was wearing to support me for a while. I shrugged. I can be realistic when I want. So he helped me up the ladder and into this cramped ship of his. He closed the hatch and started punching buttons and turning wheels. There was an incredible rocking motion like the A train between Fifty-ninth Street and 125th Street. I thought I was going to *tossez mes doughnuts* right there or something. "We're making good speed," Rod goes.

"Wonderful." I felt sick as the proverbial dog.

Well, Bitsy, it was a rough ride home. There weren't any windows because there was only rock going by. I mean, I *suppose* Rod's invention was brilliant and amazing and all, but it will be a long time before the guy books *cruises* or anything. The Love Boat it ain't—in more ways than one. I'll have to tell you *all* about this Rod Marquand sometime. He was dedicated, Bitsy. I mean *dedicated. To science and fighting crime. He figured we were almost home, see, and I go, "Why don't we have lunch or something?" He turned me down,* sweeties, do you believe *that*? His uncle, the physicist, would be waiting for a report, and besides, there was a whole rash of unsolved crimes recently in New York, and he owed it to his parents to hurry right home, and by then I told him to just *forget* it.

"Where are we now?"

"We're just passing through the lowest level of Penn Station," he goes.

"You can let me out here," I go. I was in a *huff.* Look, not even this boy genius can turn down Mo-reen, She-God of the Muck People.

"But—"

"*Let me out!*" I go, kind of brandishing Old Betsy. I was frustrated that I never did get my licks in against Yag-Nash, and I was just *dying* to start a fight.

Rod stopped the machine and opened the hatch. I squeezed on by him and went up the ladder and looked around. We were now on the second level, not far from the escalator that takes you up to Thirty-Fourth Street. I looked down at Rod and I go, "You better sail on out of here, honey, people are gawking." Then I climbed down the outside of the ladder. The hatch clanged behind me, and the subterrine dived into the floor. I walked toward the escalator, swishing my sword in little angry circles. People got out of my way, *fast.*

I had to walk to the diamond district, but it wasn't that far. You should have seen the looks I got from the old guys in the place I went into! I mean, wearing this golden bra and G-string and slashing around with

Old Betsy and all. I wonder what I looked like to them. I pried a little emerald out of my raiment and sold it. They gave me a big song and dance about how illegal it all was, but I could see they wanted to get their greedy hands on the emerald and all the rest of it. They offered me a hundred bucks—like I was from out of town, right? I laughed. It was like dickering with Pammy, my stepmother. I ended up getting my price for it, but only by promising that I wouldn't let anyone else buy any of the other jewels. The emeralds are rare and perfect or something. I was going to pay you back the money I owed you out of that cash—see, I *didn't* forget—but when you went on your vacation instead of seeing me, I figured "The hell with *her.*" Instead, you'll find a nice-sized emerald on your coffee table, and let you go through all the red tape trying to explain where you got it and everything. If you ever do, pay your mother back for me.

The tape's about finished, Bitsy. I'll see you when you get back from your trip. I hope you're sunburned as hell.

Well, she wasn't there when I got back. There were only the tape cassette, the emerald, and one god-awful mess in the kitchen. You'd have thought the Marines had camped out there on their way to the Halls of Montezuma or something. I can't imagine why Muffy—I mean, Maureen—didn't wait for me. She must have this itch for adventure now, I guess, and went whushing off to some new aggravation somewhere, sometime.

Speaking of aggravation, I got more than she bargained for with that god-damn emerald. I mean, I almost did time in jail on account of it. I'm still not square with the IRS or anybody. I really want to talk to Maureen about that, believe me. Sword or no sword, she's going to walk out of here with at least a bloody nose.

With any kind of luck, I'll hear from her soon. It will be worth having to sit through her whole stupid recitation to paste her one in the face. I can't wait.

Bill Wallace and Joe Pumilia

Back in 1976, Bill Wallace and Joe Pumilia created the H. P. Lovecraft parody figure, M. M. Moamrath, and science fiction had its answer to P.D.Q. Bach. A lot of the material consisted of little sidebars and paragraphs that worked in the magazine format where it first appeared, but would be somewhat mystifying in book form—but I am pleased to be able to reprint Moamrath's one cowboy story, a compendium of his most famous closing lines, and a collection of his serious poetry.

THE WORKS OF M. M. MOAMRATH

Besides his typical weird mythos tales, Moamrath also did a number of off-trail, change-of-pace stories which seem to suggest that, for him at least, supernatural horror was inherently incompatible with scientifiction (The Pawns of Marzoom), detective fiction (The Maltese Trapezohedron), jungle adventure (The Thing in the Trees), boy-girl romance (Pickman's Motel), sword & sorcery (The Gent from the River Styx and other stories in the Mitra McCrom series), Caucasian superiority fiction (The Shuffler from the Stars), the opium addiction story (The Strange High in the Mist), and occult adventure (Harry Houdini—Revivifier), just to mention a few genres which Moamrath infected with his literary contagion.

The present story, one of several in the Zane Offwhite series, further extended his ineptness into the western story. It appeared in the April, 1933 issue of Weird Trails, then edited by Max Gibber who, some years later, was found dissolved under mysterious circumstances.

+

RIDERS OF THE PURPLE OOZE

by M. M. Moamrath

THE SQUAMOUS LUNARY SPHERE gibbered its leprous beams over the shambling Apache village under the hideous dewlap of the mesa, just past the arroyo where Dead Man's Creek is wont to gurgle after spring rains. The angular shadows of the tipis and wigiwams seemed to slumber abhorrently in the necrophilious illumination. In the distance perverted coyotes howled at the waning sun nameless chants that were old when mankind was only worms squirming on the shores of the Permean sea. Elsewhere across the plains, normal coyotes howled nameless chants at the rising moon.

It was into this dread scenario that Buck Eldritch came riding on his cayuse, in his saddle bags an Apache transliteration of the dreaded *Negrognomicon* of the insane Bantu pygmy medicine man, Bundolo Kreegah. He hoped he wouldn't have to use it. He had learned from Capt. Jedidiah Gibber at Fort Archaic that Jake "Wild Willie" Cryptos was stirring up the Apaches with some sort of bull sweat about the return of the old Indian Elderly Gods, but it was the opinion of Sheriff Swiftie Thanatops that there might be something in that talk of aetherial powers after all.

"After all," Thanatops had allowed as they sipped suds at the Long Branch, "my grandma was part Mescalero and some of the tales she told me made my hair spin."

Buck was here to find out the truth. Little did Thanatops know that Buck was his distant kin, having the same grandmother, a septuagenarian crone called in Apache, "The One Who Gibbers Abhorrently In Leprous Moonlight." As Buck well knew, Granny was not named that for nothing.

It was nigh sundown when he pulled up his maverick at the Rocking Skull Ranch, now operated by Widder Skull and her two young 'uns, Num and Abner. While Buck tied up his steed at the hitching post, he examined the horizon with his mystic tetrahedron, dredged up from sunken P'u by Roman sponge divers in the year zero, shortly after the second siege of Cacciatore (Uno Maximus Mixupis, or The Big Mixup), disappearing for several years, to surface again in the court of Pharaoh Hehahotep IV, and vanishing again for six centuries after the Hyksos' remarkable recovery from supposed extinction. Buck had obtained it by chance through a stroke of luck, having won it in a faro game in Saskatchewan from a mysterious Oriental.

Buck went over the old Indian legends in his mind, legends of certain things lurking beyond the barbed wire fences of the universe...the dreaded T'on'to and the abominable Bison Thing, B'uffalo B'Hob...things that stirred memories of nightmares dreamed by ancient ancestors. Buck was only too well aware of his position as the sole defender of the West against these Red horrors.

He ascended the porch and knocked at the door of the ranch-house. It was answered by an Indian servant who regarded him with curiously malevolent eyes. This, Buck knew, was Minniewahwah, who had faithfully served the Skulls for seven generations or more. Before that she was said to have been in the service of a mysterious stranger calling himself Zane Offwhite. She showed Buck to the sitting room where he waited, and thereafter to the waiting room where he sat for a while chewing his tobacco and spitting into what he assumed was a spittoon. Only after the brass-plated object scuttled off into an opening under the player piano did he apprehend that things were not all they appeared to be.

A creaking board behind him signaled the arrival of a nameless presence. Turning, he saw it was Abner Skull. He recognized him from the old rock carvings on Dead Man's Rock. The man was abnormally tall with a protuberant proboscis and ears resembling nothing more than the outcrop of rimrock at Hanged Man's Canyon. His eyes were cavernous with no living glimmers within. His moustache was more tentacular than hairy and Buck was certain that one of the countless flies milling around that region was snatched from sight by some blurred stringy object.

"Yew thet Eld'rich feller?" asked Skull in a voice that seemed to come from the deepest pits of Dead Man's Mine itself.

"I was sent here by Capt. Gibber to check out the Apache situation," said Buck, his right thumb caressing the hammer of his silver-plated .45.

"Yew shouldn't have oughta cum. We dun't cotton to strangers roun' here. They's things—" He paused, looking over his shoulder. "I've already sed tew much."

"I wonder if the Widder Skull's to home."

"Who?"

"Your mother."

"Oh, yeh. Her. She passed on nigh two weeks agone. Injuns got 'er. Cut 'er up for jerky and hung 'er on the fence to dry. We got most o' her in the smokehouse now. No sense wastin' none."

The effect of this unexpected revelation unaccountably filled Buck with nameless dread. This sense of foreboding was further increased by Skull's next statement.

"Reckon yew'll hev ta best be movin' along. It's getting on nightfall and we 'uns got to mosey th' critters on down to New Lemuria."

"New Lemuria? Where's that?"

"Jest south o' New P'u. Goin' south, yew jest make a right turn at the anomaly."

"I never heard of moving cows at night," said Buck.

"Cows? Who said anything about cows?"

Less than an hour later by his clepsydra, Buck and his mount were waiting along the trail to New Lemuria as the Skull boys and several Mexicans moved the skull herd south. In the leprous moonlight it was hard to tell just what sort of herd was being moved. To the unclad eye it seemed that the lunar beams were filtering down onto the surface of some slick slimy substance. It was necessary to catch a look through his trusty tetrahedron. What he saw nearly sent his mind reeling and gibbering drunkenly over the rimrock of chaos into ghoul-haunted regions of madness.

For there, passing below the cliffs, leaving a trail of oozing purple slime in their wake, snorting and puffing like vitreous aquaeous humors subjected to the thermal pressures of an aeolipile, was such an accumulation of horrors as had never before been seen upon the terraquaeous globe! *It was a veritable unending stream of suggoths!*

Suggoths!

The very word struck a chord of terror in the cardiovascular organ of any recluse antiquarian with a penchant for the occult. Buck, a master of the occult in his own rite, was only too aware of the meaning of this horror. For the presence of the suggoths, hybrid amorphous creatures whose body in the forepart is that of a cockroach and in the hindpart that of a slug, and once used by the inhabitants of ancient Fuggoth as paperweights, could only signify one thing....Somewhere out beyond the rimrock of primordial chaos, in the vast badlands of the interstellar void, the Fuggothians still existed and were planning to return from their exile beyond the borders of time and space, imposed on them eons ago by S'Mucch, High Sheriff of the Aetherial Void.

It was in that instant that Buck realized that only one man stood between the Fuggothians and the destruction of the world as we know it. The Skulls, he realized, were agents of the Fuggothians. As he pondered his unenviable position, the thundering herd of suggoths oozed below him toward their abhorrent destination.

He followed them stealthily on his faithful nag, and it was while the herd sucked their fill at Obed Creek that Ngaio Marsh, a halfbreed indian, met with his Skull brothers in parley.

It was easy for Buck to see that Ngaio's other half was Fuggothian. It was the way the halfbreed had to ride side-saddle, with his pale slimy slug-like lower quarters dangling to the side. Buck was unable to hear what they were saying, but caught the names of Yuchkkoth the Beclouder, and Schlusch, Lord of Slime. The halfbreed then removed something from his saddlebags and gave it to Abner Skull. It appeared to be some sort of scroll. Following the foregoing, Ngaio was given payment in firewater and whooped into the hills half astride his pony.

Several hours of hard riding later, Buck watched from the shadowed rimrock above New Lemuria as the suggoths were herded aboard the boxcars of the Wendigo, Dunwent & Gone, which connected New Lemuria with some nameless region beyond a localized veil of eternal mist into which the narrow gauge tracks disappeared several miles out of town. Buck knew that if he was to prevent the range war between the Elderly Gods and the inhabited southwest, he would have to sneak aboard that train.

After checking the chambers of his twin .45s, he shambled down the cliff and slipped stealthily aboard the caboose just as the train pulled out. A quarter of an hour later a wall of mist loomed before him as the landscape was lost in obscurity. Buck sensed motion, but the familiar clickety-clack of the rails seemed muffled.

Then the black mouth of the tunnel loomed ahead. Buck could remember no hills or mountains in this area. As soon as his eyes became accustomed to the darkness, he perceived numerous twinned sets of glowing orbs, which he took to be eyes. Even as he recalled what the *Negrognomicon* said about things with glowing eyes, he recognized the squat, leprous shapes moving along walkways and niches carved into the tunnel walls, manipulating strange scientifictional machinery that could only have been produced by a super-science far beyond that of man. He knew then that he was in the realm of the dreaded Choo-Choo people, the best trained of the Elderly Gods' minions, who live or otherwise inhabit abandoned railroad tunnels and trestles, usually in Tibet.

Then he was no longer in the tunnel (which he now realized was a hyperspacial connection of some sort) and was back in the mist once more.

Moments later the train had pulled to a halt, and before he could get his bearings by counting the suns, he heard a noise behind him.

Poking over the edge of the caboose roof was Num Skull.

"Hold 'er rhat thar, boah. Jest unbuckl' yer belt and drap yer hardware. Now climb down offn this caboosie."

Buck perforce obeyed with a grim reluctance, promising himself that he would bushwhack Skull and escape at the first opportunity.

He was taken inside the caboose, still without having glimpsed any details of his environs. There he was securely lashed to a potbelly stove with moistened rawhide. Skull gloated all the while as Minniewahwah tied Buck up. In those dark Indian eyes lurked an unsettling gleam of ancient madness. Also, she was licking her chops.

"Reckon yew bit offn more'n yew kin chaw," drawled Skull, removing a pack of chewing tobacco from his pocket. He held it up to his lips where it was engulfed by the writhing tentacles of his moustache, which began to exude an unpleasant brown fluid that collected on his lower lip before dripping off his chin in large, greasy brown gobbets.

Skull then turned from his captive and sat down at a table with the scroll-like object Ngaio had given him. The Indian woman returned to the end of the car where she began sharpening knives and cutting herbs for supper. Turning his full attention to Skull, Buck watched him unroll the scroll. The end of it was rounded and its surface was strangely coated. Written on it were innumerable pictogryphs, hieroglyphs, inscriptions, and other cryptic marks. Buck easily recognized these as variations of the Elder Tongue.

But it was only after Skull had completely unrolled the object to its full length of nine feet that Buck understood that not only was it *written* in the Elder Tongue, but it was an elder tongue itself, probably that of Phyzzwigget, the one-eyed bohemian god who burbles and belches meaningless nothings as he hovers intoxicated at the center of chaos, attended by Durward and Kirby, two tone deaf sycophants with a proclivity for bad jive, by means of which they appease their master, The Howler Beyond the Outside.

But most important, as Buck read the dreaded script over Skull's shoulder, he could see that this was nothing less than a detailed outline whereby the Fuggothians would take over the earth.

He shuddered inwardly. Fuggothians! The very word made his mind reel with unspeakable loathing. They were native to a planet in the constellation of the Beetle, Alpha Insectus, where they engaged in various nefarious activities and dastardly pursuits under the thirteen blazing suns.

They were remarkably ugly, being part crab, part alligator, part lobster, and a little bit cocker spaniel. Their brains were completely controlled by the dreaded Fungi of Fuggoth, which were at war with streptococcus aurelius and other terrestrial micro-organisms in league with Nerg-Blavvath, Hare of a Thousand Young, for control of earth itself.

Prodded by fear, Buck's thoughts raced ahead of themselves, tripping and sliding through the synapses of his cerebral cortex, and his mind reeled with the terrible knowledge that he, of all men now alive, knew the hideous secret behind the obscure limerick revealed by Bundolo Kreegah in Chapter 67 of the dreaded *Negrognomicon*:

> In a cavern under the earth,
> Old Nerg-Blavvath gave birth
> To a dog and a cat,
> A cow and a bat,
> And all without aid of a nurse.

As he watched Minniewahwah glancing over her shoulder, licking her chops while chopping herbs and sharpening knives, Buck wondered whether he would ever escape to pass word to Capt. Gibber. But at that moment, the moving train lurched to a halt, and the mist cleared. Buck counted thirteen suns shining through the window.

"Holy hot tamales!" he blasphemed involuntarily. If only he could free himself! But it was too late, for the crone was coming at him with the knife.

"Heh, I'll jest leave yew tew alone," drawled Skull. "I know yew have privat buznuz to dee-scus." He exited. Outside, Buck could hear the suggoths being unloaded. Undoubtedly the Skulls had been raising them on earth under an agreement with the Fuggothians to exempt the ranch and its inhabitants from the general massacre which would ensue when earth was invaded.

He knew it was curtains for him, but in the last moment before she plunged her knife down, Minniewahwah slipped in a puddle of tobacco juice and fell against the stove, her knife accidently slicing Buck's bonds. Recovering his twin six-shooters, he exited via the forward door, climbing atop the boxcars to creep from car to car toward the locomotive.

Only one minion stood guard there, a slouching, lazy-looking Choo-Choo, surely an atypical example of the species. With a swipe of his pearl-handled pistol, Buck laid him low and stuffed him into the fire grate. He then released the brake, turned up the steam, and threw the engine in reverse.

The consternation among the Fuggothians was immense. The spooked suggoths panicked and slithered off in all directions, crashing through fences and outbuildings, and as the train picked up speed, Buck picked off his confused assailants with neatly placed slugs from his .45s.

Then the train was enveloped in the weird mist, and once more the huge dark shape of the tunnel engulfed him. From somewhere came a rumble of thunder, and soon the tunnel mouth behind him was illuminated by the weird hellish lightning flashes, probably the result of the train's warping the space-time continuum.

And in the darkness of the hyperspacial tunnel, he could see the glowing eyes of the Choo-Choos glaring with surprise, and he watched them frantically throwing the switches of their weird Gernsbackian devices. He watched with horror as some of them leapt aboard the train from the tunnel walls.

Grimly, he drew his guns and blazed away with both barrels as they came at him. He watched with satisfaction as pair after pair of glowing eyes winked out, but they kept coming. Already they were scuttling over the coal car even as the train burst free of the tunnel.

Amazingly, it was raining, and bullwhips of lightning flailed the rumps of black thunderheads stampeding across the sky.

Apparently the space warp caused by the reversed train had been even more powerful than he realized. He thought he saw the eyes of the Choo-Choos exude fearful gleams as they looked about them, but then his guns ran out of bullets and he prepared to be overwhelmed by the vile alien horrors. Just then, when he had already consigned his spirit to that big tally book in the sky, angry lightning forked down from the heavens and blasted the Choo-Choos to smithereens. Then he smiled grimly, for he remembered the hitherto obscure reference of Kreegah to the Choo-Choos, "...It is said that the Choo-Choos are good conductors...."

But he was not yet safe. For there, whooping along the tops of the boxcars was Minniewahwah, brandishing a tomahawk. Just then, the crone's moccasins fortuitously slipped on the rain slick boxcar roof. And she fell, impaled on her weapon.

As Buck leaned over her, he saw she was trying to croak a message, and it was then he recognized something familiar in that batrachian visage.

"Doesn't Minniewahwah mean 'The One Who Gibbers Abhorrently in Leprous Moonlight'?" he asked.

"Yes, my little buckaroo," croaked the crone. "It is I, your Granny. And Ngaio was your half-brother."

"Don't try to talk, Granny," said Buck, a tear welling in his eye.

"Must—must talk," she wheezed, "must tell you—tell you—couplet—dreaded couplet—" Then she summoned her waning strength and in a burst of lucidity gibbered abhorrently in the leprous moonlight.

"That is not led which eternally follows.

And if you're in Capistrano look out for the swallows."

With that, she expired.

By sunup, Buck was back at New Lemuria, where his cayuse was waiting. He was surprised to find that Old Paint had somehow thrown a shoe from his left middle tentacle, but fortunately there was a blacksmith in town.

Oh, well, he thought, eyeing the rising sun, the day is shot anyhow. Kissing his cayuse tenderly on the mandibles, he led it away to the smithy.

"Well, you know what they say," he told Old Paint. "If you can't ride off into the sunset, don't ride off at all."

FAMOUS LAST LINES OF M. M. MOAMRATH

Unlike most authors, who construct stories from beginning to end, Moamrath used to sneak up on a story idea from behind, usually starting with a last line he considered sufficiently eldritch or revolting and then going on from there. Many stories thus constructed oddly enough, actually saw print.

Moamrath's "Commonplace book," found after his mysterious demise, contained a number of last lines that were never enshrined between covers. It is in the interest of serious scholarship that we have resurrected these last lines. Certainly they can do nothing to harm Moamrath's reputation that he himself did not do.

✦

It was then I knew that it was the *ventriloquist* and not the *dummy* who was the master! (From a story Moamrath planned to call "The Thing on the Knee")

"...No, please—go away! Oh, it is hideous, blasphemous! Yuffoth save me! *Ia, ia, mufn 'glui ungl ungl! My God, it is coming through the window...* that hideous, slavering maw...those yellow fangs...Owch! *That hurt!*

"Yes, Willie, for you see the old rag-picker claimed vengeance *from beyond the grave.*"

"No, Herr Krautmord, I am afraid I will not be able to attend this year's Wurstfest. You see, *I have been dead for six years!*"

...And as the door closed behind me for the last time, *I knew that it was oak!*

"Ia, gnufgn ph'unglooie, ia, ia, ungluflthn ungl, ungl, Kreegah!"

Lying there in the casket that had once held the remains of the mysterious M. de la Arronax were *six egg rolls!*

"You don't understand, Beaufingle," said Lungwort cryptically, "You *are* dinner."

"You see, Mr. Hopslip, you made one mistake. The man you were impersonating is *three feet tall!*"

"Even as I write this, that hideous, shambling monstrosity is climbing from the fire-grate, its congeries of lumineferous eyes glowering in malefic anticipation. As it oozes putrescently across the floor, it exudes a nauseous pseudopod which envelopes my foot and works its way up my leg, causing a sensation of excruciating agony. It would have been better, my dear Samantha, if you had heeded my warning after all. Yours in haste, Wendigo Peaslea, Ph.D."

For there, protruding from the horrible mass of bloated fungus that covered the door of the crypt, were *three limpid strands of spaghetti!*

And in the midst of the putrescent, leprous mass that oozed disgustingly from the vicar's carpetbag lay *Lashjoi's toupee!*

"My God, Hackenbush—woven into the fabric of the Sultan's throw-rug were *the small intestines of Mujio Shambula!*"

And as the boots walked silently out the cottage door, clearly visible at the tops were *the protruding tibias of James Elmo Freebish*!

"No, Earbrass, I shall never forget what I saw in Prof. Smightrusset's sitting room. That hideous goldfish bowl of jello—and eternally imprisoned in that gelatinous mass...*Wimpy, my pet goldfish*!"

As I stared at the eldritch face leering down at me, *I realized he was taller than I was*!

"And so you must never tell a soul, Wolfram. No, you must never tell them what I saw there in the intensive care ward, surrounded by doctors and nurses...*the still-living pancreas of Japie I. Sumphole*!"

"Curse? What curse?" he snorted, as the six-eyed demon flew down from the stars and ate him.

"Yes, Commissioner, I know it's hard to believe, but Farnsworth was right...*Lester Tamboolah had claimed vengeance from beyond the grave*!"

And so now I wonder—where and *what* is Jedidiah Malapope?"

"And that, Sir Reginald, is why we never walk on the moors at night."

Suddenly it all became clear even as the monster's jaws crunched into my throat...the torn handkerchief...old Elijah's reticence...the nameless, gibbering thing in Petrovich's herb cellar...Northam's drunken mutterings...the dwarf that had accosted me in Red Hook...Rifkin's strange wounds...the graffiti on the Pompeiian orrery...Father Cacciatore's nightmares...the thing in the cubby hole...*aaarrgh*!

"For God's sake, Hermitage," the letter finished, "destroy that blasphemous horror. Your friend, Neddy."

"Invisible, eh? Well, we'll see no more of him."

"Wait a minute," said Bodoni with a strange look on his face, "there are no slime gods in Hong Kong."

"Once I was known as Akbar Khan," hissed the thing that oozed disgustingly toward me from the unsealed urn.

"Only one thing bothers me, Farkenham...*what if it comes back?*"

"Ho ho, he he, my name is Phinki' Le," the thing gibbered.

The last thing my senses recorded was the thing's foul breath—*reeking of garlic, onion and other abhorrent herbs!*

The last thing I saw as the horror descended upon me was the horror... *descending upon me!*

And there on the tapeworm protruding from the mouth of the decomposing corpse was *the face of Jedidiah Eldridge!*

"I'm sorry, Mr. Caltrap, but the man you hired to haunt your house couldn't make it...hope it didn't spoil your party."

It's not so bad finding a pile of spaghetti and jello on your living room floor...*but when it calls you by name...!*

"That's one for the books, Mr. Fort."

M. M. MOAMRATH: THE FORGOTTEN BARD

edited by Joe Pumilia and Bill Wallace

Mortimer Morbius Moamrath, though long unnoted for his fiction, is also reviled for his poems, notably the limerick sequence *The Young Guy from Fuggoth*. Herewith a sampling from that 1935 *Archaic House* collection.

> In Massachusetts is a town called Archaic,
> Just a little bit north of Passaic.
>   Those who dwell there
>   Have scales 'stead o' hair,
> And consider it all quite prosaic.

In Archaic is a church somewhat unorthodox.
The pastor wears eight pairs of sox.
   They invoke something odd—
    They say it's their god—
That they keep locked away in a box.

It only comes out at night.
Rarely does it ever bite.
   But if it is riled,
    It may take a child,
And might even take his bike.

A tentacular elder monstrosity
With poisonous and pungent viscosity
   Ingested a vicar
    On his setee of wicker
While displaying a most rude animosity.

The maid's piercing scream split the air
When they found what was left of his chair.
   There were gobbets of ooze
    In his clothes, in his shooze,
And puddles all over the stair.

That night one of Jeremy's bugs
Tried to give his sister some hugs:
   He was fast shut away
    For a night and a day,
But was later avenged by her slugs.

Then Jeremy pondered his tomes,
While uttering astounding-type groans.
   He was shut fast away
    For a night and a day,
And a mysterious man claimed his bones.

But the corpse returned from the grave
To get the revenge it so craved.
   The murderer it slew,
    And flushed down the loo,
Although that was simply depraved.

Next day in the house on the hill,
They found William all stony and still.
    On his flesh was inscribed,
    How and why he had died,
So they stood around reading the Will.

With blood his clothing was sodden,
From the icepick stuck in his noggin.
    They thought he was dead,
    But his mouth gaped and said,
"Ph'nglui m'nglui wgah'hagl fhtagn."

Of a sudden in the circle of chalk,
Was a monster with eyes on a stalk.
    It leered in their faces
    And began to say graces,
They were very surprised it could talk.

The horror thereafter continued,
"Like worms in human gore imbued."
    Not a day would call
    Without its grand Guignol,
And no one was especially amused.

A demon, arrived straight from hell,
Had a most disagreeable smell.
    He ate lots of goats,
    His skin crawled with groats,
Besides that, he wasn't at all well.

An arboreal carnivorous sloth
Ate a wandering child who was soft.
    Then smug as a bunny,
    He patted his tummy,
Saying, "Now you're in here and not lotht."

The mad doctor's phenomenal find
On his wife he tried in due time.
    It makes molecules stretch,
    And now the poor wretch,
She's trailing a long way behind.

We never talk of old Potter,
Since he crossed his son with an otter.
   He was chased through the town,
   Off a cliff, where he was drowned.
And we picked him up with a blotter.

The son's way out in Lake Erie
On an island quite strange and skeery.
   Those who go there
   Had better beware,
And also they'd better be leery.

There lived there a man named Mulhare,
Who slept at the top of a stair.
   He bought him a squid
   For only five quid,
And it strangled him then and there.

The disposal of Mulhare's remains
Was a puzzle exceedingly strange.
   Not even the flue
   Was o'erlooked for a clew,
But all they could find was his brains.

His daughter, a maiden mistrusting,
Opened a door old and rusting.
   What she found inside
   Tried to make her its bride,
Although it was foul and disgusting.

A writer of limericks grim
Found himself out on a limb
   For attempting to find
   Some kind of rhyme
For that far-off planet called Fuggoth.

On his mantle's a jar full of jello
That occasionally tells him "Hello."
   It comes out of the vaults,
   But despite all its faults,
It's really a jolly good fellow.

The parasites prey on my mind.
The muse has fled from my brain.
   I cannot make rhyme
   Though I try very hard,
And never goof off on the job.

Ungowa kowabonga Kreegah,
Umgo Archaic Vreegah
   Mfg'nnaftghthi
   Nfg,nnaftghthi
Hwufgni umgl zebra.

There was a young guy from Fuggoth
Who fell deep in love with a suggoth.
   He tried to make time,
   But was fouled by the slime
And...

The limerick sequence suffered some delay here when Moamrath had a nervous breakdown after struggling for six days to achieve a rhyme for "Fuggoth." Eventually he recovered and from time to time produced more limericks for the collection, but he was never to finish the famous "Unfinished Limerick."

Moamrath scholars are deeply indebted to Darrel Schweitzer of Pennsylvania for bringing to their attention a capable attempt by Mr. Artemis Vreeb, whereabouts now unknown. Mr. Vreeb's version follows:

There was a young guy from Fuggoth
Who fell deep in love with a suggoth.
   He tried to make time,
   But was fouled by the slime
And had to wipe it up with a tablecloth.

(The editors wish to thank the following scholars for their assistance with this manuscript: Bud Simons, Karen Moore, Dianne Kraft, Scott Cupp, Bruce Sterling and Lisa Turtle.)

Howard Waldrop

Howard Waldrop, who seems to be nominated for some major award or other every year, also fell in love with Moamrath, and unearthed a number of his unproduced screenplays. (And yes, the apostrophe is supposed to move around at will.)

CTHU'LABLANCA (AND OTHER LOST SCREENPLAYS)

MORTIMER MORBIUS MOAMRATH HAS been most closely associated with the *Depraved Tales* school of weird fiction from the Twenties and Thirties, and is best known for his inept Lovecraft imitations which graced the pages of a variety of pulp magazines.

It is little known that Moamrath, for a period of six months late in life, turned to screenplay writing and lived in Hollywood, hoping to find his fortune in that medium. It is fitting that this information should come to light for the first time for MidAmeriCon, which has one of the most distinguished film line-ups ever attempted by a convention committee.

The only mention Moamrath biographers make of his interest in film is reference to his one-sided romance with Marsha Moormist during the mid-Thirties. Pumilia and Wallace state that, "He sometimes sent her notes under various assumed names, even enclosing photos of movie stars." ("M. M. Moamrath: Notes Toward a Biography," *Nickelodeon #1*, 1975). The photos sent her include those of Andy Devine, "Gabby" Hayes, and Maria Ouspenskaya.

Research and interviews with residents of both Archaic, Mass. (Moamrath's birthplace) and Hatcheck, Conn. (where he composed most of the Moamrath "mythos" tales) turned up the story of the writer's involvement with the film world, and of his western odyssey which matches those of Faulkner, Fitzgerald and Nathaniel West, names unknown to most science fiction fans.

1. Puzzlement at First Sight

MOAMRATH, CONTRARY TO WHAT others would have us believe, was not totally ignorant of the world around him. Though not toilet-trained until the age of seven, he soon after developed an insatiable curiosity about his environment, devouring newspapers (for which his mother severely scolded him), reading books, maps and making drawings of things he didn't understand. Those which remain in his earliest notebooks are bizarre, to say the least. (The drawing, scribbled in crayon, entitled "Where I think Babies Come From," shows a piece of cheese, a pair of nylon stockings, a toothbrush, what looks like a large butterfly, and three dishes of the type in which banana splits were once served at Walgreen's drugstores. Arrows connect them in series; unfortunately the young Moamrath did not indicate his starting point.)

Film, however, does not seem to have attracted the future writer at all. We know conclusively that Moamrath saw his first motion picture on June 3, 1935 at the age of 39. His notebook indicates that he had intended to go into Hilton's Funeral Parlor to see some interesting fungi purportedly growing in the basement. By mistake he entered the theatre next door; seeing people sitting in darkness, he thought a funeral to be in progress, became entranced, and stayed through three showings of the film. Its name, unfortunately, is not indicated in the notebook entry which tells of the event.

The episode seems to have left Moamrath in consternation. His personal diary entry for the day consists of the sentence: "I thought they never would get that guy buried."

The next morning, someone in Hatcheck seems to have told him what films were, as his diary entry for the next day, heavily underlined, begins: "It was not until someone informed me that I had been to a motion picture that my mystification over yesterday's events cleared. I could not understand why I had been charged 25 cents to see a funeral..."

His confusions past, Moamrath became one of the most rabid movie fans imaginable. Piles of movie fan magazines of the period were found among his effects at the time of his death two years later.

The unnamed first movie Moamrath saw is lost to us, but not the one which sent him forward on his career as a screenwriter. That film was *The Life of Emile Zola*. It impressed Moamrath to no end. He had long wanted to do a biography of his literary idol, Jean George Marie, Marquis de Hacque, the Eighteenth Century Basque Poet. Moamrath rushed home from the movie and began to make copious notes for his projected screenplay, *The Life of the Marquis de Hacque*. He was so impressed by the biographical film form that he made many enquiries as to where he could contact the actor, Emile Zola, whom he wanted to play the part of the Marquis. Moamrath was understandably upset when told that Monsieur Zola, a Frenchman, had died late in the previous century.

Nonplussed, Mortimer Morbius Moamrath began to read all he could on movies, film-making and movie stars. Unfortunately, though he found books on films themselves, he found none on screenplay writing. So he used as his model the guide he found in the 1904 edition of *How to Write Plays for Lots of Money*. This fact in part atones for some of Moamrath's customary lack of craftsmanship, but it does not wholly excuse some of the blatant logic gaps to be found in his screenplays (examples of which follow this introduction).

2. Movie Fan to Cinema Professional

DURING THE NEXT SIX months, Moamrath outlined film works and, at the same time, learned as much as he could about films. Where he found some of the revelations about the media contained in his work diary is unknown, but they are interesting in and of themselves:

August 5, 1935: Gabby's real name is George!!!
August 21, 1935: de Mille?
September 19, 1935: Warner Bros. ???

It was on December 11 of that year that Moamrath was seized with a transport of rapture and rushed home to labor away at his outlines in a frenzy of work not experienced since he composed the "Young Guy From Yuggoth" poems six years earlier. For the preceding five months he had been, of course, seeing all-talking, all-singing, all-dancing films, the typical product of the day. He had gone far across town that day to catch up on movie going. Here is the diary entry for the day:

BREAKTHROUGH!!! I have seen, today the most marvellous film of all time, one that heralds new things to come for the moving picture. The film is called Hell's Hinges (though it is a western and is not about Hell at all). They have done something totally new and exciting with it. THEY HAVE TAK-EN OUT ALL THE TALKING AND THE MUSIC!!! Instead of having to listen to all that talk, talk, talk, you get to read what is being said. And you can hum any music you want! Will have to recast all movie work for this form. It is sure to sweep the motion picture industry overnight.

In time, of course, Moamrath learned the error of his thinking, but not before it cost him many hours of revision on his projects. He had, as yet, written not a single word in the screenplay form, but had amassed notes, drawings, scenes and outlines. Believing film to be the most important medium of the century, and the perfect way to present to the unaware world his "mythos," Moamrath made the decision to go to the filmmaking capital of the world and get a job as a screenplay writer.

On January 3, 1936, Mortimer Morbius Moamrath bid fond adieu to his faithful butler, Abner Skulker Stern, and set out on the Wendigo, Dunwent & Gone R.R's 19th Century Limited for Hollywood.

3. This or That Side of Paradise

HOLLYWOOD, NEBRASKA HAD A population of 730 hardy souls on the morning M.M. Moamrath set foot on the station platform. That he had taken a wrong connection at Grand Central Station seems never to have occurred to him, then or ever. He had ridden in a sitting car, taking occasional nips at his cod-liver oil bottle, until the conductor announced the arrival at Hollywood.

Moamrath seems to have made contact first with the owner of the town's other drugstore, where he went to establish credit for supplies of cod-liver oil, hair marcel cream, and Tootsie Rolls. He inquired as to where he might see someone about getting a job in pictures.

The druggist, a good Rotarian, sent Moamrath to the town's mayor, Mr. Halen Hardy, who also ran the newspaper, mortuary, and portrait studio. Moamrath explained himself, and the mayor, a shrewd transplanted Yankee with some conception of business and finance, hired Moamrath to write a promotional film to be shown industrialists in hopes that they would relocate their factories in the township.

For his work, Moamrath was furnished room, board, and $10 a month cod-liver oil money.

His diary entry for January 5, 1936 shows his concern:

Thought there was more money in this business. Also thought Hollywood was near the ocean. I asked a native about this. He said there was a WPA lake not far from here, but that the ocean had left sometime during the late Cretaceous. (Will have to use that as setting for the B'oogym'an series.) I do get to smell all the fungus in the mayor's darkroom. Hope to be able to flesh out some outlines for other movies while working on this one.

4. Polished Ineptitude

AND WORK HE DID, for the next six months, while he struggled with the industrial film *(Hollywood: Metropolis of the Cornfields*, like all of Moamrath's other screen works, remains unproduced. In the case of this film, it was due to interference of the City Council [Fred and Bob], hassles with the state authorities and the Mayor's insistence that a part be written for his daughter, Miss Laura Ann Hardy.) During the days when he was not in the Mayor's darkroom or checking locations, he struggled with the promotional movie. At night, Moamrath continued to write the other classics of inept movie scripting for which he is, until now, unknown.

Some words must be given here about Moamrath's lack of finesse at the screenplay form and his subject matter. He had no idea of the technical end of the business and simply described the effects he wanted on the screen, to the best of his not-too-great ability. (See examples of his scene transitions in the script fragments below.)

Also, the near-classic screenplays he wrote were intended, not for actors, but for actors dressed as the gods of the "Moamrath mythos." For those encountering this body of lore for the first time, some explanation must be given.

Moamrath had written a series of stories with the prevailing idea that a race of elder beings (The Bad Old Ones) once controlled the Earth and solar system, but, through sheer stupidity and forgetfulness, got lost and wandered away. Meanwhile, another race of elder beings (The Good Old Ones) stumbled onto the Earth and decided it would do as well as anyplace. The Good Old Ones then had a billion year spree and picnic, and then all went to sleep. The Bad Old Ones continue to stumble around in a place beyond time and space (and, we might add, reason and logic).

It was against this background that Moamrath set all his filmscripts, and it was with the elder gods that he peopled them.

It must also be mentioned that Moamrath's screenplays bear a *startling* resemblance to films actually produced by real studios throughout the next decade. It must be assumed that these are sheer coincidences, as no one other than Moamrath scholars who bought the writer's effects from

Sid, the recluse of Pine Barrens, N.J., have ever seen these scripts. Such coincidences do happen, and it should not be inferred that later films were plagiarized from the works of Moamrath.

During the spring of 1936, Moamrath saw many movies at a local theatre called the First Street Grand Guignol, and added ideas to his notebooks for movies heavily influenced by current releases. In late January, for instance, he wrote the notes for his series involving two happy-go-lucky elder gods, H'Hope and K'Krozby and their somewhat female companion LL'amo in a series of (for Moamrath) lighthearted adventures called *The Road to Oblivion*. He also thought of a tender view of how one small god can change things through its good works, called *Mr. D'Deeds Goes to Hell*.

He also saw his first Marx Bros. film. He set out to find what was available on the comedy team, and prepared a screenplay of one of the Marx Bros.' best-known works, *Das Kapital*, which Moamrath tentatively titled *Depression Feathers*.

But it was into his mythos screenplays that he poured all his inspiration and some of his talent. The screenplay fragments which follow show some of the many guises with which his near-genius masqueraded itself.

5. Goodbye to All Them

IT WAS JUNE 3, 1936 that Moamrath, his hopes dashed by making only sixty dollars in his first half-year as a screenwriter, left Hollywood, Nebraska with his packing crates full of screenplays, notes, outlines, and story treatments.

It is presumed that he used the backs of most of these many, many pages for his other writings in the two years of life left to him, as all that remains of that deadly half-year of film work are the following fragments, a few scattered notes, and a memory in the minds of the inhabitants of Hollywood, Nebr. (Those who remember him at all refer to him as "that funny writer feller from the East, or somewhere.")

It will be seen that his filmwork, like the rest of his writing, is for the most part wretched and inept, but that the film work especially contains a certain smarmy charm of its own. To the fragments themselves I have appended dates of composition, some technical data, etc. I hope the reader finds them as fascinatingly dreadful as I do.

✦

From GONE WITH THE WENDIGO
(Feb. 1936):

(Do the thing where you show R'hett on one side of the door and S'Car'lot on the other side at the same time)

R'HETT:
Open this interdimensional gateway, S'Car'lot!

S'CAR'LOT:
Go away! I'm going to have a 106-yard waistline again. I'm never going to have a thousand young at once anymore! Never!

R'HETT:
I can get a divorce for this, S'Car'lot!

S'CAR'LOT:
Go away!

R'HETT:
No non-Euclidian gateway could stop me if I really wanted in, S'Car'lot.

S'CAR'LOT:
Go away! I'm fine the way I am!

R'HETT:
Frankly, my dear, I don't give a malediction.

✦

From THE BLACK SLIME OF FALWORTH
(March 1936):

(Knights ride up to the slag heap that was the homeland of the noble deGeek family.)

YOUNG SIR GUY DE GEEK:

Yondo is duh abominations of my faddah.

From THE WIZARD OF OSHKOSH (April 1936):

DUNWITCH OF THE EAST:

Something appealing to the eye, something...red. Poppies. Poppies to soothe them to sleep.

(Camera does the thing where you go to another picture of people but doesn't go black first. Four people come down the road with a little dog. Around the little dog's neck is the Elderly Sign.)

D'ORTHI:

Oh, look, the Green Slime City. Let's go, hurry!

TIN FINGERMAN:

Hurry!

SCARECROW:

Hurry!

COWARDLY ANTLION:

I'm comin', I'm comin'.

TOJO THE DOG:

Arf! Arf! Tekel-li-li!

(They run through the poppies. The D'Orthi begins to slow.)

D'ORTHI:

Oh, I'm so sleepy!
(She lies down.)

COWARDLY ANTLION:

Come to think of it, forty thousand winks wouldn't be bad.

(He falls, Scarecrow does the same. So does dog Tojo. Only Tin Fingerman is left up.)

TIN FINGERMAN:

Help! Help!

(Do the thing where Gimpa, the Good Dunwitch of the North, waves her wand and looks pretty. Snow begins to fall on the poppy field. Tin Fingerman rusts in place. Snow continues to fall, then stops. Nothing moves. Bodies begin to decay. Tojo rots first, then D'Orthi, then Scarecrow, then Antlion. Tin Fingerman is still rusted in place. Poppy field withers. Winter comes, then spring again. Bodies are gone. Tin Fingerman has rusted to dark brown. Vines grow up into his leg and out through his head. Seasons pass. Mountains rise in background, then erode away. Tin Fingerman is now only loose collection of rusty parts. His head falls off. Glaciers appear in the background, come forward, recede. Tin Fingerman rusts completely away and disappears. Shallow seas form in background. Huge tentacle rises from the sea, writhes in the air, disappears. Southern Cross rises in the night sky. A great arthropod civilization evolves, builds cities near sea, falls into barbarism. Sea dries up. Moon appears in the sky, grows larger and nearer. Bad Old Ones return from adjacent dimension and reconquer the Earth. They wander away again. Another sea forms. Vast hulk of moon appears on horizon. Big Dipper rises in the nighttime sky. Stars move apart, become unrecognizable as a constellation(…)[1]

But it was for none of the above scripts that Moamrath has been forgotten. Nestled among his papers (along with the stirring wartime drama, *Mrs. Minotaur*, and his adaptation of his own story, *The Maltese Trapezohedron*) was what is considered to be Moamrath's masterwork in the form, *Cthu'lablanca*.

During Moamrath's sojourn in Hollywood, Nebraska, Italian troops invaded Ethiopia, the Japanese incurred into China and the Spanish Civil War had broken out. Thinking ahead, Moamrath posited a far-larger war in the future, involving most of the nations of the world. Such a situation was unthinkable to him. So he wrote a screenplay, set in a world outside time and space, against which his banished Bad Old Ones moved in their

---

1   Ellipsis mine. Moamrath's description goes on for six more closely-written pages which become very repetitive.—H.W.

intertheologic dramas, as a warning of what such a bleak future would hold.

Ct'hulablanca, a small settlement in a realm adjacent to ours, but outside the dimensional boundaries, has become a refugee center during the time of the ouster of the Bad Old Ones from Earth. Here, they wait, wait, wait until such time as they can reach the safety of Fuggoth, or gain passage to other dimensions.

The principal characters in Moamrath's screenplay are R'ick Yog, saloon owner ("Everybody Comes to Yog's") who was once the demon-lover of I'lsa Chubby-Nirath (now Mrs. Nigel R. Lathotep). Lathotep himself is the leader of the under-planet movement to regain control of the Earth for the Bad Old Ones, and as such his presence in Cthula'blanca is resented by Major NoDoz, military attaché from the government of the Good Old Ones.

Minor characters are H'Ugar'te Soth, murderer and under-planet figure; F'R'I, leader of all black market transactions in C'thulablanca and owner of the Blue Suggoth Cafe, rival to Yog's; Captain R'eyNoth, temporal authority in the refugee world, and S'am Zann, Nibbian violinist at R'ick's cafe.

All that remains of Moamrath's film are the following tantalizing fragments and a general outline—and one bizarre photograph. I have provided no transitional material or anything else. Everything is just as Moamrath wrote it.

✦

C'THU'LABLANCA

(F'R'I has come into R'ick's place. F'R'I is a huge corpulent god with more tentacles than one would think necessary to inspire fear and worship.)

F'R'I:
Nyhe-nyhe, R'ick. I want to buy S'am.

R'ICK:
I don't buy and sell the souls of people, F'R'I.

F'R'I:
You should. Mad arabs are Ct'hulablanca's greatest commodity. Nyhe-nyhe.

✦

(H'ugar'te comes into R'ick's. He is a thin dry god with a protruding eye. He opens his avuncular fold to reveal shiny objects to the owner of the cafe.)

H'UGAR'TE:
Do you know what these are, R'ick? Trapezohedrons. Trapezohedrons of transit. Free passage to any dimension, cannot be questioned or rescinded. Not even Blazazoth himself can deny them.

✦

(A few moments later, Captain R'eyNoth's men drag H'Ugar'te away after he has hidden the trapezohedrons in S'am's violin case. Someone mentions that they hope R'ick will protect them should the Good Old Ones ever come for them.)

R'ICK:
I stick my hexapodia out for nobody.

✦

(R'ick and Captain R'eyNoth sit outside the cafe. R'eynoth is speculating why R'ick can't return to Fuggoth, why he has come to Cthul'a'blanca.)

R'ICK:
I came to Cthulabl'an'ca for the horticulture.

R'EYNOTH:
Horticulture? There's no horticulture here. We're outside the dimensions of the space and time plenum!

R'ICK:
I know. I found you could lead a horticulture, but you couldn't make her take root.

✦

(Yog's, later the same millennia, after R'ick has seen I'lsa for the first time since they were banished from R'ealYeah on Earth. S'am comes in.)

S'AM:

Ain't you gonna sleep boss?

R'ICK:

Nah! *(Looks to chronomosphere)* What time is it in R'ealYeah? I bet it's the pleistocene in R'ealYeah. I bet they're all asleep.

S'AM:

Well, I ain't sleepy either.

(Begins to play screeching howls on his violin which shriek to the nether regions of interdimensional space.)

R'ICK:

What's that you're playing?

S'AM:

Just a little somethin' of my own.

R'ICK:

You know what I want to hear.

(Takes drink of cod-liver oil.)

I want maddening pipings from the dim recesses of pelagic time. If she can take it, so can I. Play it, S'am. Play, "As Aeons Go By."

S'AM:
(Begins to play, singing under his breath)

> Pn'gnuili mgl'wnafhk F'nglooie
> P'u gngah'nagl Fhtghngnn,
> I sing it with a sigh
> On the dead you can't rely.
> And with weird time even death may die,
> As aeons go by.

Hearts full of worship,
N'Glalal sets the date,
Bats got to swim,
Blazazoth must have a mate,
Oh that you can't deny.
When stars move into place
Set table and say grace
The meat is gonna fly.
When the islands rise,
The Good Ones we'll despise.
With weird time even death may die,
As aeons go by.

(R'ick's eyes brim over. He buries his head in his tentacles.)

✦

(I'lsa has come to explain to R'ick why she abandoned him in R'ealYeah when the Good Old Ones took over. R'ick interrupts.)

R'ICK:

Is it a good story? Does it have a zowie finish? I remember a story. A god, standing on the C'chu-C'chu platform with a comical look on his mandibles because his thorax has just been kicked in.

I'LSA:

R'ick, I…

✦

(Go to the next scene with one of those things where you just see another picture right through the first one. We are at the gate of transit to other dimensions. A huge coleopterous bug sits in the background while R'ick, I'lsa, Lathotep, R'eyNoth and others move in the foreground, slowly and sluggishly. A glistening ammonia fog drifts slowly over the bugport. Two aphidious creatures in uniforms feed the coleopt raw meat of a disturbingly familiar texture. Lathotep goes toward them. R'ick turns to I'lsa.)

R'ICK:

You're going to get on that beetle!

I'LSA:

But R'ick...

R'ICK:

You're going with him. You're part of the things that keep him going. What I'm going to start, you can't be part of. It's easy to see the problems of three gods don't amount to a Hill of Dreams in a crazy non-Euclidian universe like this...

I'LSA:

I said I'd never leave you...

R'ICK:

You won't. We lost it in R'ealYeah, but we got it back last aeon. We'll always have that.

(Lathotep comes back through ammonia fog. Sound: BYYEEEHHHH!! Beetle's left wing begins to flap. I'lsa looks at R'ick, R'ick looks at I'lsa, Lathotep looks at both. Sound: BYYEEEHHHH!! Beetle's right wing begins to flap.)

R'ICK:

Last Millennia, your wife came to me. She tried everything to get those trapezohedrons from me, pretending she still loved me. I let her pretend. She said she'd do anything to get them. Anything!

LATHOTEP:

And you let her pretend? A god of your stature?

R'ICK:

It was a lot of fun. Anyway, here are the trapezohedrons. Sealed in your names, Mr. and Mrs. Nigel R. Lathotep.

LATHOTEP:

Next time, I'm sure our side will win.

✦

(R'eyNoth and R'ick stand in the fog, R'ick is holding a smoking suggoth-prod in his hand. Major NoDoz' uniform lies crumpled on the bugport runway. R'eyNoth's men arrive.)

R'EYNOTH:

Major NoDoz has been transmogrified.

(pause)

Round up the most loathesomely unusual suspects.

(The men leave.)

I think we should go to the Free Bad Ones garrison in the Plateau of S'ing, among the C'chu-C'chu people.

(Sound of beetle flying away into interstitial space overhead. They watch it go.)

And the suggoths you owe me should just about pay our expenses.

R'ICK:

Our expenses? Fnglooie, this could be the start of a beautiful pantheon.

Thanks to Moamrath scholars Joe Pumilia and Ray Files for technical assistance.

Richard Lupoff

Ova Hamlet strikes again—this time at Fritz Leiber's beloved sword-and-sorcery heroes, Fafhrd and the Gray Mouser, who made their debut in "Two Sought Adventure," and have been waging literate, tongue-in-cheek battles against wizards, villains, and their own appetites for just about half a century.

TWO SORT-OF ADVENTURES

by Ova Hamlet

FLAYSHIG AND THE GOYISH Meshugge were sitting at a crude formica table in Silver's Deli on Fleegle Street, the foulest and most ill-reputed thoroughfare in Hotzeplotz. Flayshig, an immensely fat pattern-cutter whose origin in remote Gaulizia was spoken of only in subdued whispers (or behind closed doors) was holding a corned-beef-on-rye in one huge, fleshy hand, and a bottle of celery tonic in the other.

He leaned forward, his massive body almost hiding the table, and spoke to his companion. "You know, Meshugge, this is an awfully boring night. I could really use some excitement. An adventure of some sort. An encounter with a band of cutpurses or wizards, or a meeting with a couple of cozy girls mayhap. It's been a while since we were invited to tarry with Fryx and Frex that time in Schnipposhok."

"And lucky we were to escape with whole hides!" replied his companion, an incredibly thin and sharp-featured man dressed all in purple, orange, blue, green, red, vermilion, turquoise, chartreuse and a very few other colors. "Why, I had to leave my toad-sticker behind when we scooted out through the window. And there we were, forgetting that Fryx and Frex's cozy-chamber was in the top of an old battlement."

"Yes," Flayshig commented. "It must have been our two patron spirits, Kvetcherkeh of the Loud Complaints and Nayfish of the Cowardly Manner, who saved us!"

"More like it was the handy placement of Fryx and Frex's daddy's hog-wallow. It made for a soft, albeit a smelly, landing place."

"But don't you think it was our foresightful familiars who saw to it that we chose two girls whose daddy raised pigs for a living, instead of, say, the daughters of an iron monger? What if we'd tumbled into a forge instead of that nice, easy muck?"

"You may be right," the Meshugge conceded, although not with the sound of total conviction in his voice. "But here I am sitting in Silver's Deli, noshing on gefilte fish and Maneschewitz wine, with nothing to look forward to afterwards except a cold pallet and the awesome sounds of you snoring away on its companion."

Flayshig downed the last of his sandwich and smothered a belch as grand as his wobbly belt.

The Meshugge left half his gefilte fish behind, finished off his wine, and fastidiously wiped his chin with a corner of his companion's billowing shmatte. "I don't like the looks of dark Fleegle street," he rapped out. "I'll self-sacrificingly venture outside and make sure that the coast is clear, while you settle up our account with Silver over there." He jerked a pointed thumb at the be-aproned deli-keeper glaring suspiciously at them from behind the potato salad and cole slaw.

Scant moments later Flayshig joined the Meshugge outside in the street. The world of Nuvhen's moon shone balefully through demon-haunted (or perhaps merely storm-driven) clouds, giving Nuvhen the appearance of a watery ghost of itself. "You owe me for your share of the tab," the heavy-set Gaulizianer demanded of his friend.

"Not so," Meshugge snapped in reply. "Didn't I leave the deli first and scout out Fleegle Street at the risk of life and limb? Surely those services are worth at least as much as a plate of noshes. If anything, 'tis you who owe me a small token of gratitude. But I'm ever willing to let ride the debt, in view of our ancient friendship and the many scrapes we've been through together. But at least some expression of gratitude would be welcome!"

Flayshig shrugged. "I suppose you're right, Meshugge. But somehow it seems that I always get stuck with paying our bills, while you get first pick of loot, fruit and playmates."

"Yes, and charge you not a krupnik for all the extra work I do in tasting and sampling various wares to make sure that you get nothing less that you deserve, Flayshig. You ought to send thanks up (or perhaps some other direction would be more appropriate) for the day that Kvetcherkeh and Nayfish conspired to make us companions in our journey through life and Hotzeplotz."

The twain of them rounded the corner of Goniff's Alley, and their conversation was brought to an abrupt halt at the sight of two ladies leaning languorously against a municipal cresset-holder.

"Surely Nayfish of the Cowardly Manner heard our deli dialog," the Goyish Meshugge hissed beneath his fishy breath.

"Aye, and Kvetcherkeh of the Loud Complaints sent us upon the path we've taken, or we'd never come upon the two morsels of delight yonder!" Flayshig let go a loud krechtz. "Pardon. I shouldn't have had so much celery tonic."

"Hello, there, you two swells," one of the cresset-dumplings cooed.

Flayshig peered through the murky atmosphere of Goniff's Alley in a vain attempt to ascertain which of the charmers had spoken. The two were an oddly like and yet oddly unlike pair. One was all bosom and hips, curled red tresses and curved red lips, and great round eyes that flashed a russet hue in the flickering cresset-flame. The other was slim and willowy, as thin-fleshed as her companion was generously endowed, and her coloring was the complete opposite of her sister-of-the-night, with pale skin, nearly sallow in the darkness of the alley. Her eyes shone with a tint like that of the Bay of Brunx beneath a wind-whipped autumn tempest and her black locks hung in straight, glossy strands that seemed to catch a greenish glare from the oil-flame above.

"Wow!" the corpulent Gaulizian exclaimed, "I never saw any pair of ladies to compare with these two! How about you, Meshugge? You ever see the likes?"

"A few times," the Goyish Meshugge provided. "Once when an officer of the city watch foolishly mistook me for an infamous second story man who'd been trying to prevent revolution in Schnipposhok, and offered me free lodging at the courtesy of the Schnipposhok municipality."

"Oh, you mean the times you got thrown in the clink over t'Schnip for lifting ladies' jewels out of their bedrooms in the middle of the night. I remember, I had to bribe the chief gaoler of Schnip to get you out of that one, Meshugge. It took all of my savings and then when we got you home you loaned me money to live on until I could earn some more. And you charged me interest."

"Less than the going rate among the temple usurers, Flayshig. Although in fact 'tis I who should receive your gratitude and mayhap some more tangible token thereof, for that little escapade. Why, the whores in the Schnipposhok lockup were clamouring to provide for my needs and comforts. I could have raffled myself off and turned a handsome profit for a mere few days of not unpleasant work. But I permitted you to bribe me out of there because I knew you'd just get into trouble without me around.

"Still and all, Flayshig, still and all..." The Meshugge's eyes grew distant with recollection. "'Twas the high priests of Shubbo-Nyarlaphap who pressured the municipality into trying to clear up the streetwalker situation so's to eliminate competition for their own temple whores, as were responsible for there being any such comfort in the municipal pokey."

All during this exchange, the two lissome individuals whose presence inspired the conversation had not been unmoving. The ruddy and generously-formed one had made two circles about the Meshugge and his fleshy friend Flayshig, moving clockwise, while the darker and somewhat sharp-boned sister had done similarly, only widdershins. It was as if these two were such opposites of one another that anything either did, the other had to do backwards, or in some manner to offset the effort of the first.

"Uhh, do you two ladies think you might like some, ahh, company of an evening?" Flayshig asked, his goggling eyes and pumpkin-shaped head seeming to revolve from right to left, or mayhap it were from left to right, as he kept the green sister in sight.

"We've a marvelous set of chambers on the Street of Shmegegges. A desert-bearskin rug with fur as thick as swamp-grass, a fireplace to warm one's bones on a night of chill and damp, a full wineskin bulging with rich sweet squeezings of the lushest vines!" the Meshugge took up.

The rounder of the two cupcakes-of-the-evening ceased her clockwise sashaying and pressed her ample endowments against the Goyish Meshugge. "Hmm," she commented appraisingly, "a trifle on the scrawny side, but not without a certain potential. I'd like to see the cut of this purse, sister."

The slimmer of the maidens (or, at least, they must once have been maidens) dispensed with her widdershinning and poked a bony elbow into the pendulous belly of Flayshig.

"Methinks that skeletal lizard you're pressing against would make a fair cauldron of stew, if you'd first crack his bones to let the marrow out. For there's surely not enough meat on his bones to make a proper meal for a cub.

"But this nice bubee *ahah!*" She patted big Flayshig on his belly, holding one slim hand on either side of his rounded tum-tum slapping it alternately to the left and right until it jiggled. "This one, sister, could feed a platoon of the likes of thee and me."

Now Flayshig, while not noticeably a tall man because of his generally rounded configuration, was actually as high as a Greenpointnik stallion or the door-lintel at Silver's Deli (where, in fact, Silver had finally installed a kind of bumping-pad, not to protect Flayshig who should have known better but kept bumping his noggin anyway, but to keep the wood from being damaged by the repeated collisions). And the Goyish Meshugge, more than a trifle vain about his appearance, tended to go in for tall-heeled boots that gave him the appearance of a stature greater than that provided by the gods of Nuvhen.

The two swaggers were thus able to peer over the heads of their winsome companions, and exchanged a worldly-wise wink.

They made their way together through dank alleyways and echoing courtyards where all of the spirits of Nuvhen seemed to gather in the shadows and peer at the quartet with eyes like luminous fungus, or maybe burglars' bull's eye lanterns, for Flayshig and the Meshugge were by no means the only thieves in Hotzeplotz. When they reached the dwelling-place in the Street of Shmegegges where the rotund Gaulizianer and the diminutive Goyisher shared digs, the two men drew their new found friends into an alcove and a whispered conversation ensued.

"What's the trouble, swittniks?" the ruddy wench inquired.

And, "This don't look like such a palace to me," the greenish woman said.

The Meshugge hissed for silence. "We'll have to sneak up the back way," he whispered. "Flayshig and I don't want the lendlady should see us."

"And why not?" the rounded wench inquired, leaning back from the Meshugge, who had drawn a conservative cloak of tangerine, peach, mauve, buff, beige and turquoise over his more colorful buskin to keep the night air out.

"Why not? Why not!" Flayshig put in. "We're not behind on the rent again, are we, Meshugge?"

"Oh, no," the Goyisher replied.

"Because I remember, you told me that you had only a gold fardl and the lendlady couldn't make change from it, so I had to give you money for my half of the rent and yours, too. You paid the lendlady, no?"

"Well," the Goyish Meshugge explained, "in fact, I was going to, but I met a fellow who'd just come off a sailing caravel from Pinsk—"

"From Pinsk?" the Gaulizianer echoed.

"Well, or maybe it was Minsk."

"Ah-*hah*."

"And he had some smuggled gems with him that were worth a fortune, Flayshig old friend. For just a gold fardl and two grupniks, he was willing to sell me—"

"Oh, no!" Flayshig exclaimed. "You spent our money on cutglass, Meshugge? Is that what you're telling me? And now the lendlady will want her rent..."

The Meshugge pressed a long finger to his thin lips. "Shhh! Just keep quiet on the way in and she'll never see us."

Astonishingly, they succeeded in getting up to the adventurers' loft unchallenged. After all, the lendlady was a deep sleeper, or maybe she was just feeling soft-hearted for a change. Hoo-*hah*!

At the boys' place, the dark-haired, willowy-torsoed wench detached herself from the giant Flayshig and stood in the middle of the much-advertised desert-bearskin rug. "This is the luxurious rug you wanted us to lie on?" she inquired. "Such a rug, no wonder the bear wanted to get rid of it. *Feh!*"

The red-haired, generously-rounded miss stepped away from the Goyish Meshugge who had doffed his cloak and buskin to stand in a simple shmatte that showed only a few stains and rips here and there. "Well," the girlie said, "so how's about that marvey wine you were talking about?"

"It's right in the corner," Flayshig interjected. "Here." He made his way to the shadowiest part of the room, ignoring the terrifying scraping and scuttling sounds made by the spirits who hid there in the dark (or maybe the noises came from rats or cockroaches), and returned with a greasy old wineskin. He pulled the stopper from its neck and upended the skin above his gaping mouth but all that came out were a few drops of bitter dregs.

"Meshugges!" the Gaulizianer barbarian complained.

Even the darkness of the midnight chamber couldn't hide the embarrassed blush that reddened the cheeks of the Goyisher. "I just had a teeny sip, Flayshig," he whined. "Or maybe two teeny sips, I don't remember. You know how it is when you get tipsy. Heh-Heh."

The two girlies had withdrawn to another corner of the room and were conversing sibilantly, or perhaps gutterally. From time to time one or the other of them would cast a scornful glance at the two adventurers, then make a gutteral, or perhaps a sibilant, comment to her companion.

Finally they returned to the desert-bearskin rug and pulled their dresskeles over their heads, tossing them into the corner of the room. "Come on fellas," they murmured in unison.

✦

The philosophers of Nuvhen have been discussing for thousands of years the exact nature of the sun that rises over the Bay of Brunx and sets behind the Hills of Hoybinkyn every morning and every night. There are some who hold that the sun is a child's ball thrown across the dome of heaven by a playful tyke who lives somewhere in a land beneath the Bay of Brunx, to a companion who lives far past the Hills of Hoybinkyn. The companion then rolls the ball back through a secret tunnel dug deep beneath the land of Nuvhen, for otherwise (the philosophers point out) the sun would alternately rise in the Brunx and set in Hoybinkyn, and rise in Hoybinkyn and set in the Brunx, which clearly it does not.

Still, there are others who consider the explanation of the nature of the sun and its diurnal path across Nuvhen's sky as a bit of naive casuistry, and prefer a simpler theory, such as that of the supernal dialectical antithesis, or perhaps the aspirated partifragmentated calamari.

All of this is as it may be, for in due course the sun *did* rise over the Bay of Brunx and cast its yellow rays through the high, grimy windows of the dusty loft on the Street of Shmegegges.

The Goyish Meshugge sat up in the middle of the desert-bearskin rug, stretched and yawned luxuriantly, and reached for the warm curves of his companion of the previous night. He was thinking of a little morning's refresher, or maybe of trying to hit her up for a little loan.

Instead of delectably curvy flesh, his bony digits found only the mangy fur of a once noble desert bear.

The Meshugge leaped to his feet and glared around the room, looking for the two girlies of the night and/or his chubby Gaulizianer companion. There was no one to be seen!

A yellow ray of sunlight coming all the way from the glowing orange ball over the Bay of Brunx managed to struggle through the grimy window of the loft over the Street of Shmegegges and pierce the dusty air of the room. It illuminated the oaken door where the Goyish Meshugge's auburn, maroon, burnt sienna, gray, black, xanthic and ultramarine hat hung from its peg. The Meshugge lifted the hat and found a message stuck in its greasy leather band. The Meshugge squatted crosslegged and painstakingly traced out the message.

The writing was large and crude and hard to make out.

The Goyish Meshugge moved his lips and whispered as he read.

DERE GOYISHERE—the message ran—ME & TEH GIRLEIS HAS GIVVEN UPP ON YUO & WE AR GOWING AWUAY TO MINSK—or maybe, for the penmanship assuredly left a great deal to be desired, it said PINSK—& FINED US THUOSE GEMMS. DONET TRIY & FOLOW US ORR IL'L CRACK YUOR HEDD WEYED OPUN!!!

LOVE,
  (signed)
FLAYSHIG

Jayge Carr

I originally felt that most sci-ence fiction films and television shows are self-parodies, and needed no help from writers on that score. Jayge Carr stopped writing her excellent string of novels long enough to prove me wrong, with this little parody of George Lucas' brainchildren.

STAR SPATS

FAR, FAR AGO IN a Galaxy long, long away...

"Ouch, that *hurt!*" complained boyish-but-mature Kook Shytalker, a simple farmboy from the simple farm planet of YouTwoie, rubbing himself aggrievedly. "That was a terrible landing. Why were you going so fast when nobody was chasing us? Even I, a simple farmboy from a simple farm planet of YouTwoie, know better than that. I've got bruises on my bruises!"

"Habit, kid," growled his companion, mature-but-boyish Con Duet, the merciless mercenary who'd do anything for money and nothing for free. "Besides, you know what they say—any landing you can walk away from is a *good* landing."

"But *I* didn't walk away," Kook pointed out; "you dragged me. Where is this place, anyway? Why did you bring me here? I'm just a simple farmboy! Why did you come and haul me away from my simple farm on my simple farm planet YouTwoie?"

"Sorry 'bout that, kid." Con had been hauling the simple farmboy Kook by a rope knotted around the simple farmboy's waist; now he knotted the other end of the rope to a conveniently-sited handle on a large piece of secret, mysterious equipment which had, besides the convenient handle, lots of blinking, secret, mysterious lights. "But money talks"—he gave the knot one final jerk—"and this money said, 'Abduct Kook Shytalker and bring him to the secret, mysterious hideout of the dread Dread Raider.'" Con stepped back, dusting his hands in satisfaction.

"I'm only a simple farmboy." Kook glared at the knot and jerked on the rope below it, naturally tightening it further. "Who's Redred Razor?"

"Not Redred, kid." Con pulled a thick stack of crispies out of his space-pouch and began riffling through it gleefully. "And not Razor. It's the *dread* Dread Raider. Dread's his name, and Dread's his game, see?"

"No," said Kook petulantly, alternately jerking on the knot around his waist and the one around the handle. "No, I don't see. And I don't want to see this Redfred Reindeer at all! I'm just a simple farmboy. I want to go back to my simple farm on my simple farm planet of YouTwoie."

"Tough, kid." (Fifty, eighty, one hundred...) "But this money talks louder than you do." (One-twenty, one-forty-five, one-ninety-five...)

"I'M JUST A SIMPLE FARMBOY! I WANT TO GO BACK TO MY SIMPLE FARM PLANET YOUTWOIE!"

Completely oblivious, Con kept on counting. (Four-ten, four-thirty...)

Kook glared at his captor and made another fierce attack on the two knots that held him. He had only succeeded in tightening them further when Con stuffed the wad back in his spacepouch and said, grinning broadly, "Kid, you're forgetting one thing. I'm a merciless mercenary who'll do *anything* for money, (and nothing for free, of course). Now if you were to offer me *more* money, it would talk louder than *this* money, and naturally I'd take you back aboard my battered tin can—that is, my good ship, the Week Sparrow, and—"

Sullenly: "I'm *a poor* simple farmboy."

Con shrugged. "In that case, kid, I guess we'll both have to wait here for the dread Dread Raider—"

As if on cue, there was the sound of heavy, labored breathing. Framed in the doorway was the black-clad villainous figure of the dread Dread Raider, mysterious evil follower of the evil dark side of the mysterious power known only as the Power. "Merciless mercenary Con Duet," he husked between wheezes, "master of the Week Sparrow, who will do anything for money and nothing for free, have you accomplished your mission for which, contrary to my usual cheap policy, I paid you half in advance?"

"Yes," Con nodded, "yes, dread Dread Raider, mysterious evil follower of the evil dark side of the mysterious power known only as the Power,

I succeeded in kidnapping and bringing here to your secret mysterious hideout the simple farmboy Kook Shytalker—"

Outraged, Kook elbowed Con aside. "That's my line, you thief! I'm only a simple farmboy—"

Con elbowed Kook back. "Brought the simple-*minded* farmboy, Kook Shytalker, in my battered tin ca—good ship, the Week Sparrow—"

"Good ship, ha!" Kook sneered. "I may be only a simple farmboy, but I know a pile of *junk* when I see it."

"Don't knock it, kid. It got you here in one—in almost one piece, didn't it? Now you, dread Dread Raider, mysterious evil follower of the evil dark side of the mysterious power known only as the Power—pay me." Con held out his empty hand, palm up.

But instead of his spacewallet, dread Dread Raider pulled out an energy pistol. There was a momentary blinding flash and thin whine of an energy bolt, followed by the acrid taint of ozone and the meaty thunk of a falling body.

Kook gazed down incredulously at the limp Con. "You killed him! Even a simple farmboy can see that!"

The dread Dread Raider shrugged. "What else did you expect from the mysterious evil follower of the evil dark side of the mysterious power known only as the Power?" He worked the used energy bolt out of his gun and sighted down the barrel at Kook. "Besides, energy bolts are cheap, and he was expensive. But don't let it bother you. After all, he's the one who kidnapped you from your simple farm planet of YouTwoie—"

"Another villain! See, this one's stealing my line, too!"

The dread Dread Raider rammed the muzzle of his energy pistol against Kook's forehead. "Energy bolts are *cheap*. And, as I was saying, he brought you here from your simple farm planet of YouTwoie." He ground the muzzle in a little; Kook gulped and said nothing. "Just forget him. I'll have one of my vicious swarm trappers in later to clean up the garbage."

Kook nervously moved the muzzle out of line with his forehead. "When you put things that simply, Bedred Spader, even a simple farmboy like me can understand. Say Redlead Strayer, did you know that you've got a vicious case of asthma there? My simple—" His voice stopped, because he had spotted Obi-Qui Etkantyu, hermit, philosopher, and last of the valiant, noble Dead-Eye Mights, cautiously crawling in through the open doorway, a glittering light-scimitar tightly clutched in one aged, trembling hand.

Ignorant of the entrance of yet another player in this thrilling drama, the dread Dread Raider re-aligned the muzzle to the center of Kook's forehead. "But we're really going to have *two* disposal problems, aren't we?" He shrugged. "Oh, well, energy bolts are cheap."

Kook stuck his finger in the muzzle and spoke *very* rapidly. "Look here, Bledbed Blader, even a simple farmboy can be *extremely* useful. For example, my aunt, the simple farmer's wife, Trueblue, has this positively miraculous cure for asthma. Why, it never fails. I'll bet I could whip some up right now—"

But Obi-Qui Etkantyu had crawled into position. Suddenly he rose, and poised the point of his light-scimitar a scant centimeter from the dread Dread Raider's ribs. "Aha, I might have known, even before I stowed away on that battered tin can, the Week Sparrow. It was you, dread Dread Raider, former pupil of mine, now mysterious evil follower of the evil dark side of the mysterious power known only as the Power. You are responsible for the kidnapping of my dear young friend, the son of my late associate and colleague, the next to last of the Dead-Eye Mights."

But Kook reached over and began shaking Obi-Qui's hand—the one with the scimitar—vigorously, talking six to the second. Obi-Qui, who was old as well as being a hermit, etc., dropped the scimitar, and the dread Dread Raider caught it before it cut off anything more important than a few bits of secret mysterious equipment, shut it off, and stuffed it smugly in his own belt. "Why, it's Drop Etkantyu," Kook was saying, "the solitary old hermit who lives near our simple farm on the simple farm planet of YouTwoie. Have you come to rescue me from this villain, Fred-said Trader, Drop, old pal, old chum, old buddy? Glad to see you, Drop, old pal, old chum, old buddy, glad to see you." Finally, far too late, he dropped Drop's hand.

"Arrrrrgh," replied poor old Obi-Qui (Drop) Etkantyu, as he sadly eyed his scimitar, safely ensconced in the dread Dread Raider's belt.

"Obi-Qui Etkantyu," wheezed the dread Dread Raider, in tones of deep satisfaction.

"I may be a simple farmboy," Kook shook his fist under the villain's nose, "but nobody tells *me* when to shut up!"

The dread Dread Raider's energy gun swung back to center on Kook's forehead. "Energy bolts are cheap."

"Even a simple farmboy," Kook slid under the muzzle, "knows when to be polite. Especially when the villain has the drop on us, right, Drop?"

"Kook, my dear young friend." Obi-Qui put his arm around Kook's shoulders. "I'm afraid it's past time to tell you what you should have been told long ago. I'm not merely your neighbor, the solitary old hermit, Drop

Etkantyu. In reality, I am the hermit, philosopher, and last of the valiant Dead-Eye Mights, Obi-Qui Etkantyu."

Kook sullenly shook off the arm. "Just because I'm a simple farmboy, even old friends tell me to shut up."

"Kook, Kook," Obi-Qui replaced his arm around Kook's shoulders, "dear young friend, the son of my late colleague and associate, the next to the last of the Dead-Eye Mights, I am only telling you my true name. I *am* Obi-Qui Etkantyu."

As he shifted the muzzle from the center of Kook's forehead to the center of Obi-Qui's, the dread Dread Raider spoke. "I hesitate to correct the former teacher of my youth, before I became the mysterious evil follower of the evil dark side of the mysterious power known only as the Power, but you had better *not* be Obi-Qui Etkantyu."

"As long as you're holding that energy gun on me," said Obi-Qui (Drop) Etkantyu, swallowing loudly, "you can call me whatever you choose, old one-time pupil."

"Energy bolts are cheap. You can be the *late* Obi-Qui Etkantyu, if you prefer."

"Actually, I prefer being a nice quiet hermit on the nice quiet farm planet YouTwoie," Obi-Qui (or Drop) said. "But tell me, old one-time pupil, why did you kidnap my dear young friend, the son of my late colleague and associate, the next to last of the Dead-Eye Mights?"

"What's all this about my simple farmer father? He wasn't a Red-eyed Kite. He was only a simple farmer, as I, his son, am a simple farmboy."

"Kook, Kook, my dear young friend." Obi-Qui drew Kook closer to him, while taking a step sideways; the muzzle now pointed at Kook. "This is something else you should have been told long ago. Your dear dead father was *not* a farmer like the uncle who raised you. In reality, he was a Dead-eye Might, the next to last of the Dead-Eye Mights. As I, his colleague and associate, am the last of the Dead-Eye Mights."

The dread Dread Raider swung the muzzle back to Obi-Qui. "You are going to be the *late* last of the Dead-Eye Mights and the *late* simple farmboy if you don't quit stepping on *my* lines. You asked me why I had the kid kooknapped, I mean the kook kidnapped, I mean—why explain it at all. Energy bolts are cheap."

"Look, I'm only a simple farmboy." Kook swung the muzzle away from Obi-Qui. "I don't understand any of this Lead-Tie Lights business. But I tell you what." He realized, horrified, that the muzzle now pointed at *him*. "I promise, if you let me and poor old harmless hermit Drop, here"—he returned the muzzle to its original position—"go back to our simple farm planet of YouTwoie, you'll never see or hear of us again." Obi-Qui took a sideways step, so the muzzle was pointing back at Kook, "and we'll never, ever breathe a *word* about the location of your secret mysterious hideout." Kook stepped sideways, so the muzzle was again pointing at Obi-Qui.

"Energy bolts are cheaper than passages to YouTwoie."

"Of course"—Kook shook off Obi-Qui's arm and moved as far away from him as his rope would let him—"if you have some sort of score to settle with old Drop here, even a simple farmboy knows when to make himself scarce. I could leave for my simple farm planet of YouTwoie *right now.*"

"Energy bolts are cheaper than passages to YouTwoie," the dread Dread Raider repeated, shoving Kook back conveniently close to Obi-Qui. "But I will explain why I cannot let you go back to YouTwoie, even if you promise never to let me see or hear of you again, and never, ever breathe a word about my secret, mysterious hideout."

"Go ahead and explain, old one-time pupil who has become a mysterious evil follower of the evil dark side of the mysterious power known only as the Power. Explain, and do a good thorough job of it. Take your time, take as much time as you need. Explanations are easier on my ears than energy bolts, any day."

"Energy bolts are cheap, but my time is valuable. I'll be brief. See this solido reproduction?" He reached into a pocket of his capacious black villain's costume with his free hand and pulled out a small figurine.

Kook gave a long wolf whistle and grabbed the figurine. "Even a simple farmboy can appreciate that!"

"Beautiful, intelligent, and spunky," agreed Obi-Qui, studying the figurine over Kook's shoulder. "But I'm sure I've never even met her."

"Me, neither. Even a simple farmboy would remember a sexy—"

"Beautiful, intelligent, and spunky lady like that," Obi-Qui finished for him. "But if neither Kook or I have even met her..."

"You are correct as always, old one-time teacher. She is the Princess Playa Pianna, and she *is* beautiful, intelligent, and spunky." A short phrase was lost in the wheezing; it might have been: also sexy! "Further, she has more up her sleeve than her arm." He retrieved the figurine from Kook—with some difficulty—and stowed it away in one of his secret, mysterious pockets. "Also, you are correct in saying that neither of you have met her—yet. But it is because of her that I will have to use two of my energy bolts—which aren't really that cheap—on you two."

"But why? I'm only a simple farmboy, I don't understand. What can a woman we haven't even met have to do with us?"

"Because you will meet her," the dread Dread Raider's already deep voice deepened noticeably; this was his big speech, and he knew it. "The Princess Playa Pianna, though she believes I don't know it, is helping those pitiful royalist rebels against our glorious benevolent democratic tyranny." He slapped Kook's hands away from his secret, mysterious pocket. "My computers have told me what is going to happen. I will kidnap the Princess, to find out from her the location of the rebel's pitiful main base, such as it is. She will smuggle a desperate message out. You, Kook, and you, old one-time teacher, will be sucked into her pitiful struggle, along with the garbage I've already taken care of, here." He was so intent on his speech that he didn't notice the Princess Playa Pianna in person, beautiful, intelligent, and spunky, with more up her sleeve than her arm, sneaking surreptitiously up behind him.

"You two will have many harrowing adventures," Raider continued. (Obi-Qui shuddered.) "Many dangerous, hair's-breadth escapes. It will seem all too often that you have failed and I have won. You will be forced to the limits of your endurance, and past. But in the end, thanks to Kook's daring and courage and talents, and my one-time teacher's heroic self-sacrifice—" Obi-Qui moaned softly—"you will win. I will be forced to flee, my evil, mysterious planet in ruins. *Two* energy bolts are a cheap enough price to pay to prevent *that*." As he finished speaking, Princess Playa Pianna's indubitably well-endowed leg flashed up, and his energy gun went flying over the bank of equipment to land with a tantalizing clunk somewhere on the far side. Everybody—except Kook, who only managed to tangle himself in his rope—went over or around the equipment after it.

"Hey, look at her!" Kook enthused. "Even a simple farmboy like me can see she kicked the gun right out of his hand."

"Correct, Kook. I am not only beautiful, intelligent, and spunky, but I have more up my sleeve than my arm." She also had a head start and spotted the gun first, but Raider was too close behind her, so she simply kicked it again into the furthest corner, and said, "Not another step, Raidie baby. As you can plainly see, what I have up my sleeve besides my arm is a gun!"

He could see, so he stopped, and raised his arms carefully. "And energy bolts are as cheap for princesses as they are for villains."

"You arrived in the nick of time, Princess," said Obi-Qui, retrieving Raider's gun and sticking it gleefully in his own belt. "But how could *you* know the plans of my one-time pupil, now the mysterious evil follower of the evil dark side of the mysterious power known only as the Power?"

Without taking her eyes or her gun off Raider, the princess reached over with her free hand and plucked the gun out of Obi-Qui's belt and thrust it securely into her own. "I am not only beautiful, intelligent, and spunky, with more up my sleeve than my arm, *but*—" A broad smile, as Obi-Qui's turned-off light-scimitar was neatly moved from Raider's belt to hers "—I, too, have computers. Our computers, like his, predicted what would happen after the villain Raider kidnaps me to learn the location of our secret rebel base. Naturally, since Kook and Obi-Qui's roles will be crucial, we've been keeping an eye on them. When they both disappeared, the only vessel that had left YouTwoie was Con Duet's Week Sparrow; and its badly tuned engine left a trail easy to follow. So come on, Obi-Qui, I've come to rescue you and take you back to YouTwoie, so you can be ready to start your glorious adventures."

"I don't know," Kook said, moving as far away from her as his rope would let him. "I'm grateful to you for rescuing us and all that, Princess. But I'm just a simple farmboy; that glorious adventure bit bothers me. If something this vital is going to rest on *my* skill and daring and all that, I think you'd better just drop me and Drop off on our simple farm planet of YouTwoie and pick yourself another hero."

"That goes double for me, Princess," Obi-Qui seconded, sidling slyly toward a porthole he had spotted.

"You, too, Obi-Qui Etkantyu?" said the princess, turning to face him. Sheerest coincidence, no doubt, that the gun in her hand now faced him, too. "But you are the last of the Dead-Eye Mights!"

"Right, Princess," said Obi-Qui, fumbling behind himself for the bolts on the porthole. "But how do you think I got to be the last of the Dead-Eye Mights, anyway? Laser bolts and bombs and assassinations all around me! It's knowing how to be a poor harmless old hermit that's saved my skin up to now, and I intend to keep up the good work for a long time to come."

"You said it, Drop old hermit pal. I'd rather be a live simple farmboy than a dead hero, any day."

"Ha, ha, ha!" Raider guffawed, still keeping his hands carefully high. "Maybe I won't need my cheap energy bolts after all, Princess."

"Obi-Qui Etkantyu, do you mean to tell me that the last of the noble, valiant Dead-Eye Mights refuses to sacrifice himself heroically for the cause he has served so long?"

"Princess, you are beautiful, intelligent, and spunky, with more up your sleeve than your arm. And, this time, you are dead right; I don't want to be dead." He was still trying to open the porthole as he spoke, but fortunately for all concerned, the bolts holding it were old, cheap, and rusted shut. "I just want to go back to being a poor hermit on the poor world of YouTwoie. And if I ever have another adventure, glorious or not, it will be *too soon.*"

"But you will be known throughout the Galaxy as the great Obi-Qui Etkantyu."

"True. But more important, I will be the *late* Obi-Qui Etkantyu. You can't deny it, even though you are beautiful, intelligent, and spunky, with more up your sleeve than your arm."

"But, you, Kook, don't you thirst for adventure? Don't you look up at the stars at night and wish yourself out there, thundering through space, fighting for truth, justice, and the Galactic Way? Don't you long for a hero's reward? Does it take a princess who is beautiful, intelligent, and spunky, with more up her sleeve than her arm, to tell you what *that* is?"

"Princess, even a simple farmboy has dreams."

"Make them come true, then. Though you were raised simply by your aunt and uncle on the faraway planet YouTwoie, your heritage is too strong to be denied. Take up your scimitar of light! Embrace your glorious destiny! Embrace...Kook, what can you possibly have against a princess who is beautiful, intelligent, and spunky, with more up her sleeve than her arm?"

"No simple farmboy can have anything against a princess, Princess."

"Then I'll return you to YouTwoie and you'll wait impatiently—"

"Hey!" husked Raider, who was getting awfully tired of holding his hands up. "Hey, don't let her pull the bull over your eyes, kid. Talk's cheaper than energy bolts, even. Never forget—she's asking you to *risk your life.*"

"Hey, you're right. Even a simple farmboy can see that."

"And for what, I ask you. Promises. Well, promises are cheaper than energy bolts, too. Listen kid, there's something I ought to tell you. Something about your princess."

"Even a simple farmboy likes to hear about princesses."

"Now Raidie baby, let's not tell tales out of school!"

"Princess Playa Pianna is beautiful,—" she nodded "—intelligent,—" she nodded "—and spunky." She was distracted by Obi-Qui, still working on the rusted bolts. "And she has more up her sleeve than her arm. But, listen, kid," he dropped his husky bass voice even lower, "more important than those—or cheap energy bolts, even—*she always has to have the last word.*"

"Ohhhhh." Kook's eyes and mouth got very round. "Even a simple farmboy knows that having to have the last word is 'way more important than being beautiful, intelligent, and spunky, or even having more up your sleeve than your arm."

"Attaboy, Kook!" said Obi-Qui, who had been hauled away from the porthole by brute—more accurately, brutess—force. "Being a live poor hermit is lots better than being a dead hero."

"Well, you haven't any choice, either of you." The princess petulantly stamped her delicate, princessy foot. "You're coming back with me to YouTwoie and then you'll jolly well be live heroes, the both of you—or you'll be dead ones. Raidie baby will see to that."

"Why don't you just leave them with me, Princess, since they won't co-operate? Simpler all around, and I'll gladly donate a couple of nice cheap energy bolts to the cause."

"Thank you kindly, Raidie baby, but I'll save you your energy bolts. I'm going to return them both to YouTwoie, and I'm sure they'll find, when the swarm trappers are firing at them, and the energy bolts are sizzling about their ears—"

"Ohhhh! What a fate for a simple farmboy!"

"Cheer up, Kook. At least the computers say you'll come out of this a *live* hero."

"Say, that's right, isn't it? Not bad for a simple farmboy. And say, Sled Fader, old boy, as long as we're fated to meet again, I'll get some of Aunt Trueblue's asthma remedy—"

"You do, simple farmboy, and I'll waste *two* cheap energy bolts on it!"

"You don't have to get huffy." To Obi-Qui: "See, he's stealing my simple farmboy line again."

"It isn't *fair*!" Raider paced up and down, still keeping his hands up. "It just isn't fair! Here I am, a villain of the blackest dye I can get—cheap, of course!—a mysterious evil follower of the evil dark side of the mysterious power known only as the Power. And I can't win out over even a simple farmboy,"—Kook opened his mouth to protest, but Obi-Qui had had a bit too much already and clapped a trembling old hand over it—"an old hermit who only wants to go on being an old hermit, and an uppity prin-cess, who, it's true, is beautiful, intelligent, and spunky, with more up her sleeve than her arm, but who—also and most important—always has to have the last word. Why? Why? Why? Where have I gone wrong? Maybe I should have gotten a double supply of cheap energy bolts…"

"Even a simple farmboy knows that a villain who goes around stealing other people's lines can never win in the end." (Obi-Qui, for all his deter-mination, was after all an *old hermit*, philosopher, and last of the valiant, noble Dead-Eye Mights.) "If you say simple farmboy one more time, so help me, by the evil dark side of the mysterious power known only as the Power, I'll get you if it takes *three* cheap energy bolts—"

"Now, Raidie baby, don't have a stroke." The princess slinked up to him. "And don't cry, either. You know it rusts your energy bolts." Keeping her gun shoved against his ribs, she put her free hand behind his back and embraced him fervently. Steam swirled slowly out from behind his mask, and the black hem of his villainous costume curled up. There was a long silence. Then she stepped back, cheeks delicately flushed and eyes sparkling. "That's all for now, Raidie baby. But I'll see you later. I don't think you'll forget you have a date to—abduct me. For now, I'll just take the boys and say—not farewell, but—*au revoir.*"

"And *I'll* bring along me simple farmboy remedy for asthma—"

"Grrrrrrr! *Four* cheap energy bolts!"

"Obi-Qui," said the princess, smiling, "it's no good trying to hide behind that equipment. It's really much better to come with me, than to stay here and let Raidie zap you with one of his energy bolts."

"I'm coming, Princess, I'm coming." He leaned over to whisper in Kook's ear. "Don't worry, dear young friend. I can outfox her any day, even if she is beautiful, intelligent, and spunky, with more up her sleeve than her arm. I'll find us a *good* hiding place, and we'll both be solitary hermits; let the Galaxy spin around without us."

"Better a live solitary hermit than a dead simple farmboy hero!"

The princess winked broadly at Raider. "That's what *they* think," she snickered.

"Just once," Raider was still brooding aloud about the injustice of it all. "Just *once*. Why can't I win just once? It isn't fair, it isn't fair, it isn't— Hmmm…Maybe if I don't try to get her to tell me where the rebel base is; maybe if I just zap her right away with a cheap energy bolt…"

"Now, Raidie baby, you know you have to play the game by the rules."

"Why? I always lose by the rules! If I'm the villain, why can't I break the rules—just this once! If I'm the mysterious evil follower of the evil dark side of the mysterious power known only as the Power, why can't I do what I want to do! I want to win! I'll do anything, anything; it's got to be my turn sometimes. Maybe I'll sneak onto YouTwoie and zap that simple farmboy with one of my cheap energy bolts! Maybe I'll—"

"You villainous villain, you! You stole my simple farmboy line again! You deserve to lose!"

"Five cheap energy bolts! Six! Ten!"

"You keep thinking about that, Raidie baby. We've got to go now." With one neat zap of her energy gun, she freed Kook from his tether, ignoring his scream of anguish and frantic beating out of tiny flames all over his simple farmboy costume. "Now come along—Oh!" she snapped her fingers; genteelly, as princesses always do. "I almost forgot. You come along, too, Con."

"What do you want with him?" Obi-Qui asked. "He's dead. My old one-time pupil zapped him back at the beginning."

"Nonsense. He's very much alive." Her voice dropped an octave. "Aren't you, Conzie baby?" she purred. To the others, in her normal voice, "He's just been shamming. A girl always knows when a man's been shamming. Come along, Con. You're going to have glorious adventures, too."

A voice came from the limp figure on the floor. "Will I get paid?"

"Of course. Much more than that tightwad Raidie promised you."

"Enough for two? The way you were talking, this job may take a little more than a single merciless mercenary—no matter how well-paid—can supply. Now I have this Wackie friend, lots of muscle and brains—" To himself: "Just not enough brains to cheat *me*—successfully."

"He can't get up," Raider protested violently. "I zapped him with one of my cheap energy bolts."

"Enough for two, Con, and I only hope your friend isn't as wacky as you are." She reached down with her free hand and helped him to his feet. "See, he's fine, Raidie baby. Next time don't use *quite* such cheap energy bolts."

(Darkly.) "Next time I may use them on myself."

"Nonsense. Of course you won't, *I* say so. And I am a princess, beautiful, intelligent, and spunky, with more up my sleeve than my arm. But—most important of all—I *always* have the last word."

The end.

(Or rather—The Beginning.)

Joel Rosenberg

Very few novels of recent memory have had an impact on the field even remotely approximating Larry Niven's award-winning RINGWORLD. It obviously had a profound effect on Joel Rosenberg, himself a best-selling author, and Joel takes a full measure of tongue-in-cheek revenge.

BAGGIEWORLD: A TALE OF PRETTY WELL KNOWN SPACE

In the middle of the night, in the heart of downtown Muncie, Indiana, Huir Yu flicked into reality, a look comprised of boredom and determination on his smooth, hepitatic face.

He was swearing—a common occurrence—and sweating, a rare condition caused at the present by the worldwide shortage of Right Guard, and aggravated by the apparent breakdown of the Dubbletak Module of the InsTrans booth, a device intended to violate, nay, ravage into senseless torpor the First Law of Thermodynamics by preventing him from roasting as he gained energy teleporting downhill.

Why, he asked himself, absent-mindedly rubbing his bald pate, had he left his two-hundredth birthday party? The answer came quickly, although it was not reassuring: anyone who'd come to a party held by someone as dull as Yu would make for pretty dreadful company at any gathering. Hell, at the time he'd left, a whole bunch of his guests were discussing practical jokes of the twentieth century; they'd gone through the joy buzzer, fake dog vomit, the whoopie cushion, and were almost up to cyberpunk.

But Muncie wasn't the place to assuage his boredom. His fingers fell on the booth's keyboard. Where? Where would he find something interesting to do? As he stood there in thought, the InsTrans booth—apparently of its own volition—came to life again. The lights in the booth flickered, the booth shook, and a loud mechanical whine reached volumes and pitches of magnitudes of obnoxiousness unheard of outside Punk Rock.

The whole world outside wavered, then disappeared.

✦

He emerged from the booth in a sleazy, albeit sunlit, room.

"What the *fuck*?" he wondered. "I knew that the stuff Gil laid on me was rancid, but *this* is ridiculous."

As he looked out through the dusty windows of the booth, he saw something as strange as anything he'd seen in his sordid two centuries. It stood on two bony appendages that, for lack of a proper insult, he decided to call legs, but there any resemblance to a human ended. It was almost three meters tall and covered with yellow feathers, its long neck sitting atop a vaguely spherical body. The head on the end of the neck changed position constantly, the bleary eyes searching the room; it stood watching Yu.

The creature reminded Yu of an ostrich, save that an ostrich, even on a bad day, could never look quite so disreputable.

And then a memory oozed up from the cesspool of Yu's admittedly less-than-sublime unconscious mind: it was a Hensen's Muppetteer. That entire species had vanished from Pretty Well Known Space more than three centuries ago, fleeing in fear during the most acute stage of the Fiberfil shortage.

"Who are you, and what the fuck are you up to?" he gently queried.

The Muppetteer answered in a soft voice, reminiscent of Andy Devine with the croup.

"You may call me Nexus," it said. Nobody really knew why, but Muppetteers were known for taking mathematical concepts as use-names. Yu's father—the word 'father' is used on the violent recommendation of the author's attorney—had known one called Indefinite Integral, another who liked to be addressed as Pi, and yet another who referred to itself as LotsAndLots.

"I must speak with you, Huir Yu," it went on.

"But," Yu whined, "You look like a Big—"

"—shh. We don't want to get involved in a suit for trademark viola-tion; we're in enough danger of that, as well as one for libel, at this very moment."

Looking back up the whitish page, Yu nodded in agreement. "That's right," Yu said, "now I remember. All members of your race are terrified of lawsuits."

"And what sapient being wouldn't be? You humans are too careless, tort-prone and litigious to be allowed to run loose."

"Don't give me any of that nonsense," Yu shot back. "I could get a megastar—at least—from any court of the planet for the emotional trau-ma you just put me through, by interfering with the InsTrans. Watch it, eagle-beak."

"No, *no, NO!*" Nexus screamed, tucking its head under a nearby rug. "Make it go *away.*"

Yu was, rather surprisingly, moved to an act of mercy. He stepped for-ward and stroked the downy feathers of the creature's neck.

"Okay, okay, relax," he said, sighing, "I'm not going to sue you. Why don't you calm down and tell me about the gig?"

Nexus withdrew its head from beneath the rug, stifling a sob.

"I can't," Nexus whined, a sound as light and as pleasant as a dentist's drill, "but I can show you this." A bag, inscribed with the ancient label "J.M. Fields," hung from its scrawny neck. Nexus reached its beak into it, and pulled out a hologram cube.

"What do you make of this?" it inquired.

"Nothing. You can't read a holo cube without a laser."

"Oops," Nexus rejoined, "how's this?" It dipped into the bag again, ex-tracted a laser, and pointed it at the cube, which Yu was holding in front of his face. Nexus tongued the laser on.

"Sorry," it said, turning the intensity knob down from SCORCH to VIEW, "I didn't mean to singe your brows."

Both the pain from his scorched flesh and the smoke from his eye-brows had momentarily blinded Yu. While he rubbed his eyes to clear the smoke from them he changed his mind about his earlier act of kindness, fantasizing about the size of a later out-of-court settlement.

But when the pain eased enough so that he could open his eyes, all thoughts of writs and torts were evicted from his mind by the holographic image in front of him. Before Yu's recovering eyes, the image seemed to hang in space, stars in the background shining like pinpoint beacons. The object, whatever it was, resembled a dim star that was somehow encased in a sort of barely-translucent, somewhat squared-off oblate spheroid of a plastic-like material kind of stuff.

Yu, not a subtle person, put it more simply: "It looks," he said, "like a star in a Baggie. What is it?"

"I cannot tell you that yet. First, we must locate the other members of our crew."

"But…"

"Save your breath to cool your soup." Nexus reached into the InsTrans booth, punched a combination, then used its beak to nudge Yu back into the booth.

"I'll be with you in a moment, but I must take care of some personal matters," Nexus informed Yu, as it stood outside the booth.

"Eh?"

"I must see a man about a horse."

"Huh?"

"I'm going to hit the can, bozo. You gonna go or you gonna watch?"

Yu hit ACTIVATE.

An electronic shudder later, Yu flicked into Joe's Bar and Grill in Piedmont, Montana. He exited the booth and waited patiently.

Within a few seconds, the Muppetteer flicked in.

"That was fast," Yu said.

"Number three," Nexus explained.

A human headwaiter, both distinguished and obnoxious, led the two to their table, after the Muppetteer had explained that they both had a reservation and were inclined toward violence.

"For someone of your species, you sure take a lot of chances of getting sued," Yu commented, sitting down.

"I should inform you," the Muppetteer admitted, "that most members of my species consider me insane."

"Peachy keen."

✦

Joe's Bar and Grill, despite its unprepossessing name, is one of the favored eating spots in this corner of Pretty Well Known Space of both gourmets and chowhounds of many species.

Piggians, for example, have been known to travel parsecs for a helping of Joe's famous beernuts, which are included—at no charge!—with a pitcher. Then again, it is commonly acknowledged that Piggians will go anywhere for a free feed. At one of the six tables surrounding Yu and his feathery companion there were four of them with their snouts immersed in their glasses, pausing only occasionally to warble a porcine German drinking song, snort out an order for a fresh half-dozen steins, or gobble a trotter full of nuts.

At another table, two rather ordinary-looking humans sat, engaged in a heated conversation. Both were fairly tall, dark-haired, and sporting mustaches. One had a beard as well, and his smiling countenance positively radiated inherited wealth. He was speaking, Yu noted.

"You know how I love doing sequels. And you wouldn't believe the offers we're getting on the *Paradisio*—"

The Muppetteer interrupted Yu's eavesdropping with a firm peck on the top of his shiny head.

"Do not, Huir Yu, let those two writers notice you, particularly the rich one."

"Why?"

"I may—by the accepted standards of my race—be insane. Still, do not think me totally out of touch with literary and legal reality, nor question me further on this issue, unless you wish to see someone we both owe our existence to slapped with a vicious lawsuit."

After another, markedly less humorous glance up the page, Yu, fortunately for the author, tuned the two humans out, following the pointed suggestion.

Nexus pointed its beak at another table. There sat several large, green, vaguely humanoid creatures, each dressed only in a yellow fringed collar. They were members of a rather violent and hungry species with which humans had engaged in several important athletic competitions, as a method of solving boundary disputes. The results had been mixed; humans tended to win most events of skill, but invariably lost the jumping and swimming events, which was reasonable enough, all things considered.

Yu tried to listen in on their conversation (he was, after all, a graduate of the G. Gordon Liddy Memorial Eavesdropping School), but was unable to decipher the croaks and groans that the Phroggians, with some little justice, claim is a language.

The waitress stumbled, staggered and tripped up to Yu's table. The off-center ruby on her forehead declared that she was a *schlemeil*, a person genetically designed to raise clumsiness to a high artform. The name tag pasted on her too-ample hips read: HELLO—MY NAME IS 'PHELIA BROWN.

"Hey, Nexus, how ya doin' and who's your bald friend?" she inquired, carefully setting the water glasses on the table. Sideways.

As she wiped the spill off the pseudoak and onto Yu's lap, Nexus replied, "Never mind, for now. Come back in a few minutes with a pitcher, four glasses…and a bowl of nuts."

She tottered off with its order.

"I take it you've been here before?" Yu inquired, trying to blot his lap with his napkin. "Doesn't impress me as your kind of place."

"One need not be a Piggian to like beernuts," Nexus replied.

"True enough. I'm sort of fond of the Buffalo hot wings."

"That's not the best," Nexus raised its voice. "Yu, have you ever had the delicious *frogs' legs* they serve here?"

"Take me now, Lord," Yu muttered, burying his face in his hands.

The nearest Phroggian stood up, making a gesture to its companions to remain seated. Its skin, glistening from the *schlemeil* waitress' attempt to serve its beer, was covered with huge, grotesque warts. The creature opened its mouth to reveal a tongue that could have easily made it very popular in certain circles as it hopped over to the table where Yu cringed in anticipation of his companion's impending death. Yu may have been less than bright, he may have been less than hirsute, but it could not be said that his heart wouldn't bleed for a friend.

He pulled his chair back a bit from the table. There was no need, though, for Nexus to bleed all over him.

"Hey, YOU!" the massive Phroggian boomed. "Who, by Kdapt's Krotch, do you think you are, that you expect to live after that?"

"Err, umm, well, you see," Yu riposted, for the Phroggian was speaking directly to him, apparently having mistaken the source of the unfortunate comment.

One of the other Phroggians interrupted the impending slaughter with a series of plaintive croaks. The creature left Yu's table and returned to its own, addressed a series of croaks to the carrot and onion casserole on the plates of its companions, and then came back, patently to take up where it had left off.

"What was that all about?" Yu asked, stalling for time.

"In our religion," the immense Phroggian responded, hunkering down beside Yu, "it is customary to say a few words to our meal prior to dining. These phrases, the function of the caste to which I belong, vary greatly, according to the time of day, type of food—there is but one simple phrase to be addressed to all types of meat, however—the number of Phroggians present, and so forth. Doing this work is the function of my caste, and I am addressed by a title, in recognition."

"Yes?" Yu inquired, now almost as bored as he was afraid.

"I am called 'Speaker-to-Vegetables,'" it said, making a mystic sign with its webbed middle foredigit. "Now what is this about Phroggs' legs?"

"It was it," Yu bravely responded, once more preparing to pity his new friend, as he pointed to Nexus.

The Phroggian drew itself up to its full height.

Just as the endproducts of the defecatory process were poised to impact the rapidly revolving blades, 'Phelia Brown inserted her ample bosom and laden tray between Nexus and Speaker-to-Vegetables.

"Join us in a brew?" Yu asked her, including Speaker in his invitation with an airy wave of his hand.

"Sure," Speaker responded. "I can always beat up on Mr. Chicken a bit later."

Nexus, who had been uncharacteristically silent throughout the whole proceedings brought on by its outburst, spoke up.

"You had best understand, Speaker-to-Vegetables, that my species' legendary caution is limited to action-at-law, not attempted physical damage. Should you desire to engage in such," it grated, thickly enough to sprinkle on a pizza, "I will oblige you after having finished the business proposition for which I have gathered the three of you together here."

It gobbled a few beernuts before continuing. "Now do I have your agreements to keep this matter in confidence?"

"Very well," Yu said.

"Sure; why not?"

"I don't see a problem with that."

"Good. Sign here," Nexus said, dipping its beak into its bag, producing three pens and three sheafs of releases. After the customary signing, notarization, blood oath and pinky swear, Nexus again reached into its bag, beak-flipped the holo cube to Yu, and brought out the laser. Yu snatched it out of its mouth and adjusted the setting to VIEW, rather than FRY.

Yu gave the laser back and Nexus activated it with a quick tongue-flick. The picture was unchanged; it still looked like a star in a dirty Baggie.

"Go ahead," he urged. "What the hell is that thing, anyway?"

Nexus hesitated a moment before responding. "*Ophelia Brown*, kindly pay attention rather than continuing to stare at the tongue of Speaker-to-Vegetables."

Nexus gave her a peck in the solar plexus to drive the point home, as Yu whispered to her, "Don't threaten to sue; I think it's in its manic phase."

"Oof!" she gasped. "Oh, sure."

Nexus reactivated the laser.

"This is either a Dyson sphere, or the final set of the *Starlost*. Both possibilities seem equally preposterous, although Those-Who-Manipulate-From-Below seem to lean toward the former—when they are sober, that is."

'Phelia gestured, striking a salt shaker with the back of her hand, sending it flying toward Yu. He brushed the salt off his face as she spoke.

"What is a Dyson sphere, anyway?"

Nexus stuck its beak in the pitcher, draining it. "The concept has been around for centuries. Given that a civilization can expand without limits, eventually it will need to utilize more than the paltry amount of energy from its sun that a planet, or a number of planets, can trap. If the civilization has achieved interstellar travel by that time, that will solve the problem; the civilization will colonize other stars, either starving the home planet to death, or not, depending on the economics of the particular interstellar drive and the whim of the author.

"But, if they have *not* achieved interstellar travel, they might choose to trap more of the energy of their sun. A Dyson sphere is the maximally productive way to do this.

"If this is, indeed, a Dyson sphere, as it appears to be, what the natives have done is to encase their star with a huge plastic-like bag, totally—or almost, since we can take pictures of it—trapping the energy streaming from the sun. And—"

"Wait a minute," Yu interrupted. "Wouldn't they fall into their sun? Unless they spin the plastic sphere, but then they'd—"

"—they would cause the poles of their spinning sphere to impact the star. True. What these sentients have done, apparently, is to build a liner inside the original bag, attached to the outer bag at perhaps only millions of points, and inflated the entire thing, the atmosphere giving it enough rigidity to fight the gravitational pull of their star."

As Nexus paused to send 'Phelia for another pitcher, Speaker spoke up. "I am enough of a mathematician to know that such a system would not be stable; a solar flare on one side would push it out, sending the other side of the sphere crashing into the sun."

Nexus leaned over, and picked the huge Phroggian up by its collar, talking out of the side of its beak.

"If you, Speaker-to-Vegetables, are trying to mess up this sequel, this physical combat that you have suggested may occur earlier than you had intended."

Nexus set the Phrogg down. "If there are no further interruptions," Nexus continued, a trifle petulantly, "here is the proposition: I wish to hire you three, a two-hundred-year-old human, a *schlemeil*, and a large, violent, dangerous-to-be-in-the-same-room-with Phroggian, to explore the Baggieworld with me. I know that seems unwise, but," it leaned over, whispering conspiratorially, "what the hell, anyway."

Speaker rose angrily. "I don't mind the klutz, but you think I'm going along with the slaver-stasishead?" it said, waving at Yu's gleaming pate. "Forget it."

Yu was angry now, and in one of the fits of bravado that made his continued existence for two centuries a notion of the level of credibility of the old saw about the Grog bringing babies, he stood up.

"I have had it, Fly-breath! I challenge you to a fight, Man-to-Phrogg, since we cannot share the universe in peace without you making nasty cracks."

What Yu did not notice, although Speaker did, was Nexus ostentatiously switching the laser from VIEW to BURN YOU SO BADLY YOU WOULDN'T *BELIEVE*, and pointing same at Speaker's thorax, tongue poised on the trigger.

"Okay, okay," Speaker said, "I take it back. Sit down, I'm in." It sat meekly in its chair. "Incidentally, Huir Yu," it muttered in an aside, "I found your challenge verbose. When you challenge a Phroggian, you croak and you leap, and..."

"And?"

"And...you croak."

"Great."

"Your pay," Nexus continued as if nothing interesting or out of the ordinary had happened, which was at least half right, "will be a spaceship of a new and untested design, which is supposed to go faster than anything else ever built, assuming that it doesn't go too fast and crash into a star or something."

Nexus replaced the laser in its bag, the handle protruding menacingly. "Shall we go and take a look at it?" it asked. "And, of course, sign a waiver or two?"

"Certainly," Speaker said, nodding its green head.

"Just as soon as I punch out," 'Phelia Brown said, heading for the space behind the bar.

Huir Yu sighed. "It can't hurt to look."

The four headed for the InsTrans booths, just as the two authors, who they and we have been studiously ignoring, flicked out of the booth, the restaurant, and the story. (Whew!) Yu and 'Phelia shared a booth, the Muppetteer calling out a series of numbers which Yu fed into the keyboard.

In a moment, they were emerging from a booth in the middle of a desert.

✦

Yu couldn't tell which desert it was; it looked like any other desert: bright sun beating down, rolling sand dunes stretching from horizon to horizon, the hot beige expanse punctuated only by the sporadic scorpion, the occasional cactus, the huge spaceship shaped like a trumpet, the infrequent sagebrush, the—The huge spaceship shaped like a trumpet? Nexus stepped from the booth, followed moments later by Speaker-to-Vegetables.

"It's a new starship, of a rather remarkable design," Nexus explained. "It uses the Quantum Two hyperdrive."

"My people have done the mathematics on the Quantum Two hyperdrive." Speaker's green brow furrowed. "It would require huge amounts of energy—what's your source?"

"Ah. We travel via standard hyperdrive to a star with no occupied planets, then trigger that module there—the thing about the size of a locomotive? That makes the star go nova."

"A thing the size of a locomotive that makes a star go nova? Right."

The Muppetteer shrugged. "We then circle the expanding cloud of gas, gathering mass with the hornlike protuberance in front of the ship…"

"Eating the carrion of the dead star," 'Phelia Brown breathed.

"Yes," Nexus said. "The power source of the Quantum Two hyperdrive is a…."

"Don't say it!"

"…a Buzzard Ramjet."

"And you want us to go with you in this thing?" Yu asked, trying to keep his voice casual.

"Exactly.—Err, where are you going, Yu?"

"Back in a minute, I promise," Yu said, crossing his fingers behind his back as he stepped back inside the InsTrans booth and punched a quick combination.

In a moment, he was back in the study of his home, and scant seconds later was using a nearby fireaxe to persuade the booth not to admit any unwanted visitors.

Ever.

He breathed a sigh of relief as he walked upstairs. The discussion of twentieth century practical jokes was still going on; in a few moments he was happily engaged in a lengthy discussion of the dribble glass, the fake flower that squirts water, and, of course, cyberpunk.

He had no regrets in turning down the Muppetteer's proposal. Huir Yu may have been dull, he may have been bald, he may have been boring, but you didn't get to be two hundred years old by being *stupid*.

Marc Laidlaw

The newest phenomenon in science fiction is "Cyberpunk," best exemplified by William Gibson's award-winning NEUROMANCER. Marc Laidlaw manages to prove, once again, that there is no school of writing so important or so serious that someone can't poke some good-natured fun at it.

NUTRIMANCER

IMAGINE A TV DINNER, baked to a crisp. Silver foil peeled back by the heat of a toaster oven. Charred clots of chicken stew, succotash, nameless dessert, further blurred by a microfrost of recombinant mold like a diseased painter's nightmare of verdigris.

Fungoid cityscape.

Metaphor stretched to the breaking point.

Lunch.

ONE: NEON SUSHI

SOMEONE HAD FOUND A new use for an old fryboy. At the Lazy-Ate Gar & Krill, 6Pack was swabbing shrimp-racks with an 80-baud prosthetic dishrag when a Mongol stammer cut through the sleazy pinions of his hangover, sharp as a bitter mnemonic twist of Viennese coffee rinds tossed from a cathedral window into a turgid canal where rainbow trout drowned in petroleum jelly.

"6Pack?" said the Mongol. "Want a new job?"

He glanced up from the remnants of crustaceans curled like roseate spiral galaxies and saw:

—Limpid pools of Asian eyeliner aswirl in a violaceous haze of pain and pastry crumbs.

—Bank check skin with "Cash" spelled out on the lines of a furrowed brow.

—Some pretty bodacious special effects. To his typographic implants it looked like this:

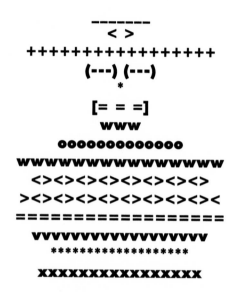

6Pack scrabbled for a purchase on reality but found only the dishrag. "Man, that sweater hurts my eyes!"

The Mongol stepped between 6Pack and the sushi counter. "It's pixel-implanted Angola wool, under hermeneutic control. Come with me or I will induce a convincing epileptic seizure by altering stripe frequency and then take you away in the guise of your doctor."

6Pack considered his options. A nearby heap of batter-fried squid tentacles quivered like golden-brown weaponry hauled from the ancient trenches of the sea. The Mongol tipped back the brass spittoon that served him as a hat, exposing an Oster ionized water-bazooka stitched among his sukiyaki corn-rows.

"What do you want with me?"

"Surely you can guess, fryboy."

"No one calls me that without hearing my story. You've gotta hear what happened, what th-they d-d-did to me!"

"Now, now," said the Mongol. "Don't cry. I'm listening."

It had all happened too fast for words.

Whiz!

  Bang!

    Whirr-ee-rr-ee-rr-ee!

      Snip!

        Clunkata—clunkata-clunkata…

          Prrrrang!

"And when it was over, I woke up. The East Anglians had rewired my tastebuds." He waved at the racks full of squirming periwinkles, octopus eyes, mackerel intestines. "Now all this tastes horrible to me. I eat the finest chocolates from Brussels—" he cannot avoid the memory of the heavy matron who served him sourly from behind the polished glass counters, shoving a gift-wrapped box of butter-creams into his hands "—and it tastes like dirt."

"If you eat dirt, does it taste like butter-creams?" asked the Mongol. "But no matter. I know your story. What if I told you that my employers can restore your tongue to its previous sensitivity?"

6Pack sneered at him. "No one's got the technology to unsplice my tongue, short of the EASA, who did the damage in the first place."

The Mongol produced a 3D business card from some fold of his sweater and handed it to 6Pack: "I am a deaf-mute," it read.

"Wrong card," the Mongol said, snatching it back and handing him another, which spelled out in tiny blinking lights: EAST ANGLIAN SMORGASBORD AUTHORITY.

"What's the matter, fryboy? Swallow something you don't like?" Hands trembling, seeing the future unfolding before him like an origami *hors d'oeuvre*, 6Pack knelt to kiss the Mongol's fingers. "I'll do anything to have my palate restored," he pleaded. "Tell them I'm sorry. Tell them I'll never confuse mayonnaise with Miracle Whip again."

"You're hired," said the Mongol and drew his hands away.

The knuckles left a taste of Kentucky bluegrass on 6Pack's lips.

TWO: WIRED TO SHOP

HE WAS AT THE Grocery Boutique when his shopping cart's guidance system failed. Narrowly averting disaster, he switched on to manual and swerved past an oncoming cart. Heart pounding, he looked up apologetically at the other driver. That was when he saw her.

A peach recomb-polyester scarf enshrouded permed and frosted curls. From platform heels of rich Corinthian vinyl, tiny blood-colored toenails oozed forth like delicate ornaments from a cake decorator. Rhinestone-rimmed videospex hid her eyes; her face was as sterile and empty as the corridors of General Hospital that held her attention.

"Pardon me," 6Pack murmured.

"Chet, you moron, she just wanted to get into the MRI with Emilio!"

He couldn't help gazing into her cart as he passed.

Sara Lee Weightless Cake.

Betty Crocker Astro-Cookies.

He remembered sitting in a Parisian cafe, the tip of his croissant immersed in a demitasse as a pathetic screech made him look up abruptly into a—

Bird's Eye Frozen Creamed Corn.

Instinctively, he shied from the selection, but somehow she sensed him and drifted nearer, like a platinum-blonde manta ray in the aquarium aisle. Her lips parted, gushing warm air that smelled like a stagnant wind coursing from all the demolished bakeries that had ever harbored starving mice. She smiled with green lips. A particle of biftek swayed like an electric eel, trapped between her teeth.

"I'm Polly Pantry," she said. "Join me for lunch?"

She caught his arm, pressed her mouth to his ear, and tickled the tiny waxen hairs with her tongue as she whispered, "Courtesy of EASA, 6Pack. You can't refuse."

THREE: ZERO GEE WHIZ

Menu.

Foodstuffs.

Out of the ovens of Earth they come tumbling, but in the radar ranges of the orbital kitchens there is no force that can cause a souffle to fall. Jaunts into shallow space for a nulldinner are common as dirt among the filthy rich. Even in his prime, 6Pack had not dined in space. Tonight he would remedy that.

The Pixie Fatline, EASA's Artificial Conscience Module, sang in 6Pack's ear-receiver as the shuttle pulled into the neat chrome pancreas called Waiter's Heaven: "Shoofly pie and apple pan dowdy make your eyes light up and your tongue say howdy!"

"I don't understand why the EASA's being so nice to me," 6Pack paravocalized. "First they give me back my sense of taste and now they're treating me to dinner."

"Shh," said the Fatline. "Incoming message from Polly."

"Hi, 6Pack! Howrya doin'? You eat that sandwich I sent up with you?"

"Sure did, Polly," he lied. "Tasty."

Deviled ham on Wonder Bread. He hoped that the shuttle stewardess wouldn't guess who'd clogged the flight toilet.

"Okay, hon, when you get off that ship you're to go straight to Chez Cosmique. The reservations are in your name, for a party of six. Tell them that you're waiting for friends, then go ahead and order. Make them bring it right away."

"When you are in trouble and you don't know right from wrong, give a little—"

"Shut up, Fatline, I'm talking! Now, 6Pack, I want you—"

6Pack fiddled with the dial in his nostril and tuned out both of them. A six-course meal for six, he thought. Good thing he hadn't eaten that sandwich.

"There's salt in this cream puff," he complained, after the last course had come and gone and dessert floated before him. The EASA had equipped him with a false gullet that compressed his meals and packed them into tiny blocks of bullion to be deposited one by one in his Swiss bank account. He had complained about everything Chez Cosmique served, while the staff milled about wishing that his supposed companions would come claim some of the food. 6Pack had eaten it all, and now—

"I refuse to pay."

The cafe grew hushed. Aristocrats with tame prairie dogs and live coelentrates embedded in their coiffures turned upon him the incredibly credible eyes of luxury. The nearest, a thin old man wearing nothing but tightly laced black undergarments and a bonnet of jellyfish, leaned close enough to whisper, "Are you a fryboy?"

"What's it to you?"

"I am in need of a fryboy with exquisite discrimination and a hearty appetite."

The manager slunk up to 6Pack's nulltable, where the ruins of his feast lingered, untouched by waiters who had rightly guessed that there would be no gratuity forthcoming. Five cream puffs floated in the diningspace, bouncing between invisible restraining fields with tiny detonations of powdered sugar at every impact.

"Sir, have you a question about your bill?"

"Yeah, you should be paying me to dispose of this garbage you call food."

"But—but this is impossible. Perhaps there is something wrong with your tongue. Each item is carefully prepared and tasted by our chef."

"He's a fake. Bring him in so that I can insult him to his face. Then you might make up for your incredible error by giving his job to me."

"Now don't be so hard on the poor guy," said the Pixie Fatline.

"My dear fellow," said the lean tycoon at the next table. "I have a position for a private chef. Besides, I own this establishment. You'd be wasted here."

"That's our man," said the Fatline. "Tempura-Hashbraun himself."

6Pack removed his seat belt and drifted toward the aristocrat. "What's it pay?"

FOUR: THE STAYLITE RUNS

"MAY I INTRODUCE MY daughter?" said Tempura-Hashbraun, guiding 6Pack through an entryway. "Lady 3Bean, this is our new fryboy."

She was both cat and canary, a hybrid of starving piranha and fat guppy, all sharp fangs and soft feathers. But there wasn't time to ogle her or quiver in dread. The old man led him through the split-level satellite to the infokitchen.

He had never seen anything like it. Never dreamed that such a thing could be.

Imagine an oven designed by the old Dutch masters. Its rails and racks had been forged by the brow-heat of the oppressed masses, then plunged sizzling into the vast oceans of their driven sweat, while the Tempura-Hashbrauns climbed their limp ladder of slaves to the stars. The dials blinded him with their intensity until the old man found the rheostat and turned them down.

"6Pack, meet Nutrimancer. Nutrimancer, 6Pack. I hope you do better than my last fryboy."

"What happened to him?"

Tempura-Hashbraun smiled for the first time, showing that he had replaced his teeth with credit registers.

"Nutrimancer fired him," he said. "Thirty seconds under the broiler and he was done to perfection." He licked his lips.

6Pack slipped his tongue into the jack, checked the pilot light, and hit the ON switch. For an instant he smelled scallions sizzling in butter, the iron tang of an omelette pan, and then he was inside.

"Wheeee!" cried the Fatline. "You're back."

Ahead of him, a ziggurat rose halfway to infinity, looking like a corporate bar chart. But it was not a savings and loan, nor a humongous tax shelter. It was a wedding cake.

He rushed forward, surpassing the rate of inflation. Tier upon tier leapt into clarity, as an army of menacing custard eclairs streaked past below.

"Watch out!" the Fatline cried. "It's covered in ICING!"[1]

In the instant before collision, he found his bearings and soared upward. The tiers dropped below, but not before he had read the message written in ICING upon the topmost layer: "YOU'RE DEAD, FRYBOY!"

Now he settled into the evasion routines with which the EASA had equipped him. As soon as a cocktail olive drew close enough, he snagged it by the pimento and followed it back to the foodbanks. Kaleidoscope of the tongue: Mint and parsley, vanilla haggis, pecans, and hundred-year eggs.

As the tastes passed through his mind, he peeped into the twisted guts of the infokitchen, sorting through spice racks and rifling iceboxes. He ignored the cross-referenced accounting files that tracked the expense of every meal and ordered supplies when they were low. He ignored the brain of that vast system.

"Go!" sang the Fatline.

Straight for the stomach.

"What are you doing in my kitchen?"

His inquisitor was a rotund chef wearing a white suit and a tall white cap; he held a wooden spoon menacingly cocked. They stood on a wild mountain peak; tennis balls whipped past and the sky was full of steel engravings.

"You're Nutrimancer," 6Pack said.

"So what if I am? This kitchen is too small for two. I don't need a fryboy. I'm self-motivated. What are you?"

Memories of Earth: hot Florida sand burning his kneecaps, his first smorgasbord, popsicles in Cannes, Judy Dixon sucking his tongue till it hurt like hell.

---

1   Incredibly Complicated Information Never Given.

"You have a messy mind," Nutrimancer announced. "You can't cook with all that confusion inside you. Let me clean it out for you."

6Pack cried out for the Fatline, but he'd been cut off. He gave a little whistle but it didn't help. Nutrimancer's laughter sounded like tricycle tires rushing over a sidewalk covered with worms and roaches.

"EASA can't help you now," said the chef. "I know they sent you to stop me, but I control the diet of the most powerful man on or off Earth. Soon I will have replaced every cell of his body with nutrients tailored for world domination. And old Tempura-Hashbraun has developed quite an appetite for human flesh. I'm sure he won't mind if another fryboy ends up under glass with an apple in his mouth."

Something was rising over the mountains, unseen by the deranged chef, like a pale and enormous yellow moon lofting through the clouds. Without letting himself follow the arc of its rise, 6Pack calculated the path of its descent. He took a few steps back, drawing the chef into the point of impact.

"It's no use trying to escape. No one knows where you are. And soon the old man will have disposed of the remains."

The shadow of the falling sphere began to grow around Nutrimancer's feet. At the last instant, the chef glanced up and cried, "Aiee! Wintermelon!"

As the titan fruit smashed upon the peak, flattening the chef, 6Pack leapt from the crag. The sky went black and so did he.

He awoke in a soft bed, an extravagant suite, as Lady 3Bean walked through the door with a breakfast tray in her hands.

"You were wonderful," she said. "Would you like something to eat?"

6Pack shook his head and regarded the rashers and cantaloupe with distaste.

"Never again," he said.

(With thanks and apologies to William Gibson)

CPSIA information can be obtained at www.ICGtesting.com
Printed in the USA
BVOW070351170812

297913BV00002B/4/P